WHITE LINES III:
ALL FALLS DOWN

WHITE LINES III:
ALL FALLS DOWN

A WHITE LINES NOVEL

TRACY BROWN

ST. MARTIN'S GRIFFIN
NEW YORK

WHITE LINES III: ALL FALLS DOWN. Copyright © 2015 by Tracy Brown. All rights reserved. Printed in the United States of America. For information, address St. Martin's Press, 175 Fifth Avenue, New York, N.Y. 10010.

www.stmartins.com

Library of Congress Cataloging-in-Publication Data

Brown, Tracy, 1974–
    White lines III : all falls down / Tracy Brown. First edition.
        p. cm
    ISBN 978-1-250-04299-6 (trade paperback)
    ISBN 978-1-4668-4098-0 (e-book)
    1. African American women—Fiction.   2. Man-woman relationships—Fiction.
3. Life change events—Fiction.   4. Drug addiction—Fiction.
    I. Title.
    PS3602.R723W49 2015
    813'.6—dc23

                                                                2015019393

Our books may be purchased in bulk for promotional, educational, or business use. Please contact your local bookseller or the Macmillan Corporate and Premium Sales Department at (800) 221-7945, extension 5442, or by e-mail at MacmillanSpecial Markets@macmillan.com.

First Edition: November 2015

D   10   9   8   7   6   5

For Dee Dee

May your beautiful soul rest happily ever after in Heaven

ACKNOWLEDGMENTS

Monique Patterson, you are my biggest motivator, my most honest critic, a true visionary, an overall genius, and best of all, an excellent friend! I will never be able to thank you enough for your role in my career.

Sara Camilli, you are a tremendous asset to my career. You give me great advice, you push me when I need it, and you look out for my best interests. On top of that, you are an incredible woman who juggles many roles at once. I am grateful for the opportunity to work with you, and I look forward to what the future has in store for us as a team.

My readers, you are so very special to me. Please know that I read all of your feedback with a smile. It's an honor and a privilege to write stories that make you happy, sad, angry, or a combination of all three. I appreciate your support so very much. Thank you from the bottom of my heart.

WHITE LINES III:
ALL FALLS DOWN

1
MOMENT OF TRUTH

Sunny looked around her cell helplessly. She sat in a small, dirty room with one tiny, grime-coated window, a filthy cement floor, a toilet that smelled and looked as if it had never been cleaned, and one old wooden bench upon which she sat now.

Sunny's tearstained face was set in a grimace. She had stopped crying long ago, but the tracks of her tears were still evident, colored in by streaks of her mascara. Her usually bright eyes were vacant, as she stared down at her hands and tried to wrap her mind around what had happened thirty-one hours ago. She had counted each one of those hours as she stared at the clock on the wall, its second hand ticking by like a bell tolling in her head.

She squeezed her eyes shut and shook her head in disbelief, fighting back the tears that threatened to rush forth once more. The reality of her situation was just too terrible. Sunny was in a Mexican prison cell, charged with cocaine possession. The baggie she had tucked into her purse when Malcolm surprised her on the seedy side of town had been discovered by customs agents at the airport. She cursed herself for forgetting about it. She had slipped. BIG time.

Sunny had been interrogated in hostile tones for hours. Like rapid fire, the police hurled questions and accusations at her in broken English, demanding to know where she had gotten the drugs. They spoke amongst themselves in Spanish after questioning her nonstop all night. When she heard them discussing all of the American money they had discovered in her purse, she couldn't resist telling them in fluent Spanish that every penny of it was theirs to keep if they would only let her go. One of the rough-looking female guards had gotten pissed off instantly. Sunny wasn't sure if the woman was pissed off that she had offered a bribe or if it was the fact that her Spanish was better than theirs. But the next thing Sunny knew, the guard had snatched her by the collar of her shirt. Glaring, she had gotten in Sunny's face so close that Sunny could smell her hot, vile breath.

"*Pendeja*! It's already ours to keep and you're *still* going to jail!" The guard had spat on the floor in front of Sunny and then sealed it with a look of pure contempt. Since then, all of the guards had been speaking to Sunny rudely in Spanish, and watching what they said to one another while in her presence. They seemed to be convinced that she was part of some big cartel. They had accused her of attempting to smuggle the small amount of coke as some kind of trial run to test the customs agents' thoroughness. They wanted to know whose drugs they were, how long Sunny had been working for them, and what role Malcolm played in all of it.

Malcolm.

As her thoughts turned to him, Sunny closed her eyes once more to keep the tears at bay. She had really fucked up now. She wondered where they had taken him after separating the two of them immediately after they discovered the cocaine in her possession. She imagined that they must have interrogated him just as mercilessly as they had her. She prayed that he knew to keep his mouth shut and say absolutely nothing. Malcolm wasn't from her world. He didn't think like she did, wasn't as quick on his feet. She began to pick at her nails, absentmindedly, chipping away at her fill-in. She was tired, hungry, and scared to death.

She imagined that Malcolm must be, too. And then there was the issue of the man they'd left to bleed to death in a cab ride gone horribly wrong. She needed to get the fuck out of Mexico.

Her thoughts were interrupted by the sound of the door opening. One of the guards entered the room. He was accompanied by a stout Mexican man wearing a cheap suit and run-over shoes.

"*Abuego*," the scowling guard mumbled before leaving as suddenly as he had appeared, leaving Stubby behind. Sunny sized up the poorly dressed man standing before her, who would be acting as her attorney. She felt a pang of guilt as she thought about her *real* attorney—Malcolm—being detained in a room nearby.

The man introduced himself as Marcos Gomez. He sat down beside her on the wooden bench, and set his briefcase down on the floor in front of him. He smelled of unfamiliar cologne and hand sanitizer, an oddly comforting combination that put Sunny at ease. She felt optimistic. Hopefully, he could find a way for her and Malcolm to get out of this mess.

Sunny began talking animatedly to her makeshift attorney, telling him in anxious, hurried Spanish that she hadn't been given a chance to call anyone since her arrest. She thought that surely inmates were allowed one phone call here as they were in America. Anything else seemed inhumane.

Mr. Gomez tried to suppress a smirk at Sunny's audacious outrage. Here she was, under arrest for drug possession in a foreign country and indignant still. He asked her if she had ever been arrested before. Sunny shrugged, unsure how that was relevant. He read between the lines, and assumed that her shrug was a "yes."

"*Para drogas?*" he asked. For drugs?

Sunny hesitated before answering. "Once for marijuana. The other time was for driving with a suspended license." She watched him write that down.

"But, I was booked, given a phone call and released both

times. Nothing like this!" She hadn't brushed her teeth nor been given an opportunity to shower since her arrest. She had no access to her luggage, and had sat in the same panties for far longer than she cared to. Sunny had barely been given anything to eat and she wondered how long she would be forced to endure this nightmare. She felt disgusting.

Mr. Gomez listed the charges against her.

"Drug smuggling, possession of narcotics, and conspiracy."

"I wasn't smuggling anything or conspiring with anybody! Those drugs are not mine!" Even though she was aware that she was lying, Sunny convinced herself that this was all just a misunderstanding. She hadn't been smuggling *on purpose*, and the small amount of coke she had in her possession certainly didn't warrant her being held for this long under these conditions.

Gomez nodded, seeming to understand her frustration.

Sunny sighed, heavily. She dragged her fingers through her hair in exasperation. "Who was I supposedly conspiring with?" she demanded. Her thoughts turned to Malcolm again. Oh, no! Did they think that *he* was her coconspirator in this imaginary drug-smuggling ring?

"Are you representing Malcolm, too?" she asked.

Gomez frowned, confused. "Who is *Malcolm*?"

Sunny looked at him like he was crazy. "My codefendant," she said. "The guy I was with at the airport."

Gomez, still looking bewildered, sifted through some papers in his briefcase. He seemed to find what he was looking for, paused on one page in particular, and slowly read a section of it. He shook his head.

Sunny cleared her throat, impatiently.

"*Señor* Dean, yes?" he asked.

"Yes!" Sunny was growing impatient with this man.

Gomez shook his head again. His expression was bleak, and she knew instantly that there was bad news.

"Malcolm Dean has already been released. He flew back to the U.S. yesterday."

Sunny's heartbeat quickened and her stomach turned. She heard a ringing in her ears. *"What?"* Suddenly she felt sick, bile rising in her throat and sweat pooling at her brow.

Gomez scanned the document in his hand once again. "He gave a statement. He *said* that the drugs belonged to you alone, and he had no idea about any of it. Since the drugs were found in *your* luggage and not in his, they allowed him to pay a sum and leave Mexico immediately."

Sunny felt like she might pass out. "He gave a statement?" she repeated, incredulously.

"Si," Gomez confirmed. He shook his head, and Sunny felt comforted by this gesture. Even he knew that Malcolm was a bitch for abandoning her this way.

"Apparently, he is an attorney in the States, and assured us that he had no knowledge of your drug-related activities. He has paid his way out."

Sunny sat in stunned silence. *That muthafuckin' bitchass bastard!* she thought. She was seething. But above all, she was hurt. She had fallen for Malcolm despite all of the alarm bells ringing in her head telling her not to. And now, here she was, crushed and abandoned. Locked up abroad. She should have known better than to trust him.

"Okay, so I need to do the same thing," Sunny said, snapping her fingers to illustrate how quickly she needed this all to be dealt with. Malcolm was a coward, she decided, and she would deal with his punk ass when she got back to the States. But, right now, she needed to get the hell out of Mexico before someone connected her to more than that small amount of drugs in her bag. "How much do I need to get out of here?"

Gomez stared at her for a moment, silently. Finally, he responded.

"The price for *you* could be very high. Your friend is an attorney, and he did not have the drugs in his possession. He claimed that he barely knew you, and that he had no idea what your involvement is in the cocaine trade. His situation was different. Yours will be tougher."

Sunny's blood boiled. Malcolm was claiming that he hardly knew her, when, just days ago, he'd had his face buried in her pussy. The two of them had children who played together. He had met her family. They were a couple. But, not anymore. Right now, she could just kill him.

Mr. Gomez snapped her back to the issue at hand.

"We can maybe work something out for you, *Señorita*." He looked her in the eyes. His suggestive tone of voice conveyed the message loud and clear.

She dismissed her thoughts of Malcolm that instant. "How much?" she asked, anxiously.

Mr. Gomez shrugged. "Ten thousand U.S. should do the trick." He rubbed his thumb against the rest of his fingertips in the universal symbol for cash.

"Are you crazy?" Sunny snapped. "I had $100 worth of yayo and you muthafuckas want ten grand?" She was appalled.

Gomez suppressed a smirk. For someone who had been framed, she certainly knew the market price of the drugs she'd been carrying.

"You must think I'm crazy. You must be out of your mind!"

Gomez watched silently while she had her temper tantrum. Sunny was on her feet, pacing her tiny cell, muttering how ridiculous this was. She thought about Malcolm. Had his corny, dumb ass ponied up that much to get himself out of this hell? She shook her head at the thought.

"I don't have that kind of money," she said, lying.

Gomez held her gaze, unblinkingly. "It is no good lying to your lawyer, *Señorita* Cruz." He pulled out a cigarette and lit it.

Exhaling the smoke, he leaned back against the wall. "The police at the airport discovered that you and your companion were traveling home with $7,000 in cash—$6,000 of which was in *your* bag. You have expensive jewelry, expensive clothes, and shoes. And your traveling companion told his interrogators that he was working with you, that you are scheduled to do a film. So you are a high-profile American woman. It is very easy to search your name on the Internet to find out exactly who you are and whether we can get more money from a tabloid instead." He took another puff of his cigarette. The cost is $10,000 or they Google."

Sunny was snarling at him and he took notice. He softened his tone a bit.

"I am not your enemy," he said.

"All you muthafuckas are my enemy," Sunny snapped. "Somebody must have planted those drugs on me. I'm telling you it wasn't mine."

He looked at her doubtfully.

"What else did Mr. Dean say in his statement?" She figured that he hadn't told about the incident with the driver because they never would have offered her a way out if they knew that she was a murderer. Still, she asked out of curiosity.

"He said basically that the two of you met recently. That he was your attorney, maybe sometimes more than that. But that he doesn't really know *who* you are."

"He's lying." Sunny fought the emotions that she was truly feeling, and looked Gomez squarely in the eyes. "All of that's a lie."

Gomez stared back at her silently. He pondered what would be the best route to take in order to convey his message to his fiery client. The lovely lady before him had all the markings of a chameleon. Sunny slipped between Spanish and English so easily, and switched demeanors at will. Her duality was evident, as she looked lost and sad one moment, then angry and defiant the next. Gomez wondered what her story was, how she had learned to be two people at the same time. Even though he was a stranger to her, it was easy even for him to ascertain that Sunny was into something, and she was in way over her head.

Sunny felt trapped between a rock and a hard place. She was being extorted. "I don't have that amount of money." She spoke slowly, emphasizing every word. "You said yourself that I only have six grand with me. I don't have ten."

Gomez balanced his cigarette between his lips, and began to pack away his paperwork. "That six grand has already been taken as evidence," he said, calmly. "You will need to produce an additional $10,000."

Sunny was furious, but she kept her mouth shut. She was aware that it was futile to try to reason with these people. Involuntary tears flooded her eyes. As Gomez zipped his briefcase, Sunny faced the facts. Either she was going to see her reputation publicly torn into pieces, or she would have to call someone close to her and explain her predicament. Someone would have to bring the money—and fast! Her carefully guarded secret was now being exposed, and she had never felt like such a failure in her whole life.

"You do not want to remain in jail here in *Mexico*. Nothing nice about it." Gomez gestured at her surroundings. "The real thing is far worse than this." He hoped he was getting through to her.

Sunny was trembling. She knew better than anybody that she had to get the hell out of Mexico immediately. Malcolm had left her with a dead body and a bag of cocaine on her hands in a foreign country. She had to figure out who she could turn to for help. For the first time, she was the one who needed a lifeline. Sunny cried in silence.

Gomez took pity on her as he rose to leave. "I will see to it that you get a shower, a decent meal, and a phone call home." He offered a weak smile. "I'll see you tomorrow."

And then Sunny was alone again.

Jada and Sheldon sat together eating dinner quietly at the dining room table. The silence was eerily familiar. It had been three days since Sheldon's release from the psych ward of Staten Island University Hospital. Three days of awkward conversations and unspoken tension. Both Jada and Sheldon had found comfort in the silence that continually fell between them. In that silence, each of them was able to think things that would have been too dreadful to give voice to.

Jada blamed her son for the fact that her relationship with Born was in ruins. She hadn't spoken to the man she loved since the day she'd walked away from him at the hospital weeks ago. He texted her from time to time to see how she was holding up. She would respond and let him know that she was hanging in there, that she needed some time alone with her son to sort things out. Sheldon had made it clear through his suicide attempt that he was not happy with his mother and Born's relationship. Jada had martyred herself in the weeks since then, depriving herself of Born's love as a way to make up for all the damage she had done to her only child. But the truth was that a large part of Jada hated Sheldon for forcing her and Born apart. It felt as if Sheldon's father, Jamari, was torturing her all over again from the grave. She hated it so intensely that she had to make a conscious effort to be kind to her son. She reminded herself that she had no one to blame but herself for Sheldon's struggles. Still, it was hard not to think negatively about the young man who had taken such control of her life.

Sheldon, on the other hand, was having his own sinister

thoughts. He was glad that Born was gone, gladder that Jada was clearly upset about it. *Good for her!* he thought. She deserved to suffer for being a crackhead, for making him so different from other kids his age. She was to blame for the urges he felt to lash out and misbehave. All the doctors at the psychiatric center pointed to his being born a crack baby as an explanation for his imbalance. He had heard them discussing his problems and their roots in Jada's drug use. Toward the end of his stay at the hospital, Sheldon had reduced his own medication. He didn't like the way it made him feel—all loopy and lethargic. He had no energy when his meds kicked in. Even his thoughts slowed to a crawl. He didn't like it. So, he began to find ways to avoid taking it. He couldn't get away with it all the time. The aides were usually extremely vigilant. But, at times, while one of the lazier aides waited and watched to ensure that he swallowed his pill, he'd create a distraction—sometimes sneezing and spitting it into his palm, other times dropping something on the floor so that he could stash the pill while the aide bent down to pick up the dropped item. Each time he would dutifully open his mouth and lift his tongue to prove that he had swallowed his meds. And once the aide was gone, Sheldon observed what was being said and done around him. Without the medication, he felt more like himself. He had perfected his listless gaze and would stare off into space as the doctors discussed his medical history. It was during one such conversation that he overheard a discussion about his parents' battle for custody of him. As he sat staring blankly at the bare white wall, Sheldon listened closely.

His father had been killed, he learned, in the midst of his parents' custody war. It was something his mother had never told him. She hadn't told him much of anything, in fact—not about his father, not about her drug use.

As they sat in silence now, eating curry chicken, yellow rice, and asparagus, Sheldon watched her. Her eyes were focused on her plate as she seemed lost in thought. *Probably thinking about Born,* Sheldon thought bitterly. He cleared his throat.

Jada seemed to snap out of her trance and she looked up at him. Their eyes locked for several seconds.

"What's wrong?" Jada asked. *What's wrong NOW?* she thought.

Sheldon set down his fork and sat back in his chair, looking his mother in the eye. "I want to know everything," he said. Seeing a look of confusion flash across her face, he explained. "About my father. And about you. And how I got here."

Jada's jaw clenched. For Sheldon's whole life, she had avoided talking about his father or about the ugly and traumatic things that transpired between them. But her policy of "don't ask, don't tell" clearly hadn't worked. Born was not around for her to seek his strength and reassurance. Alone with her son, Jada took a deep breath, sat back in her seat, and threw up her hands.

"What do you want to know, Sheldon? I already told you . . . I was addicted to coke . . . cocaine. Your father accepted that. He gave me crack to smoke. He lied to me—

"Lied to you about what?"

Jada sighed. "A lot of things. He hated Born."

Sheldon frowned. "Why?"

Jada shrugged. She shook her head. Sheldon was so young, too young to fully understand. But she forged ahead. "Your father was jealous of Born." She ignored Sheldon, who sucked his teeth in disbelief. "Born and Jamari grew up together. They were close friends. Jamari's mother was addicted to drugs. So was Born's father. So, Jamari and Born bonded since they had that in common." Jada could tell that she had Sheldon's undivided attention. She went on.

"Jamari's mom told him that he and Born had the same father. She claimed that Born's father, Leo, had never acknowledged Jamari because Leo was married to Miss Ingrid."

Sheldon's brow furrowed as his young mind tried to process all of this information. "My father and Born were brothers?"

Jada shook her head. "We don't know that for sure. That was what Jamari's mother told him. But she died, and Leo never mentioned anything about it before he died, too. So, we'll never really know for sure."

"Why would my grandmother lie about that? If she said it, I believe her."

Jada noticed Sheldon's choice of words. *My grandmother.* He said it with such conviction that she was slightly taken aback by how he had aligned himself with his father's side of the family so instantaneously. He had never met his paternal grandmother and couldn't even remember his father. Yet, he had such faith in their truthfulness. Jada didn't address it, opting to continue instead.

"Jamari was jealous because Born's father gave him everything. Meanwhile, Jamari and his mother struggled. So, all the time that he was friends with Born, he wanted what Born had. And then Jamari stole money from Born."

Sheldon blinked a couple of times. "He *prolly* needed it since him and his mother were broke," he suggested.

Jada's jaw clenched again. Clearly, Sheldon refused to believe the worst about his father. She wanted to end the conversation, but she pressed on. "When Born realized that Jamari stole the money—"

"How much money was it?" Sheldon interjected. *Bet it was like $20!* Born seemed like the type to make a big deal out of nothing.

"Five thousand dollars."

Jada waited for a reaction from her son but got nothing.

"Anyway, Born cut him off. He stopped being friends with him and I never knew the whole story between them until years later. All I knew was that Born didn't like him, didn't trust him. And Jamari didn't like Born either."

She took a sip of water and swallowed slowly before continuing.

"After Born found out that I had started getting high again, he broke up with me and I had no place to go. I had a bad drug problem, and my family had abandoned me. Jamari and I got closer and . . . we started a relationship."

"Did you love each other?" Sheldon asked.

Jada wished she could self-destruct. She knew what Sheldon wanted to hear. Every kid wanted to believe that they were conceived in love. But the truth was far uglier. She recalled Jamari's lies, the way he had manipulated her. She could still picture his outstretched hand with the crack vial in it.

"Go ahead and take it. I'm not gonna judge you. I understand."

She could hear Jamari's voice as clearly now as she had all those years ago.

"Sheldon," she explained. "I was so addicted to drugs that I couldn't love anybody. Not even myself."

"Did he love you?"

She shook her head no. Seeing the hopeful expression on Sheldon's face melt into dejectedness, she lied a little. "He did at first," she said. "But my addiction made him turn against me eventually." Jada knew that, in truth, Jamari had never loved her. He only saw her as a pawn in his sick game against Born. His control over every aspect of her life was all in an effort to flaunt his "trophy" in Born's face.

"Why did y'all break up?" Sheldon asked.

Jada sipped her water again and swallowed hard. She fought the urge to smile at the memory of stealing Jamari's re-up and exiting his life for good. Revenge had been sweet. Still, she couldn't tell Sheldon the truth—she had stolen his father's crack, sold it, and binged. She had to find a way to cushion the truth.

"When you were born, and I had made up my mind that it was time to get clean . . . I started seeing things differently. Once

I was out of the fog, I realized that Jamari had manipulated the whole situation. I felt like he used me to make Born jealous. So I ended our relationship, and I focused on doing everything I could to be a good mother for you."

Jada sat back in her chair and looked into Sheldon's eyes. She had given him the abridged version, but it was the truth nonetheless. She prayed that Sheldon would stop seeing her as his enemy.

"Sheldon . . . I love you," she said, sincerely. "I've loved you from the first moment I laid eyes on you. I *fought* for you. When you were born, your father was mad at me. He was angry because I had been selfish, and he had every right to feel the way that he did. But I was sorry, and I had made up my mind to stop using drugs. He didn't believe me. He hated me. And to be honest with you, I hated myself. I felt like dying."

Sheldon watched his mother closely, saw the tears that welled up in her eyes. He heard the emotion in her voice and he believed her. He realized, maybe for the first time, how sorry Jada was—how much she cared for him.

"But then Sunny would bring me pictures of you. Every time I saw those pictures, I felt stronger, more determined to fight for the right to be your mom. When I got out of jail, I was in court just about every week to get visitation rights and trying to get custody. You were the only thing I had to live for anymore. Your father did everything he could to keep me from seeing you. But the judge slowly made it possible for you and I to build a relationship. And then your father was killed." Jada said that last part flatly. She felt no remorse that she and Sunny had left Jamari to die alone in that parking lot in the dead of winter.

"Once he wasn't around to fight me anymore, I was finally able to be your mom."

Sheldon stared at his hands, letting it all sink in. He wondered how his life would be different if his father hadn't been killed.

He knew that Jamari had loved him. Somehow, he had always known that in his heart. But now Jada had confirmed it for him. His father had loved him so much that he had fought to keep his drug-addicted mother out of his life. Sheldon watched Jada wiping the tears from her eyes. He replayed her words in his mind.

"Sheldon, I love you."

He looked at his mother, thought to himself about how pretty she was. She wasn't a terrible person. He had seen some of his classmates' mothers, so he knew that horrible parents existed. The kind who talked loud and cussed all the time. The ones who wore scarves on their head in public, and barked orders at their kids. Jada was nothing like that. Whatever she had been in the past was far behind her now. He decided that maybe it was time to forgive Jada. Clearly, she was sorry and had already paid dearly for her transgressions. Sheldon would turn over a new leaf with his mother. But Born was a different story.

"Why did you name me Sheldon Marquis? Why don't I have my father's name instead of Born's?"

Jada's eyes narrowed. *What an odd question!* she thought. After all of what she had just told him, after hearing how determined Jamari had been to keep her away from her child, after hearing about his jealousy towards Born . . . all Sheldon had to ask was what had inspired his name?

"I named you after the two men who had been most important in my life. My father and Born."

"Did you wish that Born was my father?"

Jada hesitated before answering. "I did," she admitted.

Silence engulfed them again.

Finally, Sheldon spoke. "I bet my dad didn't like my name." He toyed with his napkin.

Jada didn't know how to respond, so she said nothing; instead, allowing his words to float unanswered.

"Thank you for telling me the truth," Sheldon said softly. "You coulda lied about a lot of stuff. But you didn't. I'm glad that I know the whole story now." He set down his napkin, pushed his chair away from the table, stood up, and looked his mother in the eye.

"I love you, too," he said.

And, with that, he walked out and went upstairs to his room.

Jada sat there alone, wondering if she should get her hopes up. She couldn't help but pray that this signaled a light at the end of what had been a very long and dark tunnel. Only time would tell.

2
BIG DREAMS

"Go, DJ!" the crowd yelled. Glasses clinked, congratulations abounded, and the music resumed its pulsing beat through the speakers. DJ was all smiles as people crowded around him to offer their well wishes and praise for his latest CD—one that was sure to be labeled a classic in years to come. Tonight's event was in DJ's honor, a party to celebrate his album debuting at number one on the Billboard charts. His career was at an all-time high, and Born looked like a proud father as he watched DJ soaking up all the accolades. Not one to get easily emotional, Born felt himself getting choked up and, quickly, covertly wiped a tear from his eye.

"I saw that," Dominique said, smiling at Born as she appeared at his side. "Don't try to hide it. It's okay to get choked up seeing your boy succeed the way that he is." She clinked glasses with Born and watched a shy smile creep across his sexy lips.

"I was just thinking about his father," Born explained. "I wish Dorian was alive to see this. He'd be so proud of his son."

Dominique nodded. "I know the feeling. Whenever I reach a milestone in my career, I wish my dad was still around to witness it. But I believe that he looks down on me and sees the strides I'm making. I'm sure the same is true for DJ's father. He *must* have a guardian angel watching over him, because the first-week sales he's gotten are unbelievable in this day and age. Almost a million records sold in an industry that is struggling. . . . I'd say that's divine intervention mixed with some incredible talent. This young man is at the top of his game!"

Born agreed. "The kid is good."

A photographer approached the pair, and gestured for the two of them to stand closer together for a picture. Born held Dominique around the waist and drew her closer to him. Dominique felt a chill up her spine. The two of them smiled brightly as the camera flashed. The photographer thanked them and walked off to capture other partygoers.

Dominique wasn't sure if it was the wine or Born's close proximity that had her feeling lightheaded. She noticed that he still held her waist even though the moment had passed.

The deejay was excellent, and the dance floor was so packed that the floor beneath them shook from all of the movement. Born was feeling good. "Wanna dance?" he asked.

Dominique beamed. "Sure."

They set down their glasses on a nearby table and headed to the dance floor to join the crowd. As they danced, Dominique laughed as Born did "The Wop," a throwback to their heyday. She pop-locked to show him that she had some old-school moves in her arsenal as well. Born cracked up and they moved together happily, enjoying themselves for several more songs.

DJ watched from across the room where he was surrounded by a group of friends and fellow entertainers. He smiled, happy to see Born enjoying himself. It was the first time he'd seen him laugh in weeks, since Jada had pushed him away. DJ knew that Born was hurt by it, but he had put on a brave face and helped promote DJ's newest release full time.

DJ had mixed feelings about Jada. On one hand, it was clear to him that she made Born happy. Never was his smile as broad or his laughter as hearty as when Jada was near. Born came alive in her presence. Even a stranger could observe them for mere minutes and surmise that they shared a long history together, one full of private jokes, happy memories, and fun. The love between the two of them was unmistakable. Jada had always been kind to DJ, especially after his father was killed and Born became a constant presence in the young man's life. Once DJ expressed an interest in rapping as opposed to the street life his uncles were grooming him for, Born had become like a father to him. Finding the right beats for DJ to rhyme to, accompanying him to studio sessions that lasted all night, eventually tours that took them to the far reaches of the world—Born had been there through it all from the very start. Whenever things seemed grim or challenging, Born reminded the young man that anything worth having is worth fighting for. He gave him advice about girls, taught him how to make his money work for him, showed him the ropes of grown-man games like chess. Born was the closest thing to a dad that DJ had known since Dorian's demise. And, eventually, once Jada and Born reunited, DJ had grown close to her, too.

But this situation with Sheldon had changed everything. All of a sudden, Sheldon seemed to be in control of everything, and it was clear to everybody that he wasn't feeling Born and Jada's relationship. So for weeks Jada had kept Born at bay. For weeks, Born had been walking around nursing a broken heart while doing his best to keep his poker face on. DJ didn't appreciate the pain his father figure was enduring. And he wasn't sure if he was pissed at Jada about it or if Sheldon alone was to blame.

Tonight, though, Born was having a good time. And so was Dominique. DJ had always taken note of her beauty, her swag. She seemed like the kind of lady who could make Born forget about Jada.

For tonight, at least, DJ hoped that was exactly what Born would do. From across the room, he caught Born's eye. They raised their glasses in a silent toast, and partied the night away.

Olivia was in a late meeting with buyers for Vintage, her clothing line. In a conference room on the top floor of the Solomon Bryan building, she sold them on the luxe fabrics and cutting-edge designs set before them. Solomon Bryan was a media conglomerate that was fast becoming known as "the black Condé Nast." They published just about every major magazine that appealed to the black and Latino demographic, which was quickly growing. Tonight's meeting was being held in the mega-company's flagship building in the fashion district, in office space that the buyers leased. Being in such close proximity to fashion's elite was a reality not lost on Olivia. These buyers worked for reputable department stores, major stylists, boutiques, and clothiers. This long running meeting was one of the most important of her career, and Olivia knew it. She had dressed the part today, wearing a Vintage electric-blue jumpsuit with a pair of nude Jimmy Choos and subtle jewelry. The look had been edgy and fashion-forward by day. But their meeting had gone on far longer than she planned, and at this late hour she was beginning to wish that she had opted for something that translated better from day to evening. In fact, she had spent so much of the past four hours second-guessing everything from the fabrics she had chosen to use for her line to the color palette she had chosen to present for the buyers today. She was high off a mixture of adrenaline and angst.

Her cell phone buzzed, and a crazy international number displayed on her caller ID. She sent it to voice mail, unaware that it was Sunny calling. She turned off her phone and tossed it into her Bottega Veneta bag. Whirling around to face the buyers, she flashed them her most alluring smile.

"So, guys, is it a yes?"

Malcolm stifled a yawn and glanced at his watch. He had sent his secretary home hours ago, and now it was so late that even the associates and paralegals had gone home for the night. It was nearly nine o'clock, and he had been working since seven o'clock that morning. In an effort to get Sunny off his mind, he had worked the whole day as if his life depended on it. It was the only way to distract himself from the feelings of self-loathing that crept up on him whenever he was idle. He had left her, the woman he loved, in Mexico with no one to help her. He felt terrible, having allowed his fear to take over. While he had been there in Mexico, being questioned mercilessly and threatened with jail time, all he had been able to think about was his career; how he could lose everything because of Sunny's crazy ass. She had deceived him into thinking that she was clean. But the truth was that even as they vacationed—a trip that Malcolm had imagined as a precursor to the honeymoon he imagined they would enjoy someday—Sunny had been getting high the whole time. Now there was a dead man on the side of some Mexican dirt road, and Sunny was under arrest for cocaine possession. He had gotten the hell out of there as fast as he could.

But now guilt had set in. Malcolm couldn't face himself. It didn't help that she had called the office three times that day for assistance—surely desperate for answers—as she faced the music all alone in Mexico. He hadn't answered any of the calls from the international number, knowing that an angry Sunny was on the other end. Malcolm felt torn. Part of him believed that whatever happened to her would be justified. After all, she had killed a man. She had been buying and using cocaine while he had been oblivious. She had lied to him. She deserved to pay for those things. But, the other part felt horrible for abandoning her. He loved her. And instead of sticking around to help her, he had fled as soon as they said that he was free to leave.

He had turned off his cell phone hours ago, after Sunny's third call. He glanced at it now, made up his mind that tomorrow he would change the number. He stuck it in the top drawer of his desk, turned off the desktop lamp, and pushed back his chair. He stood up, stretched, and willed himself to think of anything but her. Malcolm grabbed his briefcase, and headed home for the night, telling himself that he had done the only thing he could. He had saved himself.

Jada lay in bed, not sleeping, but only half awake. She had tried everything from meditating to masturbating, and nothing seemed to bring her enough relief from her thoughts of Born. She thought about calling him, but worried that Sheldon might overhear her. She resented Sheldon for the distance she had been forced to put between her and the man she loved. Each night after dinner, Jada turned off the ringers on all the phones so that the noise wouldn't disturb Sheldon while he slept. If Born tried calling her late at night after studio sessions with DJ, Jada usually missed the calls as a result. She hated this. Still, she didn't dare to risk upsetting the calm that had finally settled in her home. Jada wanted her son to be happy, even if it meant sacrificing her own joy.

She tried, for the thousandth time, to think of a way that they could all be a family. She kept coming up empty. The thought of it made her weary. It seemed that no matter how badly she wanted things to work out, there was no way. Through his suicide attempt, Sheldon had presented Jada with an ultimatum—him or

Born. She couldn't have both. Exhausted, she yawned several times, snuggling into the pillow. She glanced at her cell phone to ensure that she hadn't missed any calls or texts. There was nothing. She set the phone back on the nightstand and settled back into her cozy spot. She wondered where Born was and what he was doing. She yawned again, and this time, shut her eyes and settled into perfect relaxation. As sleep finally overtook Jada, her cell phone screen lit up with an incoming call. Tonight, it wasn't Born calling.

Sunny muttered under her breath with each ring. "Please, be there, Jada."

But Jada was already gone, blissfully dreaming of the happily-ever-after that seemed to elude her in her waking hours.

It was after three in the morning when Born walked Dominique to the parking garage at the end of the block. It was a warm, June evening and the two of them were grateful for the fresh spring breeze on their faces. The party venue had been packed, and both of them had sweated considerably as they danced, mixed, and mingled while celebrating DJ's success. Dominique's curls had all fallen, and she self-consciously raked her fingers through her hair in an attempt to make herself more presentable. Born noticed.

"Cut it out," he said, smiling and showcasing his irresistible dimples. "You look beautiful."

Dominique blushed, and felt her pulse quicken. Despite the breeze, she fanned herself with her hand, suddenly hotter than ever. "Thanks," she managed.

The pair walked on in awkward silence for several paces, both of them deluged with thoughts. Born realized just how much he dreaded saying good-bye to Dominique now that the fresh air was helping to clear his mind. He had spent the past couple of hours intoxicated by the scent of Dominique's perfume and by her disarming smile. Now, as they neared the parking garage, he hated for the night to end.

Dominique was dreading saying good night to Born as well. She stole a glance at him as they walked.

"Where's Jada?" she found herself asking. "I expected to see her tonight, toasting it up with you and DJ."

Born shook his head. "I'm not sure where she is." Noticing Dominique's confused expression, he elaborated. "We're not together anymore." Saying it aloud for the first time; Born felt an incredible sadness wash over him. He had been in denial about it, but there it was. There was no sense avoiding the truth any longer. Things had come to a standstill between him and Jada. Ever since Sheldon had regained consciousness after his suicide attempt, Jada had refused to see him. They still talked from time to time, but things were not the same. Three months had passed without any real contact with her. In Born's opinion, Jada had let Sheldon win. And, truth be told, he was hurt by it.

Dominique was surprised by the revelation. The couple had seemed unbreakable. "I'm sorry to hear that," she said.

Born shrugged. "Shit happens," he said. He pushed the pain of his failed relationship deep down inside of him, and forced a weak smile.

They reached the parking garage, and Dominique gave the ticket to the attendant, who then left to retrieve her car.

"How about you?" Born asked. "You still in love with ole boy?" Born had met Archie on a number of occasions when he had accompanied Dominique to events. He had always felt that the guy was lucky to be with her, and had never really warmed up to him as a result.

Dominique shook her head and sighed. "Nope. He got himself in some legal trouble, and I decided that I didn't need those kinds of complications in my life. Been there, done that, you know?"

Born nodded. He understood completely. Having grown beyond his hustling days, he appreciated that Dominique had outgrown her attraction to that lifestyle as well.

"Well . . . a beautiful woman like you won't be single long."

Dominique smiled. The sexual tension between the two of them was palpable. Born felt emboldened by the Hennessy coursing through his system. He brushed his hand across her cheek, then caressed her pouty lips with the pad of his thumb. Dominique swooned, completely swept up in the moment. Before she could formulate a thought, Born leaned in and kissed her passionately, drawing her close to him by her small waist. Her hands instinctively cupped his face, their tongues moving together erotically. They both lost themselves in the kiss, until the sound of the attendant pulling up in Dominique's car snapped them out of their trance.

Pulling away from Born, Dominique cursed under her breath. "Shit!" She shook her head, silently berating herself. "This is not cool. I'm DJ's rep at the label. I can't do this with . . . you're his manager . . ."

Born stepped back, the spell broken.

The attendant approached, and Dominique fished around in her clutch bag for some cash to pay him. Born placed his hand over hers, stopping her.

"I got it," he said. "Don't worry about it. He handed the attendant a crisp fifty and looked at Dominique, apologetically. "Sorry about that," he said. "You're right. I crossed the line."

Dominique felt bad. She had wanted that kiss as much as he had. But she had worked hard to climb to where she was in her career. The last thing she wanted was to allow her horniness to screw it all up.

"It's not your fault," she said. "I kissed you too. I held on to you so tight that you couldn't escape."

Born laughed at that, and she did, too. The tension dissolved. "Let's chalk this up to too much alcohol and pretend it didn't happen." Born held out his hand.

Dominique took it, and shook it firmly. She chuckled. "Deal."

Born held open her car door while she climbed inside. "Drive safe," he said. "We'll talk tomorrow."

Dominique winked at him, fastened her seat belt, and sped off before she threw caution to the wind and invited Born home with her.

Born headed off in the direction of his own car. Checking his watch, he saw that it was much later than he thought. He considered calling Jada, but decided against it. She seldom answered his calls anymore, and he was sick of the rejection. He reached his truck, climbed inside, and instinctively headed straight to Anisa's house instead.

He turned up the music in his truck, the bass pounding throughout the vehicle. He thought about Anisa as he headed to her house. For years now, their relationship had been restricted to co-parenting Ethan. But Born was noticing that Ethan liked having him around on a daily basis. Truth be told, Born liked being in the family atmosphere with his son and with Anisa. It felt good. Especially with Jada giving him the cold shoulder the way that she was. He was beginning to wonder if he had played his cards right all those years ago when he ended things with Anisa in order to give his heart to Jada once again.

Lately, Born had been spending more time than ever at the home he provided for Anisa and Ethan. Though he had a place of his own, he was comfortable falling asleep in Ethan's room, or in the home's spare bedroom. He even held meetings with DJ and his management team there. Those meetings used to take place at Jada's home, but Jada had abandoned Born in favor of her son.

Born had also taken notice of Anisa's new outlook on life. She had once been very superficial, and it was for that very reason that his mother still didn't like her, even after all these years. Ingrid thought Anisa was stuck up, self-absorbed, and a gold digger. After all, she had abandoned Born when he was locked up. Wisely, she had secured her position in Born's life forever by having his son almost immediately after his release.

But this new and improved Anisa seemed changed somehow. She still enjoyed the finer things in life. However, motherhood had settled her in ways that Born found endearing. Anisa was a great mother. Attentive and caring. The more he was around her, the more he realized that she had grown a great deal over the years. He found himself actually listening when she talked to him about the things that piqued her interest. There had been a time when he instinctively tuned her out. Both of them had matured in the years since their split, and at the very least Anisa and Born had developed a close friendship in the time since Jada had gone MIA.

He arrived, parked his car in the driveway, and saw a light burning dimly in the living room. He opened the door with his key and saw Anisa sitting on the chaise, a pair of glasses perched on the tip of her nose as she read a book. She seemed surprised to see him.

"Hey," she said, smiling at him.

"Hey," he replied. "Ethan's asleep?" As soon as the words left his mouth, he realized what a silly question it was.

"Yeah," Anisa said. "It's late."

He nodded. "Yeah. You're still up."

She nodded.

"I just left DJ's party. I was . . . I know it's late." He realized that he was practically stuttering. He cleared his throat. "I was thinking about you, so I thought I'd stop by . . . see if you were still awake."

Anisa's heart skipped. Her pulse started to pound so hard that she could feel it in her temples.

He was here to see *her*! She had been on his mind. All the time he'd been spending there over the past several weeks had seemed to be for Ethan's benefit. But here he was. Ethan was fast asleep, and Born had come over anyway. She took off her glasses, set them and the book down on the table beside her, and slowly stood to her feet. She wondered what this was all about, what he had to say to her.

"You want to talk?" she asked.

Born shook his head no. He walked over to where she stood. Their faces were inches apart, he leaned down and kissed her softly. He saw the shocked expression on her face, and felt an unexpected fury overtake him. In that moment, he hated Jada for rejecting him. He had never been unfaithful to her—not once in all their years together. He was tired of being pushed aside. And he was well aware that Anisa would give anything for even one night in his arms. It made him feel good, knowing that someone still wanted him, even if it wasn't the woman he truly loved.

He gripped her face in his large and powerful hands and kissed her like he meant it; his other hand fisted a handful of her hair and tugged at it roughly. Anisa didn't mutter a protest. Instead, she wrapped her arms around his neck and kissed him back with equal fervor. Her prayers had been answered at last.

3

SLEEPLESS NIGHT

Jada woke up in a panic. She had a terrible dream that she was being followed by a man dressed in black, though she hadn't been able to see his face. The stranger had followed her down a dark and deserted road before trapping her in a blacked-out corner. Just as he drew near, she had awakened with a start. From the way that her heart was pounding, it took her several long and agonizing seconds before she could convince herself that she had been only dreaming. Breathlessly, she sat up in bed, and fumbled for her bedside lamp. She hugged her knees close to her chest and exhaled deeply. She thought of Sheldon, and got out of bed to check on him. Opening her bedroom door, she jumped in terror at the sight of a figure standing there. Her heart skipped a beat, and she nearly fell backward. Already shaken from the nightmare, a sense of fear and dread washed over her. Her pulse calmed only slightly when she saw that it was Sheldon standing there.

She shook her head, confused. "Why are you just standing there?" Her head whipped around and she looked at the clock. "It's three in the morning. What are you doing up?"

He stared at her, frowning.

"I couldn't sleep," he said. "I saw your light on."

Jada held her hand over her heart, willing herself to calm down. "Why didn't you knock or say something?"

"I was just about to." He stepped into the room. "What's wrong with you?"

She trembled now, and grabbed a blanket off of her bed, and wrapped herself in it. "Nothing," she said. "You just scared me."

He stared at her silently for several long moments. "I didn't mean to scare you."

Jada nodded. "It's alright. Go back to bed. I'll see you in the morning."

Sheldon nodded, then turned and left. Jada stood staring at the closed bedroom door for a long time afterward. She couldn't shake the eerie feeling that lingered there. She climbed back into bed, but left the light on. She turned on the TV, and sat wrapped in the blanket, lost in her thoughts. She didn't sleep for the rest of the night.

Sunny was wide awake, though it was still dark outside the little window above the raggedy cot on which she lay. The sun had not yet risen, and the typically noisy facility where she was housed was oddly quiet at this time of morning. She had barely slept a wink at all, but spent most of the night lying awake thinking about the predicament she found herself in. Throughout the night, Sunny had come to terms with certain truths. First, that she had everything any woman could possibly dream of, and she had managed to fuck it all up. Also, that she was angry and disappointed—not just with bitchass Malcolm, but with herself. And to make the situation even worse, she finally admitted to herself—as she longed throughout the night for one good snort of cocaine—that she had an addiction. She had been in denial about that fact for far too long. But she was torturously fiending for a hit of coke, even as she was locked up for possession. Her cravings showed no signs of subsiding, and all through the night she'd tossed and turned—sleep evading her despite the fact that she was physically, emotionally, and mentally exhausted.

Sunny had cried in the dark as she thought about her life and the predicament she found herself in now. She had a beautiful daughter who was happy and healthy. The home they lived in was opulent and their lifestyle lush. She had money, fame, a career as a model at an age when most women are cast aside in the youth-obsessed beauty industry. She had every material thing that her heart desired. The only thing she didn't have was Dorian, and the absence of him—the void that was left—had driven her back to the drug that had nearly destroyed her life in the first place. This time, her addiction had gotten her in more trouble than she could manage.

Sunny had dialed Malcolm's office numerous times the previous day. Each time, his secretary insisted that he was in meetings and couldn't be disturbed. His cell phone number had been changed. He had left her for dead, and gone back to life as if Sunny never existed.

"I might as well walk away from you now, while I still can." Malcolm had said those words to her back in New York, before he convinced her to fly to Mexico with him. Sunny wished desperately that she had let him walk away.

He had never been the right man for her, and she had known it all along. She had pretended that their differences were no big deal, had forced herself to fit into his world. Jazz, ice-skating, ballroom dancing, golfing—she had experienced those things for the first time in her life while dating Malcolm. Malcolm was a starched, white-collar guy, who wore flip-flops on vacation. He was a cornball from the suburbs of Maryland. Sunny was a Brooklyn chick through and through. She saw so clearly now that it could never have worked out.

But this? She could never have imagined this. He had

abandoned her. And Sunny vowed that she would make him pay for it.

Anisa woke up in Born's arms the next morning and was so overcome with emotion that tears of joy pooled in her eyes. With her head resting on his chest, Born's hand still cupped her ass as he snored softly. Anisa breathed in his scent and smiled. Born was *back*. Back in her home, in her bed, back in that place in her heart that she had never really allowed him to vacate in the first place. She wondered if the Hennessy she had smelled and tasted on his breath the night before had been the only thing that prompted this blissful reunion. She prayed that it wasn't.

Born had ravaged her last night. He had scooped her up in his arms and unceremoniously carried her upstairs to her spacious bedroom. Caveman style, he had tossed her on the bed and tore her nightgown in his eagerness to undress her. He had muffled her moans with passionate kisses as he slid his long fingers in and out of her wetness. He had bitten at her lips, neck, and breasts with such force that she slapped him to calm him down. It had only seemed to arouse him more, and he plunged himself into her, raw, her nails gripping into his skin as she clung to him in a glorious mixture of pleasure and pain. A guttural moan escaped her lips as Anisa reached her climax. Born seemed to enjoy the effect that he clearly had on her. Placing her legs on his shoulders, he had growled with the ferocity of an animal uncaged as he took her. Anisa had responded in kind, winding her hips to meet his, mirroring his urgency, and giving him her all. She was aware that this was her big chance to blow his mind. Switching positions, she had ridden him so expertly and with such reckless abandon that Born had held her close to him and moaned her name as he spent himself within her. Breathlessly, he had lain beneath her afterward, clinging to her so tightly that she could feel his heartbeat. He had fallen asleep that way and had slept the whole night without moving from that position.

Anisa felt understandably sore between her legs now, but she didn't mind it one bit. It was proof that she hadn't dreamed this, that this was all reality. She shut her eyes again, wanting to freeze this moment in time.

Born's eyes fluttered open, and he was instantly aware of the dry, cottony taste in his mouth, the pounding in his head, and the fact that he was not in his own bed. His eyes scanned the room and he realized where he was, recalled the events of last night. Anisa lay on top of him, and he dared not move. The scent of her hair wafted up to his nostrils, and he closed his eyes once more, berating himself. Last night had been a mistake.

Miss Ingrid had raised him to never toy with women's emotions. She had drilled it into his head over the years, insisting that he not profess his love for anyone unless he truly meant it. He lay there now, trying to recall all of the details of the night before. He didn't remember saying anything close to "I love you," but he knew that it didn't really matter. Just having sex with Anisa was enough to give her the wrong impression, and he knew it. Born closed his eyes once more. He thought of Jada, and felt guilty. Last night had temporarily helped him to forget about her. But now she was back on his mind again, and he knew that he had made a mistake giving Anisa a night of passionate sex while his heart still belonged to someone else.

He opened his eyes again, cleared his throat, and stirred slightly. Anisa lifted her head and met his gaze. A bright smile spread across her pretty face, and it caused Born to smile, too, involuntarily. It had been years since they had woken up together this way.

"Good morning," she said.

"Good morning." His voice was gravelly with sleep. Glancing at the bedside clock, he saw that it was just after nine a.m. Sunlight poured through the partially open blinds, illuminating

Anisa's face. She looked angelic in this light, and Born felt his heart melt a little. He searched for something to say, but it was Anisa that spoke first.

"What a night!"

She chuckled as she said it, and Born grinned, uneasily. He wasn't sure how he should respond. He was almost embarrassed by what they'd done.

Anisa, too, seemed a bit shy lying naked on top of him. She sighed. "Ethan's gonna be waking up soon . . . I'm gonna freshen up and go make breakfast so he doesn't catch us like this."

Born agreed, grateful for the reprieve, and watched as Anisa climbed out of bed and walked, naked, into the bathroom to take a shower. He admired her body as she strode across the room. Anisa still looked good, and he had to resist the urge to go after her and satisfy his morning woody. Instead, he waited until he heard the shower running, and climbed out of bed himself. He could hear Anisa singing softly in the shower, as he pulled his cell phone out of the pocket of his jeans lying crumpled on the floor. No missed calls, no texts. He was disappointed. He rose each morning hopeful that this would be the day that Jada would walk back into his life. Riddled with guilt, he dialed her number.

"Hello?" she answered on the second ring.

"Hey, baby, it's me. I—"

"I can't talk right now," Jada interrupted abruptly. "I'm having breakfast with Sheldon. I'll call you back." She hung up without waiting for a response.

Born sat there staring at the phone long after the call had ended. He felt dismissed, his pride wounded. He chuckled uneasily to himself and shook his head. For several moments he sat there in disbelief, berating himself for the heartache he was enduring. Here he was feeling guilty for enjoying the affection of a woman who still loved him after all these years, and Jada couldn't care less. He thought himself a fool.

Born turned off his cell phone, and tossed it on top of his jeans lying on the floor. He strolled into the bathroom to join Anisa in the shower, and smiled when she giggled like a schoolgirl at the sight of him. This time, he promised not to bite.

Sunny's hands trembled as she held the phone. The receiver was gross—greasy and caked with grime. But she only half noticed. She held the receiver with both hands, her eyes squeezed shut in order to keep the tears at bay. This was the hardest thing she had ever had to do. The cord on the old-fashioned phone was coiled tightly, leaving her little room to move about. She felt the tears stream down her face as she held the phone gingerly and avoided having it rub up against her face. Slowly, painstakingly, she dialed the number.

The stubby guard was back again, standing nearby and listening.

Marisol answered after several rings, confused by the international number on the caller ID.

"Yes? Hello?"

"Ma . . ." Sunny's voice quivered. "I need your help."

Marisol could sense the urgency in her daughter's voice, even though Sunny spoke softly. She knew Sunny well enough to sense that if she needed help, it was a serious situation.

"What's wrong, Sunny? Where are you?"

"I'm in Mexico. I'm in jail." Sunny squeezed her eyes even tighter then, hearing those awful words coming from her own mouth.

"Jail?" Marisol repeated. She said it loudly, and drew the attention of Sunny's father seated nearby. Marisol locked eyes with him, their worst fears realized. "What happened?"

"Ma, I can't explain it right now. Not over the phone. But I will tell you everything when you get here." She took a deep breath. "They're shaking me down," she said. "They will let me go, but they want money. Ten thousand to get me out of here."

"*WHAT?*"

Marisol's voice was so loud that Sunny held the phone even farther away from her ear.

"What do they think you did?"

Sunny let the tears stream down then, aware as she was that her carefully crafted façade had all come crumbling down around her. Soon, her family would have to know that she had been getting high again. Soon. But not now.

"Ma, just get the money, get here, and get me out . . . please," Sunny cried.

Marisol didn't need to hear her daughter say it. She had gone through this with Sunny before—rescuing her. Jada, too. She had helped Sunny battle her addiction before, had even had suspicions that her daughter might be sliding back down that slippery slope of drugs again. Dorian had introduced their family to a very ugly lifestyle full of arrests, shootings, addictions, and a myriad of other unsavory occurrences. But the ugly underbelly of their lives was masked by the wealth they had accumulated as a result. Indeed, Marisol knew better than anyone that her family had paid a handsome price in exchange for an existence that shined like diamonds in the sunshine to those who were watching.

She snapped into action. "Calm down, *mija*. I'm on my way."

4

EVOLUTION

"You's a dumb bitch!"

Toya's voice boomed so loudly that Dominique winced. "You're telling me that *fine* ass man kissed you, and you ran like a scared little girl? You have got to be kidding me!"

Dominique shook her head at her friend. The two of them were getting pedicures at Oasis Nail Spa in Midtown Manhattan. As their feet soaked, they sipped Cosmopolitans and discussed the events at DJ's party the night before. The typically quiet atmosphere was completely different today. Toya's voice thundered each time she spoke. Her laughter echoed off the walls. But the staff wouldn't dare to try and hush her. She was one of their best tippers.

Dominique swished her toes around in the green tea–scented water. "We have a business relationship."

Toya frowned. "So?"

"I can't work on DJ's behalf while screwing his manager."

"Why not?"

"Because my other artists might think I was showing favoritism."

"And?"

"I don't want anybody questioning the integrity of my work."

"Save that shit, Dominique!"

Lucy, the nail technician working on Toya's feet, chuckled. Dominique pretended not to notice.

"What are you talking about?"

Toya glared at her. "Your ass is scared."

"Scared?"

"To death."

"Of what?" Dominique laughed off Toya's ridiculous statement, and sipped her Cosmo.

"Of getting involved in another relationship. Of letting down your guard and being hurt again. You don't fool me. All this talk of professional integrity and business relationships is bullshit! Your ass is scared."

Lucy nodded in agreement. Perched on her stool at Toya's feet, she spoke in Korean to the nail tech beside her who was pumicing Dominique's heels. Dominique sucked her teeth loudly, aware that both ladies agreed with Toya. Rolling her eyes at them, she turned back to her friend.

"I am not scared, Toya. I can honestly say that I'm enjoying the single life."

Toya looked skeptical.

"I am!" Dominique noticed that Lucy wasn't buying it either. "But let's face it. I haven't made the best relationship choices in the past—Octavia's absentee dad, Jamel, Archie. This time around, I'm not forcing it. I'm gonna stay single until the right guy comes along. And something tells me that Born is not that man."

"You don't know that," Toya said, squirming slightly as Lucy's scrubbing tickled her feet.

"I *do* know it. Yes, he's handsome, and he has that mixture of intelligence and street savvy that I love. But for as long as I've known him, he's been in love with Jada. He says they're not together anymore, and maybe that's true. But I don't want anyone else's sloppy seconds. Born isn't the right guy for me. And I'm not gonna waste my time spreading my legs for somebody who I know in my gut won't love me how I deserve to be loved in the long run." Dominique shrugged.

Toya stared at her silently for a minute. Dominique didn't sound like the same lovestruck fool she had been during her relationship with Jamel. Secretly, Toya was impressed.

"What? You thinking like a man now?"

Dominique laughed hard, and Toya joined her, snickering. "I'm just saying, you sound like you went to the Steve Harvey School and graduated at the top of your class."

Dominique looked on, as her pedicurist polished her toes. "Well, he does make some good points."

Toya sipped her Cosmo. She waved her hand dismissively. "Whatever."

"What about you?" Dominique asked. "You're dishing out all this advice and I don't hear you talking about Russell at all lately. What's going on with you two?"

"Not a damn thing. I kicked his ass to the curb."

Dominique's eyes widened. "Uh-uh! Why? I thought you were in *love*!"

"I used to love him." Toya nodded. "But I don't now."

Dominique arched an eyebrow. "Wasn't that a Lauryn Hill song?"

Toya shrugged. "My life is a Lauryn Hill song." She drained her glass and gestured impatiently for a refill. One of the pretty young staffers rushed over with a pitcher in hand.

Dominique wasn't letting her off the hook that easy. "You just spent the past hour digging all up in my business with Born. If you think I'm gonna let you slide with that weak explanation for what happened with you and Russell, you must be crazy. Spill it!"

Toya sighed. "He started talking marriage and kids, and that was a turnoff. I'm not interested in either one of those things.

He won't budge, and neither will I. He wants a family and he's ready to settle down. And me . . . as much as I cared about him, I'm not the marrying kind. Been there, done that."

She waved her hand dismissively as if it were all water under the bridge, but Dominique could see right through her. The two of them had been friends long enough for her to see that Toya's breakup with Russell wasn't as easy as she made it seem.

"Mm-hmm." Dominique sipped the rest of her drink and gave Toya a side eye. "But *I'm* the one who's scared, right?"

Toya glared at her, playfully. "Don't get cute, bitch!"

This time, Lucy and her coworker didn't bother to hide their laughter. Dominique giggled as well. Toya was a trip, but she loved her like a sister. She smiled at the thought of the two of them single once again. This was going to be a great summer!

Gillian sat across from Frankie and Zion at Beso and savored her salmon. The food in this place was divine, but Frankie was making the meal less enjoyable for her with his sour mood. She pretended not to notice him picking at his food, scowling, as Zion filled him in on the new developments in their crew.

Frankie hadn't been himself around her for a long time. Ever since she had walked away from their relationship two years prior, and replaced him as head of the Nobles crime family, Frankie had been quietly brooding. Gillian paid him no mind. Business was business and, as far as she was concerned, that was all that remained between the two of them.

She gave Zion her attention.

"So," Zion said. "Grant told us that Angelle and the doctors she works for are hot right now. It's not safe to keep doing business with her. So we're gonna go another route."

Grant Keys was an attorney working in the Brooklyn DA's office. He was also an associate of the Nobles crime family. An insider, who was well connected with judges and members of all levels of law enforcement, Grant gave them information about who was on the government's radar. In return he was paid handsomely—far more than the salary he made courtesy of the State of New York. Grant was trusted, and for good reason. He had never steered them wrong.

Frankie frowned. "What do you mean we're not gonna work with her anymore? We've been working with Angelle for years. What did Grant say exactly?"

Gillian sipped her water before responding. She didn't appreciate her decision being questioned, but since it was Frankie she let it slide.

"He said that Angelle is under the microscope. Some jocks got caught out there with a bunch of pills and Dr. Tatum's name came up during questioning." Gillian set down her fork, sat back, and looked Frankie in the eye. "Remember her little song and dance about how she couldn't keep running the risk of forging prescriptions? How she insisted that she needed more money and sold you on that bullshit about getting pills directly from Dr. Tatum's brother-in-law who owns the pharmaceutical company?" She waited as Frankie recalled the conversation in which he'd been so quick to give Angelle what she asked for. He nodded, and Gillian smirked and shook her head. "Well, she lied. Turns out she's still forging prescriptions, and the dudes that got arrested had quite a few of them. So the DA set up some type of sting operation to see if they can catch the doctor—or whoever is writing those prescriptions—in the act. So with all that going on, we're shutting down Angelle. It was never a good idea to do business with her to begin with. I went along with it because it was a relationship that you and Baron had already established before I got involved. But, clearly, that was a mistake."

Frankie sucked his teeth. "I've known Angelle for years. Since we were kids in the projects back in the day. She's thorough. All

Grant said is that the doctor is being *investigated*. If we stop working with everybody who's under investigation, that's gonna shut down this whole operation."

Zion sensed Frankie's resistance. "I hear you, Frankie. But she's hot, so we're gonna move on. It's not smart for us to keep playing with fire. We're gonna cut out the middlemen and deal directly with my Russian connect."

Frankie was livid, and was doing a poor job of hiding it. "So who made this decision?" he asked loudly, glowering at Gillian, who was chewing as if she hadn't a care in the world.

Gillian had to resist the urge to laugh at Frankie's pathetic temper tantrum. She could tell that he was pissed. To rub a little salt in the wound, she said, "Zion and I have been discussing this for a while. We made the decision together."

Frankie gripped his glass so tightly, that Gillian expected it to crack in his hands. "I feel like you're trying to piss me off," Frankie said.

Gillian frowned. "Piss *you* off?" she repeated. "What would you have to be pissed off about?"

"Because you're not coming to me for any type of feedback before you just make big decisions like that. Since when is that the way we do things in this family?"

She took a sip of water. "I already told you," she said, calmly. "I talked to Zion about it."

Frankie let her words, and their underlying meaning hang in the air. He took a deep breath, willed himself to calm down, and blew it out.

"Why not have a conversation with Angelle? Why not warn her that shit is heating up?"

"Frankie, I'm not interested in warning anybody. Angelle is cut off. It's too risky to keep doing business with her," Gillian looked him in the eye. "Zion's guy is reliable. He's done business with him before, and there's far less risk with him than with our usual way of doing things."

"I don't think that's smart," Frankie said. "So what, she's hot? Every member of this crew has been on the DA's radar at some point. Why should we mess up a good thing?"

"I just told you why." Gillian held Frankie's gaze, unflinchingly.

"I'm saying . . . you making these kinds of decisions without even talking to me all of a sudden?" Frankie's voice cracked. He was clearly hurt by being overlooked.

Zion was sick of watching Frankie practically fall apart. "Gillian don't have to consult with nobody," he clarified. "At the end of the day, she's in charge. She made an executive decision." He sipped his Patrón, thinking Frankie was sounding like a little bitch.

Frankie's jaw clenched. If he didn't get out of there fast, he would hit Zion. He balled up his napkin and tossed it in his plate. Tossing several twenties on the table, he rose abruptly. "Fuck it then. Since you two got it all figured out, ain't no point in me sitting here." He shot a glance at Gillian. "Let me know when you need me." He turned and stormed out without looking back.

Gillian shook her head as she watched Frankie take his tantrum on the road. At one time, Frankie had been the only man she wanted. They had shared an intense love affair that was all-consuming and taboo. Frankie's marriage had been the only thing that stood in their way. In the end, however, their passion for one another was quelled by the realization that Frankie's family drama was more than Gillian cared to tolerate. She walked away from him for good almost two years ago. Despite the passage of time, Frankie was still as salty about it now as he had been then.

Gillian sighed, glad that she had ended their relationship. It hadn't been easy. Frankie and Gillian had shared one last moment of passion, which had resulted in a pregnancy. Gillian had never told Frankie about it, knowing that if she had that he would have taken it as a sign that they were meant to be together. Instead, she had aborted his baby in secret. After witnessing his behavior today, she had no regrets. She couldn't imagine being burdened with a kid by such an emotional wreck.

Zion took a swig of his drink. "I guess Frankie don't like change."

Gillian shrugged. "Change is good. Frankie can either get on board or get gone."

Camille smiled as she stepped out of the car. Eli held open the door and held an umbrella above her head. The rain beat down nonstop, but neither of them seemed to mind. It only added to the romance of the night. Once they had stepped up on the curb, he took her by the hand. Together, they walked into Amy Ruth's restaurant, Eli's favorite. It was his birthday, so Camille had secured Misa as a babysitter for her daughter, Bria, and tonight she and Eli had some rare time to themselves.

Camille watched him as he interacted with the servers. She couldn't take her eyes off of him. Her relationship with Eli was completely opposite of what she had shared with Frankie. She was happy to trade in the grand public overtures like the outrageous parties Frankie used to throw for her in exchange for this more intimate and romantic celebration. While Frankie had been secretive and emotionally unavailable, Eli was honest, affectionate, and caring. Camille was in love.

They sat at a table in the corner.

"It feels weird being out without Bria," Eli said.

Camille beamed at the mention of her daughter. Bria was the light of her life. The past three years transitioning into the role of motherhood had been the most incredible years of her life so far. Shane, too, was a joy to behold. Her nephew had survived so much turmoil in his young life, but was still such a happy kid.

"It is strange, right? She's usually right here making a mess and saying 'hi' to all the people at the next table." Camille's smile was radiant. Eli loved to see her eyes light up that way at the mere mention of her child. He couldn't wait to be a parent. But, in the meantime, being a significant figure in little Bria's life was sufficient.

Camille was grateful. Frankie had been nearly invisible in Bria's life. Fatherhood had changed him in ways that weren't necessarily positive. "I want to say how much I appreciate the way that you've been there. Not just for me. But for Bria, too. Having you around has been . . . it's been really nice, Eli." She reached across the table and gently stroked his hand.

Eli squeezed her hand in silent response, lifted it to his lips, and kissed it gently. "I love you," he said. "I love Bria, too. She might as well be my baby. To be honest, sometimes I forget that she's not. Frankie comes around only once in a blue moon." Eli shook his head, but caught himself. He didn't make a habit of speaking negatively about Camille's ex-husband. "Oh, well," he said. "He's the one who's missing out on watching his beautiful baby girl grow up."

Camille couldn't agree more. "I remember a time when I would have given anything to save that marriage. Anything! But ever since Bria was born, I realize that all I ever really wanted was unconditional love. Frankie never gave me that. But I've found it in my daughter. And in you. I'm good now."

Eli smiled. His cell phone vibrated, and he excused himself briefly to answer it. Camille did not protest. Ever since being transferred to the Narcotics Division, Eli was more and more secretive during his phone conversations. Camille understood it, although she worried about his safety in such a notoriously deadly unit. Still, she had spent enough time on the other side of the drug war that she was fine with having no involvement in it at all these days.

While Eli was away from the table, Camille checked her own messages, and was relieved to find that she had none. For once, things were calm and she was happy. After so much drama, she and her family had found peace at last, and she was grateful. Her sister Misa and little Shane were thriving with the second chance they'd been given. Camille's mom had been instrumental in keeping the family united. She had once believed that she could never make it without Frankie. But, she was doing just fine.

Eli returned and so did the waitress, bringing them water and silverware. "Are you ready to order?" she asked.

Camille had only glanced at the menu, so Eli asked for another moment or two. While they decided what to order, Eli stroked her hand.

"You want to go out after this?" Camille asked.

Eli looked at her, though he seemed distracted. "What?"

Camille sipped her water. "There's a nice little spot on Fortieth Street. We could swing by there after dinner."

"Oh," Eli said. He shook his head. "It's my birthday, so I get to have it my way, right?" He smiled, and Camille melted.

"Right."

"So, let's just eat and go home and make the headboard knock."

Camille laughed.

"Word," Eli continued. "We can make as much noise as we want because Bria's with your sister."

The waitress came back, and both of them placed their orders. As they waited for their meal, they looked forward to the night ahead and all of the fireworks that lay in store.

The kids were asleep. Misa lay across her bed, talking to Baron on the phone. She wished he was with her tonight. It was a rainy and romantic night, and right now his voice was like smooth, creamy chocolate melting all over her.

"What you got on?" Baron asked. He sat on the edge of his bed. He was relaxed and comfortable at home after a long day grinding. Despite his previous misfortune in the game, he was still putting in a little work. Gillian kept him under her thumb, though. Still, he managed to carve out a good life for himself. As their father's firstborn, Baron had inherited much. His mother, too, as Doug Nobles' first wife, was a very wealthy woman. And despite their wealth, Baron had a thing for the game. He had been raised in it for as long as he could remember, groomed to be his father's heir apparent. After his shooting and all the time it took to recover, he had unwillingly relinquished control to his sister. Now, whenever he walked into a room—his leg injury had resulted in an odd limp that Baron somehow made cool—he still garnered respect, though not the kind he felt he truly deserved. Baron believed that he belonged on top.

"The kids are here," Misa reminded him, "so, I'm not wearing nothing sexy tonight. I'm in some shorts and a T-shirt."

"That's sexy on you," he said, flirting. "I miss you." It was true. Baron had a thing for Misa.

"I miss you, too. I'm coming over tomorrow." She smiled at the thought of it. She needed a physical tune-up. Baron had gotten help for his anger-management problems. He was a changed man to Misa. Despite their past together, the pair were growing more serious as time went by.

"Did you think about what I said?"

"You were serious?" Misa sat up in bed. Baron had suggested that they pack up, move away, and start a family together. Misa wasn't so sure she wanted the very thing she had once desired more than anything in the world.

"Yeah," he said. "You thought I was playing?"

Misa laughed a little. "Yeah," she said. "Baron, you're not ready to leave your mother behind."

"She can come, too, if she wants. But I'm a grown man. I feel like as long as I stay around here, I'll always be my father's son. I'm living in his shadow. I feel like it's time for me to get away from here and be my own man."

"What about Gillian?" Misa asked.

"What about her?" Baron laid back across his bed. "My sister don't need nobody but herself. She has everything under control. Let's see if she can keep it going without me."

Misa wasn't sure she believed him. Baron and his sister had a complicated relationship. They loved each other one minute, and hated each other the next. Still, Misa wondered if Baron was truly ready to walk away from the game and all the notoriety that came with it.

"Okay, well . . . I'll think about it some more and let you know tomorrow when I come over." Misa clicked off the light and lay in the darkness.

"Shane starts school soon," Baron reminded her. Since Misa's trial, he had bonded with the kid. "We could go somewhere with a good school district and all that. And then we can start working on a new baby."

Misa's smile lit up the dark room. "I can't believe this is you, Baron. You're like a completely different guy since . . ." Misa's voice trailed off, not knowing what to say.

"Since I damn near died!" Baron said. "I feel different. I want to get out of here." He closed his eyes and imagined the new life he wanted. "Call me tomorrow, and let me know what time you're ready. I'll pick you up."

Misa could hardly wait to see him. "Good night, baby."

"Good night."

5

BLOWN

Acapulco, Mexico

Marisol's heart sank as soon as she caught sight of her daughter. Sunny looked strung out for the first time in her life. Her face was drawn, and her already slim frame now looked gaunt and frail. Sunny avoided her mother's gaze as she was led into the room. She felt sick to her stomach and fought back the bile rising in her throat.

Marisol had arrived in Mexico that morning with her son Reuben in tow. They had met with the prison officials and paid the exorbitant price to free Sunny from prison. The exchange had been quick and easy, but the wait for Sunny's release had been a long one. Marisol had paced nervously while the guards went to retrieve Sunny and her belongings. She told herself that she would hold it together when Sunny got there, that she would not cry or fall apart. But nothing had prepared her for seeing her daughter this way, clearly broken by her ordeal.

Tears pooled in Marisol's eyes and she cried out, *"Mija!"* Sunny ran to her mother, and the two women wept as they embraced.

Reuben wiped tears from his own eyes as he stood to greet his sister. Sunny had clearly lost control. Reuben hugged her tightly, feeling her bones through her clothes. He held her face in his hands and shook his head. "You're a mess."

Sunny nodded, tearfully. "I know." She looked at him seriously and spoke over the lump in her throat. "Reuben, I have to get the fuck out of this country. Now!"

He felt her urgency, and knew that there was probably more to the story than they already knew. He didn't need to hear anything more. "Let's go."

He grabbed her luggage, while Marisol grabbed Sunny's hand. They hurried through the doors that the guards held open for them, Sunny's heart racing the whole time. She said a silent prayer of thanks that she was finally free. But she wouldn't feel relieved until her plane was in the air. She half expected someone to rush in at any moment and announce that they had discovered the dead body of the man she killed. As they rushed to the airport, she promised God that if He got her out of this mess, she would never get high again.

Frankie watched Angelle strolling toward him and couldn't resist the urge to leer. Angelle had a body that wouldn't quit. The two of them had known one another since they were kids and had gotten closer over the years. Frankie and his deceased brother had been cool with Angelle's older brother, who was serving a lengthy federal prison sentence. In his absence, Angelle had stepped up and proven to be an asset to the team. That is, until now.

Frankie had called her and asked her to meet him at the corner of Fifty-Seventh Street and Fifth Avenue so that they could discuss the crew's recent decision to sever ties with Angelle and the doctors she worked for. Even in the sea of people out shopping and sightseeing on the busy stretch of Midtown Manhattan, Angelle was easy to spot. She smiled when she saw him and greeted Frankie with a hug and a quick kiss on the cheek.

"What's up, Frankie B?"

"Nah, the question is, what's up with you?" Frankie frowned slightly. "Why do I have to hear from other people that your office is under investigation? Why didn't I hear that directly from you?"

Angelle shook her head. "Cuz I ain't even know about it, that's why." She gestured animatedly with her hands as she spoke. "Dr. Tatum got greedy. Instead of being happy with all the money we've been making off prescriptions with your crew, he decided to get involved with steroids and all that type of shit. He had been doing that for a while with no problems. But he fucked around and gave steroids and HGH to a bodybuilder who had a heart transplant . . . it was a mess. The guy died. I had no clue about any of this until Zion called to tell me that y'all wasn't dealing with us anymore. He said that Grant let him know about the investigation."

Frankie frowned at her. "Zion called you? Since when do you talk to him?" Frankie had always been the middleman in the business Angelle did with the crew.

Angelle nodded. "Yeah, he called me yesterday. He was on some real bullshit. But that shit with Dr. Tatum and the steroids . . . that shouldn't matter. Nobody knows nothing about the prescription pills we've been moving. I work with the brother-in-law directly on that, and he's not on nobody's radar."

"The whole damn office is under investigation, Angelle. You can't be sure that they don't know about the pills, too."

She shrugged. "I hear you, Frankie. I know you're in a tough position. But to tell you the truth, it's been all good even without y'all. It's not like the operation shut down just cuz Gillian said so. I'm still making money. Good money. So it is what it is."

Frankie looked at her sidelong. He knew that Gillian had overreacted. It sounded like Angelle's situation may have been overblown. "Come walk with me to Niketown." Frankie nodded toward the flagship sneaker store. "Let's talk and see if we can figure something out."

Angelle adjusted her Louis bag on her shoulder and walked alongside Frankie gladly.

Born felt like he was experiencing a bad case of déjà vu. Years ago, he had done the same thing that he was doing now—attempting to assuage his longing for Jada by spending time with Anisa. This time, though, he intended to be up front about what was going on. He sat on a stool in Anisa's kitchen, as she packed a lunch for Ethan to take to school. Their son was upstairs getting dressed, and Born seized the opportunity to clear the air.

"I want to talk to you," he said.

Anisa paused and looked at him. "About what?"

"Us. What we're doing." Born searched for the right way to begin.

Anisa saved him the trouble. "You mean you want to let me know that we're not back together." She shrugged. "I know that, Born. I'm not dumb."

He was caught off guard. He hadn't expected that. "I never called you dumb."

She retrieved a juice box from the refrigerator and stuck it in Ethan's lunch bag. "It would be dumb to think that you and I can just snap our fingers and go back to being a couple. I know that you're still not over Jada."

Born stared at her, speechless. He didn't know what to make of her matter-of-factness.

Anisa continued. "We don't have to label this . . . . thing that's happening between us. It is what it is. I'm not the young girl you knocked up years ago."

Born laughed at that depiction, and Anisa chuckled, too.

"I see the situation clearly. So don't worry." She turned to place the cutting board in the sink. He checked her out from behind. Anisa always looked good. There had never been any doubt about that. But, she was a handful. Not that Jada wasn't, too. The difference was that Jada had stolen his heart long before Anisa sauntered on the scene.

Still, Born had to admit that Anisa was beautiful, even after all these years. She had grown out her hair, rocking it in its naturally curly state, and her hair looked like a glorious crown on her head. It was wild, full, and free-flowing, and Born thought it looked so sexy. Anisa caught him staring.

"What you looking at?" she demanded, suppressing a smile.

Born grinned, aware that he was caught. "What made you go all Erykah Badu with your hair?"

Anisa laughed, displaying all of her pretty teeth. "I don't know. I just got sick of relaxers, and weaves, and decided to go natural." She shrugged. Changing her hair had made her feel liberated. "You like it?"

Born nodded. "I do."

Anisa sipped her tea and winked at him. Even after all these years, no man she ever dated compared to Born. And, she compared them *all* to Born. Truthfully, she thought Jada was stupid for allowing Born to slip away. But, it was clear that that the Bonnie and Clyde team had broken up. Jada had abandoned Born in favor of her son. Anisa didn't blame her. She just found it funny how things worked out after all.

Born listened as Anisa told him all about her new outlook on life and about the classes she was taking at Wagner College. After a few minutes, she caught herself babbling, and felt embarrassed.

She was beginning to like having Born around, and she didn't want to scare him off with all of her talking about natural hair and psychology class.

"Want more?" she asked, holding up the kettle.

Born licked his lips. "More what?"

Anisa's smile widened. "Don't start nothing you can't finish."

Ethan entered the room, interrupting their exchange. He grabbed his lunch bag off the counter and kissed his mother good-bye. "Ready, Dad?"

Born chuckled. "Yup. Let's go." He rubbed Ethan's head, playfully, as they headed out the door. He glanced back at Anisa, liking what he was feeling. No pressure. Just going with the flow. He could get used to this.

Jada sat in Silver Lake Park, alone with her thoughts for the first time in weeks. A soft breeze blew. The sun shone on her face, and she wished that she could somehow freeze this moment in time.

Sheldon was at home with the tutor who came to their house each day to give him home instruction. The administrators at his school had determined that his unpredictable behavior warranted him sitting out the rest of the school year. A child who was a danger to himself and others couldn't be trusted to function in a traditional classroom setting. With only three weeks left of school, Sheldon had been assigned a teacher—Mr. Baez—who was well versed in Sheldon's brand of dysfunctional behavior. From day one, Mr. Baez had made it clear that he meant business. Sheldon seemed to sense that this guy wasn't worth testing, and during the four hours they spent together each weekday, Sheldon willingly complied with whatever Mr. Baez said. Today, Jada had seized the opportunity to unwind alone during Sheldon's schooling.

She had an uneasy feeling in the pit of her stomach that she just couldn't seem to shake. Again, she had awakened from a terrible nightmare. In this one, she had the sense that she was alone in a pitch-black room, but a paralyzing fear gripped her anyway. She didn't know how she'd gotten there or how she would get out. The absence of light was one thing. But what really sent her into a state of hysteria was a sound—like a humming noise—that started off low. Then slowly it swelled into a full crescendo of laughter. Sinister, menacing laughter. And it was familiar. It was Jamari.

Fear gripped Jada's throat, preventing her from crying out. She was petrified. She couldn't make out Jamari in the blackness of the room, but there was no mistaking the sound of that voice. She stood pinned by terror in the corner against a wall. The sound got closer. Louder. Within moments, she could feel his hot breath on her face as he stood before her and laughed ominously inches from her. Jada lashed out, swinging wildly, scratching and clawing. And she had awakened from her nightmare that way, tearing at the sheets on her bed as if she were fighting for her life.

In the hours since then, she hadn't been able to shake this feeling of anxiety. She sensed that her conversation with Sheldon the other day had brought some long suppressed memories to the surface. She hadn't allowed herself to give much thought to her past. Doing so usually sank her into depression. But Sheldon had questions. In the process of answering them, it was as if she had raised Jamari from the dead. In her mind, she could still hear him taunting her, having the last laugh. It made her sick to her stomach.

She inhaled deeply, breathing in the scent of flowers in bloom, willing herself to feel relaxed and refreshed. But no wave of calm washed over her. Instead, she felt a flood of tears build up, and then unwillingly plunge forth. She tried in vain to push her emotions back down deep inside but those feelings would no longer allow themselves to be brushed aside. It was as if her sadness, loneliness, and helplessness were demanding an audience now.

Though she frantically wiped away her tears, they still poured forth, streaming down her face endlessly.

She looked around, praying that no one saw her. Realizing that she was alone, she let herself go and sobbed bitterly. She cried for the years she had smoked crack while she was pregnant with Sheldon, for ever getting involved with Jamari in the first place. She cried because she knew that her past decisions had caused Sheldon to be born with the odds stacked against him. Her son was crazy. Just as twisted and cruel as his father had been. And his actions had cost her the love of her life.

Jada laughed aloud at the absurdity of having ever believed that she could find a "happily ever after" despite the madness of her past. She must have been crazy to ever expect any outcome other than this. It occurred to her that she had spent most of her life being selfish. Just about every action, every choice had been influenced by her own self-serving desires. She had hurt everyone she had ever claimed to love—everyone who had ever truly loved her in return.

And here she was, sitting alone in the park crying over what she was being forced to atone for. Jada was well aware that by pushing away Born she risked losing him for good this time. No one could be expected to tolerate the things that she had done to him. She had gotten high behind his back, stolen his drugs, blamed his workers for something she had done herself. She had slept with his arch enemy—albeit unwittingly—and had his child. And now that child had grown up and decided that he was not cool with their relationship. Only a fool would put up with all that she had done to Born.

The devil on her shoulder urged her to go and get high again— to snort something or smoke something to clear her mind. To escape. Those thoughts only made her hate herself more.

What kind of animal am I? she wondered. She had done enough harm to herself and to those she loved.

Disgusted with herself, she wiped away her tears, berating herself silently. She didn't deserve to escape her reality; didn't deserve to have a normal son or a normal life. She didn't deserve Born. And crying about it wasn't going to change anything.

Jada took a long, deep breath, put her sunglasses back on, and stood up. She strolled back to her car, promising herself that she would not get high ever again, that she would do whatever it took to help Sheldon regain his sanity and his happiness, even if it meant sacrificing her own.

Sunny's stomach was still uneasy. As the plane taxied down the runway at JFK airport, she wanted nothing more than to be back in her luxury apartment. Visions of a long, hot bath, a drink, and some much-needed sleep in her own bed danced through her head. She did her best to ignore her longing to get high again, reminding herself that coke was what had gotten her into this mess in the first place. Absentmindedly, she sniffled and wiped her nose. Marisol noticed, and shot her daughter a look of disgust, disapproval, and disappointment that broke Sunny's heart. Sunny looked away, ashamed.

Reuben sat in a seat across the aisle from them, and she caught his eye. Sunny felt convicted as she looked at her brother. She had fucked up, had let her whole family down, and she knew it would be a long, hard road to win back their respect.

Once the flight attendants turned off the fasten seatbelt signs, they stood along with the other passengers as they retrieved their luggage from the overhead compartments and prepared to disembark. Sunny noticed some stares from some of the other passengers in first class, but she ignored them. This was one time that she wanted to go unnoticed. Her eyes shielded behind shades, she waited impatiently as she listened to the pings of cell phones being turned back on as people reconnected to their busy lives. Sunny didn't bother turning on hers. All she wanted was to get back home to her daughter.

They stepped off the plane, and walked through the tunnel that led to the terminal. Marisol had called Dale while they were at the airport in Mexico and given him their flight number and arrival time. They all expected to find him waiting for them at the gate. But Sunny's heart seized in her chest when she spotted the throng of reporters and photographers who awaited her instead. Her shock was evident as her mouth fell open at the sight of them. Shutters clicked rapidly as they snapped pictures of her and her family.

"What the fuck!" she cried, looking around frantically at all the people swarming them. As Sunny was being ambushed, rage flooded through her. She had been set up. She had paid those Mexican bastards and they had tipped off the press anyway.

Reuben sprang into action and took off his track jacket. He used it to shield Sunny from the photographers. Marisol's gaze darted throughout the crowd as they pushed their way through. She was looking for Dale, but he was nowhere in sight.

The photographers got aggressive, pushing toward Sunny in hopes of getting another shot of her stunned face. They hurled questions at her in rapid-fire succession.

"Sunny, why were you arrested in Mexico?"

"Are you addicted to cocaine?"

"Where did you get the drugs, Sunny?"

"Are you going to rehab?"

"Sunny, over here!"

She began to cry, and pulled her brother's jacket tighter around her face as he held her close and ushered her through the swarm.

In the midst of the fracas, Marisol felt her cell phone vibrating in the pocket of her jeans. She pulled it out as she trotted alongside Sunny, who was sandwiched between her and Reuben.

To her relief, she saw Dale's photo and number flash across the screen. She answered breathlessly.

"Where are you?"

"I'm in the car right outside of baggage claim. Come straight out. The whole place is packed with paparazzi. I had to cover up Mercedes and rush her back to the car because they kept trying to take her picture and ask her questions."

Marisol's heart sank. "She's here?"

Mercedes' presence was the last thing they needed right now.

"Yeah," Dale confirmed. "She wanted to surprise Sunny." He realized the irony in that. Until they'd arrived at the airport, Mercedes hadn't known about her mother's arrest. She had been told that Marisol had gone to get Sunny because Sunny's passport had been stolen. But the truth came from one of the paparazzi. Mercedes sat, devastated in the backseat. "Just come straight outside," Dale repeated. "We'll send Raul back for the luggage later on."

It was the longest trip of their lives, walking from the airport terminal to the exit. The bloodthirsty paparazzi grew increasingly aggressive. Reuben shoved one of them as he jostled the trio while they maneuvered through the crowd. Marisol bitterly cursed at them in Spanish. All Sunny could do was cry as she walked, her head down and Reuben's jacket shielding her face. She had never been more humiliated.

At last, they reached the outdoors and Reuben spotted his father's Benz. Dale sped up to the curb and Reuben did his best to block Sunny and Marisol as they quickly slid into the backseat beside Mercedes. He shut the door once they were inside and then scrambled into the passenger seat. He quickly shut the door as Dale sped off. Mercedes sat crying silently, and at the sight of her Sunny broke down sobbing, too. She pulled her daughter close and hugged her as they both bawled amid the flashing lights of the paparazzi.

6

DÉJÀ VU

Sunny stared at Mercedes, who pretended not to notice. They sat on opposite ends of the sofa in Sunny's parents' living room. Her brothers and her parents stared at her expectantly. She eyed her daughter closely, wishing that she could find the words to make it alright, but coming up empty. Mercedes had barely uttered a word since their escape from the airport. In fact, no one really had. Reporters were staked out at Sunny's apartment building in Manhattan. Jenny G had warned Dale there was no way for Sunny and Mercedes to get into the high-rise undetected. There were vans full of mysterious looking strangers armed with cameras and microphones at every one of the building's entrances. So Sunny and Mercedes had taken refuge at her parents' home in Brooklyn, at least until things died down. Sunny felt trapped. She felt like a child who had messed up majorly, and was awaiting the wrath of her parents with a mixture of fear and anxiety. Only it wasn't her parents she was worried about the most. It was her daughter.

Sunny had been here before. Years ago, when Dorian had come to meet her family for the first time, she had sat surrounded by her family as nervous and anxious as she was at this moment. Back then, her nervousness had been due to her concern over whether or not her family would like Dorian as much as she did. Thinking back on that now it seemed so trivial. This time, she was on the hot seat for real. The people she loved were demanding to know how she could thoughtlessly risk everything for the sake of getting high again.

Sunny decided that she owed it to them to tell them the whole truth, no matter how painful it was. She took a deep breath, glanced over at thirteen-year-old Mercedes who was staring at her blankly, and Sunny began.

"I was bored," she said, honestly. "I know that sounds crazy, but it's the truth. I was bored, and I was lonely. I don't think I ever got over Dorian's death. I wake up every day and I do what I have to do, but I haven't really lived since he died." She wiped the tears that had begun to stream down her cheeks. "I had the money, and my career was going good . . . but I was not *happy*."

"Not happy?" Marisol asked, incredulously. "How can you be unhappy with all the shit you have going for you, Sunny?"

Dale touched Marisol gently on her arm, willing her to hush and let Sunny continue. Marisol shook her head in frustration, folded her arms across her chest, and sat back in her seat. She wanted to wring Sunny's neck, but first she wanted to hear the whole story. She had to know how things had gone so horribly wrong.

Sunny could see the disappointment and anger in her mother's eyes. She could hear the condemnation in her tone. Still, she continued.

"I know it was selfish. Obviously, I see that now. But I convinced myself that I could handle it. I handled it before, I thought I could do it again."

Marisol sucked her teeth loudly. Sunny did her best to ignore her. Her father cleared his throat.

"When did you relapse? I didn't see any signs that you were getting high again." Dale seemed genuinely perplexed. "Did you start back again recently?"

Sunny shot a glance at her mother. It was Marisol's turn to squirm in her seat. Sunny knew that her mother had suspected that she was getting high again. On a couple of occasions, Marisol had stopped just short of accusing Sunny. Sunny suspected that her mother's reluctance to call her out was due to her fear of being cut off financially. Marisol avoided Sunny's gaze.

Sunny tore her eyes away and looked at her father. "I started using again during my trip to L.A. It was my first time using cocaine in ten years."

Dale shook his head in dismay. He should have known there was more to that trip than Sunny had let on. The press had relentlessly covered the story of the groupie found dead in Sean Hardy's mansion. Dale had watched the coverage of Malcolm leading Sunny through a swarm of photographers and reporters after she was questioned at the police station about the events that led up to the young lady's death. He should have known that there was more to the story of that night than Sunny had let on.

Reuben, too, realized that he had missed the signs that the L.A. trip had brought back the old Sunny. He had picked her up at the airport when she returned, had watched her stroll over to his car with her eyes masked behind dark shades. He remembered her bursting into tears at the sight of Mercedes, and realized now that it had been guilt eating away at his sister then.

Sunny thought back to the night in Sean's bedroom when she'd gotten high, and danced away the night locked in a room with a stranger who had overdosed. It was one of the lowest points of her life. But at the time it had felt like pure bliss.

"It was like being reunited with an old friend," she said, softly. "I missed getting high so much. It made me forget about the loneliness, forget about the boredom. When I started using again, I had a secret that nobody knew about—not Jada, Malcolm, nobody. And it was like old times again." She shrugged, shook her head, and the tears came again. "Then I got to Mexico with Malcolm, and I told myself that I was going to stop using. I realized that I had so much going for myself." She looked over at Mercedes and saw the blank expression on her daughter's face as she sat silently in the corner, her legs curled beneath her in the armchair as she listened intently to her mother's story. Her face betrayed no emotion as she listened, uttering not even the slightest sound. That hurt Sunny more than anything, knowing that her baby was disappointed in her to the point of stone silence. She knew that behind Mercedes' blank expression was tremendous disgust.

Sunny could only imagine the thoughts that were going through her child's head at the moment. Contempt, bitterness, embarrassment, just to name a few. The knowledge that she was no longer her daughter's hero was what broke her heart the most. Tears flowed down Sunny's cheeks and she sobbed softly.

"I got to Mexico and I met these ladies in the bathroom. They were snorting coke, so I asked them where I could get some. They put me in touch with this guy, and I went to meet him to buy drugs. Malcolm found out about it." She intentionally left out the attempted robbery, the fact that she had slit a man's throat and left him dead on the side of the road. She wasn't going to confess that to anyone, and she wondered if she could trust Malcolm's cowardly ass to keep his mouth shut. She was so angry with him and so unsure of his loyalty that she was seriously contemplating killing him to ease her mind about the whole thing.

"When he found out, we had an argument and we decided to cut our trip short. But I was so upset and so focused on getting back home, getting away from him . . . that I forgot about the bag of blow I had in my purse. And when we got to the airport they found it in my bag."

Sunny's brother Ronnie asked what they all were wondering. "So where's Malcolm now?"

She shrugged. "They let him go after he paid a fine. So he left me there and came back home."

Dale hung his head. Marisol dabbed at her eyes. Her brothers looked on in shame and pity. She hated being looked at that way. Her whole family was sitting there judging her, making her feel worse than she already did. As if they weren't guilty themselves of enabling her for all these years. She thought back on Malcolm's words during their trip.

To be honest, I feel a little sorry for you. Your family basically pimped you out from the age of seventeen.

An unexpected rage welled up inside of her and she wiped away the tears roughly and her eyes flashed with anger.

"Let's not all sit here and act like this is a complete shock, okay?" She glared at her mother. "I know that you probably suspected that something was off. But you didn't dare to say a word about it because it's always been about the money to you."

"Sunny!" Dale's voice boomed as he sat forward in his chair.

Sunny's eyes widened, defiantly. "What? I'm lying? The minute you figured out who Dorian was and what he was worth, you both turned a blind fucking eye to everything. Nobody would challenge me because you're all scared that I'll cut the cash flow. You sit there and you shake your heads at me, and you judge me. But it was all good until the media found out about it. Until today you all wondered and speculated behind closed doors, but had your hands out whenever I came around. You're a bunch of fucking leeches."

Dale was on his feet now. He stormed toward Sunny, but Ronnie stopped him. Marisol was crying now, the truth of what Sunny had said hitting her like a ton of bricks. Mercedes, seeing her family in turmoil and feeling overwhelmed by the events of the day, ran out of the room in tears and upstairs to the spare bedroom. The sound of Mercedes slamming the bedroom door reverberated throughout the home. Reuben looked around and felt like his family was falling apart right in front of his eyes.

"She's right!" Reuben said, yelling over the noise of his mother's sobs and his brother's attempt to calm their father down. "She's right."

Marisol looked at her oldest child with pain in her eyes. "How can you say that, Reuben?"

He sighed. "Ma, come on. Be honest. All of us wondered whether that girl who OD'd was the only one getting high in the house that night in L.A. But none of us wanted to accuse her because we didn't want to piss her off."

Marisol and Dale stared at him, incredulously. Ronnie avoided eye contact and cast his eyes downward, convicted.

Reuben looked at Sunny. "The truth is, none of us would have been okay with you dating a guy like Dorian in the first place, unless he was as powerful and well-connected as he was. He paid off this house, he brought me into the game, and we all benefited from it. All of us did."

Guilty silence filled the room. Dale slunk back to his seat on the sofa and buried his face in his hands. Marisol stared at the floor. Ronnie leaned against the wall and stared at a spot on the floor, digesting what Reuben had just said. It was true. They'd all come up as a result of Dorian's relationship with Sunny.

But Reuben wasn't about to allow his family to shoulder all the blame. He walked over to where Sunny sat and squatted down in front of her until they were eye to eye. Sunny met his gaze, grateful that at least one of them was willing to face the truth. Reuben had more to say, though.

"We fucked up by letting you get involved in this lifestyle. The money wasn't worth what we got in exchange. Dorian is dead. All the money in the world can't bring him back. And you're a fucking cokehead."

Sunny's heart broke hearing her beloved brother describe her that way. She choked back a sob and looked down at her hands, but Reuben tilted her face back upward, staring her in the eyes.

"Don't pass your blame around. Nobody stuck that shit up your nose but *you*, sis. You chose that lifestyle. You chose that man, and brought him here and told us to love him because you loved him. You're right. We got blinded by the money and all his power. But you chose that life. And you're the one who got caught up in it. You're the one who decided that you was bored with having everything. So don't go looking around for somebody else to take the fall for it." Reuben wiped the tears from Sunny's eyes. "You are a coke addict. You relapsed, and this time it cost you. Your name and face are gonna be all over the news, and for all the wrong reasons. Your daughter is mortified."

"You think I don't know that?" Sunny was angry at hearing the truth.

"Okay, so you know it. Now what are you gonna do about it? Point fingers at everybody else? It's Mom and Dad's fault for letting you be with Dorian in the first place. It's my fault and Ronnie's fault for having suspicions and not confronting you about it. It's Malcolm's fault for leaving you in Mexico. Everybody's at fault, but you, huh, Sunny?"

"I'm not saying that!"

"So what are you saying?"

Sunny didn't know how to respond. She stared back at Reuben in silence.

He shook his head at her, disappointed. "You did all the talking tonight and I didn't hear you apologize to your daughter once! How do you think she feels hearing you say that you were bored and lonely when she's been by your side all these years? Huh? How do you think she feels hearing you say that you haven't lived since her father died? What does that say about her? That she's not enough for you?"

"No, she is *everything* to me. That's not what I meant!" Sunny couldn't stop the tears now even if she tried.

"So I'm asking you again. What are you gonna do about it?"

Sunny threw up her hands in frustration. "I don't know what to do, Reuben! You got all the answers. Why don't you fucking tell me? What am I supposed to do?"

Reuben shook his head at her. "You get help. You check into rehab."

"Rehab? I don't need no damn rehab, Reuben! I been to rehab before."

"Go again. It didn't work last time."

"It worked! I just . . . slipped up. I can get myself together again."

"You're in denial. You're trying to blame everybody else but yourself. You need to stop bullshitting yourself, Sunny. You need help." He stood up, straightened out his clothes, and looked down at his sister as she sat in the chair. "You told your story. We heard you out. And I'm telling you that we're gonna take responsibility for enabling you for too many years. But it ends tonight. You need to go to rehab, and you need to make this shit right with your daughter. Until you do that, I have nothing to say to you. And I mean that shit sincerely."

With that, Reuben turned and walked out the door. No one said a word in the long silent moments that followed. Soon, Marisol got up and went upstairs. Dale followed behind her. Ronnie stared at his sister for a long time before he said anything. When he did, his voice was low and restrained.

"Reuben is right. You don't have to go through it by yourself. We're your family. We got your back. We'll support you. But you do need help." He looked at his sister sympathetically. "Sleep on it at least. Don't be so stubborn."

He grabbed his car keys off the couch, walked out the door, and left Sunny sitting alone with the weight of the world on her shoulders. She sat there in silence and solitude for over an hour before she pulled herself together enough to head upstairs. She found that Mercedes had locked herself inside of Sunny's old bedroom. So Sunny retired to one of the spare bedrooms, not even bothering to flip on the light switch. She sat on the edge of the bed, feeling defeated and completely spent after the day's events.

Her mind was going nonstop. On one hand, she was so relieved to be back in New York after her Mexican ordeal. On the other hand, she wished that she could escape from her family and their scrutiny. The prospect of sitting across from them at the breakfast table in the morning filled Sunny with dread. She had never felt more torn apart. For the time being, she and her child were captives because of the media frenzy surrounding her arrest in Mexico. Sunny chuckled bitterly at the irony that her D-list celebrity status had been upgraded to at least a B since the cocaine scandal broke. She shook her head at the fact that being locked up abroad would likely land her on the front pages where her modeling career had never placed her.

Her thoughts drifted to Malcolm. She wondered if he had anything to do with the press being tipped off about her arrest. It was clearly not beneath him to be so grimy, since he had abandoned her while she was jailed in a foreign country. Maybe in his bitterness he had betrayed her. She wondered when they would be face to face again. It was inevitable that they would cross paths. After all, he had brokered her movie deal. He was one of the partners at Ava's firm.

Ava. The thought of her reminded Sunny of Jada. Damn. Sunny's tears returned as she thought of her friend. *Jesus.* She had disappointed everyone she cared about. She shook her head in dismay. It would be a long, hard road to redemption.

7

UNFORGIVEN

Jada couldn't believe her eyes as she tuned into the *Mindy Milford Show* the next morning. The scandal-obsessed talk show queen was on TV talking about Sunny's arrest in Mexico, complete with pictures of Sunny's arrival at JFK. Jada watched openmouthed as Mindy Milford filled in her audience on Sunny's misfortune.

"Did you all hear about what happened to professional girlfriend, Sunny Cruz?" Mindy asked, as the cameras zoomed in on a photo of Sunny shielding her face from the cameras, surrounded by paparazzi and protected by her family who looked distressed and caught off guard.

The audience gasped, shook their heads, and rolled their eyes. Mindy chuckled. "Don't get mad at me! It's not my fault that Sunny can't seem to leave those white lines alone." On cue, the show's producers played the chorus from the rap song by the same name. Grandmaster Flash and the Furious Five's "White Lines" played as Mindy cackled and the audience clapped. Jada cringed, as she watched her friend being made fun of.

Mindy fought to control her laughter before resuming her report. "Those of you who have followed me since my radio days will recall that Sunny Cruz and her friend Jada Ford came on my show a few years ago. They had just written their bestseller

Truth Is Stranger Than Fiction," and Sunny was one of the spiciest guests I ever had on my show. Both ladies arrived at the studio draped in diamonds and expensive clothes. They looked the part of the women they had written about. Their book was this salacious novel about life as the wives of drug kingpins—and this was back when there really *were* drug kingpins. Not these wannabes that you see nowadays. Her story and Jada Ford's story was a "fictionalized account" of their own experiences on the arms of two notorious power players in the drug game." Mindy paused to sip from her teacup as the audience waited with baited breath for her to continue. "Now, keep in mind that Sunny and Jada did not deny that this 'fictional story'"—Mindy used air quotes to drive home her point that the story was anything but—"was based on their own truth. So I asked if Sunny was getting high like her character in the book was."

Again, the audience laughed and applauded Mindy's brazenness.

"Well . . . Sunny didn't deny it! She told me point-blank that she used to get high, just like the character Charlene in the book!"

The gasps and laughter again. Jada felt herself growing angrier by the minute. Nothing about being an addict was a laughing matter.

As if reading her mind, Mindy gave a caveat.

"Now, I've always been honest about my own years as an offender. I had my struggles with cocaine addiction, and I've spoken about that in my books, on this show, and on my radio show back in the day. So, I'm not condemning Sunny for her affinity for the powder. What I did take offense to was that she threatened to fight me! Imagine that! This woman wrote a book chronicling a cocaine-filled lifestyle of money, parties, gunplay, and steamy sex, and when I asked about the truth behind the story, she got so defensive that it frankly caught me by surprise. When one opens themselves up to scrutiny by penning a novel about their life, one cannot start pulling off earrings and kicking off shoes to fight when someone asks a simple question!"

The audience agreed. Mindy seemed to be gloating about Sunny's relapse. The look on her face screamed, I told you so!

"Well, it looks like those demons that Sunny didn't want to face back then have reemerged today. So the report is that Sunny was in Mexico and as she was returning to the States, her luggage was searched and they discovered a bag of cocaine. Sunny was arrested, and managed to pay her way out of jail . . . allegedly." Mindy winked as she said it, then sipped from her cup again. "Her family went down there to get her, but you know how shady those Mexican police officers can be. They ratted her out, and the paparazzi was waiting for her when she landed in New York."

The photo of Sunny flashed across the screen once more. "This is so unfortunate. This is a tragic situation for Sunny's career. She caused quite a stir at New York Fashion Week earlier this year when she strutted that runway with such fierceness that her breasts broke loose and made their debut." The audience cracked up, as they had all heard about that. "And now we see why she didn't notice!" Mindy laughed some more, and then composed herself. "Seriously, though. Sunny has dated many high-profile men in recent years. She dated football player Michael Warren, and later his teammate Sean Hardy." Mindy gave the camera a side eye that said everything that she didn't verbalize. "She accompanied the actor Jamie Knox to the Golden Globe awards years ago. So, this is why I call her a professional girlfriend. She has no problem snagging a great catch. But until she leaves that coke alone, she is going to be doomed to follow in the footsteps of the Lohans and Sheens of this world. And I'm praying that she pulls it together before it's too late." The audience clapped and cheered. Then Mindy was on to the next story.

Jada grabbed her car keys and her purse and ran toward the

door. "Mr. Baez, I have to go out for a minute!" she yelled over her shoulder. "Call me if you need me." Jada raced out the door without waiting for a response. She had to get to her friend immediately.

Sunny heard voices in her parents' living room, and approached warily. The voices were lowered, hushed, as if the speaker didn't want her to overhear. It was approaching noon, and Mercedes had just returned from her last day of school—a half-day schedule in which the students only had to report to homeroom class to pick up their final report cards for the semester. Raul had driven her to school, waited for her around the corner, and then returned her to Sunny's parents' home. It hadn't gone well, by the looks of it, because Mercedes had come in, stormed up to the bedroom, and slammed the door. She hadn't emerged since then. Sunny half expected to find her mother and father talking to some school administrator. As she got closer, though, she recognized the familiar Southern drawl of Dorian's mother, Gladys, as she addressed Marisol.

"You know that I have always loved Sunny. No matter what ups and downs her and Dorian went through, I always stayed out of it. And soon enough, they always got back on track."

"I know," Sunny heard her mom reply. "I remember the way those two went back and forth. In love one day, and at each other's throat the next."

The two ladies chuckled at the memory.

"Dorian loved Sunny so much that it would be impossible for me not to love her, too. When he died . . ." Gladys's voice trailed off. "Sunny did a good job picking up the pieces. Mercedes is a smart young lady. This time, I think she's too smart to ignore what's going on. Sunny's all over the news. BET, *TMZ*, Mindy

Milford's show. This is gonna embarrass Mercedes, and the entire family for that matter."

Marisol's heavily accented voice sounded unusually shaky. "Gladys, this was a mistake that Sunny made. Everybody makes mistakes sometimes."

"This mistake keeps happening with Sunny, though," a deep voice countered.

Sunny recognized it instantly. It was Patrick, Dorian's brother. Sunny was convinced that he and his brother Christian wanted nothing more than to get their hands on Dorian's money. Ever since his death, Sunny had been constantly on guard against Mercedes' greedy uncles. In the days after Dorian's funeral, Sunny had fled to her mother's family home in Puerto Rico to escape the danger she felt existed for her as the sole beneficiary of Dorian's money. Everybody knew how ruthless his brothers were. Patrick's presence now only confirmed that.

Sunny stepped into the room. "What's all this about?" she asked, gesturing toward Gladys and Patrick. "Why are you here?"

All eyes turned to her, and an awkward silence followed as they all searched for what to say. Finally, Gladys spoke up.

"Sunny, we came over here to talk about Mercedes." Gladys sized up Sunny, noting that she'd lost some weight since the last time she saw her. "Maybe it's time she came to stay with us, since you need to get yourself together."

"Get myself together?" Sunny smirked. "Miss Gladys . . . with all due respect. When have I ever looked to you or your family for help?"

"Sunny . . ."

"No, seriously." Sunny stepped closer. "You came over here to be nosy. Because you heard about some *lies* they put out there. You don't have to worry about my daughter. She's fine."

"Dorian would want me to look out for Mercedes. She's my

granddaughter," Gladys reminded her. "I have a right to question the way she's being raised."

"Okay, you asked your questions. I answered them. Now it's time for you to go."

"Sunny—" Marisol hated to hear her speak to Gladys so dismissingly.

Gladys held up her hand to halt Marisol. "It's okay. She's right. It's probably best for us to leave now." Gladys turned to look at her son. "Let's go, Patrick."

Patrick watched as his mother pulled her purse strap up on her shoulder and rose to leave. Despite these signs of readiness, Patrick remained seated, staring at Sunny. She noticed, and glared at him.

"What, Patrick? What the fuck is *your* problem?"

"Sunny!" Marisol was livid. She didn't like Dorian's family sniffing around any more than Sunny did. But she was old-fashioned. And the thought of having guests in her home cussed at and yelled at was just too much for her.

Patrick looked sympathetically at Sunny's mom. "It's okay," he said. "She's not herself right now." He looked at Sunny and could tell that the stories were true. He had hustled drugs for years, so he knew an addict when he saw one. Sunny was fidgety, wild-eyed, and agitated. She was skinnier than the last time he'd seen her, only weeks ago. She kept sniffling absentmindedly, rubbing at the bridge of her nose. She was longing for another hit, and Patrick shook his head in pity as he watched her.

"My mother is a nicer person than I am. She likes to pray about things, and she stays calm in situations like this because she don't like confrontation. So she's willing to let you off the hook right now, because she can see that you're upset. But I'm not like her. I didn't come all the way over here to get disrespected. And I don't care how aggravated you get. You don't scare me."

Sunny sucked her teeth hard. "Please, Patrick! You don't scare me either!"

"Good," he said, calmly. "I'm not trying to. But I am gonna say what's on my mind. And after that, I'll leave."

"No," Sunny said, her voice raised. "You can leave *now*! I don't give a shit about what's on your mind!"

"Maybe you'll give a shit when you get served with papers!" Patrick was done handling Sunny with kid gloves. "I'm gonna make sure that my niece is okay."

"You don't even care about your niece! This shit is all about the cash, Patrick. And you can kiss my ass, cuz you will never get your hands on Dorian's money!"

"You're paranoid! See what I'm saying? What the hell does this have to do with money, Sunny?" Patrick demanded.

"You tell me!" she yelled back at him. "What's the plan? Get Mercedes and then sue me for support? You must be crazy!"

Patrick laughed. "Nah. You're the one who's crazy."

Jada approached the door to Sunny's parents' house and heard raised voices coming from the other side of the door. She could make out Sunny's voice above the others, and a booming baritone countering her. Jada wondered what hell had broken loose in there, and for a moment she considered leaving. Perhaps this was a bad time. But she had to see Sunny. She needed to give her friend a hug and some reassurance, and to hear her version of the events in Mexico. Jenny G had answered the phone at Sunny's apartment when Jada called, and warned her that the press was staked out all around Sunny's high-rise. She said that Sunny and Mercedes were hiding out in Brooklyn and Jada had sped right over. She couldn't leave now without seeing her friend. She took a deep breath, said a quick and silent prayer, and rang the doorbell. A minute later, amid the noise of the continuing argument, Marisol opened the door. An expression of pure exhaustion was etched on her face. She sighed with relief at the sight of Sunny's one true friend.

"Jada!" Marisol unlocked the screen door and ushered Jada inside. Pausing in the foyer, she turned to Jada and shook her head. "*Mami*, thank God you are here. Sunny really needs you." Marisol stole a glance toward her kitchen before turning back to Jada again. "Dale ran out to get us some groceries. Dorian's mother and his brother are here. They are threatening to fight her for custody of Mercedes."

Jada sighed. This was the last thing Sunny needed right now. "What the hell happened?" Jada asked in a muted whisper. "Last I heard, Sunny and Malcolm went to Mexico to celebrate her birthday. The next thing I know, Mindy Milford and *TMZ* are showing pictures of Sunny surrounded by cameras at JFK." She searched Marisol's face for answers. "Is it true what they're saying? She's getting high again?"

Marisol nodded, then looked down at her hands and burst into tears. She sobbed silently, squeezing her eyes shut as she wept. Jada hugged Sunny's mom, rubbing her back comfortingly.

"My God." Jada whispered. "Don't cry, *mami*. Sunny will get herself together, you'll see." Despite that reassurance, Jada wasn't really sure about that. She knew how hardheaded Sunny could be. This relapse could be hard to overcome.

The sound of glass shattering in the kitchen caused them to put an end to their emotional exchange. Marisol wiped her eyes brusquely, shook her head in exasperation, and the two women rushed in the direction of the kitchen.

The scene they beheld when they stepped inside was disheartening. Sunny and Patrick stood on opposite ends of the kitchen from one another. Gladys stood near the refrigerator with both hands clasped over her mouth, stunned. Mercedes stood in the center of the room near the island, surrounded by shattered glass, tears cascading down her lovely young face.

"What happened in here?" Marisol asked, her eyes scanning the room for blood or other signs of trauma.

"Mercedes overheard all the arguing and yelling, and she got upset," Gladys explained. She looked apologetically at Marisol. "She broke your vase of flowers," she explained, nodding toward the mess at Mercedes' feet. "But it's our fault because we should have left when I said we were leaving." Gladys shot her son an evil sidelong glance when she made that last comment. Patrick stared at his hands in silence.

Gladys walked slowly over to Mercedes, the sound of glass crunching under her feet audible. She stopped in front of her granddaughter and waited until Mercedes lifted her gaze to meet hers. Gladys reached forward and wiped Mercedes' tears.

"Don't cry," she said. "Crying won't fix a thing."

Somewhere down inside, those words resonated with Mercedes. Mercedes sniffled, then wiped her eyes with the back of her hand, doing her best to control her heaving chest.

Gladys stared into Mercedes' eyes. "You are your father's child. I see him in you, do you know that?"

Mercedes nodded slightly. Gladys was a warm and loving grandmother, who told her all the time how similar she was to Dorian.

Gladys smiled a bit. "If he was here, he would beat your butt for breaking your grandmother's vase.

Mercedes slowly came back to herself. "I'm sorry," she offered meekly.

Gladys nodded her approval. "Take a deep breath."

Mercedes did as she was told.

"Good." Gladys brushed an errant strand of hair out of Mercedes' face. "Now listen to Grandma. The adults in this family don't always do what we're supposed to do. That goes for all of us, not just a few. We owe you more than the nonsense you've had to deal with."

Sunny and Patrick were both quiet, convicted. Marisol and Jada looked on in silence.

"But don't stoop to our level. Don't be like us—yelling, screaming, throwing things. You're better than that. You're better than us." Gladys smiled weakly at Mercedes, winked an eye at her. "We don't get to pick our family. We have to play the hand we're dealt. And all of us know that *this* family is a mess." She laughed. "But hang in there with us. We're gonna get it together." Gladys stole a glance at Sunny. "I'm gonna call you tomorrow." Then she turned to Patrick and coldly stated, "Let's go."

This time, Patrick didn't hesitate. He quickly mumbled good-byes to Mercedes and followed his mother outside.

Mercedes was calmer now, thanks to Gladys. She took a deep breath and then walked over to the utility closet to retrieve the broom. Marisol took it from her and sent her upstairs. "Go put your shoes on. Dale and I will take you home to get some of your things."

"Ma, Raul can bring us—"

"*I'm* taking her home to get her things!" Marisol was adamant. "*You* are staying here." She shut her eyes against the pain of a migraine coming on. She took Gladys's advice to Mercedes, and took a deep breath herself. Opening her eyes, her voice was calmer when she spoke again. "It's a good chance for us to have a talk about what's been happening around here." Mercedes left the room and ran upstairs to clean her face and to get her belongings. Marisol took the opportunity to address Sunny.

"You better have a talk with her, Sunny. Today! With no one else around. Just you and her, the way it's always been. She needs to hear from *you* about what happened. She needs to be able to yell at *you*, and get mad at *you*, and tell *you* how she feels. So when she gets back here today, *you* make it happen. And I'm not fucking around, either!" Steamed, Marisol angrily swept up the glass, tied up the garbage, and marched upstairs to get her car keys.

Sunny looked over at Jada and threw up her hands in defeat. "Well," she said. "Guess who really fucked up this time?"

"*You*." Jada shook her head.

8

HEART TO HEART

Once Marisol and Mercedes had gone, Sunny and Jada sat down on stools perched around the island in the center of the kitchen. Sunny opened the fridge and snatched the container of orange juice. She was clearly still upset. She slammed the juice down on the counter and grabbed two glasses out of the cupboard.

"Mercedes is all upset," she muttered. "She has enough shit to deal with, and now these fuckin' Douglases want to come sniffing around trying to get their hands on Dorian's money. They kill me!"

Sunny sat down, but her hands kept moving, busying themselves with sweeping up miniscule crumbs, straightening the napkins in the dispenser, repositioning the salt and pepper shakers.

Jada watched her. Twisting the top off of the orange juice, she poured some into each of their glasses, her heart breaking the whole time. It was like looking in a mirror and seeing herself all those years ago when she was strung out but convinced that she still had it all under control. Jada had once believed that all of her troubles were someone else's fault. Hearing Sunny singing the same song made her sad. When she was done pouring the juice, Jada sipped hers slowly while she listened to Sunny rambling. After a couple of minutes, she couldn't stand it anymore.

"Sunny," she said. "Calm down for a minute."

"Calm down?" Sunny repeated, incredulously. She scoffed as if the very notion was unimaginable. She had to keep going—and going fast. Because if she stopped and considered the enormity of her situation—her arrest, Malcolm's abandonment, the shakedown by the authorities, the ambush by the tabloids, her daughter's disappointment, her family's judgment, the public scrutiny, Dorian's family's threat to fight for custody of Mercedes . . . If she allowed herself to calm down like Jada suggested, she might fall completely apart.

"I can't." Sunny rubbed her arms, suddenly cold despite the warm June temperature.

Jada watched her closely. Sunny stared absently at her hands while she chattered on about the conditions in the Mexican jail. She knew Sunny well enough to discern that she was unraveling. Jada had never seen her like this. She was angry, anxious, scared to death, and fighting for control all at once. Gone was the fun-loving life of the party Sunny had once been. In her place was a woman broken by her own choices. Jada stared at Sunny until her gaze bore into her. Sunny looked up. The friends locked eyes, and Sunny saw sympathy in Jada's brown eyes.

Jada offered a weak smile. "You know I've been there," she said.

Sunny laughed a bit too loud. "You've been in a Mexican jail cell?"

Jada wasn't laughing. "No. But, I know exactly what you're going through."

Tears welled in Sunny's eyes. She let out a long sigh to fight them back.

"I remember how it felt . . . fighting for custody of Sheldon, trying to convince everyone, including myself, that I had it all under control, trying not to think about how much I *missed* getting high. 'Cause that's what got me in trouble in the first place. But getting high was still the main thing on my mind. I was disgusted with myself."

A lone tear streamed down Sunny's face. It was as if Jada was reading her thoughts and emotions.

"Like I said," Jada continued. She reached across the island and held Sunny's hand. "I've been there."

Sunny squeezed Jada's hand. She shook her head in dismay. "You ever want to get high, still?"

Jada stared at Sunny, seriously. She thought about her recent excursion to Silver Lake Park. She kept it real with her friend. "Sometimes I do. But I think about all the hell I went through those other times. I think about how I lost everything and everybody, and how I lost myself."

"I hear you." Sunny sniffled, took her hand back, and wiped her nose. "Everything is just . . . so fucked up."

Jada silently agreed. "Sunny," she said, gently. "When did you start back using again?" During the drive from Jada's home in Staten Island to Sunny's parents' home in Brooklyn, Jada had rewound the events of the past few months in her mind to try to determine when Sunny had relapsed. She thought about the signs she had clearly missed, distracted as she was by Sheldon's shenanigans. Jada felt terrible, having missed the chance to save her friend from the clutches of the devilish drug that had stolen so much of their happiness already.

Sunny shook her head and averted her eyes, shamefully. She didn't answer for several long moments. Finally, she met Jada's gaze again, her expression serious.

"Remember last year when Malcolm told us about the movie deal? When I was so gung ho about going to L.A.?"

Jada squeezed her eyes shut. She remembered it all too well. Both she and Sunny were supposed to go on that trip. But when she had told Born about it, he had asked her not to go. And Sunny had gone alone. Jada had agonized over that for a long time, and she felt terrible now that she knew Sunny had reacquainted herself with cocaine during that trip.

"I went to Sean Hardy's big bash at his house. It was *crazy* in there. He had a groupie passed out in his bedroom, and he asked me to sit there with her until he came back. He had been going in and out all throughout the party to check on her. But he felt like he was neglecting his guests, so he asked if I would keep an eye on her. There was a pile of cocaine on the dresser." Sunny caught herself salivating at the memory. "Sean left me there alone with that coke. I sat there for a while and tried to fight that shit, Jada. But the urge to do it . . . it overpowered me. Before I knew it, I had snorted most of it." Sunny shook her head. She hated Sean for that. He had left her alone with a drug that was calling her name. As she reflected on it now, Sean was the devil himself, ushering her into a hell which she could not escape.

"So you were there when that girl died?" Jada asked.

Sunny shrugged. "I guess so. Jada, I was in such a trance that I don't even know when she died. I was too busy partying all by my damn self. When Sean finally brought his ass back to the room, he passed out. We woke up the next morning, and the girl was dead, and all hell broke loose. I left there with what was left of the cocaine and went back to my hotel room to get high some more."

Jada's face was twisted into a deep frown as she imagined all of this. "And Malcolm? He knew?"

Sunny wiped her tears angrily. "That muthafucka!" she hissed. "Don't even mention his name!"

Jada's head tilted slightly. "Okay," she said. "I won't say his name again. But we do have to talk about him. Where is he? And did he know that you were getting high?"

Sunny rolled her eyes. The very thought of him made her sick. "He wasn't there. I stood him up when we were supposed to meet with producers. He picked me up at the precinct after they took out the dead body and brought us all in for questioning." She licked her lips, her mouth suddenly bone dry. "He didn't know I was getting high. He found out at the airport in Mexico, after I got caught with the coke in my bag." She looked at Jada, and said the words she hated to hear come out of her own mouth. "That was the last time I saw him. He left me alone in Mexico and flew back home without me."

Jada's frown deepened. "What?"

Sunny nodded. "He's a pussy, Jada." She sipped her orange juice and slapped the glass back down on the island after she drained it. "I mean . . . I knew he was no Dorian. But to do some sucker shit like leave me alone in a foreign country to face a drug rap by myself?" Sunny's voice cracked. She toyed with a napkin just to have something to occupy her hands.

Jada's heart broke at the pain she discerned in Sunny's voice. She didn't know what to say, so for several moments they sat silently. Finally, Jada cleared her throat and broke the ice.

"Remember when Born caught me getting high years ago? How he threw me out and had Miss Ingrid come and help me pack up all my things?"

Sunny nodded.

"At the time, I thought that was the worst thing anyone could do to me. I needed help, not abandonment. At least that's how I felt at the time. But back then I was looking at the whole thing through tainted eyes. The truth is, Born had every right to throw me out of his life. I lied to him. I stole from him. And he had to find out what I was up to the hard way."

Sunny stared at Jada through narrowed eyes. "So you're saying that Malcolm had every right to run like a bitch? Why? Because I lied and hid shit from him?"

Jada shook her head. "I'm saying that people react differently to the news that someone they love is an addict."

"Don't call me that." Sunny's voice was even.

Jada frowned. "Why not? That's what we are. Recovering a—"

Sunny cut her off. "I'm still not understanding how you and Born compares to me and the coward."

"I'm saying Malcolm's reaction wasn't the best one, obviously. But, in some ways it's just like what Born did. If he hadn't left me then, I might still be getting high." Jada thought about it for a moment. "When he left me, it forced me to hit rock bottom. And that's what I needed. It was a scary, crazy journey back to myself, Sunny. But if I did it, you can definitely do it."

Sunny shrugged. She wasn't in the mood for a pep talk. It felt to her like she had lost her best friend. In the old days, Jada might have been the kind of friend Sunny could trust to bring her a line or two to even herself out. More than anything, Sunny wanted to get high right now. Just one or two quick hits would set her right. But Jada wasn't the same anymore.

Sunny's facial expression and tone were condescending as she spoke. "Your situation with Born is completely different from mine with bitchass Malcolm. Born is the love of your life. So of course he was hurt and reacted the way that he did. Malcom is not the great love of my life."

"No. Dorian was."

"Exactly."

"And if he was alive, he would be so mad at you, and you know it."

Rage bubbled up in Sunny so quickly that she didn't even have a chance to think about it. *"FUCK YOU, JADA!"* Sunny's voice boomed, echoing off the kitchen walls. "If he was alive, I wouldn't be doing this shit!"

Jada wasn't letting her off the hook just because she was pissed off. "Sunny, you can't believe that."

"Shut the fuck up, Jada! Now all of a sudden you're Miss Holier Than Thou!"

"No, I'm not!"

"Sitting here acting like you didn't use to snort as much of that shit as I did."

"I'm not acting like that!" Jada insisted. "I was right there doing it with you. You know what? Just the other day I was sitting in the park by myself, stressed out over Sheldon and missing Born. And I wanted to get high so bad!"

"But you didn't, right?" She felt like Jada was gloating, looking down on her.

"That's not because I'm better than you," Jada insisted. "I'm not saying that."

Sunny shook her head. "*No*. It's not because you're better than me." Sunny's voice was mocking. "It's because your man deserted you and forced you out on the streets to get knocked up by some bum-ass nigga. Then you had your baby and BAM! It was a miracle! You never got high again. And you owe it all to Born!" Sunny sucked her teeth dramatically. "Get the fuck outta here with that. Take a long, hard look at your son. Poor Sheldon."

Sunny let the words linger in the air. She looked at Jada sitting there, trembling with rage and hopefully guilt. *Finally*, Sunny thought. Jada was feeling the way she did for the first time in ages. "I *know* you, remember? Save the sound bites for your interviews."

Jada sat in stunned silence for several long and awkward moments. Sunny's words stung.

Sunny wasn't done. She shook her head, disappointed.

"You know what, Jada? I thought you were my friend. All these years . . . me and you on some Oprah and Gayle type shit. But those days are gone. They've been gone for a long time. You gonna sit here and tell me that Dorian would be mad at me. How could I expect you to understand? Matter of fact, who are you? I hardly ever even fucking see you anymore. Truth be told, you forgot about me the minute Born came back into your life."

"That's a lie." Jada denied it, but thought about it. Had she?

"You forgot about the good times. You used to be *fun*! But look at you now. You're so fucking dry and boring and *stuck up*! Don't come over here with your Dr. Drew speeches about how far you came because you got kicked down to nothing. Good for you! You forgave the bastard who threw you out when you needed him most." Sunny applauded dramatically and then stopped. "Well, not me! You can keep that testimony. That's *your* story. Not mine."

Sunny stood to put the glasses in the sink, even though Jada had barely touched hers. Jada watched her and tried not to be hurt by the things her friend had just said. But it was no use. Sunny had cut her verbally and Jada's heart ached. She was either going to cry or hit Sunny below the belt, and she didn't like either of those options. Instead, she got up off the stool, retrieved her bag, and walked out in silence.

Sunny watched her go, and tried to ignore her own heart's aching. She knew deep down inside that she was fiending. Her longing for a hit of cocaine was taking control of her every waking moment. *Fuck it,* she thought. Jada, and anyone else who judged her, could go to hell!

9

HALF CRAZY

Zion rang the doorbell, took a deep breath, and waited. Lately, his every interaction with Olivia felt forced. He wasn't in the mood for a fight today. All he wanted was to drop off his daughter, keep his conversation with her mother short and sweet, and get out of there. He looked down at Adiva and smiled. She reassuringly squeezed his hand, as if sensing his apprehension.

Zion winked at her. "You're getting taller every day, you know that?"

Adiva nodded.

"Soon you'll be tall enough to model for your mother's clothing line."

On cue, Olivia opened the door.

"You don't have to ring the bell, Zion," she said, flatly, her voice void of any warmth. "You have a key."

He nodded. "I know. Just trying to be respectful."

Olivia scoffed. Shaking her head, she turned and walked inside as Zion followed her into the house. She was beginning to wonder if this arrangement of theirs would ever change. Zion had moved out months ago. Since then, they had been co-parenting well together, with Olivia dropping Adiva off at school each day and Zion picking her up in the afternoon. Typically, Zion dropped her off curbside in order to avoid a confrontation with Olivia. But this time it was early in the afternoon, since Adiva's school had a half-day schedule. And, he wanted to talk to Olivia about a couple of things. Reluctantly, he entered the home that they once shared.

Olivia kissed Adiva on the forehead. "How was the last day of school?" she asked.

"It was great. I got my report card." Adiva handed it to her mother and watched as a proud smile spread across Olivia's face.

"All fours!" Olivia proclaimed. "That's my girl!" She gave Adiva a high five, and hugged her tightly. "I'm proud of you."

"Thanks, Mommy." Adiva was beaming. She looked at her father. "Daddy said he's gonna take me shopping this weekend." Adiva could barely contain her excitement at the thought of it. Like her mother, she loved to shop.

"Is that right?" Olivia cut a side eye at Zion.

Adiva nodded, smiling brightly. "Yup!"

Zion didn't want Adiva to tell her mother what else they had discussed, so he interjected. "Adiva, go upstairs and let me talk to Mommy for a minute. I'll come up when we're finished."

Obediently, Adiva did as she was told, still excited at the idea of the shopping spree.

"You heard about Sunny?" Zion sat down at the kitchen table.

"Who hasn't?" Olivia snapped. "It's all over the radio and Mindy Milford practically did a whole damn segment on her show about it today. It's one of the reasons that I'm home so early. I got nothing accomplished with all the phone calls from the press."

As the face of Olivia's clothing line, Vintage, Sunny had caused quite a stir at New York Fashion Week prior to leaving for Mexico when her breasts had broken free from one of the garments. Sunny's in-your-face behavior had been an asset for the company, garnering lots of press for Olivia's label. But Sunny's drug-related arrest was not the kind of attention Olivia wanted.

The thought of it made her blood boil. She looked at Zion. "Just when I was starting to make progress. Now it's all falling apart." Olivia wasn't just talking about her clothing line. She felt like her whole life was in an out-of-control tailspin. She felt overwhelmed by the magnitude of it all.

"I mean . . . it's definitely not good publicity," Zion agreed. "But it's not the end of the world either. Sunny's the one who has to explain, not you."

"Yeah, but now I have to fire my friend. That's not a good position to be in."

He nodded. "Sunny needs to step out of the spotlight for a while. I'm sure she knows that."

Olivia shrugged. "It's all a big mess. Now I have to save face with the buyers and pray that they don't renege on our deal."

Zion nodded. "Well, maybe I can help you out with that."

Olivia laughed. "I remember a time when this whole conversation between us would have had a different meaning."

Zion chuckled at the irony, too. "Seriously, though. Let me help."

Olivia frowned. "Help me with what? My work?"

Zion nodded. "Yeah. It's summer now, and Adiva's out of school. You're working all the time, trying to grow your business. I was thinking that instead of her staying with your grandmother, Adiva can just stay at my place for the summer."

"Listen." Olivia took a deep breath to keep from going off. She was waiting each night for Zion to come home. And here he was talking about a whole summer. "She is *not* staying at your apartment, for the last time."

"Why not?"

"Cuz only God knows what goes on over there. You're lucky I even let her come there after school."

Zion stared at Olivia. At times like this, he wondered what he had ever seen in her in the first place. When they were younger, the two of them had such a volatile and passionate relationship, and it excited him then. Lately, though, he was mostly turned off by her loud mouth, scathing words, and her unwillingness to compromise. Her career had taken off, and he was happy for her. But her success was causing a disruption in Adiva's usual routine, and Zion wanted to be the one to fill that void. He didn't want Adiva being raised by her great-grandmother while Olivia was busy working hard. She usually went to Olivia's grandmother's house after school. But Grandma had recently been diagnosed with heart disease and hypertension, which required her to take it easy. Most days, Zion handled all of his business early in the morning. In the afternoons, he drove to Staten Island and picked Adiva up after school. He'd take her back to his apartment in Tribeca and they would discuss her school day, go over her home-work, watch TV, and bond as father and daughter. Zion loved the time he had with her, especially since it was time spent with-out Olivia's nasty attitude, eye rolling, and teeth sucking looming large and killing the mood. But as of late, Olivia's responsibili-ties were causing her to be away from home more frequently than ever before. Several times a week, she got home long after most kids Adiva's age had been asleep for hours. Often he had to rouse Adiva from a peaceful sleep just so that he could bring her home. Olivia was adamant that Adiva should be at home each night, and she often reminded Zion that if he had any sense he would come home, too. But Zion was enjoying his freedom. Be-ing without Olivia's nonsense was like stepping out of a pair of shoes that had caused you great discomfort all day long. There was no way he was going back to that anytime soon.

"You don't *let* her come to my apartment," he corrected. "She's my daughter. What's mine is hers. My home is her home. Period."

Olivia shook her head. "You're jealous," she hissed.

"Of what? You?" He laughed. "You're the most miserable per-son I know."

Olivia wanted to hit him. She wanted to spit at him, scratch him, cause him pain as he had done to her. She had been so close to having it all—the man she loved, a beautiful daughter, the career she'd dreamed of. But Zion had fucked everything up.

"You wish I was miserable," she said. "That's why you're trying to punish me by moving out."

Zion laughed again. "You're crazy." He shook his head. "I moved out because your mouth is too reckless. Eventually, you were gonna make me put my hands on you, and I'm not that type of man. I don't believe in hitting women. But you . . . you tempt me and I think you're almost daring me sometimes." He shook his head again as he thought about all the times Olivia had emasculated him in front of company—or worse, in front of their daughter. "I'm really happy for you with your work and everything. In fact, I'm proud of you. Really. It's not easy to dream about something and then go out there and make it happen. You're doing your thing." He smiled a little. "But until you can admit that you need to change your attitude with me, I can't see us being together anymore."

She knew he was right. She did have a terrible attitude. She had been quite a handful in their years together. But in her opinion, that wasn't the only thing coming between them. "So I guess the fact that you're still dealing drugs after all these years has nothing to do with the problems between us?"

Zion glanced toward the stairs, praying that Adiva wasn't within earshot.

Olivia continued. "We both need things to change. You need me to work on my attitude. I'm willing to do that. In exchange, I need you to stop hustling. Are you okay with that?"

Zion shook his head in frustration. Olivia made the shit sound so easy. "It's not like it's a job and I can go in and quit tomorrow," he said. "It's not that simple."

"Sure it is. Hustling drugs is playing little boy games, and you're a grown-ass man. What's that scripture that Grandma's always throwing at Lamin? 'When I was a child, I acted like a child. But now that I'm a man, I put away childish things.' Something like that. It's time for you to stop being childish."

Zion laughed hard. "You quoting scriptures now? Never thought I'd see the day. I remember when the only time you called God's name was if I was hitting it."

Olivia glared at him with contempt. "You see that's the shit I'm talking about, Zion. I'm trying to have a serious conversation with you, and you can't even stop your jokes and sarcasm long enough to give me a grown-up response."

Zion sighed. "Listen, Olivia . . . what do you want me to say that I haven't said already?"

"That you'll stop hustling and find a legitimate way to get money. That you'll come back home and love me the way that I deserve, for once."

"For once?" His face contorted into a deep frown. "Damn, Olivia. So all these years, you don't think I've been loving you right?"

Olivia stared at him without responding.

Zion knew then that their relationship was over for good. He knew that Olivia loved him. He loved her, too. But, they had grown in opposite directions. When they met as young adults, Olivia had been just as entrenched in street life as he was. They made trips out of town together when he was hustling hand to hand. As his role got bigger and his empire grew, Olivia had been right by his side looking gorgeous with her deep chocolate skin tone, her sassy mouth, and her unique style. They had been unstoppable once. But then she started demanding that he get out of the game. And the game was all that Zion had ever known.

"I'm gonna . . . what . . . sit around and let you support me financially?" He stuck his hands in his pockets. "I'm a man, Olivia. And a man has to make money. You knew how I made money the minute you met me. But now all of a sudden it's not good enough for you anymore?"

Olivia shook her head. "It's not good enough for *you* anymore, Zion. You said it yourself. You're a man. Not a boy. When we met, we were kids. The shit I used to think was sexy and exciting doesn't do it for me anymore." She shrugged her shoulders. "I want more."

He nodded, let her words sink in. Finally, he offered her a weak smile. "I hope you find it."

Rage built up within Olivia so quickly that she couldn't seem to stop herself. She yelled, her voice raised so high that she even surprised herself.

"Fuck you, Zion!"

He didn't reply. Instead, he walked to the foot of the stairs and called up to Adiva. After a moment or two, she peeked her head out and looked down at her father. "Bring your bag, and come on. I'll bring you back to Mommy on Friday night."

Adiva nodded and scampered off to get her bag, which she had already packed as part of the plan she and her father had worked out on the way over.

Olivia stared at Zion, incredulously. "Zion, you do know that if you leave here tonight it's over between us for good, right?"

Silence.

"HELLO?" she shrieked. "Answer the fucking question!"

He pretended not to hear.

"You mutha—"

"Watch your mouth," he warned. His voice was even, and his tone was serious. Zion was through with Olivia's nonsense.

She grunted angrily and paced the room in frustration. "You know what?" A maniacal smile graced her lips. "I hope those streets choke the fucking life out of you. You're gonna lose *everything*! Watch!" She shook her head in bewilderment, then laughed, although she found the situation anything but funny. "You'd rather walk away from me, from all these years and all that we built—to be a fucking *drug dealer*?" She grimaced in disgust. "Every minute I spent with you has been a complete waste of my time."

Zion searched her eyes and saw the blind fury within them. She stood with her arms at her side and her chest heaving, out of breath. "Are you done?"

"Yeah, nigga! I'm done!" Even as she said the words, Olivia knew that she didn't mean it.

Adiva came downstairs just then, and Zion smiled at her. He took her duffel bag and slung it over his shoulder. Then he took Adiva's hand in his. He looked at Olivia and wondered how a woman so beautiful could say such ugly things. He promised himself that this would be the last time Adiva would have to hear her parents arguing.

Olivia walked over to the door, opened it, and held it ajar for him. "Good-bye, Zion," she said. She looked at Adiva and forced a smile. "Good night, sweetie. I'll call you tomorrow."

Relieved and happy to be dismissed, Zion left with Adiva by his side and Olivia fuming in his wake.

Sunny's cell phone buzzed for the thousandth time. She would need to change her number as it had apparently gotten out somehow. One unrecognized number after another buzzed across her screen every few seconds. She dared not answer, knowing that it would likely be some nosy people wanting to know the scoop. But then she saw one familiar number light up the screen. Abe Childs. He was the vice president of Kaleidoscope Films, and the producer of her movie in the works. She answered.

"Sunny, it's Abe. Is everything okay?"

"Hi . . . yes! Everything is fine, Abe. I just have a misunderstanding to clear up, but everything is good." Sunny's heart galloped relentlessly.

"Well, I'm sure things will work out for the best," Abe said. "If you need, um, you know . . . referrals for any resources, just let me know and I'll gladly give you some numbers to call."

Sunny stopped pacing the room. "Resources?"

"Well, yeah." Abe seemed to hesitate before continuing. "You know, Sunny, there's nothing wrong with admitting that you need some help. My brother Rick just got out of rehab, and he's doing well for the first time in years. The place is discreet. No paparazzi in the bushes, no leaks to the tabloids. It's the real deal. If you want the number—"

"Abe, I don't need rehab." Sunny's voice was stern. "As I said, it was a misunderstanding."

"Sure. No, Sunny, I didn't mean to imply anything. I'm just saying if you need anything—a lawyer, anything—you can let me know."

"Thanks so much," she said, softer this time. "I'll keep that in mind."

"Sunny, that's not the only reason I called." Abe cleared his throat. "Listen, Kaleidoscope decided to go in a different direction this year. We had a meeting yesterday with Malcolm about his involvement with the project. I'm sure you're aware by now that he's pulled out and won't be acting as your attorney any longer."

Sunny felt so lightheaded with rage and shock that she nearly collapsed onto the sofa. "No," she managed. "I wasn't aware."

"Well, he did tell us that his office was looking to get in contact with you, but was understandably having trouble reaching you." He tapped a pencil on his desk absentmindedly as he spoke.

"Anyway, Sunny, listen. You've got one hell of a story. It's just not gonna be a good fit for us at this time."

"Abe, come on." Sunny was nearly panting. She needed that movie deal. It was her one ray of hope in a very gloomy reality. "Whether Malcolm works with us or not, we can still make this movie."

"It's not just Malcolm, you know? We've just decided to take our focus in another direction altogether. That's the truth. But Sunny, I meant what I said about those resources. If you need anything, I'm just a phone call away. Okay? Take care."

Sunny sat frozen in place on the sofa for several moments after Abe hung up. She felt completely blindsided. Malcolm, that cowardly bastard. She thought about him abandoning her in Mexico. Now he had pulled the rug out from under her movie deal. He had quit on her without the benefit of any discussion. Sunny was enraged.

Before she knew it, she was on her feet. She ran up the stairs, two at a time, and hurriedly dressed. She grabbed her father's car keys off the table in the hallway, and dashed out the front door, headed for Manhattan.

Sunny and Ava had never been close. Over the years, Sunny had viewed Jada's little sister as her snobby sidekick. Ava, on the other hand, viewed Sunny with an odd mixture of admiration and condescension. They had in common a genuine love for Jada, and that was what united them. That, and Sunny and Jada's dealings with Ava as their attorney in their publishing ventures. Sunny had all of Ava's contact numbers stored in her cell phone for the latter reason. She dialed Ava's office number and quickly shushed her secretary when she answered the line.

"Bradwell, Foster, and—"

"Fuckin' . . . 'scuse me, Miss. I'm sorry to cut you off, but I need to speak to Ava Ford immediately."

The frazzled secretary took a moment to recover before responding. "She's in a meeting right now. Can I take—"

Sunny hung up and dialed Ava's cell phone. Ava answered as Sunny sped across the Brooklyn Bridge.

"Sunny, let me call you back," Ava said.

"Ava, let me tell you about your bitchass boy Malcolm!" Sunny was so angry that she felt the words spilling forth quickly and yet she couldn't say it fast enough. "He's a fucking *snake*, Ava!"

"Sunny, I can't talk right now. I'm in a meeting."

"Ava, listen to me!"

The line went dead. Sunny gunned the engine.

Ava sat across from Malcolm in her office. He had been crying. She had never seen him like this. Since returning from Mexico, Malcolm had been avoiding her. Until today. Word around the office was that Malcolm's sexy girlfriend had turned into a psycho stalker, speed-dialing and terrorizing his secretary for days straight. Finally, after days of avoiding her, Malcolm had run into Ava in a department meeting and joined her on the elevator going down. Once the doors closed Ava turned to him.

"So, how was Mexico?"

"Terrible." Malcolm let out a deep sigh. He ran his hand across his face. "Evidently, um . . . Sunny's using cocaine again. She got arrested at the checkpoint. And I left her there." It was the first time he had said the words aloud. Malcolm felt a wave of nausea, and forced himself to man up.

The elevator doors opened, but neither of them got off.

Malcolm had turned to her. "I left her there, Ava."

They both let the doors shut again, staring at each other in silence.

For the next half hour, Malcolm sat in Ava's office telling her about Sunny—"She's so beautiful, and so intoxicating."—and their love—"I fell for her hard." He regurgitated the details of their trip, their detainment—leaving out the incident by the side of the road—in such detail that Ava almost felt that she was watching a movie. She couldn't help thinking that it all might be an interesting twist in the film Sunny was planning with Abe Childs. She also couldn't help but remember that she had set her sights on Malcolm first. Sunny had swooped in and stolen the spotlight as usual. But it had been Ava who fell for him first.

Then Sunny called, and Malcolm could hear her screaming through the phone, although Ava sat on the edge of her desk a good distance from where he stood looking out the window. Ava hung up and he turned toward her.

"See what I mean?" he asked. "How can I face her?"

"You just have to." Ava sent Sunny's next call to voice mail. "Start with 'I'm sorry,' and take it from there."

"You don't understand." Malcolm hung his head in his hands. Only Sunny and he knew the magnitude of what he'd left Sunny holding. Sure, it was the cocaine, the detainment, and all of the bad publicity. But there had been more. Sunny had saved their lives, and he had run.

"Malcolm . . . well at least you know she's okay." She sighed. "Why don't you answer her calls? It's worth it just to get it over with."

Malcolm shook his head. "And say what?" His voice was at a higher pitch than he intended, making him sound like a girl. He cleared his throat. He was exhausted, up all night and in meetings all day. And Sunny was out for blood. His stress level was at its highest peak. Or so he thought. "I have nothing to say to her."

Suddenly Ava could hear a commotion near the office reception area.

"Bring him out here *now!*" a voice was loudly demanding. "I'm not leaving until I see him. *Punk ass Malcolm Dean!*"

Malcolm raised his head and met Ava's gaze. An intense sense of dread filled the room.

Ava ran out of her office toward reception to see what was going on. Her mouth fell open in shock when she saw Sunny without makeup and her hair snatched back into a sloppy pony-tail. Security surrounded her, holding her back as she caught sight of Ava and tried to rush forward.

"Miss, we told you to calm down!" One officer was in her face. Sunny was furiously pointing in the guy's face, and unleashing a verbal fury.

"Sunny!" Ava rushed toward her. "What's your problem?" Ava spoke through clenched teeth, aware that all of her uptight colleagues were peering out of their office doors to see what all the commotion was.

"Where is he, Ava? Huh? Where's Malcolm? Let him bring his punk ass out here!"

One of the security guys was on his walkie-talkie calling for police.

Ava spoke in a hushed voice. "You can't come up here like this. Why don't you just call Malcolm?" She knew, of course, that Malcolm was avoiding Sunny's calls, but she would say anything to get her to leave.

Sunny sucked her teeth. "Are you kidding me? I've been call-ing him for days, Ava!"

"Come on. Let's step inside my office and—" Ava prodded.

"*No!*" Sunny's voice was purposely raised loud enough for the whole floor to hear. "I just want this whole fucking firm to know that Malcolm Dean is a punk ass, bitchass coward who abandons his friends and his clients when they need him the most."

As Ava thought of what to say next, Malcolm came out of his

office and sheepishly approached Sunny. Security held her back as she called him every variety of bitch imaginable. Ava watched it all unfold with her mouth agape.

People were pouring out of their offices now, and Malcolm looked like he wanted to cry.

Her jaw set in a firm line, Sunny spoke through nearly clenched teeth.

"It took you this long to face me? You fucking coward!"

"Sunny . . ." Ava found her words at last.

"You're a real pussy, you know that?"

"Sunny, my secretary's been calling you all morning. She left you three messages." Malcolm stood a safe distance from Sunny as he spoke.

"Your *secretary* called me." Sunny repeated his words as if pondering the absurdity of them. "Why didn't you call me yourself, Malcolm? Huh? You scared little—"

"I'm not gonna stand here and let you insult me."

"You could never stand like a man. That's the problem. You crawl your way out of every situation and you leave other people to stand alone."

The elevator doors opened and six police officers stepped off.

"What's the problem?" the first cop asked, looking at the black guy immediately.

Malcolm held up his hands. "This is a misunderstanding. We don't need the police," he protested.

"Someone called us," one officer replied.

Sunny glared at Malcolm. "Probably this b—"

"Listen, I don't know who called you," Malcolm said. "But, we don't need any police, thank you. We're just having a disagreement and we can talk in private."

"The young lady is the aggressor," the security guard explained. "We called you. Mr. Dean works here. We had instructions not to let her upstairs, but she got past one of our workers who's new on the job."

Sunny glared at him. "*Instructions.* From this pussycat?"

"Listen," Ava said. "We don't need the police. The two of them can talk in my office."

"You think that's smart?" the officer asked, looking at Sunny as if she might be able to kick his ass. She was clearly pissed all the way off. Her chest was heaving, and the look in her eyes made it clear that she meant business.

Malcolm looked around. Truthfully, he didn't want to be alone with Sunny. The security guards stepped to the perimeter, but stayed on the scene. Along with the handful of employees who milled about, the presence of all the police and security officers was overwhelming.

Sunny did her best to calm down now that there were police involved. The last thing she wanted was for her loved ones to discover she'd gotten herself arrested again.

"Ava can come with us. I just need a few minutes." Her voice was much calmer, but her body language was saying something altogether different. Her fists were clenched at her side, and she looked ready to pounce.

Everyone looked at Malcolm.

He thought about what Ava said about Sunny deserving a chance to have her say. He looked at the cops and said, "You can go. I'm going to talk to her in private."

Malcolm looked at the building security officers lurking nearby. "You guys stay out here, please?" They agreed, and he led the way to Ava's office.

Sunny wished the cops would leave so she could punch him in the back of his head. Sensing Sunny's tension, Ava trotted to catch up to her.

"Calm down," she hissed in a harsh whisper. "You don't want

to get thrown out of here. Those cops would love to drag you out of here."

Sunny heard her, but her focus was on the man she thought she could love. As soon as the door was shut behind them, Sunny went in.

"I never met a bigger pussy in my whole entire life."

Malcolm didn't flinch.

"You ran like a bitch." Sunny stared him in the eyes as she said it.

"I had to leave. I have a career to protect, Sunny."

"What about protecting me?" Her voice caught on the last word and she was so angry with herself for allowing her vulnerability to show. "You got no balls, no integrity, no loyalty."

"Sunny, I'm sorry," Malcolm pleaded. He felt terrible seeing the hurt that she masked with her anger. He had not meant to hurt Sunny. He stepped closer to her, aware that Ava was watching. He didn't care. "I got scared. You lied to me. You put my whole life in danger." He thought about the man Sunny had killed in Mexico, about being detained at the airport. He loved her, but she was too much trouble.

"Don't you think *I* was scared? Did you even give a shit?" Sunny glared at Malcolm. "Did you tell anybody?" she asked. The question hung between them alone, although Ava, and probably security on the other side of the door, was listening.

Malcolm locked eyes with her, and wished he never left her. "No," he said. "I swear."

He couldn't believe what happened. But he would take their secret to his grave. "Never."

Sunny stared at him with contempt.

"Sunny, I don't expect you to forgive me. But at least try to put yourself in my shoes. I was scared. I never thought I would be in a situation like that. I panicked. I'm sorry."

Sunny's eyes narrowed. "You left me there. And now you backed out of the deal with Abe. So now he dropped the project altogether."

"Abe was on the fence about the whole thing from the beginning, Sunny. My backing out has nothing to do with it."

"That's a lie!" Sunny was seething. "I let you get close to my daughter, my family. I left my best friend here to deal with her son's suicide attempt by herself. All so I could be with you." Sunny was full-on sobbing now.

"I'm sorry. I swear. I'm sorry. Sunny—"

"I hate you."

"Please—"

"Go exactly the fuck to hell!" Sunny's eyes flashed with rage. She shook her head in frustration. Her whole life was in ruins. Mercedes pissed at her, her family disappointed in her, her movie opportunity gone. The whole world knew what she'd done. The sting of Malcolm's abandonment was like salt in an already festering wound.

Sunny took a deep breath. She pulled herself together. "I swear that I will pay you back. I promise you. No matter what, I will get you back for this," she hissed. She stormed out of the office, and Ava followed her. Security joined them to ensure that Sunny exited the building. Malcolm wasn't sure what he wanted to say to Sunny. But he couldn't shake the nagging feeling that there was so much that he needed to express to her. He followed her to the elevator, and stood there amid all the whispers and stares as she boarded the elevator and the doors slowly closed.

10

INTERVENTION

Sunny stared out the window in the passenger seat of her father's car. Ava was driving it while Sunny did her best to pull herself together. Sunny prided herself on being tough and unemotional. But right now she couldn't stop crying.

When they left Ava's office building, Ava had called Jada, and told her what happened. In return, Ava had gotten a brief rundown of the confrontation between the friends earlier that morning. Jada told her sister to bring Sunny to Staten Island. Jada had already been in touch with Sunny's mother, Marisol, and she, too, was on her way to Jada's house with Mercedes in tow. It was time for an intervention.

Sunny had led Ava to the garage where she had paid to park her car, but found herself too frantic to drive it herself. It had all come falling down on her. All of it. She'd lost everything today, including her dignity. Now, aware that they were heading to Staten Island, Sunny began to pull herself together. She rummaged around in her bag until she came out with some tissues. She wiped her eyes, pushed her pain back down, and turned to Ava.

"I know you don't like me."

Ava glanced at Sunny before putting her attention back on the road. "What are you talking about?" She shook her head. "You don't know what you're saying. I like you."

"Don't talk down to me just because you have degrees and I don't."

"I'm not!"

"So don't say that I don't know what I'm talking about. Clearly, I don't make the smartest decisions all the time, but I know exactly what I'm saying."

"Fine, Sunny."

"'Zactly." Sunny rolled her eyes, fidgeted with the ring Malcolm gave her, now too loose on her thinner fingers. She had meant to give it back to him. But in the moment, she forgot all her lines, all the things she'd meant to say to Malcolm once she finally cornered him.

"Anyway, as I was saying, I know you don't like me. I'm not all reserved and composed like you. I know you don't approve of who I am or how I get down."

Ava merged onto the Verrazano Bridge. "It's not my place to approve or disapprove of how you live your life, Sunny. I learned that a long time ago. All I'm saying to you today is that you can't come into a place of business—"

"I couldn't care less about Malcolm's place of business, Ava." Sunny shook her head, thinking that Ava just didn't get it. "He's a coward. I'm upset because he left me in Mexico. He changed his number, stopped taking my calls. I deserved to have my say."

"I don't think you're looking at it from both sides, Sunny. Malcolm isn't like you. He panicked. I'm not making excuses for him. But right before you came to the office, he was telling me how sorry he was that he left you behind, and how he just didn't know what to say to you."

"I don't care how scared I might be, I would never leave somebody that I cared about all alone in another country under those circumstances."

Ava nodded. "He was wrong for that."

Sunny finally addressed the fact that they were pulling into

Jada's driveway. "What are we doing here?" she asked. "I'm sure Jada doesn't want to see me right now. We had words this morning."

Ava put the car in park and cut the engine. "I heard. You're on a roll today." She climbed out of the car, and waited until Sunny followed suit. Together they approached Jada's door. Ava rang the bell and waited, marveling at what a lovely day it had turned out to be, but aware that a storm was brewing on the other side of the door.

Jada opened the door, greeted the women, and ushered them into her home. Sunny stepped inside, but stopped in her tracks when she saw her mother, Jenny G, and Mercedes sitting side by side on Jada's sofa. Mercedes avoided making eye contact with her mom. Instead, she kept her eyes fixed on Sheldon, who sat on the floor close by.

"What's all this?" Sunny asked, eyeing Jenny G so intensely that the woman averted her gaze. Sunny turned her attention to Marisol. "Ma, what are you doing here?"

Jada stepped forward. "Come in and sit down, Sunny." She motioned toward the armchair. Born's chair, or at least it used to be.

Sunny looked around the room. She had a ton of questions but she surmised that no answers would be forthcoming until she sat down as she had been asked.

She walked over to the chair and sat down, unaware of how small she looked now. Her clothes, and even her jewelry, seemed to swallow her thin frame.

Marisol spoke first. "Sunny, this is an intervention." Marisol's heavy accent couldn't go unnoticed.

Sunny actually laughed, amused by the fact that her loved ones found this necessary. She looked around the room, her gaze resting on Jada. "You're kidding, right?"

Jada shook her head. "No, we're not. This is serious."

Sunny's smile faded. "Come on, man. Don't be ridiculous!"

Marisol sighed. "Sunny, listen to me." Marisol's voice wavered, her eyes flooded with tears. "I hate . . . *hate* that I have to have this conversation with you, *mija*. It is breaking my heart that the shit has come down to this." Marisol shook her head as several tears made their descent down her face. "You have a problem, Sunny. It is not a game. All of these years, I've watched you out here living life like it's all about bling, and power, and having fun. There's more to life than that. And you are going to lose all of the things, all of the people that really matter to you if you don't get it together."

Marisol wept softly, clearly agonizing over her daughter's plight. Jada cleared her throat and tried to steer the conversation smoothly.

"Sunny, after I saw you earlier, I called your mom to discuss the whole situation. I was talking to her when Ava called to tell me about what happened at the firm today. So we all decided that it was time for this. We all love you so much. And one of the things that we love about you is your outlook toward everything. You're the queen of keeping it real. So we want you to let us say what we have to say, and then we'll all come up with a plan for the best way to move forward. Deal?"

Sunny stared at her friend without answering. She wanted to storm out of there and tell each and every one of them where to stick their fucking intervention. But when she glanced over at Mercedes, Sunny's cold heart melted. She saw Mercedes watching her through hopeful eyes, and any thoughts of resistance dissipated. Sunny nodded.

Jada breathed a sigh of relief. "Okay," she said. "I think your mom should go first. Then we'll each have a chance to say what we need to say." Jada glanced over at Sheldon, then looked at Sunny apologetically. "Your mom feels that Mercedes needs to be here for this, too. She has a lot that she wants to say. And Mercedes insisted that she needs Sheldon here for moral support."

Sunny looked at her daughter. So Mercedes had a lot to say. Sunny was on pins and needles to hear it, since Mercedes had barely spoken two words to her since she'd gotten back from Mexico. Again, Sunny nodded in agreement.

"But just because the kids are here doesn't mean that we're going to hold back. Because we're not." Having said that, Jada took a seat on the large leather ottoman and Ava sat beside her.

Marisol had pulled herself together by this point. The wet and teary eyes were replaced by a steely, determined gaze, which she fixed now on her daughter. Marisol was no longer the weeping, grieving mother. Instead Sunny looked into the eyes of a fed-up mother, who was willing to do whatever was necessary to get through to her child.

"*Mija,* this is no joke. We have been down this road before, so let's not pretend." Marisol clapped her hands together loudly to punctuate her words, and sat forward in her seat. "Enough is enough. It's been too many years of this . . . shit! I've known about it for years, God help me. I've known that you like to—" Marisol sniffed dramatically, wiping her nose animatedly to spare herself the horror of having to utter the words in front of her grandchild. "I've known ever since Dorian died, God rest his soul. You were a mess, and after you had Mercedes, you went completely crazy. We got you in rehab, cleaned you up, and you swore to me, Sunny . . . you *swore* to me . . . that you would be clean for the rest of your life so that you could raise this baby girl. And now this. What the fuck happened? Where did it go wrong, I want to know? What would make you choose sticking that shit up your nose over your baby?"

Sunny tapped her foot rapidly as she listened to her mother. Anger bubbled up within her like a volcano. Her mother's words echoed in her head in a warped loop.

"You risked everything you worked so hard for. And for what, Sunny? To be high?" Marisol continued on and on.

"Ma," Sunny shifted in her seat. "You only knew that I was getting high when Dorian died?" Sunny watched her mother's face morph into an expression of utter horror. "Are we being serious? I thought this was 'Keep it 100 Day.' So let's keep it one-hundred percent real, *Mami*. You said it yourself. You've known about it for years. But how many years? Huh? Ten years, twelve years, fifteen years? Maybe twenty years?"

Marisol shook her head defiantly. "No, I did not! I did not know that you were getting high back then."

"Why not? Weren't you being the perfect parent watching over me all the time?"

"I never said I was."

"Well, that's what you said I need to be doing for Mercedes, right? I'm choosing other things over my baby, that's what you said. So what did you choose over me, *Madre*?"

"Sunny—" Jada interrupted.

"Nah, Jada, fuck that." Sunny frowned, looking at her mother and noting that Marisol's tears had returned now. "Didn't you know that I was dating one of the biggest fuckin' hustlers in New York City? Didn't you know that Dorian's name carried so much weight that he lifted the whole family out of a paycheck-to-paycheck lifestyle?" Sunny looked at her mother innocently as if she really wanted answers to her questions. Inside, though, she was enraged. "Didn't you think that maybe he was an older man? More experienced than me." She shook her head sadly. "Who could I talk to when I got bored sitting at home while he built his empire? Did you ever think I might get bored? Eighteen years old and stuck at home with thousands of dollars and nothing to do. Nobody asked me if I was having fun. So I looked the part, while Dorian paid the way, and as long as he was paying nobody asked any questions. And I came to you, *Mami*. You remember? When I first got wind that he was cheating on me, I came to you crying. You stroked my hair." Sunny's voice cracked.

Jada looked away, unable to watch her friend cry.

"I had my head in your lap, and you stroked my hair, and you said, *'Mija*, he loves you, what more do you want?'" Sunny looked at Jada and Ava and laughed through her tears. "I said, 'Ma, what if love is not enough?'" Sunny looked at her mother. "And, what did you say?"

Marisol closed her eyes and shook her head.

"You told me that the mortgage was two payments away from being paid off. And you reminded me that Reuben worked with him, and Daddy had enough to retire now, and Dorian was part of the family now." Sunny shook her head. "I knew right then that I couldn't come to you anymore. Dorian was family, but what was I?"

Marisol was flooded with guilty tears. Ava spoke next.

"So, is that when you started 'partying'?" Ava used air quotes as she repeated the term that she'd heard Jada use over the years when she and Sunny were out getting high and carrying on.

Sunny nodded. She sat back in her chair, and willed herself to relax. "Yeah. I was hanging with all the fancy people, wealthy people. Dorian was well connected. It was a glamorous life. And the girls on the arms of the ballers back then were getting high. Dorian warned me, but I was young." She looked at Mercedes. "I was dumb." She shook her head. "I started it, and it seemed like . . . like I could stand it as long as I was having my own little party."

Jada nodded. "I know what that feels like."

Sheldon watched his mother. He watched everyone silently, analyzing each person's reaction.

Sunny looked at Jada. "When you and me were out there taking this city by storm and in love with the men of our dreams, I was on top of the world, Jada. And then Dorian died."

The weight of those words resounded in the otherwise silent room for several moments after she said it. Dorian had been her world for most of her life. Losing him had sent her life into a tailspin.

"I looked around and the party was over, and then I had Mercedes." She thought back on holding her beautiful brown bundle of joy in her arms for the first time. She had been so lonely without Dorian there to share in the happiness with her. Soon she found herself back on drugs again. "I cleaned myself up again, and I didn't relapse until about a year ago." Sunny knew the moment she said it that the words had come out all wrong. "It's not an excuse," she insisted. "But, once again, I found myself needing to feel . . . needing to feel *something*." Sunny feverishly laid out her case, doing her best to explain what had driven her to coke again.

"So, why couldn't you come to me now?" Marisol asked. "I know what I said years ago . . . it was wrong. But I have always loved you, Sunny."

Sunny had never doubted that. "I know," she said. "I love you, too. But our relationship changed once I became old enough to make my own decisions. I started being responsible for everything. It's never been just about me and what I need or what I want. I can't turn to anybody because I'm the one everybody depends on."

"You could come to me," Jada offered. "Sunny, we've been friends for so many years. You are my best friend. And I've been down that road myself. So why not come to me when you felt yourself slipping?"

Sunny sighed. "Do you come to me every time you feel the urge to get high again?"

Jada wanted to say that she would, but it was not true. Over the years she had fought each day for her sobriety, and it had not always been an easy battle. She usually waged those wars alone, and understood the point that Sunny was making.

"You still want to get high sometimes?" Sheldon asked, his eyes on his mother.

Jada shrugged. "Not really." She looked at Sunny, and thought her friend could use a lifeline right now. She decided to be honest. "Sometimes I do. Being addicted to something is like going to war every day with the same enemy. So when things get bad and I feel stressed, yes. Sometimes I do have to fight the urge to get high again." She looked at Sunny. "But I took my rehab seriously, and I use the tools they gave me to stay sober."

Sunny lit a cigarette, a nasty habit she'd resumed while locked up in Mexico. "Well, rehab didn't work for me. Clearly."

"You could have called me," Jada said. She walked to the nearby kitchen. Filled a plastic cup halfway with tap water, and brought it to Sunny to use as an ashtray. "Why didn't you?"

Sunny blew out some smoke, which Ava discreetly fanned away.

"Because you have your own life, Jada."

"That's bullshit, Sunny. You're family to me."

"You have Sheldon and his problems," Sunny reminded her. "And where's Born?" Sunny wasn't saying it meanly. Still, the poignancy of the question struck a lull in the conversation as booming as a bell tolling in the center of the room. "I wasn't gonna burden you with my problems on top of everything else." Sunny took another drag.

"What about me?"

All heads turned toward the speaker, and Sunny slowly doused her cigarette inside of Jada's makeshift ashtray.

Mercedes watched her mother through narrowed eyes. "Why couldn't you talk to me?"

Sunny felt her heart shatter in a thousand pieces.

"You always say that I can come and talk to you about any and everything. So why should I come to you if you won't come to me and tell me the truth?"

"Mercedes, you don't understand." Sunny shook her head.

"You're right. I don't." Mercedes shook her head as well, almost mockingly. "I don't understand why I have to go to school with kids who already think they're better than me because of who their parents are. My dad is dead, and my mom is all over the magazines that all the boys jerk off to at home."

Ava shifted uneasily in her seat.

"Then you go and get arrested with cocaine. And I have to go to school and hear all of the kids call me 'crack baby' in the hallways."

"You are not a crack baby!" Sunny said, defensively. She realized too late that Sheldon was paying close attention, and she shot a look in his direction. "I'm saying that those kids don't know what they're talking about, Mercedes."

"Now I'm the school joke. Last day of school and all the kids go home laughing at the girl whose mother got arrested for trying to sneak coke on a plane home from Mexico."

"Mercedes . . ." Sunny's voice was pleading, though the right words escaped her once again. "I don't know what to say to you."

"Tell me why you did it. Why did you do it, Mommy?" Mercedes was crying, though doing her best to keep a brave face.

Sunny looked at her daughter for a long time. "Baby girl, there is no answer I can give you that will be enough."

Mercedes wasn't satisfied with that. "What happened to Malcolm?" she asked. "Why wasn't he doing the perp walk with you at the airport?"

Sunny was tempted to ask her thirteen-year-old daughter what the hell she knew about a perp walk.

Mercedes didn't leave time for Sunny's questions. She had enough of her own. "Does Malcolm get high, too?"

Sunny shook her head. "No, he doesn't. Malcolm had nothing to do with what happened in Mexico." In that moment, for the first time, Sunny realized how true that sentence was. None of what happened there had been anyone's fault but her own. The cocaine, the dead man, the arrest, their breakup. It had all been Sunny's own doing. The gravity of it hit her for the first time.

Mercedes looked at Sunny as if seeing a stranger, or a distant relative. Sunny was usually all glammed up. But today she looked worn down. Her hair was a mess, and she wore no makeup. Her nails were chewed down to the gristle, and she looked sick. Mercedes wasn't used to seeing her mother this way. This was not the Sunny she had grown up in the glow of. Mercedes wanted her mother back, the old Sunny. She cleared her throat, and reminded all the adults in the room that she was Sunny Cruz's and Dorian Douglas's daughter, and wise beyond her years.

"Aunt Jada," she said. "The reason I wanted Sheldon to be here for this conversation is because he needed to hear all this as much as I did. Lately, Sheldon's been giving you a hard time about the drugs you used to use. He found out that you got high, and he can't seem to let it go. Somebody told him that your drug use is the reason he has a hard time behaving in school. So now he uses it as an excuse."

"I do not."

"Shut up, yes you do!" Mercedes was tired of everybody bullshitting. The time had come for some truth telling. "You use it as an excuse for all the dumb stuff you do." She looked at Jada again. "It's all because he's mad. He's mad and he can't forgive you for getting high. So I told him that my mom got high, too. But Sheldon likes to pretend that he's the only one who ever had to deal with a parent who was addicted to something." Mercedes looked at him now. "So now you see. My mother's still using cocaine. At least yours quit like she said she would."

"Mercedes!" Marisol chastened.

Mercedes shrugged her off and continued. "Sheldon, I understand how you feel. In fact, I feel worse because I can't even go home because of the cameramen hiding outside. At least the whole world is not talking about your mother right now." She looked at her mother. "But even though they talk about her, I still love her." She watched Sunny's hands tremble with emotion.

"You embarrassed me, Mommy. I'm so mad at you for using drugs again." Mercedes fought the tears back. "But I love you. And I can forgive you as long as you get help. If you go into rehab that will make me so happy."

Sheldon stared at the floor. He felt convicted. He loved his mother, and he knew that she was miserable since Born was gone. Sheldon couldn't really understand why he did the things that he did. What he knew for sure was that he was getting his way, and he loved that. He was also enjoying having his mother all to himself. He didn't have to share her attention and affection. Sheldon envied Ethan, because Ethan had his dad. Sheldon had no memory of his. And he was torn somewhere between wishing that Born was his dad, too, and hating him because he wasn't. But as he watched Mercedes pleading with her mother to get help, Sheldon felt terrible for the way he had treated Jada. Jada had proven more than once that she would do anything for Sheldon. He sat there watching the exchange between Mercedes and Sunny, and felt guilty that he hadn't been more cooperative lately.

"Mercedes," Sunny pleaded. "I don't need rehab, baby."

Mercedes shook her head, defiantly. "That's the only way we can move on. It's rehab or nothing. Either go get clean once and for all or I want to go and live with Grandma Gladys."

Sunny felt like someone had a gun to her head. Marisol looked at her granddaughter with a mixture of awe and pride. Mercedes had told the truth and thrown down the gauntlet. Ava, too, was impressed. She thought to herself that the young lady would have a brilliant future in law.

Sunny looked around the room, helplessly.

Nervously, Jenny G spoke up. As Sunny's housekeeper/nanny, she was afraid that participating in this intervention might get her fired. Still, Jenny had grown to love Sunny like a daughter over the years. She cleared her throat, and her voice quivered as she spoke. "Sunny, Mercedes is right. I'm not saying that rehab is all that you need. Because you need God, too. But you need to go somewhere and get your head together. You have to clean yourself up."

Sunny glared at Jenny G, but was snapped out of it by Mercedes' voice.

"You look terrible, Mommy." Mercedes shook her head, sadly. "I'm not saying it to hurt your feelings. I'm just telling the truth. I've never seen you like this before. I don't like it at all. This is not you."

Ava marveled at Mercedes' candor, but silently agreed. Sunny wasn't herself at all.

"Sunny," Ava said. "Earlier in the car, you said that you think I don't like you. But the truth is I've kind of looked up to you all these years. You and my sister." Ava looked slightly embarrassed. "Maybe I was even a little jealous," she admitted. "Even when I didn't agree with how you lived your life, I always admired you for keeping it together. You always maintained your composure, and made it look effortless. You're such a go-getter. You're not afraid of anything, always in control. But the woman I saw today charging into that law firm was not the Sunny I know and love. I listened to you talking today and I think your story explains a lot. I see why you got hooked and I understand your family dynamics and all of that. But you've got an incredible daughter here. She's just like you. Tough, sassy, and smart. You have to meet her halfway and go into a program. We can find you someplace discreet."

Sunny covered her face with her hands. This was a nightmare. She didn't want to go into rehab. What she wanted was to hit rewind, and have the events of the past week erased completely so that she could start over. She wanted to rewind to that day in

Acapulco when she'd stormed off after Malcolm told her the truth she wasn't ready for. She had vowed not to get high anymore, and she had let herself and everyone else down. She looked up and saw Mercedes looking at her. An unspoken conversation took place between them then. Sunny's eyes said, *I'm lost and I'm so sorry.* Mercedes' said, *I forgive you. We can do this together.*

Sunny wept openly. "Okay," she said. "Okay."

Mercedes went to her mother and hugged her. Sunny threw her arms around her and hugged her back tightly. The two of them cried, so many raw emotions overtaking them at once. Soon, Marisol encircled them, and the three generations of women embraced tearfully, ready to face their challenges as a united front.

Afterward, Sunny looked Jada in the eyes. "I'm sorry for the things that I said earlier, about you and Born." Jada nodded. "He loves you, Jada. You have to make things work between you."

Jada looked over at Sheldon, and Sunny read her thoughts.

"He'll have to get over it. You have to be happy, too," Sunny said.

Jada squeezed her hand and smiled weakly. "Right now, I'm just worried about you."

Sunny winked at her. "Everything is gonna be just fine." She wished she believed it. Somehow, she couldn't shake the feeling in the pit of her stomach warning her that her troubles were far from over.

Sunny noticed Jenny G standing nearby, looking unsure. Sunny gestured toward the seat next to her, her lips curled into a slight smile. "Come sit with me, Jenny G."

At fifty-nine years old, Jenny Gonzalez had seen it all. Having worked as a domestic all of her adult life, she had learned the art of understanding her employers. She had to know when to become invisible, and when to make her presence felt. She had worked for Sunny for years, ever since Sunny moved into her fancy Manhattan apartment after Dorian's death. She had seen

Sunny up and had seen her down, too. But she had never crossed the line and intervened in Sunny's personal life. Until today.

Jenny sat now beside Sunny, unsure of what to expect from her unpredictable boss. They had a good relationship, but Jenny had rolled the dice when she agreed to be a part of Jada and Marisol's plan. Jenny had walked into Jada's apartment that day, knowing that Sunny might fire her for daring to question her behavior.

Her heart beat rapidly as she sat beside Sunny. She stared at her hands, wondering what she would do or where she would go if Sunny sent her packing. Jenny was an illegal Mexican immigrant, and had given up her rundown Bronx apartment years ago to move in with Sunny full time. She knew that she had enough money saved to start over, but the truth was that Jenny didn't want to go. She loved Sunny and Mercedes like family. Jenny fought the urge to burst into tears as she waited for Sunny to speak.

Sunny watched her housekeeper struggling with her emotions, and knew instinctively why Jenny was so anxious. She reached out and took the older woman's soft hands in hers, and met her gaze.

"Jenny, it's okay," Sunny said, soothingly.

Jenny's tears plunged forth, and a lone sob escaped her. Sunny pulled her close and Jenny rested her head on Sunny's shoulder in relief.

Sunny resisted the urge to cry herself. She patted Jenny reassuringly, and comforted her. "You have nothing to worry about. You hear me?"

Jenny nodded, sat up, and retrieved a tissue from her pocket. She blew her nose, softly, and did her best to pull herself together.

Sunny took a deep breath. "I just want to tell you that I'm grateful." Her voice cracked as she spoke, and she looked at Jenny intently, willing herself to hold it together. "You have been one of the few people that I can really trust. You've always had my back. You are loyal, and you only told me the truth—you, Jada, my mom . . . you were *all* right. I need to get help." Sunny wiped the corners of her eyes where her tears had gathered. "I just want to say thank you for looking out for me and Mercedes all these years. You're like a second mom to me, Jenny."

Jenny nodded, happy tears slowly falling from her eyes. "I feel the same way. I really love you and Mercedes. I want you to be happy, Sunny. You deserve that after everything you've been through."

Sunny couldn't agree more. "You're right, Jenny." Sunny nodded. "And from now on, I will be happy." She gripped Jenny's hand. "Thank you. I don't trust people very easily. But I trust you. And I know that you've got my back, even though I'm not the easiest person to work for."

Jenny laughed, knowing that last statement was true. "I wouldn't want to work for anybody else. You are like family to me." She smiled.

"Good," Sunny said, wiping her eyes one last time. "No more crying."

"Okay," Jenny agreed.

Hand in hand, Sunny and Jenny G joined the rest of the women to plot her return to rehab.

11

OLD NEWS

Born heard the doorbell ring. He wasn't expecting company. In fact, this was his first time at home in days. He'd been spending a lot of time at Anisa's place. Too much time, he feared, since the last thing he wanted was for Anisa to get the wrong idea. He did enjoy her company, as well as the sex and the attention. But he knew that all of it was merely a substitute for what he was missing, which was Jada. He hoped it might be Jada at the door now, and he quickened his pace in eagerness. He looked through the tiny peephole and was surprised to find no one there.

He stood back. Something didn't feel right. His time in the streets had taught him to trust his instinct. Stepping away from the door, he went to the coat closet nearby to get one of the two guns he kept in the house. As he reached for the .45 on the top shelf, he was rocked by a force so powerful it deafened him. He felt as if he'd been pushed with an incredible amount of force, and found himself thrown feet first across the room, landing on top of the door to the coat closet he'd just been standing near. Debris was scattered everywhere. There was a gaping hole where his front door had been, and through it he could see nothing but smoke and flames. As his hearing slowly returned, he heard the faint sound of the smoke alarms squalling. Born was dazed and confused. It took him several minutes to register that a bomb had just gone off at his front door. And if he had stepped outside instead of stepping back, he'd be dead right now. The realization hit him so hard that he passed out cold.

Jada raced through the halls of Richmond University Medical Center in search of his room. She passed nurses and staff members who asked whether they could help. She had to find him.

Jada was spent. After a long and emotional day with Sunny and her family, she had gotten a call from DJ that Born had been in an accident. It was all he was willing to say over the phone. Jada finally spotted him as she rounded the corner. DJ saw her, too, and came rushing toward her.

"Calm down," he said. Jada had panic etched all over her face.

"Where is he?" She was breathless. "What happened?"

"He's okay. There was some kind of explosion. They don't know if it was a gas leak, but they said something about a suitcase at the front door. They ain't saying much, but he's okay. Some neighbors called nine-one-one and they got him here. They called Miss Ingrid, and she got in touch with me. We've all been trying to get in touch with you for hours."

Jada groaned in frustration. She had been staging Sunny's intervention all day. "Where is he?"

"Listen." DJ took a deep breath. He put his hands on Jada's shoulders, looked her in the eyes. "Anisa's here. She's in there with Born right now."

Jada held his gaze. Her heart raced. With her jaw clenched, she narrowed her eyes at DJ.

"Where's Ethan?"

"He's with Miss Ingrid. She took him to get something to eat."

Jada glanced around. "Which room is he in?"

DJ led the way. They stopped outside of Born's room, and Jada could hear Anisa laughing softly.

"Now I *know* you're okay. You're back to being fresh again."

Jada heard Born mumble something she couldn't hear, but she had heard enough. Her blood was at a brisk boil.

She stepped into the room, and saw Born lying in the bed with his head and right arm bandaged heavily. Anisa had basically draped herself across him, despite the IV and other monitors connected to him. Born looked at her as she stepped in.

"Hey, Jada."

He seemed groggy. Jada wasn't sure whether they had him doped up or if he was still mumbling as a result of the explosion.

"Hey," she said. "Why is she here?"

"Excuse you?" Anisa frowned as she sat upright. "I'm right here. Why don't you ask me?"

Jada side eyed her.

"Nah," Born said. "Don't ask nobody nothing." He wasn't that groggy, and he could tell that this was not about to go well. "Listen." He tried to sit up, but his right side was racked with pain. His head was pounding, and it hurt to move. He spoke in a jumbled whisper in an effort to keep his head from throbbing worse than it already was. "Listen, 'Neece, let me talk to Jada for a while. Please."

He watched Anisa contemplate it. This was her big chance. She could blow it all up, and tell Jada the truth about their reunion. Or she could play it cool and let Born handle things his way. Anisa was the type who could go either way. She was a live wire. But Born counted on the fact that they'd bonded recently. He hoped that they had an understanding. She sighed, gathered her sweater, and touched Born tenderly on the leg. "I'll be outside."

She walked past Jada without a second glance. And it was then, as Born looked at Jada, that he saw the pain etched on her face. She stood close to his bedside with her hands in the pockets of her hoodie, her eyes heavy with tears. "She's ''Neece' now?"

Born shook his head slowly. "Don't start."

Jada wiped her eyes quickly. She was an emotional wreck, and she knew it. Seeing Born like this wasn't helping. "Are you alright?"

"I will be. Right now everything hurts." Born licked his lips. They felt dry as hell.

"She was all over you," Jada said. She gestured with her chin toward the door. "What's up with that?"

Born cleared his throat. "My lips are dry. She was putting some Vaseline on for me."

"I bet she was," Jada sniffed. She snatched the small jar of Vaseline from Born's bedside table and applied it to his lips with her fingertip. "What else has she been doing with your lips?"

"Oh, you care now?" Born tried to move into a more comfortable position, and winced a little at the pain that shot through his right side. He resigned himself to his uncomfortable fate, and looked at Jada standing there with the nerve to be mad. "It's hard to tell if you even know I'm alive."

Jada's eyes watered unexpectedly hearing him say that. It was true. "Come on, Born. You know what I'm dealing with. Sheldon is—"

"Sheldon is what?" He sucked his teeth. "He's a fucking brat."

Jada's tears turned to rage then. "What did you just say?"

"You heard me." Born was done playing. Somebody was out to get him, and he wanted to know who it was. Being so close to death had put things into fresh perspective for him. "Word. That's how I feel. For months I been calling you, texting you. Nothing. You want to blame Sheldon, but you're the parent. He's not in charge."

Jada shook her head. "It's not that simple."

"I think we have different definitions of family."

"He tried to kill himself, Born."

"Right. So now you give him what he wants for the rest of his life. That's smart." His sarcasm was evident despite the rasp in his voice. "We're talking marriage and making future plans, and then he does that and—*BAM*! Silence." Born's hurt was evident. "You just disappeared on me."

Miss Ingrid returned with Ethan. Jada greeted Born's mother warmly, but she couldn't help being annoyed with the interruption.

Born, on the other hand, was grateful for it. He wasn't interested in talking to Jada about their relationship since it was clear that she was still feeding into Sheldon's bullshit. All he cared about at the moment was figuring out who had rang his doorbell that afternoon.

Ingrid sat at the foot of Born's hospital bed. She was still terribly shaken after finding out that her son had a close brush with death. Ethan, too, had been so afraid that his father was harmed. It had taken much reassurance from Born to calm him down.

Jada managed a weak smile, and greeted Ethan with a hug. He seemed to have grown in the months since the last time she'd seen him. Jada hadn't realized how much time had passed while she was being held hostage to Sheldon's wishes.

As if reading her thoughts, Ingrid asked, "How's Sheldon doing?"

Jada glanced at Born. "He's okay. Ava's with him now."

Ethan sat in the chair next to his father's bed. He didn't miss Sheldon one bit, and wished his grandmother hadn't asked about him. Ethan was no punk. But he was smart enough to realize that Sheldon was crazy.

"Tell me what happened." Jada looked at Born with genuine concern in her eyes. She wished that they hadn't been interrupted. She wanted to tell Born that she thought about him all the time. That she missed him. He was her warrior. Seeing him lying there so helpless was killing her softly.

He cleared his throat again. "I was home, and the doorbell

rang. I went and looked through the peephole and I didn't see anybody. I just got this feeling that something wasn't right. I wasn't expecting nobody. So I went to the closet to get that thing." He looked at his mother as he said it, because Ingrid knew better than anybody what her son was into. "Next thing I knew . . . it was just a big-ass blast. The door flew off the frame, and the whole front of the house is blown apart. I'm lucky to be alive, for real."

"Oh my God," Jada said. She thought of who might be responsible, but came up empty.

Ingrid didn't like it one bit. "I called Zion and he's sending some of his friends down here to keep an eye on your room around the clock."

"Ma—" Born protested.

"Ma, nothing. We don't know who rang that doorbell. I heard the detectives talking about a black suitcase. Until we know what's going on, I want you protected. And like it or not, you're not in the position to protect yourself." Her tone of voice made it clear that the subject was not up for debate. "And what about that thing you keep in the closet? You know they're gonna mess with you about that now." Ingrid didn't miss a thing.

Born smirked at her. "You worry too much."

"We're all worried about you," Anisa said, as she stepped back into the room. She was tired of standing in the hallway.

Jada scowled at her, and Anisa pretended not to notice. DJ stepped into the room, too, and stood quietly in the corner.

Anisa filled Born in. "The doctor said you can have more painkillers soon. I told him the last dose was wearing off." Anisa walked over to Ethan and stroked his well-groomed head affectionately.

Jada was pissed. All of a sudden Anisa was the one speaking to Born's doctors and acquainting herself with the staff. She re-

minded herself that Ethan was present, that Anisa was his mother. Jada didn't want to make a scene. But she needed this bitch
to know that Born was not hers for the taking. "Thanks for filling us in," she said, her eyes boring into Anisa's. "I'm here now.
I'll take it from here."

Anisa smirked a little. There were so many things she could
say to shatter Jada's heart. Born had been in her bed and in every
crevice of her body for many nights. Anisa held her tongue, but
was cackling on the inside.

A nurse came in and checked Born's vitals. She injected something into his IV, and then left quietly.

No one spoke after she left. The tension was palpable, and Ingrid sought to relieve it. "Marquis, you have a concussion. You
should get some rest." She stood to leave. The ladies reluctantly
followed suit. Ethan stood near his father's bedside.

"I don't want to leave, Dad. I feel better when you're home
with us."

Jada listened closely. *Us?*

"I'm gonna be home soon," Born said. "Trust me."

"Can I come back tomorrow?" Ethan asked.

"I'll bring you back tomorrow, baby. Don't worry." Anisa knew
that Jada was listening and she didn't care. She couldn't just run in
and out of Born's life as she pleased. As far as Anisa was concerned,
you snooze you lose. And Jada had fallen asleep on the job.

Jada was livid. She looked at Miss Ingrid and was met with
an expression of understanding. Ingrid shook her head and Jada
understood that she was not to play into Anisa's hands. Jada was
fed up though.

"Good night, you all," she said. "I'm going to stay and talk to
Born for just a little longer."

Anisa seemed to want to say something, but Miss Ingrid took
her by the elbow and led her and Ethan to the door. "Good night,

Marquis. Good night, Jada," she called over her shoulder as she left. Jada was so grateful for her.

DJ lingered behind. "I'm gonna stay for a while until Tremaine gets here. I'll be in the lounge right by the elevators."

Born thanked him, and DJ followed everyone out.

Once they were gone, Jada turned to Born. "You want to tell me what's going on?"

"What are you talking about?" he asked.

"Don't act dumb. You know exactly what I'm talking about. Anisa. What's up with you two?"

"Jada, what do you want me to say?" Born was tired. He was dazed. He didn't want to do this right now. "She's Ethan's mother. I'm not gonna stop her from coming around."

Jada stared at him for a while in silence. Her gut told her that there was more to the story than just that. But her concern for him took over.

"Who would want to hurt you?" she asked. "Who do you think it was?"

Born shook his head. "I have no idea. Far as I know, I'm a pretty nice guy."

Jada was really worried. "Is anything going on with the crew?"

"That's none of my business. I don't deal with that," he reminded her. "I haven't for years. You know that."

Jada nodded. She did know that, but felt she had to ask. Suddenly explosives were going off and the crew was being called to stand guard. She didn't like this.

"Listen, Born," she said. "I love you. I know I haven't been around like I should be. I just don't know how to deal with everything. Sheldon is my son. He didn't ask to be here. But now that he is, I owe it to him to do whatever I can to make him . . . okay. I'm not trying to push you away, baby. I swear."

Born nodded his head, his eyes lowering from a mixture of exhaustion and medication.

Jada watched him with her heart so full of words to say. She didn't know why she felt like this was her last chance to say what was on her mind. But as she watched him drift off, she knew that it would have to wait another day.

"I'll be here in the morning," she said. She leaned over and kissed his forehead, and then left him alone.

Jada arrived home and parked her car outside her condo. She stopped at her mailbox and used her key to open it, removing a small stack of mail. She flipped through it as she walked back to her door. One piece stood out among the rest. It was a blue envelope. Fancy stationery with her first name only, and no address. She wondered how the mailman had known to place it in her locked mailbox with no address and only her first name. As Jada unlocked her door, a chill ran down her spine, and for no real reason, she rushed inside and quickly locked the door behind her. She called out to her sister.

"We're in here!" Ava yelled from the living room.

Jada walked in and found them sitting together watching *The Pursuit of Happyness*. She breathed a sigh of relief that they were okay, and told herself to relax. Seeing Born laid up in the hospital, and hearing talk of explosions and black suitcases . . . it had all left her feeling ill at ease. The nightmares she had been having didn't help matters at all.

Ava made eye contact with her. "How's everything?" She didn't mention Born by name since she was aware that Sheldon didn't know where Jada had gone.

"Okay. I'll fill you in later on." Jada took off her sweater, and sat down on the ottoman to open her mail. She started with the mysterious envelope. She opened it and froze in her seat. Inside the small envelope, she found a single crack vial and a small note card that read, "For old time's sake."

Jada's adrenaline rushed. She stood up and marched to the bathroom and flushed the crack vial down the drain. She hadn't held one in her hands in years, and they shook now as she watched it disappear. The note was still in her left hand, and she stared at it now. Trembling, she held it up to the light. The lettering was bold and etched in black Sharpie. All of the words were written in capital letters. Jada jumped when she heard a noise behind her, and breathed a sigh of relief when she saw that Ava had followed her into the bathroom.

The words came flooding forth like a river. "This is crazy, Ava. Somebody's playing games."

"Wait, what are you talking about?" Ava held up her hands in an effort to calm her sister.

Jada shook her head in frustration. "Born got hurt. Somebody rang his doorbell and left a suitcase at his doorstep. The suitcase exploded, and thankfully he survived. But he's bandaged up, cracked ribs, a concussion, hurt his collar bone."

"My God!" Ava exclaimed.

"Just now I came home and found this in the mailbox." Jada shoved the cryptic note and the envelope into Ava's hand. "It had a crack vial inside."

Ava's eyes widened. "Where is it?" she asked, looking around for the drugs.

"I flushed it."

"Why, Jada? That's evidence." Ava held the envelope by its edges.

"It was just a reaction. I wanted it gone. Ava, I haven't held a crack vial in my hand in over ten years." Jada couldn't control the trembling. "Plus, I can't go to the police," Jada said.

Ava frowned. "Why not? You didn't do anything wrong. This all sounds crazy."

Jada shook her head. Though she had nothing to hide, she still didn't trust the police. Old feelings from her days behind bars resurfaced. It had never occurred to her to contact the cops.

"I just have to think," she said. She thought about the nightmares she'd had about Jamari. She could hear his voice now, laughing at her. Jada shivered, and her sister noticed.

"You okay?" Ava asked.

Jada nodded, though it wasn't true. She was far from okay. "Where was Sheldon all afternoon?" she asked. "Did he leave the house?" Jada wondered if her son was crafty enough to pull this off. Could he have gotten his hands on a vial of crack and met the mailman when he made his delivery? And would he be cruel enough to do something so heartless?

"No, he was in here with me the whole time. He hasn't left my side." Ava glanced at the note again. "This is scary, Jada. Who would do something like this? And who would do that to Born?"

Jada shrugged. "I just can't stop thinking about Jamari." He had been on her mind ever since she awoke from that dream.

Ava looked at her sister like she might be losing it a little. "Jamari is dead. I don't think you need to be worried about him anymore."

Jada knew it sounded bizarre. "I've been having crazy nightmares about him. I could hear his voice so clearly." She shook her head. "It's like he's haunting me."

Ava knew all that Jada had endured at Jamari's hands. She listened sympathetically. "What was he saying in these dreams?"

"He just kept laughing. Like he was teasing me, mocking me. It was pitch-black, and I couldn't see him. But I could hear him. I could feel him." She shuddered again. "I'm scared, girl. I feel like something ain't right."

Ava nodded. She understood why she felt that way. The whole thing was eerie. She felt her cell phone vibrate, and pulled it out of her suit pocket. She saw a text from Zion: "Come over tonight. Adiva's asleep, and I'm lonely."

Ava smiled. They had been living dangerously, she and Zion. On plenty of occasions over the past few weeks, Ava hung out with Zion and his daughter at the park, over dinner, even playing board games after school at Zion's place. So far, Adiva hadn't told her mother. But Ava knew that if Olivia ever got wind of the fact that she was not only sleeping with Zion, but interacting with their child, all hell would break loose. But she couldn't help it. There was something so sexy about Zion; something so intoxicatingly erotic about sneaking around with him this way. She texted him back: "Just leaving Jada's house. I should be there in about forty minutes."

"Well, just keep the doors locked, and the phone charged," she advised Jada. "I'm gonna leave soon because I have a court appearance tomorrow." She was lying. "I was supposed to be preparing for it today, but I got caught up with Sunny and Malcolm and all of their drama."

A moment later, Zion texted back: "Okay."

Jada hated to see her sister go. She didn't want to admit that she was afraid to be alone in the house with only Sheldon as company. But she understood that work came first. "I'm going back to the hospital in the morning. I'll tell Born about the note. Maybe it's all connected. I'll let you know if anything else happens." Jada looked at her sister, thoughtfully. "Be careful please."

Ava smiled weakly. "I will."

They returned to the living room where Sheldon was watching the end of the movie. Ava called a car service for a ride to Tribeca. She didn't even ask the cost. After the day she'd had, all she cared about was getting back into Zion's arms again.

12
SLIPPING

Sunny was on the phone with her PR people, while Marisol cleaned up after dinner. Sunny had agreed to check into rehab in the morning. First, she would make an appearance on *The Mindy Milford Show* to answer a series of preapproved questions. This interview would be her attempt at spinning the scandal with the Mexican authorities in her favor. If they could convince America that the arrest had spurred Sunny to get the help she needed, it could work to her benefit. After the interview with Mindy, Sunny would check into Crossroads, a drug rehabilitation facility in Pennsylvania.

The family had shared dinner and more discussion about Sunny's future. She seemed serene, quieter, and more resigned to the fact that she needed help. She had called Abe Childs and gotten a referral from him for the rehab center, which he described as discreet and effective. She, Mercedes, and Marisol had spent some time talking privately as well. The three generations of women had a lot of healing to do, and it began that day. After the intervention at Jada's house, Sunny had donned a hat, sunglasses, and an oversized hoodie in order to gain access to her apartment building. Along with Jenny G, Marisol, and Mercedes, Sunny had gone home and gathered as much of her things as she would need for the next several weeks. Her driver, Raul, had met them in the underground garage and helped them load up the car with four suitcases worth of Sunny and Mercedes' belongings. Sunny had bid a tearful farewell to Jenny G. The woman was like a second mother to her, and it touched Sunny's heart when Jenny promised to pick her up from rehab on the day she was discharged. Sunny had cried watching Jenny go.

Now it was getting late, and Marisol wanted to get some sleep in anticipation of the next day. She and Sunny had finally discussed the elephant in the room—Sunny's family prospering as a result of her relationship with Dorian. Marisol had tried not to think about it over the years. But today it had been brought to the forefront. She admitted that she had allowed Dorian's money, power, and status to cloud her judgment years ago.

"At the time you brought Dorian home, the family was struggling. We didn't tell you about it. We didn't tell your brothers about it. But Dale and I were praying every night for a miracle. We were about to lose the house, the car payments were behind. It was so bad that the gas company was threatening to come and take our meter. I'm not saying that's an excuse. But it definitely felt like an answer to our prayers when Dorian showed up with all of his generosity toward the family. And it was obvious that he loved you. And you loved him, too."

Sunny had listened to her mother, thinking back to those days.

"When we drove to the restaurant that first night you brought him home, he rode in the car with your father, remember?"

Sunny nodded. She did remember it like it was yesterday.

"Well, Dale told me later on that Dorian knew about our problems with money. How he knew, I'm not sure. But being a powerful man like he was, I guess he used his resources and he found out that we were struggling. He told your father that he wanted to help. He offered to pay off the mortgage and give us a monthly stipend if we didn't stand in the way of him getting to know you."

Sunny had shaken her head, sadly. "That sounds like you sold me off to the highest bidder."

"It does sound like that," Marisol admitted. "But that's not what it was. You loved him. And he swore to your father that he would not touch you in any way until you turned eighteen. We had our reservations about him because of his age and because we were not dumb. We knew the life that he was living. But it was obvious that you cared about him. It seemed like a win-win thing at the time because we were in a bind. Your father figured that if things didn't work out, he could always pay Dorian back somewhere down the line. But it turned out that you fell in love and stayed together until he passed away." Marisol had dabbed at her eyes. "I won't make any excuses for what we did. We threw you into a life that you were not ready for, and we didn't realize that you were getting in over your head. Over the years, I cannot tell you how many times I have hated myself for letting you get caught up in this craziness."

That conversation had taken place hours ago. Still, Mercedes was enthralled by it. As she prepared to go to bed, she approached her grandmother.

"*Bella*," she said, softly. "I love you."

"I love you, too, Mercedes."

"Tomorrow, after Mommy checks herself in, I want to go and stay with Grandma Gladys."

Marisol's face betrayed her emotions. She felt hurt that Mercedes did not want to stay with her and Dale. "Why?"

Mercedes knew that her grandmother was disappointed. But her mind was made up. "I just want to get away from all of the stuff going on with Mommy. I don't want to sleep in her old room, and see all of the reminders of her. I think spending the summer with Grandma Gladys and my uncles will be better for me." Satisfied with her answer, she waited for Marisol's response. The truth was that Mercedes had a lot of emotions to sort through. Since hearing about her grandparents' prospering from Sunny's relationship with her father, Mercedes had a lot to think about. She understood her mother's story a little more, and why she might have felt like no one really loved her. No one except Mercedes. It wasn't that Mercedes resented Marisol and Dale, and her uncles Reuben and Ronnie. But she was beginning to see them through new eyes. She thought it would be a good idea to wait out Sunny's rehab stint in the company of her father's side of the family, for once.

Marisol reluctantly agreed. "If that's what you want to do, Mercedes, okay." She was too tired to argue. She kissed her granddaughter on the cheek and headed up for bed. Sunny came in and stopped her when she was halfway up the stairs.

Sunny looked at her mother and her daughter and offered them a sad smile. "I love you guys. I want to thank you for hanging in there with me. And I want to apologize for the ways I embarrassed you. The ways that I embarrassed myself."

Marisol descended the stairs and stood face-to-face with her daughter. Sunny looked so defeated, and yet so determined. She hugged her for a long time, stroking her back reassuringly. "You're not going through this alone. We're all with you." She held Sunny tightly, then pulled back and held her face in her hands, smiling at her. "I'm proud of you, Sunny." Marisol turned and walked slowly upstairs to bed.

Mercedes looked at her mother. "I'm proud of you, too, Mommy. Don't be too hard on yourself. You're gonna turn things around in no time."

Sunny looked into her daughter's eyes. She saw Dorian in there. She saw herself, her young and impressionable self. There were so many things she wanted to say to Mercedes. But there were more pressing matters at hand.

Sunny sighed, heavily. "Thank you, sweetie." She hugged Mercedes and smothered her with kisses. "Get some sleep. Tomorrow is my big day."

Mercedes squeezed her mother tight, and inhaled her warm, powdery scent. She wanted to cling to her forever, and keep her all for herself. No more paparazzi, fashion shows, and photographers. Mercedes just wanted her Mama back. "I love you," she said. Then she went upstairs to say a prayer that God would make it all better.

Sunny stood in the solitude of her mother's kitchen, and toyed with the baggie of cocaine she had retrieved from her bureau at home that afternoon. Tucked in the corner of her panty drawer, the coke was exactly where she'd left it prior to her trip to Mexico. She had stuck it in her pocket hours ago, and had been waiting with bated breath for the chance to be alone. It had been the longest day of her life waiting for this moment. Now that everyone had gone to bed, Sunny willed her hands to stop shaking as she walked out of the kitchen. Mercedes voice lingered in her head. *"I love you."* She whispered, "I love you, too." Then she locked herself in the first-floor bathroom with the bag of white powder. Just one more high before she gave it all up for good.

Born lay awake in his hospital bed that night, unable to sleep. So much was going on at once, and his sixth sense was telling him that something big was about to go down. Dorian had always taught him to be aware of subtle changes, the ripples caused by even the smallest pebbles hitting the water. So much was changing in his life at that moment. Instead of ripples in the water, the explosion that had injured him was more like a great wave sweeping through and leaving catastrophe in its wake. He wondered who was out there.

He wasn't the only one wondering.

Jada stuck the mysterious note inside her desk drawer and continued her nightly routine. She fixed dinner for Sheldon, and picked at the food on her own plate. She wasn't hungry. Consumed instead by thoughts of who was taunting her, she was distracted all night. She wondered who it was and what they wanted from her after all this time. Sheldon was especially quiet tonight. After the things they'd all discussed during Sunny's intervention, it seemed that he was lost in his thoughts. Jada always worried when he spent too much time thinking. So she lay awake for most of the night, unable to get her mind or her body to rest.

Zion heard the shower go off and the curtain pull back as Ava finished freshening up after a long day. She had arrived about a half hour ago, looking corporate in a navy blue dress and nude heels. It turned him on to see her that way. Ava was a beautiful, buttoned-up lawyer by day and a wildcat in his bed at night. To Zion, she reminded him of a naughty librarian, ready and eager to be spanked for her dirty deeds.

She came into the bedroom wrapped in a towel, her makeup washed off. He thought she was beautiful.

"Come here," he said. "Drop the towel on the floor and come here."

Ava hesitated. Beautiful though she was, Ava had insecurities, the same as most women. Zion watched her think about it. She was different from Olivia in that regard. Olivia was a performer. She liked to be watched, seen, heard, adored. Olivia would have dropped that towel and sauntered over to him as seductively as a cat. But Ava was different. He liked it. She was shy, despite the fact that she was sexy as hell. Once she got warmed up, she was insatiable. But he liked the thrill of working her up to that.

"Come here," he demanded again.

Ava took a deep breath and let the towel go. Beads of water dotted her naked skin, as she walked over to the bed where Zion lay. He watched her every move, and felt his manhood rise within his Hanes. She crawled into bed on top of him. The feeling of her skin against his own made Zion moan with pleasure as he kissed her. Ava sank her nails into the taut skin of his back, and held on for dear life.

Gillian extinguished the blunt she'd been smoking and sat up in bed, folding her legs Indian-style beneath her. Her Upper West Side townhouse was dead silent except for her breathing. The noise on the streets outside was the only other sound that filled her space. She sat there thinking about her father.

Doug Nobles had been quite a man. He was old school. An original gangster. As his daughter, Gillian had been pampered, protected, and taught from an early age how to make power moves. His death had drawn a wedge between her and her brother Baron, who she still blamed for it. She wondered if Doug would be proud of the way that she had carried the family torch in his absence. She prayed that he would be.

Doug had been particularly fond of Frankie. In fact, he had practically raised him and taught him everything he knew. In the days after his death, Frankie had guided Gillian into the game, teaching her the ins and outs of the family business. The two of them had been a team at first, and Gillian knew that her father would have approved. But Frankie had let his feelings get in the way of the business. He couldn't accept the fact that

Gillian was not willing to be with him anymore. Unlike his ex-wife, Camille, Gillian didn't cry, beg, or even appear to lose sleep over her breakup with Frankie. Instead, she had forged ahead and taken the helm of the business with ease. Because he couldn't let go of his romantic hopes for the two of them, Gillian had ceased to rely on his advice. She trusted her gut instead, and the years of wisdom she had gained at her father's knee. She was loved by her crew, respected by her business associates, and feared because of the power she held.

Still, she wished her father was alive. Doug would tell her if she was missing something, if she was making any wrong decisions. Without him or Frankie to depend on, Gillian had to trust only her instincts. And something felt out of sync. She was uneasy for some reason. She couldn't quite put her finger on it, but whatever it was, it was keeping her up at night.

Sunny turned on the faucet, in order to drown out the sound of her snorting. She held one nostril and sucked up the crystalized powder with the other. In one long sniff, she took a big hit. She wiggled her nose around, sniffled a bit, and then bent forward and did it again. Another long and exaggerated snort. She wanted her last time to be a memorable one. Standing upright, she felt it all hit her at once. She shook her head vigorously, taken over by the intense sensation. The whole room looked like a kaleidoscope. Colors swirled in and out, and she heard music. It sounded at once far away and in stereo surround sound. Pulsing, throbbing, uptempo music. She hadn't been this high in a long time.

Sunny found her own reflection in the mirror, and gripped the pedestal sink for support. Staring at her reflection, she was amazed by what she saw. All sorts of colors shot out of her face. Blues and greens, red, orange, sparkles and shimmering lights. It was a neon light show taking place across her face, and techno music audible only to her blared loudly. She began to sweat profusely, and beads of sweat dripped from her forehead. Her heartbeat quickened to a rapid pace. She hadn't gotten high for a long time, and she had been fiending. This was some good shit. She took another hit. She wanted to go out with a bang. Afterward, she looked at her reflection in the mirror once again.

The music slowly faded, and the colors became less vibrant. While staring at herself, she was aware of a figure standing behind her. She leaned in closer to the mirror to get a better look at the reflection. The vision shocked her, and she squeezed her eyes closed in order to refocus. She suddenly felt dizzy. When she opened her eyes again, the vision was clearer, closer, standing directly behind her. It was Dorian.

Her eyes filled with tears as she stared at his reflection in the mirror. She was afraid that he'd disappear, so she dared not turn around, dared not even to blink. She held his gaze for long and tender moments, sweat still falling from her face. Standing behind her, he watched her through despondent eyes. "Baby, why? Why didn't you listen to me?"

His voice caused the tears to spill forth. She shook her head in dismay.

"You messed up this time," he said, sadly. "You got more chances than you were supposed to get."

Sunny felt herself laughing despite the tears falling from her eyes. A tingling sensation began in her toes and her fingertips. It felt funny. "What, baby?" she asked, smiling at him through the mirror. "What are you saying?" She dared not turn around, afraid that she might discover that she was hallucinating. If this was an illusion, it was one that she wanted to hold onto desperately.

Dorian wasn't smiling. "No more chances, Sunny. This is it."

Sunny's smile faded.

"This is it." Dorian's image began to fade, and Sunny frantically reached out toward the mirror. As he faded altogether, she spun around to see if he was there, and found that his image had disappeared.

She tried to cry out to him, but her voice got caught in her throat. Her chest tightened, and her breathing became labored. Her heart was galloping in her chest, and pain racked her so violently that she braced herself against the wall. She willed herself to calm down, but the room felt suddenly smaller. Her lungs weren't filling with air. Sunny lunged for the locked door, but fell thrashing to the floor with her hands clutching her heart. It felt as if someone was sitting on her chest, and she wanted desperately to call for help, but could not find her voice. Dorian's voice called to her as everything faded to black. "Sunny!" he cried. "Why didn't you listen to me?"

13

FALLING

Zion lay sprawled out across his king-size bed. Ava was spread out across his chest, her long hair hanging loosely around her. He ran his fingers through it as they lay there, spent from their lovemaking. It was three o'clock in the morning, and they had been going at it for hours. Ava was smiling. Zion had taken his time. Slowly and passionately he had made love to her. Now, his fingers working her scalp, she closed her eyes and smiled contently as they lay together.

"I think you're beautiful, Ava." His voice was throaty and sexy.

Ava stroked his stomach. "Thank you. I think you are, too." She wished she could pause this moment. The time she spent with Zion was the sweetest thing. Her thoughts drifted to Olivia. She felt a pang of guilt as she lay with her friend's man. She reminded herself that she and Olivia were only friendly because of Jada. Thinking of Olivia as Jada's friend somehow made it easier for Ava to admit that she was falling for Zion.

"What are we doing?" She asked the question before she gave herself a chance to rethink it.

Zion shifted slightly. "What do you mean?"

"What are we doing?" she asked again. "What is this? Is it just sex? Are we together? Are we friends with benefits?"

Zion sighed. "Nah, it's more than that. For me, it's more."

Ava turned to face him. "For me, too. But what about Olivia?"

Zion shook his head. "It's over with us. I saw her earlier and she's just . . . we're not meant to be together anymore."

Ava was glad to hear that, but still skeptical. "You still love her?"

Zion looked at her. He decided not to lie. "I'll probably always love Olivia. But she's not the same anymore. The spark went out. So it's time for me to move on."

Ava thought about it. "Is that what this is? Moving on?"

Zion smiled, his sexy white teeth gleaming in the darkness. "This is more than that," he said. "This is—"

Boom! Boom! Boom!

"Open up!"

Boom! Boom! Boom!

They looked at each other in stunned silence.

"Police! Open up!"

Boom! Boom! Boom!

Zion's shut his eyes in dismay. This was it. Ava jumped up out of bed and grabbed his T-shirt laying nearby. She hurriedly put on her panties, as he jumped into his sweatpants.

Boom! Boom! Boom!

"Police!"

Adiva came running into the room, and Zion held out his arm to her. Just then, the sound of the battering ram crashing into the door rattled them.

"Come here!" Zion yelled. Adiva ran to his side. Zion and Ava exchanged one last glance filled with terror and unspoken fear before the room was flooded with DEA agents and the sounds of walkie-talkies blaring.

"Get on the ground! Get on the ground!"

The police got them all on the floor with their arms spread above their heads, including Adiva. Ava tried not to cry as she was handcuffed. Zion was in a similar position on the other side of the room. A female agent came and took Adiva out of the room altogether. They could hear the apartment being ransacked while one of the agents explained that they had a search warrant.

"Can we see it?" Ava asked. As an attorney, she wanted to ensure that this was a legal search.

One agent roughly snatched her upright by her handcuffs and shoved the papers in her face. "See?"

"Do you have any illegal substances, guns, or anything of the sort in here?" another agent asked Zion. "It's better for you to tell us now before we find it."

Zion wanted to spit in his face. There was plenty of illegal stuff in there. But if they thought that he would make it easy for them by telling them where to look, they were fools. He ignored the question and exercised his right to remain silent.

It wasn't long before an agent called out that she had found two firearms in the bedroom, and a bag of pills in a kitchen cabinet.

One agent smiled at the two of them. "You're under arrest, guys."

Ava cried softly. In no time flat, her dreams had turned into a terrible nightmare.

At four o'clock in the morning, Jada awoke to her cell phone ringing. She yawned and looked at the screen. The number was unfamiliar, but she answered it anyway.

Ava's crying voice filled her ear. "Jada, I'm under arrest."

"What?" Jada sat up in bed.

"The cops came to Zion's house while I was there, and they arrested both of us."

"Zion?" Jada looked around the room for signs that she might be having another nightmare. She pinched herself. "What were you doing at Zion's place?"

"I'll explain that later," Ava said, impatiently. "I need you to come to court for me. They tell me I'm going to be arraigned and have a bail hearing. Please come and get me out of here, Jada."

"Calm down, okay. I'll be there. Don't worry." Jada was already out of bed, pacing the floor. "Ava?"

"Yes?"

"Be strong and don't tell them nothing."

"I know that." Ava knew that Jada was more streetwise than she was. But both of them had grown up in Brooklyn, and had learned early on what to do and what not to say if you were ever in police custody. Ava had never imagined herself in this predicament. But she knew how to handle herself.

"I love you," Jada said. "I'll be in court today. Don't cry."

"Okay," Ava said. "I love you, too." She hung up the phone, took a deep breath, and was returned to her cell.

Jada rushed into her bathroom to get ready. Everything was beginning to crumble.

Marisol awoke to a six a.m. phone call from Reuben's wife, Bridget. She was frantic. Reuben had been arrested, and the cops were still combing through their Long Island home in search of evidence. Bridget was distraught, and Marisol was, too. This was the last thing their family needed. She told Dale the news, and climbed out of bed in search of Sunny.

Marisol instantly knew that something was terribly wrong when she found Sunny's room empty, her bed unslept in. She rushed down the hall to the guest bedroom where Mercedes slept. Along the way, she prayed frantically that Sunny had slept with Mercedes rather than alone in her own room. But she knew in her heart that wasn't the case. Even before she opened Mercedes' door and found her sleeping alone, Marisol knew that this was bad. She shut the door, and ran past Dale down the stairs to the kitchen. Dale went into the living room. Both of them began calling out Sunny's name. Dale checked for their car keys, and found that all of them were accounted for. He saw Sunny's purse laying on the table in the foyer and he wondered where she could be. It didn't seem that she had left the house. His heart jumped when he heard Marisol cry out from down the hall.

Dale ran to where Marisol stood before the locked guest bathroom door. They banged on it together.

"Sunny! Sunny, open the door!"

After a few seconds, Dale told his wife to stand back, and he kicked at the door several times. Finally, with all of the force he could muster, he kicked the door until it gave way. Rushing inside, they found Sunny lying facedown on the floor. Her eyes were open, and her hands were folded beneath her body.

Marisol cried out in desperation, while Dale turned his daughter's body over and checked for her pulse. Marisol sobbed loudly as she ran quickly to get her phone to call an ambulance. She didn't see Mercedes come downstairs to see what all the commotion was.

Mercedes had a strange feeling in the pit of her stomach. She walked into the bathroom where she could hear her grandfather weeping openly. She stepped inside and saw him sitting on the floor as he cradled Sunny's lifeless body in his arms. She knew right away that her mother was gone; that this time Sunny had done it for good. A bag of powder sat on the edge of the sink, and Mercedes noticed it. Rage and fury took over her, and she hated Sunny so much in that moment. She took the scene in silently. Her mother was dead. The reality hit her hard. There was no turning back.

Slowly, Mercedes walked over to where Dale sat with Sunny in his arms. She stared down at her mother and etched the image in her mind of Sunny lying there with her eyes eerily wide open and somehow shut forever. Sunny's nose was covered in dried blood. Despite the macabre sight, Mercedes saw her mother's beauty even then. Even in death, to Mercedes she looked like an angel. She knelt down and touched Sunny's hand. It was cold and clammy. She held it up to her face, and let her tears fall like rain.

Camille was asleep when her phone rang. It was just past six in the morning and Eli never usually called this early. His shift started at five a.m. and, as usual, he had slipped out of bed soundlessly and left her sleeping, undisturbed. She answered the phone, her voice heavy with sleep.

"Hey, baby."

"Camille," he said. "Wake up. I have to tell you some news."

Camille propped herself up on her elbow and rubbed her eyes. "What's wrong?"

"It's Frankie," he said. "He's been arrested. Him and some of his friends."

Camille was wide awake now. "What? When? What happened?"

"I can't get into all that now, but he's due in court this morning. I'll tell you what I know when I see you."

"But, Eli . . . he's arrested?"

Eli tried not to be bothered by the genuine concern he heard in Camille's voice. After all, Camille and Frankie had been married for years and shared a child together. "Yeah. Listen, baby. I gotta go. I'll call you as soon as I can say more."

"Okay," Camille said. "I love you."

She hung up the phone, jumped up out of bed, and called her sister. To her surprise, Misa answered right away.

"Oh my God," Misa said. "Baron just got arrested, too. Miss Celia called to tell me that the feds raided her house in New Jersey and took Baron. She says they tore the place apart while waving around their search warrant."

Misa and Baron were entering a phase of their relationship that was unfamiliar to either of them. She believed that he was getting out of the game. During their intimate moments, he had suggested that they move away from New York, have some babies, and settle down. She had been considering it, wondering if she and Shane could survive without the warmth and comfort of her mother and sister. But now this.

Camille sat on the edge of the bed. "This is it, Misa. This is where it all comes falling down."

Born woke up early to nurses prodding him with needles, checking his blood pressure, and sticking a thermometer in his mouth. The doctor came in and explained that Born would need to remain in the hospital for at least another day or so for observation. He had a fractured clavicle, a few cracked ribs, and a concussion. He would need to be in a sling for a couple of weeks. But overall he was lucky to be alive. He dozed off for awhile after the doctor's visit, and was awakened not long after by some detectives who wanted to ask him a few questions. Their tone was relaxed, concerned.

"Do you have any enemies that might want to see you hurt? You messing around with anyone's girl, that kinda thing?"

Born told them that he had no enemies. It was true as far as he knew. Sure, in a community as small as Staten Island, there were characters that he chose not to associate with. But none of them would have a reason to go so far as to try and kill him. It bothered Born that he couldn't figure out who it might be. The reality was that someone had wanted to take his life. Whether he knew who it was or not, somebody out there was gunning for him.

He couldn't fall back asleep after they left. He lay in his bed doing his own mental detective work. Just after seven o'clock in the morning, Tremaine came in. He had to cozy up to one of the nurses on duty in order to get in before visiting hours began.

"I slept outside in the visitor's lounge near the elevator," he told Born. "That way, anybody who came up to this floor had to go past me."

Born appreciated that his boys were on high alert.

"I woke up to this text," Tremaine continued, handing Born his cell phone. He reached and turned on the TV at the foot of Born's bed. Flipping through the channels, he stopped on *Eyewitness News.*

Born read the text. "FEDS!" It was from Biggs, another associate of theirs who acted as the crew's muscle.

"Now I can't get in touch with nobody," Tremaine said.

A news bulletin stole their attention.

> *"Twenty-two people were arrested in a narcotics bust on Staten Island and in Brooklyn this morning. Prosecutors allege that the suspects are part of a drug-and-gun trafficking ring that has terrorized New York City for decades. Those arrested include an attorney from the Brooklyn DA's office. Grant Keys was among those targeted in a predawn raid coordinated in both boroughs."*

Born and Tremaine looked on in wide-eyed amazement as video rolled of Frankie being led out of his house in handcuffs. The reporter continued.

> *"Frank Bingham was arrested after selling Oxycodone on three separate occasions to an undercover NYPD officer, police*

said. He was identified as one of two dozen loosely affiliated drug dealers on Staten Island and throughout Brooklyn.

Bingham is the brother of Steven Bingham, the shooting victim in the brutal 2008 murder case that rocked the city. He will be arraigned this morning in Staten Island Criminal Court. Police arrested twenty-one other people in the operation and seized drugs from twelve different locations, including 475 Oxycodone pills, 200 Vicodin pills, 300 Xanax pills, 200 grams of cocaine, 201 glassines of heroin, and sixteen ounces of marijuana. They also seized $17,000 in cash and two loaded 380-caliber handguns from one defendant.

The suspects range in age from nineteen to forty-four and were arrested on charges including cocaine distribution, possession and criminal sale of controlled substances, burglaries, conspiracy, and weapons possession.

We'll have more on this story after today's arraignment."

Born was frozen. This was not good. Tremaine's cell phone rang. He saw DJ's phone number, and answered it quickly.

"Tell Uncle Born, the feds got 'em," DJ said, breathlessly.

"Got who?"

"Uncle Patrick, Uncle Christian, and their whole crew." DJ sounded shaken. "My grandmother just called, said they ran up in her house and Uncle Christian's house this morning."

Tremaine relayed the news to Born.

Born blew out a deep breath. "Damn! Give me the phone."

"Uncle Born, I'm going to court with Grandma this morning," DJ said. "I'll come up there afterward."

"No, you're not," Born said, adamantly. "You're not just

some dude from around the way no more, DJ. You're a celebrity. You're not gonna sit up in some courtroom watching your uncles battle a drug case. Get out of here with that. You sit your ass at home, and we'll get somebody else to go to court and let us know what happens."

DJ reluctantly agreed, and they hung up. Born called Jada next. He wasn't surprised that she didn't answer. He was used to that these days. He handed the phone back to Tremaine.

"Shit!" Born said. He felt helpless. "It sounds like they got everybody." He was grateful that he had gotten out of the drug game a long time ago. Still, many of the people he cared about were still living that lifestyle, and he worried for them. "Call Zion," he suggested.

Tremaine shook his head. "I been calling him since I got Biggs' text. No answer."

Born thought about it. "You should probably go. You never know who might be looking for you."

Tremaine had been thinking the same thing. "But, I can't leave you open here by yourself."

"I'm here," Anisa said, walking into the room. "I saw the news this morning, and I came right over after I took Ethan to Miss Ingrid's house. She'll bring him up here with her when she comes this afternoon."

Born relaxed a little when he saw Anisa. She had an uncanny knack for showing up right on time lately. "Thank you," he said.

"Don't thank me yet. The nurse acts like she wants to kick me out." Anisa hid her bag behind the curtain, and positioned herself where she couldn't be seen from the hallway.

"We'll worry about her later," Born said. He was grateful for her company. He thought about Jada and assumed that she was too busy with Sheldon to answer her phone. He forced his thoughts away from her, and said good-bye to Tremaine as he prepared to go on the run. "Be careful out there," Born said. "Keep in touch with somebody. Let us know you're alright."

Tremaine gave Born a long handshake, and assured him that he would watch his back. Then he left. Anisa touched Born's hand, caressed it.

"What the hell is going on?" she asked, rhetorically.

Born shook his head. "I wish I knew."

Gillian's phone started ringing just as the sun began to rise. The arrests had come unexpectedly in a well-orchestrated pre-dawn raid. Simultaneously, various members of her crew had been taken into custody. Zion. Baron. Reuben. The Douglas brothers. Frankie. Biggs. Even Grant Keys, and *that* was a game changer. Grant was an insider. His arrest meant that the government had established their best case yet against the Nobles crime family.

Gillian called her attorney, showered, dressed, and sipped peppermint tea as she waited for the authorities to come for her. But no one came. As the time neared when court would open and the arraignments would begin, Gillian sat anxiously by her phone, waiting for word from her people.

Jada was on her way out the door with Sheldon in tow when she got the call. She stopped with her hand on the doorknob and answered her cell phone, hurriedly.

"Hello?"

She heard Marisol crying, and instantly froze. Sheldon sensed the tension in her body, and wondered what was wrong. Even he could hear Marisol crying through the receiver. "She's dead! Jada! *Mija* . . . she's gone. Sunny is dead."

Jada fell to the floor.

The courtroom was packed. For Misa, this was eerily familiar. She had been the defendant in a high-profile murder case just a couple of years ago. Her family had rallied around her, attending her trial each day. She hated to think of those days. This time, although she wasn't the defendant, she held tightly to her sister's hand as the arraignment began.

Camille was trembling. Her mother was back at home, babysitting Bria and Shane. Before her daughters had left for court that morning, Lily gathered them together. "Listen, don't go in there trying to be heroes. Frankie and Baron are grown men. When you were in trouble, where were they? Go, show your support. But don't put that 'S' on your chest today, okay, Superwomen?"

Camille thought about that now. She remembered all the times that Frankie had abandoned her. Part of her thought of an eye for an eye. The other part opted to turn the other cheek. She looked around the room and saw a lot of familiar faces. Olivia walked in looking fabulous and stressed at the same time. She had been called to pick up her daughter after Zion was taken into police custody. Olivia had picked up Adiva from the police station, brought her to her grandmother's house, and hurried to court to see about Zion. Her brother Lamin followed close behind. Lamin was thanking his lucky stars that he hadn't been involved in any illegal activities for many years. Still, having endured his own trial in connection with his cousin's murder, he was uncomfortable being in the courtroom today as well. Lamin and Zion had started out in the game together. When Lamin went legit, he begged Zion to do the same. But Zion was hardheaded. Lamin shook his head, as he thought about what that stubborn streak might cost his friend. Assorted extended family members of some of the other defendants filed in behind him.

"It's like some kind of sad reunion," Misa whispered to Camille.

Camille nodded. "Yeah. Like a funeral."

The defendants began to enter the courtroom. The first few cases had nothing to do with them. But then Frankie led the parade into the courtroom. He was followed by a few other crew members from Staten Island. One by one the DA read the charges against them. Each of them had been charged with crimes involving drugs, guns, and money laundering. For each of them, bail was set at half a million dollars.

In courtrooms in Brooklyn and New Jersey, Baron, Grant, Reuben, and the Douglas brothers were also arraigned on similar charges. Grant was additionally charged with racketeering, obstruction of justice, possession of a controlled substance, and conspiracy. Baron, Dorian's brothers, and Reuben were granted half a million dollars bail. Grant Keys' bail was set at a million dollars.

The news funneled into Staten Island Criminal Court via covert text messages and whispered conversations. One by one, the crew was going down.

The mood was grim when Ava was led in shortly after ten a.m. She looked so ridiculous and out of place in this setting, seeming frail as she stood next to her towering attorney. She wore a pair of Zion's sweatpants, one of his T-shirts, sweat socks, and some prison issued Croc-style shoes. Although she felt foolish in this outfit, she had decided that going to jail in the alternative—a Phillip Lim suit and Jimmy Choos—would have been far worse. She had arrived at Zion's house still in her work clothes. Their passionate evening had been interrupted by the raid. The officers at the scene had made themselves quite clear.

They meant business, and had terrorized Ava thoroughly. They had pummeled her with questions all night long. This was one side of the judicial system that she had never seen up close and personal before.

Jada rushed in the door, looking a teary-eyed mess just as the DA set forth his case. "Your Honor, Ava Ford is the lady friend of Zion Williams, who is the kingpin in this operation. She was arrested in Mr. Williams's home during this morning's raid. She's an attorney, who we believe has acted in concert with Mr. Williams and his operation."

Ava's attorney interjected, explaining that Ava was in no way complicit in any illegal activities. In fact, she was just in the wrong place at the wrong time with a guy who she was just getting to know.

As the attorneys volleyed back and forth, Olivia sat boiling in the middle of the courtroom. Many of those present turned to look at her. They wondered if Olivia had known that Zion was sleeping with someone else. She did her best to keep her game face on. She noticed that Ava was wearing Zion's clothes, and quickly connected the dots. Olivia's blood boiled. Sensing this, Lamin reached over and discreetly squeezed her hand. She squeezed it back hard. She wanted to explode.

Jada, too, was confused. She thought she must be hearing wrong from where she stood way in the back of the courtroom. Ava had made no mention of being involved with Zion. She wondered what else she didn't know.

Finally, the judge set Ava's bail at two hundred and fifty thousand dollars. She was led away, and Jada prepared to meet the attorney outside. But then Zion was led into the courtroom. And everybody froze.

As incredibly handsome as he normally was, Zion now looked horrendous. An audible gasp rose from the courtroom. Zion had been beaten badly. His face was swollen and bruised, his hairline creased with dried blood. He walked slowly and hunched over, as if he was sore. Olivia cried out, and so did several onlookers. It was clear that he had suffered an intense beat down.

"What the hell did you do to him?" Olivia called out. His betrayal was momentarily forgotten.

The DA spoke over the uproar. "Your Honor, Mr. Williams has been resisting our officers' efforts to restrain him. He charged one of our officers last night and had to be physically restrained."

"That's not right!" someone yelled. A chorus of protests rose from the courtroom. Zion seemed dazed as he stood there.

The judge banged her gavel in an attempt to get her courtroom in order. But it was futile. The uproar over Zion's appearance was so great that she had to empty the courtroom. Olivia was inconsolable. Lamin ushered her out first. Once all spectators had been removed, Zion's case was set forth, and he was ordered held without bail. The judge ordered that Zion be taken to the hospital immediately.

In the lobby, families huddled with attorneys to discuss strategies. Jada stood alone, still reeling from the news of Sunny's death. She had gone to Brooklyn as soon as she was able to compose herself enough to drive. She had spent the morning at the home of Sunny's parents, consoling Mercedes and letting the realization sink in that Sunny was gone for good. Sunny's body had been removed before Jada got there. But there was a palpable misery that hung over the home in Sunny's absence. So much was happening at once. Jada felt like she had been sucked into a horrific whirlwind and everything was being turned upside down.

She was so overcome with grief that she almost hadn't made it to bail her sister out of jail. At the last minute, she had allowed Marisol to convince her to go to court and see about Ava. Simultaneously, Ronnie was being sent to the Brooklyn courthouse to bail out Reuben, if possible. Sheldon was back at Marisol's with Mercedes and the rest of Sunny's family, everyone trying to make sense of what had taken place. Sunny was gone. No one could believe it.

Jada felt a special sadness. Sunny had been her sister. She had saved her life. Together, they had taken on the world. Now they would never get to talk again. Never share a laugh. They had kept each other's secrets, and planned on being old ladies together. An overdose had stolen those dreams. Like a candle in the wind, Sunny was gone. Jada stood in the corner fighting tears, praying that she could bail Ava out quickly. She needed time to process the loss of her friend.

Finally, Ava's attorney approached, and Jada agreed to put up her home as collateral for her sister's bail. As they walked off to handle the paperwork, Olivia approached them. Jada asked the attorney to go ahead and she would catch up with him in a moment.

She turned to face Olivia.

"So how long did you know about your sister and Zion?" Olivia demanded.

"I had no idea that anything was going on between them," Jada said. "I promise you, Olivia."

Olivia stared at Jada, deciding whether to believe her or not. "What's wrong with you?" she asked. She could tell that Jada was visibly distraught, and it appeared to be more serious than just Ava's arrest. Jada's face was splotchy, and her nose was red. Her eyes were puffy, and she kept dabbing at them.

"Olivia . . . Sunny died this morning."

Olivia gasped, clutching her hands over her mouth. "What?"

"She . . . she's dead." Jada wanted to crumble, but kept her back pressed firmly against the wall for support.

Olivia closed her eyes, devastated. "Oh my God, Jada." Olivia stared at her for a few silent moments. "I'm so sorry." Olivia wiped the tears that fell from her own eyes. She and Sunny had been friends for a very long time. Olivia had weathered many storms with Sunny, and hearing this was incredibly sad news. She knew how close Sunny and Jada were. So she instinctively pulled Jada into a warm embrace. They hugged and cried softly in the corner of the courthouse lobby. Olivia had no beef with Jada. Maybe she hadn't known about Ava's affair with Zion. And even if Jada had been aware of what was going on, Ava and Zion were adults, responsible for their own actions. Still, Olivia was pissed. They pulled themselves together and stood for several silent moments. "Listen," Olivia said at last. "Let me know if there's anything I can do to help with arrangements or anything." She walked away, her shoulders hunched in sorrow.

Jada watched Olivia walk off, a then she went to meet the lawyer to bail out her sister. The process was long and arduous. After about two hours, Jada was told that her sister was being released and would be brought down to the lobby. By then, the courthouse had emptied out considerably. Jada took the opportunity to use the ladies' room before meeting her sister. She relieved herself and washed her hands. And just as she stepped out of the bathroom, a shriek was heard across the lobby, followed by the sound of scuffling feet and cries of "Stop!" "Oh my goodness!" and "Help!" Police ran toward the direction of the melee, as Jada strained to see what was happening. By the time she got a clear view, it was too late.

Olivia had reappeared, although Lamin was nowhere in sight. She had spotted Ava walking alongside her attorney after being bailed out. Without uttering a word, Olivia pounced on Ava, punching her in the face repeatedly, tearing at her hair, scratching at her face and throat, kicking her and clawing wildly. It took three police officers to pry Olivia off of Ava.

"You're supposed to be my friend, bitch!" Olivia was still trying to get loose to attack her again, but the cops held her tightly. They began to drag her into a nearby room. "Wait till I see you again, Ava!"

Jada rushed over to her wounded sister. Ava had been completely caught off guard. Several court officers lifted her up off of the floor. Zion's T-shirt was now bloody from her dripping nose.

One female officer was sympathetic. She looked at Jada. "Miss, go pull your car around front, and I'll stay with her until you get back." Jada rushed off to do that, and the cop led Ava to a quiet corner where she blocked Ava from view as best she could.

The officer looked down at Ava. "You're not having such a good day, huh?"

Ava looked up at her for several moments before laughing. She thought about her arrest, the arraignment, the high bail, and now getting beat up by Olivia. She shook her head in amazement. "No. Not a good day at all," she agreed.

"Do you want to press charges against her?" the officer asked. "She's automatically going to be charged with disorderly conduct and disturbing the peace."

Ava shook her head. "No. I just want to get out of here."

"Based on what I just saw you might need a restraining order."

Ava declined. "I'm okay. I just want to go home." Ava sat there quietly for a few moments. "How do I find out where they're taking Zion Williams?"

The officer gave Ava information on how to look up an inmate. Ava thanked her just as Jada pulled up in the front of the courthouse. The officer walked her to Jada's car, which was idling at the curb. Ava thanked her.

"No problem," the cop said.

Once they were alone, Jada turned to her sister and shook her head. "The whole world is falling apart."

14

CHECKMATE

Mindy Milford looked directly into the camera, her expression serious.

"This is a sad day here at *The Mindy Milford Show*. Today, we were supposed to conduct an exclusive interview with Sunny Cruz on the couch. You'll recall that Sunny was what I call a professional girlfriend. She was a sometime model and an author, who was seen on the arm of some high-profile men. Sunny had agreed to talk to me today, leaving no topics off limits! We were gonna talk about the modeling, the fame, the drugs, her recent arrest, and what happens now. So . . ." Mindy dabbed at her eyes with her monogrammed handkerchief for dramatic effect. "Sadly, we got word this morning that Sunny Cruz is no longer with us. She passed away this morning from an apparent overdose at the family home here in New York."

The audience gasped. The camera panned to catch their unsuspecting reactions. Mindy cleared her throat. They zoomed in for a close-up once again. "First of all, our deepest condolences go out to her family. I know that she has a young daughter. That's the biggest tragedy in this whole situation. A little girl is parentless now because of the disease of addiction. I've made no secret about my own battle with drugs years ago. So my heart really goes out to Sunny's family. It could have been my family grieving over me. I'm grateful that I found the strength to kick the habit." The audience applauded.

"For all you young kids out there who think these celebrities are living the good life, doing drugs and carrying on all the time, you see that there are consequences to that life. No one thinks it can happen to them until it does."

Mindy shook her head. "Wow. What a sad story. She was such a beautiful woman." She dabbed at her eyes again. "Well, today on the show . . ."

Jada let out a deep sigh. That's all that Sunny's life in the public spotlight had boiled down to. A cautionary tale for young people. What not to do. And now the show must go on. Everyone who knew Sunny was watching to see what Mindy would say. Jada and Ava watched together at Jada's house after picking up Sheldon from Brooklyn after court. Camille and Misa watched in Camille's living room on Long Island with their mom. Olivia, who had been released from police custody with a desk-appearance ticket, watched at home with her grandmother. Born watched while sitting in his hospital room with Anisa.

An hour later, Jada walked into his hospital room. Born had called her as soon as he heard about Sunny's passing. But Jada hadn't answered his calls, too distraught to talk over the phone.

Anisa had been standing near the window when Jada arrived. Seeing the look on Jada's face, Anisa knew that today was not the day for a confrontation. Old rivalries aside, the woman had lost her best friend. Anisa gathered her things and left without a word.

Jada collapsed at the foot of Born's bed and cried. He wished that he could pull her close to him, but he was in no position to do so. "Come here," he beckoned her. "Come here, Jada."

She got up and moved closer to him. Folding herself into the crook of his left arm, she laid her head against him and sobbed for the loss of her friend, and for what felt like the loss of her relationship with Born. She was aware that Anisa was always hanging around now. And she was too drained from grief and worry to put up a fight.

Born spoke soothingly to her, reminding her that Sunny was at peace now. But it hurt like hell anyhow. Nothing was making the loss easier to handle. Jada cried until her eyes would no longer produce tears. Once she ran out of tears, she just laid there in silence.

"Sunny wouldn't want you to be crying," he said. Born tried to think of more words of comfort, but he came up empty. In his heart, he felt that Sunny was a fool. Her overdose was a sad final chapter in what had been an incredible life. Born was sad to see her go. But he placed all of the blame for Sunny's demise at her very own feet.

Jada sat up. She wiped her face and composed herself.

"Born," she said, her voice barely above a whisper. "With everything that happened today . . ." Her voice trailed off as she recapped the past twenty-four hours in her mind. It was almost too much to process. Ava's arrest, Sunny's death, Born's injury. Jada felt her pulse quicken at the thought of it all. "I forgot to tell you this. When I went home yesterday I had an envelope in my mailbox. It had only my first name, no address or anything. And inside was a crack vial and a note that said 'For old time's sake.' I don't know who would send me something like that."

Born frowned. "Where is it?"

"I have the letter at home. I flushed the crack down the toilet."

Born thought about it. "You didn't recognize the handwriting?"

Jada shook her head. "No."

Born frowned and thought about it. He wondered if this had anything to do with the bomb left at his door, or the arrests and indictments that had swept the crew off the streets of New York City. He made up his mind right then that he had to get out of this hospital. The people he loved were vulnerable. Until they figured out who was behind everything that was happening, everybody was a possible target.

"I'm getting out of here," he said. "I can't stay in this hospital like this."

Jada sat up. "No. That's not happening. Your doctor—"

"My doctor nothing." He sat up. It took some effort, but he got his bearings and positioned himself. He rang for the nurse. "I can't have you out there in the open like that while I'm laying in here eating applesauce." He shook his head. "Your best friend just died. Your sister just got arrested. Now you're telling me somebody's leaving crack vials and notes in your mailbox. That's too much to deal with by yourself."

The nurse came in.

"I'm leaving," Born announced. "Get me discharged."

"Mr. Graham, I—"

"Just bring me the forms to sign so I can leave. I don't care about nothing else."

Anisa returned, this time with Miss Ingrid and Ethan. The nurse turned to them and threw up her hands. "He's signing himself out," she said. She left to prepare his paperwork, and Anisa charged into the room.

"Why are you leaving?" she demanded.

"'Cause there's too much going on right now out there for me to just sit in here. That's why." Born was pulling his clothes out of the little closet near his bed. His IV was still connected and he dragged it along behind him.

Ethan was smiling. "Good! I want you to come home with us, Dad."

Jada frowned slightly, perplexed by Ethan's choice of words.

Born looked at him and winked, smiling slightly. "Okay," he said, calmly. "Help me get my shoes on."

Ethan eagerly walked over to the narrow closet and retrieved his father's sneakers.

"This is not a good idea, Born. You can't go climbing on your white horse all the time to save the day." Anisa stood with her arms folded across her chest.

Jada wanted Anisa to mind her business, but she held her tongue.

Miss Ingrid chimed in. "Marquis, I heard about what happened to Sunny. But you shouldn't leave the hospital early for that. You got hurt pretty bad. You need time to heal."

Born looked at his mother. He didn't want to have this conversation right now, but he knew that she wasn't about to let it go. "That's not why I'm leaving. Jada got something crazy in the mail yesterday."

Anisa chuckled. "Of course she did," she said under her breath. "How convenient."

Jada's jaw clenched.

"Somebody sent her a threatening letter. After what happened to me, I don't want to take any chances." Born sat down as the nurse reentered and set about checking his blood pressure. He looked at his mother again. "Plus what happened with Sunny and all the trouble that Ava's in now . . ." He shrugged a little. "It's a lot to handle."

"She's a grown-up," Anisa said. "I'm sure she can survive on her own."

Jada hit her boiling point. "Keep your mouth shut, Anisa."

Anisa shook her head. "No. I won't keep my mouth shut. After all these months when you never even had a second of time to spare for him. *All* this time you disappeared from his life. And now you're the one in trouble. You're dealing with grief. So he's supposed to drop everything? Born has to get up out of his hospital bed because *you're* in a crisis? How selfish!"

Jada stepped closer. "What goes on between us has nothing to do with you. You shouldn't even be here."

Anisa stared Jada down. "Born wants me here." Her words were heavy with meaning. She sneered at Jada.

Miss Ingrid fidgeted in her seat, mumbling, "Oh, Lord," under her breath.

Jada was enraged. She waited for Born to correct Anisa, to tell her that Jada was the only one he wanted there. But instead, Jada was met with silence. Miss Ingrid looked at the floor. Ethan watched uneasily. Jada looked at Born, questioningly. He said nothing.

"Is that true?" she asked. "You want her here?"

Born stared at Jada. He wasn't sure what he wanted anymore. Silence lingered awkwardly in the room. Jada heard Anisa give a slight chuckle. It felt like a punch in the face. Finally, Born spoke.

"I just want to get out of this hospital," he said. "That's what I want."

Jada stood there for a few minutes while the nurse returned to remove Born's IV. She looked at Miss Ingrid, who was still avoiding eye contact. Then Jada glanced at Anisa, still standing there, still waiting for Born after all of these years. She came to her senses. Her worst fears had been realized. Born had wandered back into Anisa's arms. Suddenly he was calling her sweet nicknames, and she was speaking to his doctors on his behalf. Ethan wanted him to "come home with us." Jada thought back to when she'd walked in on Anisa draped across Born, the two of them giggling together. Anisa was right. Clearly, Born did want her there.

Jada stared at Born, and felt a war within herself. Part of her knew that she alone was to blame for this. She had pushed Born right into Anisa's arms. But the other part of her felt sucker punched in the gut for all the world to see. She wanted to fight, cry, and scream all at the same time. Instead, she bolted, practically running toward the exit. She didn't want to give Anisa the satisfaction of seeing her cry. She caught the elevator just as the doors were about to close, and rode the few floors down to the lobby deep in thought. She felt like her life was spiraling out of control and she was powerless to stop it. Her heart was broken in so many pieces that she wasn't sure she would ever be the same again. Sunny was dead. Ava's life was in chaos. Sheldon had her sleeping with one eye open. And now Born and Anisa were acting like the fucking Huxtables.

Reaching the lobby, Jada stared straight ahead as she barreled toward the exit. To her dismay, it was pouring rain. She had no umbrella and raindrops fell heavily on her as she darted through the parking lot toward her car. Despite the rain, there were still a few cars moving about in the parking lot. Jada saw several people dashing to their cars like she was. She hit the auto-unlock button on her key ring as she neared it, and cursed herself under her breath for leaving her umbrella in the car. She was drenched in seconds, her blue cotton dress clinging to her tightly.

Climbing behind the wheel, Jada hurriedly shut the car door and locked it. The raindrops beat down on her car with ferocity. She hugged herself, wiping the rain away and soothing her nerves at the same time. Jada wanted to cry, but had no more tears. Instead, she took a long, deep breath. She felt the weight of the world on her shoulders, but she willed herself to put the key in the ignition. Just as she leaned forward to start the car, she was startled by someone rapping on her window in rapid succession, and pulling at her car door. Jada gasped, and squinted her eyes to see if she could peer through the sheets of rain to identify the person. For a fleeting moment, she thought it might have been Born. But now the person was tapping with such ferocity that the window shattered loudly, sending shards of glass flying everywhere. Jada gasped, in fear for her life, and quickly stuck the key in the ignition and started the car.

A hand reached through the window, and punched Jada with such intensity that she was momentarily dazed. She leaned on the horn, hoping that the noise would get someone's attention. With the car still in park, Jada floored the gas, but quickly realized her mistake. Scared for her life, Jada slammed the car in reverse and peeled backward. Her perpetrator was running alongside her car.

"You fucking bitch!" he yelled. He reached inside the car, trying to open the door as he ran at top speed to keep up. Jada didn't recognize the voice. She tried to get a look at him as she sped through the lot. He wore a black hoodie pulled low over his head, and he had gloves on his hands. She couldn't make out much more than that.

She kept honking her horn, whirling the car backward at a much higher speed than she was comfortable with. But this was life or death, so she peeled backward, her tires skidding in the parking lot.

The sound of the car racing through the lot, and the horn honking got the attention of a few people passing by. Several EMTs began running in the direction of Jada's car. She slammed the car in drive and floored the engine again, finally shaking the crazy stranger loose from her car. She sped out of the parking lot and raced toward home. Her thoughts were scattered, and her hands were trembling. The wind blowing through the shattered window was a constant reminder of the ordeal she had just endured. It occurred to her after a minute that she could have sought help from the people in the parking lot. But she had been too scared to think in that moment. All she wanted was to get away from the man who was trying to kill her. About four blocks away from the hospital, Jada was pulled over by the cops. She didn't know whether to be scared or relieved.

With the police lights flashing behind her, she sat back in the driver's seat, and exhaled slowly, willing herself to calm down. The left side of her face stung from where the man had punched her with all of his might. Looking down at her hands, she noticed for the first time that she was bleeding. Heavily, it seemed, though she felt no pain. Jada trembled in fear, still as afraid as she had been the moment the man began pounding on her window, pulling at her car door. She wondered if she might go insane as she watched the two officers approach her car.

By the grace of God, one of them was a woman. Jada felt comforted just by the presence of her. They assessed her car, the blood, her shaken state.

"Did you have an accident, ma'am?" the woman asked. "We got a call about an attempted abduction. Are you alright?"

Jada shook her head. "Somebody . . . I don't know who it was. He hit me. He hit the car. He broke . . . Oh my God, who was he?" Jada's trembling intensified, and she saw looks of concern on the officer's faces. The male cop called in for backup, while the woman reassured Jada.

"It's okay, ma'am. Calm down. We're gonna get you some help."

Jada nodded, and her tears returned again. Help was exactly what she need right now.

As it turned out, an ambulance arrived and took her back to the hospital she'd fled from only a short while ago. She suffered a mean cut to her right eye, and a few scratches from the glass on her hands and arms. But she was free to go home after giving a statement to the police.

Jada kept her bearings about her when dealing with them. She didn't say too much. She told them everything that happened in the parking lot. But she left out the incident with the crack vial. She didn't want them snooping around Sheldon, asking questions. Jada was afraid of having her parental rights taken away. She had fought to rip Sheldon from the system's grasp before. She didn't want to have to go down that road again. Even with all that he had put her through, she loved him too much to lose him. She also didn't tell anyone about the dreams she'd had. Jada felt like she was living in a strange and surreal nightmare.

She told them that she didn't have any enemies that she knew of. Anisa didn't count, she reasoned. It had definitely been a man that attacked her tonight. She took them up on their offer of an escort home. Someone out there wanted her dead. Or maybe it was an attempted kidnapping as the bystanders suggested. Either way, Jada was scared stiff. Her car was taken to sweep for evidence while the officers drove Jada home.

On the way she thought about Born. She had been tempted to call him to tell him about what happened to her, but decided against it. The thought of him reminded her of her anger. She had called Ava to tell her that there had been an accident, and that she would be home soon. Jada urged her sister to lock every door and secure the alarm.

"Keep your phone charged and close by," Jada told her. "I'll tell you everything when I get home."

Arriving at her condo, the officers escorted Jada to her door, and came inside to have a look around. Sheldon was upstairs asleep, and Ava was on the couch wrapped snugly in one of Jada's bathrobes. The cops reminded Jada to call them immediately if anything happened. Jada thanked them and saw them out. Then she locked the door, secured the alarm, and collapsed on the couch next to her sister.

"What the hell happened to you?" Ava asked.

Jada shook her head. "Where do I begin?"

By the time Jada recounted all of the details, Ava was shivering with fear.

"This is serious, Jada. You need a gun."

"I can't have a gun with Sheldon in the house," Jada said.

Ava agreed. "Well, you have to do something." She nudged

her sister with her foot. "I know you're mad at Born. But you should call him and tell him what happened."

Jada shook her head. "All I want to do right now is pray and go to sleep." Jada knew that was only half true. She'd be praying alright. But sleep would elude her as it so often did these days. There was so much happening that she couldn't get her mind to relax long enough for her body to catch up.

It took a long time for Born to get through all of the red tape of getting an early discharge from the hospital. The doctor had emphasized the need for his body to rest so that his wounds could heal properly, and suggested that he remain in the hospital. But his mind was made up, and Born had stubbornly refused to be persuaded otherwise. Instead, about two and a half hours after Jada had stormed out of his hospital room, Born had walked out as well.

Now it was close to midnight, and he was propped up on Anisa's couch watching TV while Ethan snored softly in the recliner across from him. Born smiled down at his son, grateful to be back at home with him. But as his gaze shifted to Anisa, Born's smile faded. He knew that it was time for them to have a very difficult conversation.

"Come here," he said.

Anisa stopped flipping through the tests and notices in Ethan's school folder and set it aside. She came and sat beside Born on the couch, and laid her head gingerly in his lap.

"You okay?" she asked.

"Yeah. I told you it takes more than some pipe bomb to kill me."

Anisa chuckled and shook her head. "You must have a guardian angel. Some divine intervention was at work for you to survive that. Your condo was practically destroyed."

Born nodded. He hadn't been back there since leaving the hospital. But his mother had warned him that what awaited him was a pile of rubble to sift through.

He cleared his throat. Right now the condition of his home was the furthest thing from his mind. "Listen, Neece . . . earlier today . . . at the hospital . . . something happened."

Anisa sat up and faced him, concern etched all over her face. "What?"

Born eyed her, cautiously. "We always keep it 100 with each other, right?"

She nodded, a frown slowly forming on her face. "Yeah. Of course we do."

"So I want to tell you the truth of how I'm feeling." Born wiped his face with his good hand, the other held hostage in a sling. He let out a deep sigh and looked Anisa in the eyes. "There's a lot of history with me and Jada. It's like . . . the connection I have with her can't really be explained."

Anisa's eyes narrowed visibly. She didn't like where this conversation was heading at all.

Born pressed on, aware that they had reached the point of no return. "I used to wonder if she put some kind of magic on me. 'Cause it don't make sense the way . . . she plays me and I can't even stay mad at her."

Anisa let out a heavy breath. "Okay, so you're going back to her even after all the shit she's put you through? Seriously, Born? You falling for that old-ass damsel-in-distress shit again?"

Born pretended not to be bothered by Anisa's implication that he was playing a fool.

Anisa was angry now. "Months of silence. She ignores your calls, won't let you come around her son, and even hangs up on you. No respect, no love. Then the minute she sees that you might be happy with someone else, she comes running back with her pitiful stories of how she needs you." Anisa shook her head.

"You're a fool." She rolled her eyes at Born so hard that he felt slapped.

He sat silently for several moments. "I might be," he said at last. He nodded slowly, pondering the possibility. "But I love Jada."

Now it was Anisa's turn to look wounded.

"I'm not trying to hurt you," Born said. "In fact, I told you out the gate that this wasn't gonna be—"

"I already know." She cut him off, not wanting to be consoled or reminded that this dalliance with Born was supposed to be light and fun, nothing serious. But she had fallen for him all over again, despite telling herself not to. So this speech about his love for Jada stung more than it should have.

Born sighed again. "Seeing her there today, and how hurt she is about Sunny . . . I need to be with her night now." He looked at Anisa, hoping to really make her understand. "When she asked me whether I wanted you there, I realized that I wasn't sure what I really wanted right then. I care about you a lot. We got Ethan here. Shit has been good. But when I saw the pain in her eyes today, it got clear to me. I'm gonna always love Jada. So I have to make it clear to you, to her son, and to everybody else that she's the woman I want in my life. And I'm done playing games. Life is too short."

Anisa was tempted to react in anger. After all, her feelings for Born ran deep. For years she had been pining for him, hopeful that he might come to his senses and give their love another try. Then it seemed that he had done just that. But there he was now professing his love for Jada, and all Anisa wanted to do was cry.

"Okay," she said softly. "I still think you're a fool. But I respect your honesty." Anisa stood up from the couch and looked down at Born, disappointment and sadness etched all over her pretty face. "When she breaks your heart again, I might not be there to help you piece it back together." Anisa went upstairs to bed, and allowed her tears to fall in the darkness of her room.

At just after one thirty in the morning, Jada's cell phone vibrated. Her heart pounded in her chest. With shaky hands, she reached for it, half expecting that it would be a message from her tormentor. Instead, to her simultaneous relief and dismay, it was a text from Born: *Come open the door.*

Jada thought about it, and considered leaving him standing out there in the rain that was still falling, though not as heavy as it had been earlier. The thought of her tormentor out there with Born alone in the dark, sent her running quietly downstairs. Jada peered through the window, and watched Born walk toward her door. She disarmed the security system and unlocked the door, ushering him quickly inside. She reset the alarm, secured all of the locks, and pulled the blinds on the windows once again. Born had no umbrella and was wet, and Jada stood facing him in her foyer. The sling on his right arm had gotten drenched. He didn't seem to care.

"What happened to your eye?" Born asked. "Why are you all scraped up?"

Thunder roared.

"When I left the hospital somebody attacked me."

"Attacked you? Attacked you how?" Born looked ready to blow his top.

"I got in the car and some man busted the driver's-side window out." She held her arms up briefly to illustrate. "He punched me." She gestured toward her eye. "I drove off, but he ran after me. I got away."

"Why the fuck didn't you call me?" Born was furious.

Jada frowned at him. "Keep your voice down!" She was whispering herself, but with such venom that her point got across. "Call you for what? So you can pull yourself away from your old standby to come and rescue me?"

Born made a face like he had a bad taste in his mouth. "Please!" he said. "Give me a break with that bullshit, Jada. All of a sudden you care? Really? Since when?" He waited briefly for an answer, but knew that she had none. "For weeks, no word from you. I call you and text you, and nothing."

"Why did you come here?" Jada asked. "You can go back where you came from. I know Anisa must be waiting up for you."

Born looked Jada in the eye. "It's not like you think it is."

"Don't lie to me," Jada said.

"I'm not lying."

"Did you fuck her?"

"What?"

She gestured toward the door.

He sighed. "Come on, Jada!"

She looked at him and knew the truth before he told her.

"Yeah," he said.

Jada closed her eyes. Hearing him admit it cut worse than she thought it would.

Jada opened her eyes, and looked at him for a long time. Not knowing what to say, she shook her head.

"I'm sorry," he said.

So many words fought to spill forth from her lips. They fought so hard that Jada pressed her mouth closed. She said nothing. All she did was shrug her shoulders and shake her head, tears gliding down her face to the beat of the rain.

"Please don't cry," Born said, softly. "I promise you, Jada, I—"

"I just can't deal with this right now," she said. "Somebody is trying to kill me."

The thought of death brought Sunny to mind. Jada thought for a moment that Sunny might be better off than she was.

Jada chuckled through her tears at the absurdity of what she was about to say. "The last time I saw Sunny she told me that I have to make things work between me and you." Jada's eyes flooded at the memory. "She said that Sheldon will get over it."

Born smiled, too. "I think she was right."

Jada's smile faded. She looked Born in the eyes. "You gave yourself away."

Born didn't respond. Instead, he stared back at Jada unable to find the right words. Finally, Jada looked away, disappointed. She brushed away the tears.

Born stepped forward toward her. "You shut me out completely, Jada."

"So that's your excuse?" Jada was steamed.

"What was I supposed to do? I didn't want to just show up here because I know that Sheldon's not feeling me. I felt like I was stalking you! I called you constantly. Texted you. You would hang up on me, if you even answered at all. And you never even called me back." Born threw up his hands in frustration. "I don't know what you want me to say."

"I don't want you to say or do anything," she said. "You should just go. It's late. I'm tired . . ."

"No." He sounded defiant, like a child. "Not this time. I'm not leaving. I'm tired of doing things your way. You can go upstairs if you want. But eventually, you're gonna talk to me. You owe us that."

Jada stared at his lips and pictured them kissing Anisa. She rolled her eyes at him.

"Us," she repeated, mockingly. "What us? There's no us. It's you, and it's Anisa. That's the way you made it."

"I'm not in love with Anisa."

"Does she know that?" Jada felt her adrenaline surge.

He nodded. "Yeah. She knows. You know it, too."

Jada shook her head, sadly. "You hurt me for the last time, Born."

"You're right. Yes, I have," he said. He took another step closer to her. "And you hurt me for the last time, too. You ran from me. Kicked me out of your life, and out of Sheldon's. You shut me out."

"For my son."

"I asked you to marry me," Born said. "*Marry* me. You know what that means? That means it's no more you and then me. It's *us*. Your son, my son, and we're a family. How would you feel if I had a problem with Ethan, and I stopped talking to you while I solved the problem by myself? That's not a family."

Jada looked away, knowing that he spoke the truth. "Well, now you have your family," she said. "Congratulations." Jada caught the bitterness in her voice, and fought to tone it down. She pictured Born, Anisa, and Ethan as one big happy family while she was left stuck with "Jamari, Jr."

"I want to build a family with *you*."

"It's a little too late for that, Born. You're over there with that—"

"I fucked up."

"—bitch!" Jada was determined to finish her sentence. Her face was etched with disgust.

"I swear, I'll never hurt you again. I promise—"

"You couldn't *wait* to go running back to your good 'ole standby."

He inched closer. "It was nothing."

"Go home."

Born reached for her and she backed away. "I am home," he said. "This is my home. Wherever you are. That's home."

He moved another inch forward. Jada could have sworn that her heartbeat was pounding audibly.

"I love you," Born said, his lips inches from hers. "I don't love her."

Jada felt so torn between her heart, and her pride.

Born rubbed his nose through her hair and inhaled deeply.

He had missed her so much. Being alone with her now, it was taking all of his willpower to restrain himself. He pulled her chin upward toward him. When their lips touched, he kissed her slowly, deeply.

Kissing Born after so long was so magical that Jada felt like she was floating on air. After a few moments, she pulled away.

"Born . . ." she whispered. "I'm tired."

"So let's go upstairs," he pleaded. "Jada, I miss you." Born was growing visibly frustrated. Everything that meant the most to him was slipping through his grasp. Earlier, he hadn't been sure who or what he wanted. But when Jada left his hospital room, it had started to become clear to him that she was the only one his heart longed for. Hearing now that she had been attacked, that someone was trying to bring her harm, Born wanted nothing more than to forget about the past few weeks and months, pull Jada into his arms, and never let her go. "Jada, let me protect you. Let me prove to you that I love you, and only you. I made a mistake. You made a mistake, too. But I'm never leaving you again. I don't care what Sheldon has to say about it, or how Anisa feels about it. All I care about is you. Me and you."

She felt her heart give in. She was just too weak to fight anymore. She stared back at him, wanting nothing more than to fall into his arms and let him take away the pain. "Come upstairs," she said, softly.

Born followed her into the darkness of her home's upper level. Jada didn't bother to switch on any lights. She didn't want to awaken Ava or Sheldon. She ushered him into her bedroom, shutting and locking the door behind her.

Born stood watching her, so grateful to be alone with her. He stepped closer to her, and stroked her face with his left hand, his right trapped in the sling. "I missed you so much," he said, gently.

"I missed you, too," she said.

Born pulled her close with his good arm, grateful to hold her again. "I'm sorry," he said. "I love you, Jada."

Everything else slipped away. At that second, she forgot about Sheldon and Anisa and everything else. There was only Born right then, and she focused only on those three words coming out of his mouth. Her heart pounded like a drumbeat.

He led her to the bed, and they gently stripped each other out of their clothes. Their skin touching for the first time in months, Jada was breathless. Carefully, he laid her down. Born kissed her slowly, touched her tenderly. His lips traveled her body like an explorer traversing familiar territory. Having been abstinent during their separation, Jada's body responded to him in quivers and quakes. She felt intoxicated by him. Born spread her legs apart, and buried his mouth in the folds of her wetness. Born licked her, sucked her, devoured her until she wiggled away from him, her body too sensitive to his touch.

"Don't run from me," he demanded. Born sat up on his knees and pulled Jada back toward him, dragging her down the length of the bed with his one strong arm. She moaned in surrender, and he dove in again, licking and sucking her so expertly that in no time she climaxed and trembled uncontrollably. It took all of her restraint not to call out his name at the top of her lungs as he entered her. Instead, she cried softly, stuck somewhere between ecstasy and heartache. Born wiped her tears, and whispered in her ear, "I love you." He illustrated it with lovemaking so intense that both of them sweated like Olympic athletes. They rocked together, silently locked in a dance so familiar, so exquisite and beautiful, that night melted into morning before they fell asleep in each other's arms.

Jada didn't sleep for very long. She didn't want a repeat of what happened the last time Sheldon had awakened to find Born in her bed. She left Born sleeping, and slipped downstairs to make breakfast as usual.

She put on a pot of coffee. While it brewed, she thought about the night before. Born had given all of himself to her. He had been gentle, laying with her in the pauses between their lovemaking, stroking her face, her skin, rubbing her feet, playing with her hair. They had talked about their transgressions. She replayed parts of their conversation now, while staring out the kitchen window.

"I started staying over there to be close to Ethan," he explained about his relationship with Anisa.

"That was an excuse."

"No, it really wasn't. I wasn't even thinking about Anisa like that."

"So what happened?" Jada had been mad at herself for asking the question. After all, she knew what wound up happening. The thought made her nauseous.

"I kept trying to get with you, and you kept shutting me down. So I was over there a lot. I was lonely. One night, I came in twisted after a party, and . . . I made a mistake."

"And you kept making the mistake after that night, right?" She was so mad at him that she had to keep reminding herself to keep her voice down.

Born didn't know what to say to that. She was right. He had continued screwing Anisa as a way to keep his mind off of Jada. But he knew that it would be futile to try and convince her of that now.

"I cut it off," he told her, truthfully. "After you left the hospital, Anisa and I took Ethan home and I told her the truth. I told her that I love you. I'm gonna always love you." He frowned a little. "I'm not gonna front like she's cool with that. Her feelings got involved. You know what I'm saying? But I never lied to her or gave her any reason to think that I was done with you for good. I know I was wrong. But I never pretended to love her."

Jada absorbed what he was saying. She knew him well enough to know that he was being truthful. She couldn't help thinking of Sunny then. She remembered Sunny's stories about Dorian and Raquel; how Raquel refused to move on and Dorian had somewhat liked that. She knew that, like Raquel, Anisa would always make herself available to Born. As long as she was alive, she would hold a vacancy in her heart for him in case he ever returned to fill it. Jada wasn't sure that she was equipped to deal with always having to wonder if he would go running back to her.

Born seemed to read her mind. "I don't love her," he said again. "Jada, look at me."

She did, her eyes full of sadness and longing.

"I only love you." He had stared at her intently. "Marry me," he said. "For real. Be my wife."

"You make it sound so simple."

"'Cause it is. We don't even have to plan it. We can go to city hall and do it, just me and you."

"You're serious?" She had sat up in bed and looked at him. Born sat up, too, and they sat face to face in the moonlit room.

"I'm serious." He squeezed her nose playfully. "Do you love me?"

"Yes."

"You promise to honor and cherish me till death do we part?"

Jada's smile had been bright enough to light up the room. "I do."

Jada snapped back to the present when she heard footsteps on the stairs. It was Ava.

"Good morning," Jada said, smiling casually. She held up the coffeepot. "Want some?"

Ava frowned. "No. Thanks." She sat down at the kitchen table. "Umm . . . why's Born asleep in your bed?"

Jada's eyes widened in surprise. "You went in there?"

Ava looked at Jada like she was crazy. "Yes, I went in there. He's snoring like a trucker." Ava watched Jada pour cream in her coffee.

"I know," Jada said. "He's exhausted."

"What are you gonna say to Sheldon when he sees Born naked in your bed?"

Jada nearly dropped the coffee mug. "You saw him naked?" She had pulled the covers up over him before she came downstairs, but she knew that Born tossed and turned in his sleep. The thought of Ava seeing Born's pony made her claws come out.

"Relax. His johnson was hidden. But I saw enough skin poking out from under the covers to know that he didn't have no clothes on." Ava tossed a balled-up napkin at her sister.

Jada leaned against the counter and sipped her coffee. "Don't be peeking at my baby."

Ava shook her head. "What are you gonna say to Sheldon?" she asked again.

Jada looked worried. "I really don't know, Ava."

They were interrupted by more footsteps on the stairs. Sheldon stepped into the room. "Good morning," he said. He greeted both his mother and his aunt with kisses on the cheek.

"Good morning. You hungry?" Jada asked, rubbing Sheldon affectionately on his head.

"Yup! Starving!" Born said, entering the room, unexpectedly. "Good morning, everybody." Rubbing his belly, he smiled at everyone present.

An awkward silence filled the room. Born tried to make light of it. He walked over to Ava and nudged her, teasingly. "What's up?"

Ava laughed and punched him playfully on his good arm. "Good morning, Mr. Graham."

Born walked over to Jada and kissed her softly on the cheek. "Good morning, beautiful."

She smiled, awkwardly. "Good morning." Her heart raced as she looked at Sheldon to see what he would say or do. He took two steps back, staring at Born, unsmiling. Jada's smile faded as she noticed that Sheldon's chest was heaving. He was puffed up with rage.

Born held his hand out for a five. "Good morning, young man."

Sheldon left Born hanging, and continued to glare at him.

"I said good morning," Born repeated.

"FUCK YOU!" Sheldon yelled at the top of his lungs. His voice was so loud that it reverberated off the walls.

Jada gasped. Ava stood to her feet.

"Sheldon!" Jada yelled.

Sheldon backed up some more. He felt the control he'd once had slipping away. How could his mother allow Born back into their lives after Sheldon had tried to kill himself? This wasn't part of the plan.

"We don't need you!" He looked at his mother, desperately. "What's he doing here? Tell him to get out," he demanded.

Born stared at Sheldon as if he were watching a volcano erupt from a safe distance. He looked fascinated by what he was witnessing, but disturbed by it at the same time. He stood speechlessly for several moments as Sheldon huffed and puffed, his chest heaving with each breath he took.

A thousand thoughts were battling in Born's head. This little boy—Jamari's son—was terrorizing his mother. He had single-handedly destroyed all of the work that Jada and Born had done to repair their relationship. Born knew that the kid had mental problems, that he had a lot working against him. But in this moment, all he wanted to do was wring Sheldon's scrawny little neck.

Before he even realized what he was doing, he lunged at Sheldon. Vaguely, as if it were happening at a slow, warped pace, he was aware that Jada's hands had flown up to cover her mouth as if she was in shock. Sheldon's eyes widened in terror as he watched Born barreling down on him.

Born snatched Sheldon by the collar of his shirt, and flung him down to the floor with such force that Ava cried out as if she herself had been thrown down. Sheldon kicked wildly at Born while he was down there. Only able to fight with his one good arm, Born stomped him, causing the kid to fold himself over in pain. Born grabbed Sheldon's collar again and dragged him back to his feet. With his good free hand he gripped the young boy's face tightly and backed him up against the wall. Sheldon's cheeks caved in under the pressure of Born's strong grip, forcing his lips into a fishlike pucker. He looked absolutely terrified as he locked eyes with Born and saw the fury within them.

"You little fuckin' brat!" Born spoke through clenched teeth and he was so close to Sheldon that he could smell the morning on the young man's breath. "You walk around here like this is your world and everybody has to ask your permission to live in it. Let me tell you something." Born leaned in even closer so that their noses were practically touching. *I'M THE MAN IN THIS MUTHAFUCKIN' HOUSE!"*

"Born . . ." Jada's voice cracked as she called out to him. She wanted to calm him down before he went too far. But at the same time, she was so happy to see Born taking charge of the situation. Secretly, she was more turned on than ever hearing Born declare himself king of this castle.

Born ignored her halfhearted plea. He tightened his grip on Sheldon's face. "The next time you raise your voice to me or your mother, I'm gonna kick your little punk ass. The next time I hear you curse, I'm gonna *drown* your monkey ass just like you did to that puppy you had."

"Born." This time Jada's voice didn't crack.

"Nah," Born said. "This little boy thinks he's grown, Jada! So

I'm gonna talk to him like he's grown." He turned back to Sheldon, who was still pinned against the wall in Born's strong grip. "It's a wrap," he said. "Your little reign of terror around here is over. I'm here now. I'm not leaving. So you gotta deal with that. Your father is dead. Guess what? So is mine. Get the fuck over it."

"Born, calm down," Ava said, in her hostage negotiator voice. "Calm down."

A tear slid down Sheldon's face, but Born was unmoved by it. He was still inches away from Sheldon's face. "Your mother made some mistakes, and she's spent years trying to make that shit up to you. But your whiny ass is too busy playing the fuckin' victim, taking pills, bullying kids, killing dogs and shit. That shit stops *TODAY*! I'm not playing with you, either."

Born stepped back from Sheldon at last and mushed him hard, causing his head to collide with the wall behind him. Sheldon was full on crying now, and Jada felt a tug of sympathy for him. Still, she didn't move or say a word. It was refreshing having Born take charge this way. For the first time in years, Sheldon was not the one with the upper hand. He sniffled and sobbed softly as Born stood ready for whatever he might try to do.

"All this time you wasted worrying about your dead father, your dead grandmother, and shit that happened before you could even form memories in your mind. Meanwhile your mother is here. She's fuckin *HERE*. And I'm here." Born took a deep breath. "Your Aunt Sunny is dead, God rest her soul. She's never coming back. Now Mercedes has no mom, and no dad. You have a family. Your aunt Ava loves you. Your mother loves you. *I* love you."

Now Jada felt tears burning in her eyes. It was the first time she had ever heard Born say that.

"No you don't," Sheldon said, between sobs. His voice was small and childlike for the first time in ages. "It's all about DJ and Ethan. You don't care about me." He squeezed his eyes shut and silently cried harder.

"Yes I do," Born said, flatly. "I don't *like* your bad ass all the time. I want to fuck you up when you start wilding. But how would you know who loves you and who don't when all you ever do is fight everybody? *EVERYBODY!* You got a chip on your shoulder 24-7, and if shit don't go your way you cause trouble. Nobody likes a nigga like that."

Born some air blew out, feeling the anger finally beginning to wane, albeit slowly.

"But I do love you. You got a lot of people who love you. The problem is you spend so much time feeling sorry for yourself that you can't even see it." He paused and stared at Sheldon, who still had tears streaming down his face. "Man up! Stop crying. You can't walk around terrorizing everybody and then cry like a little bitch when somebody calls your bluff."

Sheldon tried his best to pull himself together. Jada watched in awe.

Born walked over to the counter and snatched a stack of napkins. He stomped over to Sheldon and gruffly handed them to him before he continued. Born towered over Sheldon.

"That's it, you heard? All the tantrums and the bullshit you put your mother through. All the trouble you cause at school, picking on the other kids, disrespecting the teachers, making them have doctors evaluate you and medicate you. None of that shit is necessary. Yeah, maybe you need a little extra time on a test than most kids. Maybe you have a hard time focusing. That's not your fault. We can help you with that. But you're taking advantage of it and using it as an excuse for all the shit that you *can* control. You don't fool me, son. I see right through you."

Sheldon stared down at his feet, confused and flooded with emotion. He was angry, having been tossed around and choked up. No one had ever raised a hand to him in his entire life, and the feeling of being physically confronted was unfamiliar to him. He was nervous because he had never seen Born this angry before, nor had he ever before heard so much rage in Born's voice. Sheldon also felt convicted, because Born was right. Mercedes continuously pointed out the same thing. Sheldon was well aware that not all of his behavior was the result of his mother's drug abuse during her pregnancy. Some of what he was doing was just an attempt at garnering attention, getting his way, and making his mother pay for the mistakes she'd made. Until now, the only person who had ever called his bluff had been Mercedes. And, although she had shown him tough love, too, her version had been nothing compared to this. Sheldon glanced sheepishly at his mother.

Jada stood near the refrigerator, her gaze fixed on them. She caught sight of Sheldon looking her way, and she met his eyes. But gone was the sympathy Sheldon usually saw there. Gone was the weakness, and in its place a look unlike Sheldon had seen before. For the first time in a very long time, Jada looked emboldened. She stared back at her son, and it was clear to him that, although she'd spoken no words, she was staunchly on Born's side.

Born gestured toward the table. "Sit down." He watched as Sheldon did as he was told, and then Born sat down across from him. Jada sat, too, while Ava leaned against the counter and listened silently.

"I don't like having to put my hands on you," Born said, his voice sincere. He locked eyes with Sheldon, who had to resist the urge to look away. "But I will do it again if you force my hand. The next time you disrespect your mother, or any adult, or intimidate Ethan; the next time you fuck up at school or talk back to someone in authority, I'm gonna kick your little ass. That's not a threat. That's a promise. You feel me?"

Sheldon wanted to defy Born. He wanted to shrug his shoulders, or suck his teeth, or ignore him altogether. But the idea of being yoked up again kept him from doing any of those things. Reluctantly, he nodded. "Yeah," he answered weakly.

"We're not having this conversation ever again," Born said. "This is it. We're gonna wipe the slate clean, and start all over." He glanced over at Jada, sitting with her hands folded in front of her. He winked at her and offered her a slight smile. "I'm in love with your mother. I'm gonna marry her. We're gonna be a family and you better learn to deal with that."

Sheldon looked at Born in silence, letting his words sink in.

"Today, you and me are gonna spend the day together."

Born saw Sheldon's eyes widen in surprise. Then he frowned, unsure.

"Just us, nobody else," Born said. "We're gonna talk man-to-man and get some shit off our chest. I'm not gonna treat you like a kid today. You walk around here like you're a grown man, so today we're gonna talk grown-man style. You have one hour to think about what you want to say to me. Nothing is off-limits. That cool?"

Sheldon was enticed by the idea of having an afternoon with Born all to himself. True, he wasn't his father. But Sheldon was beginning to realize that Born was playing hardball. He could tell that Born was there to stay this time. He nodded again.

"Good," Born said. "Now go upstairs."

Sheldon stood up slowly and looked at Born, then at his mother. It was clear to him that a shift had taken place, and he was no longer as powerful as he had once been in this house. He cleared his throat. When he spoke, his voice was barely audible. "I'm sorry."

He ran upstairs, as Born smiled victoriously, and Jada and Ava stared after him, in awe.

15
BYGONES

Gillian walked through the kitchen at *Conga*, the popular Cuban-style Manhattan restaurant formerly owned by her mother, Mayra. Prior to his death, Gillian's father had signed ownership of *Conga* over to Frankie. But in the years since then, Gillian had persuaded Frankie to give the restaurant to her. He hadn't required much convincing. It was clear to all who knew him that Frankie was still in love with Gillian. When she had asked for ownership of the restaurant, Frankie had happily signed the necessary paperwork. So as she strolled through the bustling kitchen on this day, she did so with the authority of its owner. Gillian directed the staff, gave her compliments to the chef, and chatted with the maître d' to ensure that everything was being done according to her exacting standards.

Mayra scowled at her daughter, as she watched her make the rounds. This restaurant had been Mayra's baby. It had been *her* idea, her vision that had brought this place to fruition. Doug Nobles had been happy to see his wife enjoying the day-to-day details of running a business. Mayra had loved the sense of power and accomplishment it had afforded her. But those days were long gone. Once Gillian got her hands on the place, Mayra had no choice but to sit back and watch the takeover. She suspected that Gillian took pleasure in snatching Mayra's dream out from under her. Her only solace was the fact that Gillian was so busy running the illegal Nobles empire, that she seldom found the time to stop in to *Conga* personally. But lately even that had changed. With the family under investigation and the majority of the crew locked up, Gillian was nervous. She had been spending way more time at the restaurant lately, keeping up appearances in case anyone was snooping around. She wanted to look the part of the attentive legitimate business owner.

This forced the two women to spend time together daily. Mayra refused to allow Gillian to run her completely out of the restaurant that she had created. So she stayed on, running the day-to-day operations of the place in name only, while Gillian made all of the profits and got all of the glory. It was a setup that neither of them favored. Mayra was resentful toward her daughter for taking away her business, and ensuring that she didn't inherit more than a small portion of Doug Nobles' fortune. Gillian, too, was resentful. Her mother had cheated on Doug with one of his closest friends, a torrid affair that Gillian had uncovered. Mother and daughter had a lot of tension between them these days.

So Mayra was completely caught off guard when Gillian strolled over to where she sat at a corner table going over inventory lists. Gillian pulled up a chair, sat across from her mother, and clasped her hands together.

"We need to talk," she said.

Mayra took off her glasses and set them down on the table. Meeting her daughter's gaze, she nodded. "Okay," she said. "So, talk."

Gillian let out a deep sigh. "I've been thinking a lot about Daddy lately. How he would think I've been doing since he passed away." She looked to her mother for feedback, and hated herself for feeling hopeful for her approval.

Mayra swallowed the wrong way, and choked. As she coughed to clear her throat, she apologized. It was a rare occurrence for

Gillian to spark idle conversation between them. Odder still, that she would seek her approval. Mayra cleared her throat.

"I think your father would be very proud of you," Mayra said, honestly. "You stepped into his shoes very easily. All of his businesses are still running nicely." She tilted her head to the side, knowingly. "Well, almost all of them. And even with those recent problems in the family, you've managed to steer clear of having your name dragged into it. You're doing a good job." Mayra meant what she said, even though she was still a bit resentful.

"Thanks," Gillian said, offering a smile rarely seen on her lovely face these days. Gillian had grown colder since her father's death, colder still once she and Frankie split up. In business, her iciness gave her an edge when dealing with negotiations. But that coldness had caused Mayra to wonder if Gillian would ever truly be happy. She spent so much time ensuring that she was respected that it left little time for joy. Seeing her smile now was contagious. Mayra's lips spread into a grin as she looked at her daughter.

Gillian looked away. "I need a favor."

Mayra's smile faded. *I should have known,* she thought.

"I don't really need the favor from you," Gillian explained. "Because I could ask someone else. There are other ways for me to go about this," she explained, vaguely. She met her mother's gaze. "But I'm going to ask you for the favor. As a way for us to start to bridge this gap between us." Gillian blinked, willing her emotions to stay in check. "I miss having my mother," she said, her voice wavering slightly. "I want us to fix our relationship."

Mayra's eyes welled with tears. She was all ears. Despite her resentment, she had longed for the day when she and Gillian could begin to find their way back to the close relationship they had once shared. She nodded vigorously, too choked up to respond verbally.

"I need to hide some money," Gillian said. "Quite a lot of money."

Mayra nodded. She knew about her daughter's recent concerns. The feds still had most of the crew locked up. There was no telling how much dirt they had on the family, or when they might come snooping around Gillian's finances. So far, it seemed that no one in the crew had disclosed that she was really the one in charge. But just in case that changed, Gillian needed to cover all of her tracks.

"If anyone looked into it, they would find out that I work here as the proprietor of this busy establishment." Gillian winked an eye, facetiously. "But even as a successful business owner, there's more money than I can account for. I need to correct that."

Mayra was glad that Gillian came to her with this. Still, she couldn't help pointing out that this was a huge turnaround for her. "After Doug died, and you found out about Guy, you stopped trusting me."

Gillian didn't deny it. "That's true."

"So what changed now?"

Gillian sighed. "Honestly," she said. "I thought you and Guy were both after Daddy's money. I expected him to kick you to the curb the minute he realized that you weren't inheriting anything." Gillian chuckled a little. Guy London was her godfather, her father's supposed friend, and a married millionaire record executive with whom Mayra continued to have an affair.

"Now I see that he must really like you. I know that he's separated from his wife, and now he's even been taking you out in public recently." Mayra didn't miss the subtle shade that Gillian was throwing, but she didn't interrupt. "Anyway, I see that he's cool with the fact that you have no money. I hear that he's the one paying your staff, and financing all of your shopping sprees. So maybe I was mistaken. Maybe Guy didn't want Daddy's money. He only wanted his wife."

Mayra leaned toward her daughter. "Gillian, I know that it's hard for you to understand this thing between me and Guy. But, we are in love. It's not something we planned. And we did not intentionally try to hurt anybody."

Gillian held up her hand to interrupt. "I don't care," she said, simply. "Seriously, so save your breath. Guy is a leech in my opinion. He was supposed to be Daddy's friend, my godfather. He should have spent Daddy's last days out fishing with him. Not fucking you every second he got."

"Gillian . . ."

"Like I said, I don't care about Guy. I may never understand the two of you as a couple. But that's not my concern." She popped a mint into her mouth. "Like I said, I've been thinking about Daddy a lot lately. And I know that he would not approve of us walking around here everyday not speaking to each other." Gillian looked sheepishly at her mother. "So I'm proposing this as kind of a . . . trust-building exercise."

Mayra smiled, liking the sound of that. "Okay," she said. "I'll do it. But before you tell me the particulars, I want you to know something." Mayra folded her hands in front of her. "I may not always like you. And I know that you do not always like me. But Gillian, you are my only child. I love you always, and no matter what happens between us, you can always trust me." Mayra looked down at the table in shame. "I cheated on your father. Doug had reasons not to trust me. But it was never about me trying to get my hands on his money. I loved your father. I just made some mistakes. But I won't make those mistakes again. From now on, I will never keep a secret like that from you again."

Gillian felt herself getting choked up as she listened to her mother. She nodded. "Okay," she said. She looked around to ensure that none of the workers were lurking nearby or eavesdropping. "So, here's what I need you to do."

———

"My dad died a long time ago. But even before he died, he was already gone." Born took a bite of his cheeseburger and chewed in his usual messy manner.

Sheldon frowned. "What does that mean?" The two of them were sitting in a McDonald's on Bay Street. Born had taken him there to talk after their heated confrontation earlier. In the car on the way there, Sheldon had sat in silence staring out the window at the passing scenery. But once they arrived and ordered their food, Born made it clear to him that he expected the kid to talk. *"We're not going back home until we get everything straight between me and you. So, you're gonna speak up about everything that's bothering you. We'll deal with it, move on, and everybody can live happily ever after."*

They had arrived at Mickey D's and gotten a booth in the back. They sat down with their food and Born had started the conversation off by telling him about his own childhood, in the hopes that it might humanize him more to the kid who acted as if Born was the big, bad wolf.

"I mean the drugs he was on, the wheelchair he was in, the way he was not the strong tough guy that he once was. Even before he passed away, the fact that he wasn't the man that he used to be . . . it kinda killed him inside."

Sheldon chewed his French fries. "So was he my grandfather?" he asked.

Born nearly choked on his food as he looked at Sheldon wide-eyed.

"My mom told me that you and my father were brothers," Sheldon explained.

Born shook his head. "Nah. I mean . . . not that I know of." Born cleared his throat. He wondered what else Jada had told him, and chided himself for not finding out ahead of time. "Your father used to be my friend. We were close until something happened—"

"He stole your money," Sheldon offered. "My mom told me."

Born nodded. "Yeah. We stopped being cool after that. So I'm not sure if he said that about my father and his mother because he was jealous or if it was true. Personally, I don't believe it. But it doesn't matter."

"It matters to me," Sheldon said. "I don't remember my dad. So I want to know as much about him as I can."

Born looked at Sheldon, sympathetically. He tried in vain to come up with something positive that he could say about Jamari. But he came up empty. "Listen, your father wasn't one of my favorite people, honestly. I didn't like the guy. But from what I hear, he loved you a whole lot." Born took a sip of his orange soda. "I know how it feels to have no father in your life. Mine checked out long before he passed away. But what I learned to focus on was that I still had my mother. I didn't have sisters or brothers, didn't have my dad. But I had her. I still do. And she never lets me down. She reminds me a lot of your mother." He winked at Sheldon and bit into his burger.

Sheldon thought about that.

Talking with his mouth full, Born continued. "Your mother went through a lot with you. She fought to get custody of you and she takes her job as your mother very seriously. So seriously, that she was willing to give up on our relationship in order to save her relationship with you."

Sheldon felt a pang of guilt. He had purposely driven Born and Jada apart, hopeful that he might have her all to himself for once. Part of him felt good about the wedge he had managed to create between him. But hearing Born remind him about the sacrifices she had made for him, Sheldon felt convicted.

"I know you don't have it easy, Sheldon. You have to work harder than most of the kids your age because you were born addicted. You were really sick as a baby, and maybe now there's still some problems here or there. But you're not crazy. Don't let them teachers and school psychologists tell you that you're crazy. Cuz you're not. You *act* crazy a lot. But I think that's because it gets you attention, even if it's negative attention." He waited for Sheldon to deny it, but he didn't. Instead, he continued to sit there in silence. "That shit stops now. The next time you act up, it's gonna be me and you. I'm not a fan of putting my hands on kids. But I will if it's necessary."

Sheldon nodded, stared down at his food, and twirled a fry around in a pool of ketchup. Born noticed his hunched shoulders and defeated expression. He cleared his throat.

"I'm not just here to be a disciplinarian. I love your mother. I love you, too. And I know I'm not your father. I'm not trying to take his place," Born assured the young man. "But I can be that male role model in your life if you let me. You can talk to me the same way that you would talk to your dad if he was alive. I might not respond the same way that he would. But I can promise you that I'll give you the same answer I would give to Ethan, or to DJ." He looked Sheldon in the eyes. "I'm gonna be your stepfather whether you like that or not. So you might as well get to liking it." He finished off his burger and watched Sheldon's reaction.

Sheldon stared back at him boldly. "I don't want beef with you," he said.

Born had to resist the urge to laugh. Instead, he nodded. "Good."

"So, I guess . . ." Sheldon wasn't sure what to say. "Okay." He sat back as if resigned to his fate.

Born smirked. "Don't worry," he said. "You'll grow to love me."

Sheldon forced a smile. This would take some getting used to, having Born around all the time again and having to be "brothers" with Ethan again. But this time, maybe it could be different.

Before they left, Sheldon said that he needed to use the bathroom. Born followed him into the men's room and stood near the sinks while Sheldon took a leak. A man walked in. He wore a black hoodie, dark jeans, and a pair of Timbs. He looked to be of some exotic heritage. His hair was cut into a low Caesar, and his dark eyebrows and goatee framed a hard face. He wore both the uniform of the streets, and its countenance.

The man greeted Born nonchalantly with a quick nod of the head. He walked toward the urinals along the wall and stopped at one not too far from where Sheldon stood. He fumbled with his belt, but stopped suddenly and turned to face Born.

"That's your silver Benz parked outside, right?"

Born nodded. "Yeah. Just got it about three weeks ago."

The man smiled. "That shit is beautiful," he said.

Born smiled proudly. "Thanks."

"I thought I saw it parked outside of your house the other day." The guy said it so casually that Born thought he must have heard him wrong.

"What?" Born asked, confused.

The man stared back at Born. His smile had faded. "I said I was at your house the other day," the man repeated. "I left a nice package for you on your doorstep."

Born's heart rate quickened. The man stood facing him with his hands tucked into the front pocket of his hoodie. Instinctively, Born reached for the gun on his waist. Sensing that, the man shook his head.

"You don't want to see your son here get hurt," he cautioned. He slid one hand out of his hoodie pocket, just enough for Born to see the handle of a gun. The man gestured toward Sheldon standing merely inches away. He smiled at the kid. "Stay right there, little man. This won't take long."

Sheldon wasn't sure what was going on. But he sensed the tension between the two men, and it made him uneasy.

Born's adrenaline surged. He left his gun alone, aware that

this man had the upper hand. "Who are you?" Born stared at the man and wracked his brain for some recollection of him. Had he known this man and crossed him in his past? Born was coming up empty.

The man shrugged. "Names don't matter much, do they?" He seemed to ponder his own question. "Actually, sometimes names do matter. And there's a name that's been on my mind for a lot of years now. You know what name that is?"

Born waited. He wanted to blow this clown's head off. But first he had to find out who he was and why he had tried to kill him. He took in every detail of him. He was of some kind of Mediterranean descent. He stood about five ten with a slim build and no visible tattoos. His voice was deep and melodious. He seemed to be unafraid. In fact, he was quite confident as he continued.

"Jada," he said. "You know that name?"

Born's heart raced, and his hands instinctively balled into fists at the mention of Jada's name. He stepped forward toward the guy. But the man moved closer to Sheldon, halting Born in his tracks. He forced himself to calm down, though his heart was still pounding in his chest.

"Jada?" Born repeated.

"Yeah," the man said, smiling. "You know Jada. She's a mutual friend of ours." Both of his hands were in the front pocket of his hoodie, ensuring that Born kept his distance. He glanced at Sheldon. "She's your mother, right?"

Sheldon nodded.

"I want you to give Jada a little message for me," the man continued. He fixed his gaze on Born. "Tell her that until she gives me what she owes me, I will never go away."

"What she owes you?" Born repeated. "Who are you?"

"Aaaah . . ." the stranger said, the grin widening across his face. "That's the million-dollar question. Literally. That's what it

will cost you. One million dollars and I will go away for good."
His smile faded again and he looked serious as he addressed Born.
"Jada crossed me many years ago. She did more damage than she
may realize. But it is payback time. If she does not cooperate, it
will not be good."

Again, Born resisted the urge to physically defend Jada, Sheldon, and himself. He wondered who this guy was. Born was well
aware of Jada's past. During her time as a drug addict, she had
resorted to many unfortunate means of survival. Born wondered
if this was some guy Jada had slept with, or crossed in some terrible way. But more important than anything else, he had to protect Sheldon. With his right arm in a sling, and his torso in a
brace, Born had only the gun on his left side for protection. And
he wasn't left-handed. He was at a disadvantage, so he had no
choice but to wait and see what the stranger would do next.

"I will give you a week to get the money together. I understand you have had a loss in the family, so to speak."

Born wasn't sure whether the man was eluding to Sunny's
death or to the recent rash of arrests that had occurred.

"You will hear from me in a week, exactly." He stepped closer
to Sheldon, but kept his eyes on Born. "You don't strike me as
the type to involve the police. From what I hear, you've had your
problems with them in the past. But just in case you change your
mind, I know where Ethan lives." He stared Born down as he
said it. He knew he had hit a nerve when Born's jaw clenched
involuntarily. "I know Anisa's schedule at school. And I know
how often you like to spend the night over there. It took me a
long time to get you alone at home. But I did. And I can do it
again." The man laughed, cryptically. "I'm a reasonable man. But
I don't have a problem crossing the line. When I cross it, though,
I cross it all the way. Trust me on this." He patted Sheldon on
the head and then quickly walked out of the bathroom.

Sheldon and Born stood there for a couple of moments. Born

could tell that the kid was scared. Truthfully, the encounter had left Born shaken as well, though he would never admit it. The man knew so much about Born, about Jada, their whole family. Born was terribly on edge. Still, he wanted to see which way the guy went, what kind of car he was driving, something. So he quickly reassured Sheldon, and together they hurried outside. But by the time they reached the parking lot, the guy was gone. And all four of Born's tires were slashed.

He grabbed Sheldon by the arm, and ducked into Next Level Barbershop across the street. The owner was a friend of his, so Born knew that it was a safe place to get his thoughts together. Once inside, he spoke with the owner in private, and was ushered into the back office where he could speak without being disturbed or overheard. Then he pulled out his cell phone and got busy. This was war.

Celia ushered Gillian into her home. Her visit was unexpected. It was early on a sunny Saturday morning, and Celia had just been on her way out for a jog.

"Come on in," she said. "What brings you out to Long Island so early in the morning?"

Gillian smiled graciously. "I wanted to come and talk about Baron. Are you having trouble posting his bail?" Two days had passed since Baron's arraignment. His bail had been set. And although his bail was high, there was no shortage of resources at their disposal to use as collateral.

Celia arched an eyebrow. "No," she said. "Not at all."

Gillian adjusted her clutch bag under her arm. "So why is he still sitting in jail?"

Celia's eyes narrowed. "Excuse me?"

"With all due respect, Baron has been through a lot over the past few years. I'm worried about him." Gillian's expression was serious.

Celia shook her head. "Gillian, who do you think you're fooling?"

Gillian frowned. "What do you mean?"

"First of all, I haven't bailed out Baron because he needs to sit in jail for a few days. His whole life, whenever something went wrong, his father would swoop in and fix it. Well, his father is gone now. And it's time that Baron learns to take responsibility for his own decisions."

"I understand that, Miss Celia. And I'm all for Baron taking responsibility. But it just seems kinda cruel to leave him in there like that."

"So why don't you bail him out?" Celia asked. She knew the answer, of course. But, she asked anyway.

Gillian sidestepped the question. "I came to offer my financial help if it's needed. Baron is my brother. I'm happy to help."

Celia nodded. "Okay. So will you personally go down there and bail him out? Sign your name on the paperwork?"

Gillian didn't respond.

Celia scoffed. "Of course you won't! You're not really worried about Baron at all. You're only worried about yourself."

"That's not true. I love my brother. And I don't like the idea of him sitting in jail when there's no reason why—"

"So, go get him out!" Celia yelled, her voice echoing off the walls. She shook her head. "That won't happen, will it? Because you can't figure out why no one has arrested *you* yet. And you're scared to go to court, and sign your assets over to the government, and affiliate yourself with the case. So it's not about Baron at all. It's about the fact that his is a high-profile case, and your ass is at stake. Right?"

Gillian blinked a few times. Her stepmother had never spoken to her this way before. Even though she was an adult, and the family queenpin, Gillian felt like a kid being scolded by a parent who has seen right through her bullshit.

Celia pointed her finger, inches from Gillian's face. "I never wanted my son to be a criminal. I begged your father for years to keep Baron out of it, but he didn't listen to me. Now, your father is dead. Baron was shot, and has just begun to recover physically, and *you* have the top position in the crew. And try as I might, I could not convince my son to keep his hands clean. I warned him not to keep working with you. And now here you are standing free as a bird in my foyer. Meanwhile, Baron is up on Rikers Island where his life is in danger every second."

"So why would you leave him there?" Gillian demanded. "That doesn't sound like motherly love. You leave him in that type of environment so that you can prove a point?" Truthfully, Gillian worried with each passing day that Baron would break. He wasn't strong like she was. True, he was the firstborn son and she was the baby girl. But their actual roles in the family could not have been more opposite. The longer Baron stayed behind the cold stone walls of Rikers Island, the more likely he was to turn state's evidence.

Celia shook her head and closed her eyes. "Gillian, you should go now, before I say some things to you that can never be unsaid." Celia was well aware of the sibling rivalry between Baron and Gillian. She knew that this show of concern was actually a thinly veiled attempt for Gillian to cover her own ass. Celia opened her eyes again. "I will bail my son out of jail when I get the time to do it. If I'm not moving fast enough for you, then *you* do something. Something besides sitting at home and letting everybody else go down while you get away scot-free."

"That's not what I'm trying to do."

"Good. I'll be sure to tell Baron to contact you when he gets home." Celia walked to the front door and held it open for Gillian.

Without any protest, Gillian nodded her head and walked out the door. "Thanks."

Zion walked into the visiting room, trying hard not to put too much weight on his right ankle. The cops had beaten him so badly that he twisted his right foot the wrong way and now he was in incredible pain whenever he placed too much pressure on it. Most of the swelling in his face had gone down, although his lip was still swollen. Several bruises were still visible on his skin. He walked slowly, deliberately toward Olivia. She sat at the visiting table looking radiant on this hot July day. She wore a jade green T-shirt and a pair of dark denim skinny jeans. Zion thought the color of her shirt made her smooth, chocolate brown skin glow. She wore her hair up in a neat ponytail. He smiled, thinking that she looked as gorgeous as the day they met. But as he drew closer, her beauty was overshadowed by the menacing scowl on her face. She was livid, and it showed.

He noticed other inmates in the room eyeing Olivia. She had always had that effect on men. Olivia would walk into a room full of models and shut it down. She had style and flair that was unmistakable. But beneath that stunning exterior existed a bitterness that he was all too familiar with.

Zion made it to the table and maneuvered himself into the seat. Bending down hurt him, but he did his best not to show it. "Hello, beautiful," he managed, with a weak smile. He dared not reach for a hug or a kiss. The effort would be painful, and it might not be worth it if she shut him down.

Olivia watched him through piercing eyes. "They hurt you," she said softly.

Zion saw no sense in denying it. "They tried to. But I'm the bionic man. They can't kill me." He sat back in his seat. "Where's Adiva?"

"She's with Grandma," Olivia said. "I thought it was best for me to come by myself this time."

Zion nodded. He understood. Above all of the voices in the courtroom during his arraignment, he had heard Olivia's loud and clear. He knew that she loved him, but also that she knew about Ava. He had called once he got to Rikers, but Olivia had refused to speak to him. Instead, he had spoken to Lamin, who told him that Adiva was with them, and that they had been in touch with Maury Pendelstein, his attorney. There wasn't much more to say beyond that. They couldn't talk about the particulars of the case because everyone knew that jail conversations are recorded. There was no resolution in sight, since he was being held without bail. Lamin had asked about Zion's recovery, and about his safety in the zoo that is Riker's Island. Once Zion assured him that he was fine, Lamin had put Adiva on the phone, and she had talked to her daddy until the phone clicked off.

So until this moment, Zion had not been able to speak with Olivia. He wondered if she planned to add to the bruises he already had. He wasted no time finding out. Zion put his elbows on the table and made eye contact with Olivia.

"So let's have it out. I know you came here with some things to say to me."

"I bet you have some things to say to me, too."

"I do. But ladies first."

Olivia was unsettlingly calm. She sat back in her seat and folded her arms across her chest. "The police did this to you?" She analyzed all of the scars and bruises on Zion's face and the parts of his body that were visible.

"Yeah. They ran up in my place in the middle of the night. They snatched up Adiva without even giving me a minute to talk to her and explain what was happening. The poor baby was scared to death. When they were taking me out, I wanted to know where she was, to find out if I could talk to her. One of the guards said something disrespectful, and I just lost it." He motioned toward his face. "They didn't like that too much." He shrugged it off. He left out the part about how that same cop had watched Ava put on a pair of Zion's sweatpants, and gotten a peek at Ava's thong. Zion had caught him leering, and the cop had laughed in Zion's face. Told him, "Don't worry. While you're in jail, somebody else will handle things around here for you." The remark was enough to send him over the edge. In fact, the whole arrest had come at a terrible time. Zion had relaxed, and had things in the house that he normally wouldn't. Adiva and Ava had been there. His nosy neighbors, who already gave the urban-looking man in apartment 3B the side eye, had the pleasure of watching him led out in handcuffs, beaten, and hauled off to jail. His fight with those cops had been about the disrespectful remark made about his lady. But it was also his final attempt at fighting for freedom. Zion knew that he was going down.

Olivia stared at him, looking him up and down.

"Speak your mind," he urged.

"How long have you been fucking Ava?"

He sighed. "Me and Ava got close around New Year's. You were in Paris with Adiva. I ran into her at Born and Jada's engagement party."

Olivia hated even the idea of Zion with another woman. *Any* other woman. But knowing that it was a so-called friend of hers made it far worse. "You in love?" she asked through clenched teeth.

Zion stared back at her. He wasn't sure how to answer that. But, having love for Olivia the way that he did, he decided to tell her the truth. Even if it hurt.

He took a deep breath, and sat back in his seat. *Fuck it,* he thought. He had nothing to lose. If Olivia wilded out, she would be escorted out by the mean-mugging COs that dotted the room.

"I'll tell you what I love and what I don't love. I love feeling like a lady wants to be around me. Like getting a text or a phone call from me lights up her whole day. I like being able to call her and even if she's busy, she makes time to talk to me for a minute. I like being spoken to like a man."

"I don't speak to you like a man?" Olivia challenged.

"You speak to me like *you're* a man," Zion corrected. "And that's one of the things I don't like."

"So Ava addressees you with 'yes, sir' and 'no, sir'?" Olivia asked, sarcastically.

"No, but she's not cussing at me constantly, stirring up problems. I don't like arguing all the time, Olivia. I've been telling you that for years. I don't like being yelled at like a little kid and being embarrassed out in the street."

"What did we argue about?" She waited for him to answer, but he did not. "This!" she exclaimed, gesturing at their surroundings. "I kept warning you that this would happen."

He didn't reply. Instead, he watched her growing angrier by the second.

"You don't like me having a successful career, either," she said, leaning forward as if to ensure that he words were effectively hurled across the table.

Zion shook his head. "That's a lie."

"All I was trying to do was build us an empire so that you could stop hustling. And now look what happened."

Zion didn't argue. After all, he knew that she had been waiting to say that to him—*I told you so.*

"Everything is messed up now, Zion. They're really trying to put you away this time."

"I know."

"And you had Adiva with you." Olivia shook her head. Her

eyes welled with tears. The thought of her daughter crying and afraid while her father was arrested just broke her heart.

Zion felt her pain. He squeezed his eyes closed and shook his head in shame. He lowered his head and stared down at his hands on the table for several moments. "I'm sorry, Olivia. I swear I'm sorry."

She looked away, watched a couple at the next table playing with their little boy.

Zion reached across the table and touched her hand. "Nah, listen to me." Only when Olivia turned back to face him did he continue. "Olivia, I'm sorry. I should have listened to you. You're right." He threw up his hands, conceding defeat. "But the game is all I've ever known. Think about that." Zion tapped the side of his head for emphasis. His facial expression implored her to feel his pain "It's all that I've *ever* known. I was a kid when I found myself on my own. No parents, no family whatsoever. Group homes, foster homes, juvenile detention. All that shit did was prepare me for this right here."

Olivia was disgusted at what she was hearing. "So why feed into it then? If you know that . . . if you know that's what the system is designed for, why would you keep playing with fire?"

He laughed a little because he knew it didn't make sense, but he couldn't help it. "'Cause the thought of doing something regular scares me to death." He shuddered at the thought. "Get up every day and go . . . do what? What could I do, Olivia? What am I cut out to do?"

"I have a business, Zion. You could've helped me run it."

"That's *your* business," he clarified. "How do I look working in fashion?"

"Lamin has a production company. He's been begging you for years to get on board with it." Olivia wasn't going to let him off the hook. "You could have talked to Born and worked with him and DJ. You could've started your own business, Zion. It's not like you would be the first person to ever go legit. Lots of people we know have done exactly that. You're just so damn stubborn!"

Zion waved his hand. "Come on," he said, as if none of the prospects she had listed were realistic.

"There's no excuse," Olivia insisted. "You hustled because that's what *you* wanted to do. What I wanted didn't matter. And Adiva got caught up in your bullshit. And now what? What's the plan now, Zion? Huh?"

He shook his head. When he spoke, he sounded weary. "Maury has to get me out of here," he said. "For now, they're holding me without bail. But once we go to trial, he has to win. It's just that simple." He cracked his knuckles. "Maury has money for you and Adiva put away for times like this. So if you need anything, if money runs low, go to him."

Olivia wished she was the soft and gentle type. If she was, she'd tell Zion that no amount of money could ever make up for his absence in their lives. But being as hard and tough as she was, she couldn't bring herself to say it. She stared at him, thinking of all that had brought them here to this moment in time. She remembered seeing Zion for the first time and falling in love instantly. The two of them had been quite a pair. They were fiery together, electric. They had each other's back. Together they had built a family. And it had all come falling down with his arrest and his betrayal of her love for him.

Olivia's eyes narrowed. "I've known Ava for years. Years! Her and her sister. So it wasn't bad enough for you to cheat on me with just any old ho. Of all the women you come into contact with on a day-to-day basis, you had to pick my friend?"

"I'm sorry," he said, sincerely. "It wasn't planned. It just happened."

"Bullshit."

"It's not bullshit!" Zion licked his lips and frowned slightly. "Olivia, I moved out last year during the holidays. It's been more than six months that me and you have been living apart. We don't live together. We don't sleep together. Okay, so we never officially broke up. But don't make it sound like I've been cheating on you. Cuz that's not the truth."

He was right, but Olivia ignored him. "You had her around my daughter."

Zion had no defense. Olivia stared at him hard and unrelenting. At the risk of getting her mad again, he kept it real. "It's not like she never met Ava before. Adiva and Mercedes are friends. Sunny, Jada, Ava—they were all in the same little circle."

"With me." Olivia wanted to punch him in his face.

Zion looked away.

"How would you feel if I went and fucked one of your boys? Maybe somebody you're not *that* close with. Somebody like . . . I don't know, Frankie?"

Zion felt the hairs stand up on the back of his neck. The very thought of that caused bile to rise up in his throat. He glared at her. "Where did that name come from?"

Olivia fanned her hand at him, dismissively. "Don't try to twist this around. The point is, how would you *feel*, Zion?"

He had to admit that she was right. He understood how she must feel. "If that happened, there's no telling what I would do."

"Why?"

"What do you mean, *why*?"

"Why would there be no telling what you would do?"

He took a deep breath. "Because I care about you, Olivia. We've been together for years. Through all kinds of ups and downs. You know I'm always gonna love you."

Olivia's heart broke. It sounded like this was leading up to good-bye. Even though she had known for months, maybe even years, that their relationship had run its course, she couldn't believe that this was really it. That they were going their separate ways for good, and that Zion might actually find happiness in the arms of someone else. That is, if he didn't go to jail for the rest of his life instead.

"I hate imagining you with some other dude," he said, honestly. "For real. I guess that's a double standard or whatever, but it's how I feel." He wiped his face with his hand. "The problem has never been about me not loving you or nothing like that. You're still sexy, still got that hustler's spirit that I love. I guess I just stopped liking you over the years."

"Fuck you, Zion."

He shrugged. "Okay. Fuck me, then. But that's how I feel. You got too much mouth." He opened and shut his hand rapidly in a quacking motion, demonstratively. "You stopped having my back, and I can understand that you grew up and didn't want me hustling no more. Fine. I can handle that. But sometimes it's not about what you say, it's how you say it. And instead of hearing you say, 'I love you. I'm scared. Maybe it's time to step out the game,' you came at me crazy. Snapping at me like I'm your son instead of your man. Starting fights with me in front of your family. And it turned me off." Again, he shrugged. "I probably shouldn't have got caught up with Ava. I understand why that pisses you off. But it wasn't planned. She just came around at the right time."

"Okay," Olivia said. She had heard enough. "Fine. So you go your way, and I'll go mine." She wished it was as easy as she made it sound. "You think Ava's gonna go the distance with you? Miss Corporate Attorney? You believe she's cut out for this life you got her thrown into? She's not built like us. She's from Brooklyn. She got Jada as her sister. But, she's not Jada. So I hope you know that you're stuck with that." Olivia wiped her hands together. "It's a wrap for us. Even if she lets you down. Don't come running back to me, Zion."

He knew her well enough to tell that she wanted to cry, but was fighting it with all she had. He wanted to comfort her, to tell her that he was sorry. But he knew she wasn't that type of chick. Olivia was too tough for her own good sometimes. "I deserve that," he said honestly. "I let you down. Not just with Ava. But this, too." He spread his arms and looked around at his abysmal surroundings. "You tried to tell me that it was time to move on. I just was too stubborn to listen."

Zion looked down at the table, toyed with this hands. He had gotten too comfortable in a life that wasn't meant to be long term.

Olivia felt her heart break a little more, seeing him sitting there beaten, bruised, and sad. She knew that she would never love another man the way that she had loved Zion for so long. Even though he had hurt her deeply, she wanted him to be happy. She wanted to see him anywhere but here in this cage.

Zion looked into her eyes. "I'm sorry to hear about Sunny," he said.

Olivia nodded. She was, too. She hung her head at the thought of her friend. "I can't believe she's gone."

Zion shook his head. "Old habits die hard," he said. "Sunny's old habits killed her. Mine may cost me my freedom."

"Where's Gillian?" Olivia asked.

Zion raised an eyebrow.

"I mean, why is she the only one not named in the indictment?"

Zion had wondered the same thing. "She's not the only one."

"True. But, she's the only *major* player who's not in the same position as you," Olivia reminded him.

"I don't know," he said. "I can't talk to her from in here."

Olivia shook her head. "So, suddenly *you're* the kingpin of the whole operation and she just walks away? You're okay with that?"

Everyone within the family knew that Gillian called the shots. Sure, Zion had her ear these days. But he was not the head of the crew as the indictment suggested. Tongues had started wagging about who had been swept up by the feds, and who had not.

And, like Olivia, there were many people questioning Gillian's good fortune.

Zion didn't answer right away. He trusted Gillian. In the years since she had taken the helm, she had always shown herself to be worthy of her crew's loyalty. There were others within the family who Zion wasn't so confident about. But his instinct told him that Gillian was not the reason he was sitting behind bars.

"When Maury gets me out of here, I'll handle everything," he said simply.

Olivia felt angry then. Had Ava not been in the picture, Olivia would have gone to visit Gillian. She would have asked all of the questions that Zion couldn't ask himself, given his present circumstances. She would have harassed Maury relentlessly until he argued effectively enough on Zion's behalf that bail was granted for him. She would have ensured that his commissary was maxed out, and that a lawsuit was filed against the officers who had beaten him this way. But she pictured the terror in Adiva's eyes when she had picked her up from the precinct after Zion's arrest. She remembered the pain of seeing Ava stand before the courtroom, fresh out of Zion's bed and wearing his clothes. And she reminded herself that his problems were no longer her own.

"I wish you well," she said. "I really do. I have to focus on taking care of Adiva. 'Cause whether you come home tomorrow or ten years from now, I have to make sure that she's alright. I have my company to grow, and my life to live. So . . ." She felt like she was giving a speech, and that wasn't her intention. "I just wish you well, Zion. I hope it all works out and that you can be free."

He felt himself getting emotional. "I love you, Olivia. I want you to be happy, too."

She let a tear fall, but quickly erased any trace of it. She picked up her visitor's pass, pushed back her chair, and stood up. Zion stood also. Olivia walked around the table and embraced him.

Their hug was strong and meaningful. They were aware of the COs yelling for them to separate, aware that everyone in the visiting room was looking at them. But they didn't care. Olivia kissed Zion on his cheek, as one officer neared them. She touched his face. "I love you, too," she said. "Take care of yourself."

The guards belligerently carried on about how their visit was being terminated and ordered Zion to walk over to the inmate exit. But it didn't matter. Olivia was already on her way out the door, their visit terminated the moment that tear had fallen from her eye. He had never meant to break her heart. But they both knew that this breakup was for the best. Still, as she exited the visiting room, the prison, and their relationship, Zion knew that Olivia would always be special to him for as long as he lived.

16
CROSSROADS

Camille squirmed. Eli was staring at her, his eyes probing her for the truth. She felt like a bug, trapped in a jar and being stared at by her captor. Only she wasn't trapped. She and Eli were sitting together in Central Park, discussing Frankie's case.

"I'm the only one who can help him, Eli."

He toyed with his key ring. "You're telling me this man has no family, no friends, nobody else that can step up and help him out? I don't think that's true."

"Honestly, all he has is his mom. But she's old and basically a recluse. She can barely keep herself going." Camille hadn't seen Frankie's mom since Bria was born two years ago. Sometimes it felt like she hadn't seen Frankie since then either. "I just feel bad, Eli. It has nothing to do with me and him. That's *been* over."

It was true. After Gillian rebuffed Frankie's attempts at reconciliation, he tried to come crawling back to Camille. But in the end it proved too complicated for them to dust themselves off and try again. Far too much had happened between them, not the least of which was the fact that Camille's sister had murdered Frankie's brother for molesting her child. Camille found herself falling in love with Eli, and she told Frankie so. That seemed to be the deal breaker. Soon after that conversation, Frankie's visits to see his daughter became less frequent. Since then,

Eli had been more involved in Camille's and Bria's lives than Frankie.

Eli didn't say anything for a while as he mulled it over. "Why can't his cohorts help him out?" Eli stared into Camille's eyes. They both knew what Frankie's real line of business was. Sure, he owned a barbershop, a pool hall, and had his name on a couple of other legitimate companies. But those closest to him knew the truth. Ei had been with Camille long enough to be in on the not-so-well-kept secret that Frankie was a drug dealer.

Camille didn't answer. How could she? She had no idea what was going on in Frankie's life, let alone in his business. "Fine," she said. "I won't bail him out, or visit him, or nothing."

Eli looked visibly relieved. "I know you think I'm being harsh."

Camille didn't respond.

"Do you still love him?" It was a question he hadn't asked Camille since the early days of their relationship.

Camille looked down at her hands and shook her head. "Not in the way you might think. I know the old Frankie. The guy who was ambitious, and fun. But since his brother died . . ." Camille couldn't bring herself to utter Steven's name. It disgusted her to think of what he had done to her nephew. Shane was progressing normally, but the scars remained on their family forever. "Since he died, Frankie's been going downhill. He needs help." She found Eli's eyes again. "The Frankie I love is gone for good, I think. But I just feel kinda sorry for the shell that's left behind."

Eli looked away, watching a horse-drawn carriage go by.

"I don't know why his so-called friends left him high and dry. But I do know that he's Bria's father. I just wanted to extend an olive branch." A thought occurred to her. "What if I write him a letter?" Camille took Eli's hand in hers.

"He's barely been around," Eli reminded her, sympathetically. "You can't make him have a relationship with her if he doesn't want it." He shrugged. "Write him the letter."

Camille's eyes brightened. "You can read it before I mail it," she offered.

"I trust you." Eli loved Camille. He loved her enough to understand her need to reach out to Frankie. Camille had a kind heart and an innocence about her. Perhaps, at times, she was a bit naïve. But family was important to her. And love was, too. "I don't need to read it. Just write it and see what happens. Hope for the best."

Camille smiled and kissed him on his cheek.

The next morning, as Eli left to begin his shift, he noticed a note on the coffee table. He stopped and picked it up, thinking it might be some mail. And it was. A letter from Camille to Frankie. She had left it there for him to read.

> *Frankie,*
>
> *I know that things are crazy for you right now. I wish there was something I could do to help you out. I haven't heard from you in a while. And that's the reason that I'm writing to you.*
>
> *I don't know much about what you're going through right now. But whatever happens, whether you come home or go away for a long time, Bria is growing every day. When she smiles, the corners of her eyes crease exactly like yours. She is a beautiful little girl. She's your daughter. We didn't succeed at marriage, but we did succeed in bringing forth a wonderful addition to this world. I want you to see her, Frankie. I can bring her to see you along with your mom, if you want.*
>
> *Write me back and let me know if it's okay. I'm praying for you.*
>
> *Love,*
> *Camille*

Eli folded the letter and placed it back on the table. He placed his watch on top of it, so that Camille would know that he'd seen it. Then he walked out the door, hoping that Frankie wouldn't let her down again.

Ava was in her office packing up boxes of her personal belongings. This was a sad day in her career. She had been called into the office of the managing partner, and summarily fired. The publicity from her recent arrest was hurting the firm. Plus, it didn't help that she had been associated with the raving lunatic Sunny Cruz, who had disrupted business at the firm weeks ago. The firm of Bradwell, Foster, and Knight decided that it was best that they sever ties with Ava. Sadly, she had returned to her office and began packing. She felt like such a failure.

A knock on her office door caused her to look up. Malcolm stood there, looking like hell. His face was unshaven, his eyes had bags beneath them, and he wore no tie. In fact, Ava noticed that he was rather casually dressed in a pair of Dockers, a T-shirt, and sneakers.

"Hey," Ava said.

"Hey." Malcolm's voice was barely above a whisper.

After her release on bail, Ava had called Malcolm personally to deliver the news of Sunny's overdose. Malcolm had broken down, sobbing terribly. Ava had talked to him on the phone for an hour afterward, hoping to get Malcolm to stop blaming himself. He had sounded so hopeless then. Now, two days later, he still looked unsettled and stressed. But at least he had stopped crying.

She didn't bother asking how he was. "You're dressed down today."

He leaned against the doorframe. "Yeah. I'm doing the same thing you're doing." He nodded toward the boxes on her desk.

Ava looked surprised. "They fired you, too?"

Malcolm shook his head. "No. I quit. I figured I might as well beat them to the punch." He stepped into the office and shut the door behind him. He slumped down into one of the chairs facing her desk. "Oh my God," he sighed. "Ava, how did this happen?"

Ava shook her head, coming up empty.

"This is all my fault."

Ava shook her head. "We discussed this," she reminded him. "We all thought Sunny was okay. She had agreed to go into rehab, and then . . . bam! She just . . ." Ava tossed a file into one of her boxes and sat in her high-back leather chair one last time. "This is déjà vu," she said. "The last time we were in an office together, Sunny blew through here like a tsunami."

Malcolm managed a slight laugh through the tears that welled in his eyes. "That's putting it mildly." He wiped his eyes.

Ava shook her head. "That Sunny was one of a kind." She got choked up thinking about the beautiful woman with a penchant for playing with fire.

"I miss her," Malcolm said. "I miss the time I spent with her. I just wish I could do it all over again." He seemed to shake himself out of it. "Have you heard anything about her funeral arrangements?" he asked. "Do you think it's okay if I go?"

Ava did know, of course. Sunny's funeral was the next day. But she wasn't sure that it would be safe for Malcolm to attend with Sunny's brothers present. They were aware that he had abandoned Sunny in Mexico, and that perhaps the shame of facing everyone all at once had driven her to the extreme. "You should call her parents and ask them," she suggested. "I don't think it's my place to tell you whether you should go or not."

Malcolm nodded. He understood, of course. But the situation was made all the more painful by the fact that he would never be able to say a proper good-bye to Sunny. And he had no one to blame but himself.

"You want to know the truth?" he asked.

Ava nodded, though she wondered if she really wanted to hear this.

"I thought Sunny was the total package. She was gorgeous. Had her own money, one child just like me. A daughter, just like me. Single and successful, just like me. And I convinced myself that she could fit into my world." He laughed, a bit maniacally. "And she *did*! She fit right in. She danced to jazz music with me, and sipped wine with me, and dressed the part when we went out. She was perfect. I told myself that she was perfect. But, the whole time . . ."

Malcolm stared at his hands in silence for several long and silent moments. Ava gave him the space to let it out, aware that she was probably the only person who Malcolm could talk to about this.

"She had a secret." He looked at Ava, questioningly. "You know what it was?"

Ava stared back at Malcolm, unsure how to answer. In her mind she was screaming, *Yeah, I know what it was. She was snorting coke behind your back the whole time!*

"The secret was that she had fit into my world, but she had never really let me into her world. She never exposed me to it, not once, until we got to Mexico. And then she showed me." Malcolm thought about that. The things he could never tell Ava or anybody. "She showed me and I ran. Like a bitch."

Hearing him quote Sunny, Ava felt sorry for him. He looked so sad. "You made a mistake, Malcolm, but Sunny's death was not your fault. She chose to get high after all of the trouble she found herself in. Nobody made her do it. So stop blaming yourself." She watched him mulling over what she had just said. He nodded, but Ava wasn't sure that his guilt had subsided at all. "What will you do now?" she asked. "Got another offer lined up?"

Malcolm nodded. "Yeah. I'm moving back to L.A."

Ava's mouth widened in surprise. "What? Really? I thought you hated it out there."

He shrugged. "One of my former partners opened up a firm. He invited me to come and partner with him. I figured it's time for a change of pace. Maybe I didn't give it a chance the first time. Going back now, I think I'll be more prepared."

Ava was suddenly sad. She had always liked Malcolm a lot. "I'm sorry to hear that," she said, honestly. "You'll be missed." Ava thought about how different things would have been had Malcolm expressed an interest in her when she was pining for him. Back then, Sunny had swooped in and swept Malcolm off his feet. All the while, Ava had stood on the sidelines feeling like that was the position she had always been destined to play. She was always on the bench watching the players in the starting lineup getting all of the action. But not any more. Ava had a whole new outlook these days.

Malcolm inquired, carefully. "How about your situation?" he asked. "Are they still charging you or did you get that worked out?"

"Thankfully, they dropped the charges against me," Ava said. "But a lot of good that did me." She tossed a pack of Post-it notes in one of her boxes. "They still gave me the boot."

Malcolm shrugged. "So what!" he said. "It's their loss. You go somewhere else and start over."

Ava nodded. "I'm actually thinking of switching gears," she said. "My little predicament showed me how terrible the criminal justice system is. It's really disgusting. So I'm thinking about going into criminal law. I've been thinking about changing gears for a while now. This may be just the push that I needed."

Malcolm's eyes widened in surprise. "Really? Wow, Ava," he said. "Good for you."

Ava looked at Malcolm. He was dressed like the preppy lawyer that he was. He spoke properly, held degrees from top schools, boasted an enviable stock portfolio. If someone had told her a year ago that she would end up with an incarcerated drug lord instead of a guy like Malcolm, she would have laughed in their face.

"You know," she said, "I had the biggest crush on you at first."

Malcolm smiled weakly. He was surprised by Ava's revelation. "Yeah? You never said anything." He looked at Ava through new eyes. She was beautiful. He had never taken the time to really notice that, too preoccupied with the work they did, the hours they billed.

"I know." Ava laughed. "I was shy. I kept waiting for you to make the first move, but that never happened. And then you took one look at Sunny and fell head over heels."

Malcolm nodded. It was true. Sunny had stolen his heart from the moment he laid eyes on her.

"I was just sitting here thinking about how different our lives would be if you and I had gotten together instead of . . . the way that things turned out. You wouldn't be heading back to L.A. with all these regrets, and I wouldn't be ruining my career and my reputation at the same time."

Malcolm nodded, seeming lost in thought.

Ava laughed at the absurdity of it. "It makes no sense," she said. "I spent so many years judging my sister and judging Sunny for the men they chose, and the lifestyles they lived. And now here I am in this mess." She shook her head, threw up her hands. "But I'm not gonna let it get me down. Life goes on."

Malcolm stared at her. "I'm sorry, Ava." He tried to find the right words to express what he was feeling. "I'm sorry we both wound up like this. I guess we bit off more than we could chew in our relationships and it cost us our careers." He laughed. "I'm leaving town, you're stepping into a new career. So I guess it's a new start for both of us."

Ava nodded.

"I'm gonna miss working with you," he said. "And I think

you're an amazing woman. I wish you well wherever you go in life." He looked into her eyes. "I'm so sorry about Sunny," he said. "I know you keep saying it's not my fault, but . . . I know that I could have done more. I could have helped her." He wanted so badly to go to Sunny's funeral, but knew that he wasn't welcome there. His relationship with Sunny had ended the moment he boarded the flight back to America, leaving her to fend for herself. There would be no long good-byes, no time to hash things out, no forgiveness. It left him feeling exceedingly sad.

Ava stood up and Malcolm met her at the midpoint of the room. He held his arms wide, and she hugged him. "Keep in touch," she said. "Knock 'em dead out there in L.A."

Stepping back from their embrace, he smiled down at her. "Listen," he said. "Next time you're in L.A., give me a call."

Ava nodded. "You got it," she said. She knew that she was lying. She would never look Malcolm up. This was their last good-bye, and she watched him leave her office to finish packing up his belongings. Ava was glad that she hadn't been the one to suffer the misfortune of dating Malcolm. What he had done to Sunny—abandoning her in Mexico when she needed him most and then turning into a blubbering crybaby when the shit hit the fan—was enough to show Ava that Malcolm wasn't the man she desired. Neither was Zion. She had been enamored by his lovemaking, his swagger. But there was nothing sexy about sitting in jail. The time she had spent in police custody had been enough to take the bloom off the rose. Ava wanted out. By any means necessary.

Jada and Born sat in Maury Pendelstein's office, waiting for him to get off the phone. They had come here after Born's ominous meeting with the stranger in the bathroom at McDonald's. Maury had been one of the first people Born called. As his attorney for the past two decades, Maury was trustworthy and had seen it all. He could tell from Born's tone of voice during their phone conversation that he was very upset by his run-in with the man earlier. So he had insisted that Born and Jada come to meet with him immediately. They had waited for Ava to return from packing up her Midtown Manhattan office. As soon as she got back, Jada had briefed Ava on the latest developments and insisted that Ava and Sheldon lock themselves inside the house. "Don't even answer the phone unless it's me whose calling," Jada said. Then, together, she and Born jumped into the Towncar Maury sent for the two of them. Jada's car was still in police custody, and Born's had four flat tires. He'd had it towed from the McDonald's parking lot. Their tormentor had succeeded in shaking up their lives in no time.

Maury got right down to business. "The children are secure?" he asked. "Since this guy mentioned Ethan by name, I'm concerned. Clearly, he's already done his research."

Born nodded. "I called Anisa and told her to stay inside, keep the doors locked, and the security system armed."

Jada nodded, too. "Same here. Sheldon is with my sister."

Maury nodded, satisfied. He sat back in his chair and looked Jada in the eye. "So, from what Marquis has shared with me, there's a man out there who is very unhappy with you."

Jada toyed with her hands, ashamed. She was sick of her past coming back to haunt her, and she wondered whether the rest of her life would involve these constant reminders of who and what she had once been. For years, it seemed that every time she turned around there was some aspect of the old Jada coming back to the surface like an old skeleton she thought had long ago been buried.

"Any idea who it might be?" Maury asked.

Jada shook her head. "I've been thinking about it ever since Born's accident," she said. "Then, I got this note in the mail the same day." Jada passed the cryptic note to Maury. "There was a crack vial inside of it. I threw it out." Jada watched Maury read the note.

He glanced at her when he was done. Jada could detect the question in his eyes before he asked it.

"Did you have a drug problem in the past?"

She nodded. "It was a very long time ago."

Born could sense her discomfort and embarrassment. He reached over and squeezed her hand, reassuringly.

Maury read the note again. "Back then, who was your dealer?" he asked.

Jada cringed a bit, but took a deep breath and answered the question. "Well . . . there were a few people. When I first got hooked, I was getting it from a guy named Lucas. Then I worked for a guy named Charlie in exchange for drugs." She hated rehashing this, but knew that it was necessary since they were being terrorized. "Lucas was in jail, last I heard. And Charlie is an old man. I doubt that he has anything to do with this." Jada thought back to the not-so-good old days. "Then I got involved with Sheldon's father. He used to give me crack to smoke," she said. "But Jamari has been dead since Sheldon was a baby. It can't be him." She skipped over all of the times that she had stolen from Born in order to get high. Not only wasn't it relevant, but it was an ugly old wound to reopen.

Maury scribbled notes on a legal pad, listing the names of everyone Jada had mentioned. He glanced at Born. "Did you describe the man that you met today to Jada? Maybe his physical appearance rings a bell."

Born nodded. It had been the first thing he'd done. "Yeah. No such luck."

Jada frowned. "He said that the man looked . . . interracial." She shook her head, not recalling any of her old acquaintances that might fit the description.

"Maybe Arabic or something. I couldn't tell really." Born was frustrated that he couldn't offer a better description.

Maury sat back and looked at Jada. "The fact of the matter is that this person has gone to great lengths to get your attention. The bomb at Marquis' door, the note in the mailbox, his visit today. It all seems very well thought out, very deadly. With his threatening the children, it's even worse really. It means he's capable of anything. I would take this whole thing seriously."

Born's brow was twisted in knots. "So what do we do?"

Maury took a deep breath. "He says you have a week. A million dollars is a lot of money."

Born shook his head. "So we pay him off and then what? He's gonna keep asking for more and this shit will never stop."

Maury nodded. "That's a possibility," he allowed. "Or he could keep his word and disappear, never to be heard from again. There's really no way to tell what will happen."

Jada was frowning, too. "So you think we should take our chances and give him the money?"

Maury shrugged his shoulders. "I'm just saying that it's an option. The other option is to go to the police."

"But he said not to do that," Jada reminded them.

Born waved his hand dismissively. "He ain't calling the shots," he asserted. "But for my own reasons, I'm not feeling the idea of getting the cops involved."

"Why not?" Maury pressed.

Born looked at Jada and wished that he could erase her past forever. "Jada had a hard time getting custody of Sheldon. Then, with Sheldon's recent accident . . ." Born didn't want to call it what it was—a suicide attempt. "I just don't want the police to get in contact with social services and open up a whole new case."

Jada felt her heart melt a little. Here they were rehashing her days as a crack addict and lamenting the fact that some old connect had come back to haunt them. And Born was thinking about her, about her son, and putting them first. She loved him more in that moment than she ever had before.

Maury nodded. "If you don't involve the police, you have two options left. You can pay the guy and hope that he goes away. Or you can figure out who he is and track him down, take matters into your own hands." Maury threw his hands up as if he didn't care which of the options Born chose. "As your attorney, obviously, I have to advise you to go to the police. But the ball is in your court. Your call."

Born felt conflicted. He would do anything to protect Jada and their children. But he wasn't about to pay a million dollars to some spooky stranger, and then sit around and hope that he kept his word and went away.

Sensing Born's dilemma, Maury leaned forward and looked him in the eye. "Listen, you don't have to make a decision here and now. Sleep on it. Take the week that he gave you and weigh your options. You have a lot to deal with already. You're injured. Your friend's funeral is tomorrow." Maury shook his head. He felt sorry for them both. Looking at Jada, she seemed just as lost as Born. "Try to put this out of your mind for now. One thing at a time."

They both nodded, knowing that Maury's advice was sound. Jada listened as the men discussed the details of Sunny's funeral, which was being held at the legendary Frank E. Campbell Funeral Home on Madison Avenue. Known for its opulent and detailed services, the venue was perfect for the final gathering in Sunny's honor. Jada still hadn't come to grips with the loss of her friend. Tomorrow would be tough.

"Listen," Maury said as they stood to leave. "Try to get some rest. You're gonna need it."

Jada smiled weakly and nodded as she followed Born out. Easier said than done.

17

FAREWELL

Mercedes sat in the front of the room, flanked by her grandparents. She stared straight ahead at her mother's casket, her gaze unwavering. Despite the fact that there were scores of people in attendance, she had never felt more alone. She was aware that friends and family were milling about, speaking in hushed tones to her grandparents as they offered their condolences. She was also aware that every one of the people in the room had taken the time to stare at her, to search her face for signs of what she was feeling, how she was holding up. Mercedes felt like she was in a fishbowl being gawked at by a room full of awestruck spectators. Part of her wanted to run and escape the scrutiny. But she was transfixed by the presence of her mother's body only a few feet away from where she sat.

Sunny looked like an angel. Mercedes knew with certainty that her mother was dead. After all, she had been there when Sunny's lifeless body was discovered; had sat watching in a daze as they carried her out in a body bag. Yet she couldn't help thinking that Sunny looked like she was enjoying a peaceful sleep. Lying there in her gold casket, her head resting atop plush white velvet fabric, Sunny's face was set in the most serene expression. Tears slid down Mercedes' face as she wept silently, wishing that her mother's eyes would flutter open, and that all of this would be some terrible misunderstanding. She couldn't accept that this was their final good-bye.

Jada sat two rows behind the family. She was watching Mercedes, wondering what she was thinking and feeling. Mercedes had inherited Sunny's ability to mask her emotions. It was impossible to tell whether she was holding up well or if she was falling apart on the inside. Sensing her concern, Born reached over and took Jada's hand in his own.

"You okay?" he asked.

Jada looked at him and offered a faint smile. She shrugged, then shook her head sadly.

Born understood, and squeezed her hand reassuringly. His heart broke for her. Sunny had been Jada's best friend for close to twenty years. The loss of her had broken Jada. Several times, he'd caught her staring off into space, lost in thoughts that were too painful for her to discuss. At other moments, she sat with tears pooling in her eyes, too choked up to give voice to what she was going through. Born comforted her as best he could, aware that their problem with the mystery man who was terrorizing them only added fuel to the fire. She dabbed at her eyes and he watched her, wishing all the while that he could take away her pain.

A woman approached the podium and spoke into the microphone.

"We're going to begin the service now," she said. "Can everyone please take your seats and mute all electronic devices?"

Jada kept her eyes glued to Mercedes as the wake ended and the funeral portion of the program began. Reuben had been released on bail with an electronic monitoring ankle bracelet to track his movements. While everyone else, including Sunny's parents, talked among themselves in hushed tones and prepared for the main event, Mercedes continued to stare at her mother's coffin in silence. She hadn't spoken a word to anyone all morning.

"I'm worried about her," Jada whispered to Born. "She's not taking this well."

Born frowned and looked at Jada questioningly. "Seems like she's doing alright," he said. "She's just tough like her mother, that's all."

Jada shook her head. "No," she said. "That's the problem. Sunny wasn't nearly as tough as she thought she was."

Born looked at Mercedes and put himself in her shoes. He thought about how he'd reacted to his father's death years ago. Born had been unemotional on the surface, but inside he was a mess. And he had been a grown man by the time his pops had passed away. Mercedes was barely a teenager. Sadly, he understood where Jada was coming from.

The service began with a musical prelude. A woman with the most beautiful voice Jada had ever heard sang a heartbreaking rendition of "Amazing Grace." Her velvety voice was full of the most poignant mixture of purity and pain. It brought tears to the eyes of everyone in the room. By the time the songstress took her seat, even the officiating minister had to collect himself.

Reverend Gibson was the assistant pastor at Jada's church. Sunny's family wasn't very religious and had no church affiliations. Jada had arranged for Reverend Gibson to officiate, eager to help to ease the family's burdens in any way that she could. He addressed Sunny's family, offering consoling words and reminding them that God heard even their faintest cries and would comfort them in their grief. He read Psalm 23, slowly and deliberately. Mercedes listened intently, imagining her mother lying down in green pastures, strolling beside still waters, at peace. The thought of that did little to comfort her. She wasn't content with the idea of her mother in heaven. She wanted her right there on earth, with her. Anything else just wouldn't do.

Next, Reverend Gibson called upon Sunny's brother, Ronnie, to read Sunny's obituary. Ronnie seemed to be warring with himself as he approached the podium. On one hand, he stood tall and strong, his hands gripping the funeral program firmly. But in contrast, he repeatedly dabbed at his eyes, his tears spilling forth nonstop. Ronnie struggled to find his voice, unable to control its wavering under the weight of his emotions. He looked over at his beautiful sister lying serenely in the gilded coffin, and choked back a sob.

Words of reassurance echoed through the crowd as the attendees encouraged him to take his time. After a few moments, Ronnie cleared his throat. He stole one last long glance at his sister's body, took a deep breath, and began.

"Sunny Victoria Cruz was born on May 29, 1973. She was the youngest of three children born to our parents Marisol and Dale." Ronnie stopped reading, and set the program down on the podium. He wanted to speak from his heart, not read what amounted to a prepackaged press release. He looked out into the crowd and saw so many familiar faces. Family members, Sunny's friends and neighbors, all the people who had known her well. Ronnie smiled as he thought of his sister's infectious laughter and her fiery personality. "Sunny was the life of the party from the moment she took her first breath," he said.

The crowd audibly concurred, shouting "Amen" amid laughter and smiles of agreement.

"She was a wonderful daughter, sister, mother, and friend. She had a heart of gold. But, she was tough. If you crossed Sunny, you better be ready for war."

The crowd was hyping Ronnie up now.

"She didn't take anybody's shit. I never knew her to be afraid of anything or anybody. But she had a heart of gold. Many of us in this room can remember times that we went to her for help and she made it all right. She was beautiful inside and out." Ronnie took a moment to wipe his nose before continuing. "She always seemed like she was in complete control. But underneath that tough skin . . ." Ronnie looked to the sky for strength. "My sister was struggling. She had a burden that none of us could help her carry."

Ronnie broke down in sobs, unable to continue. Many of the mourners were crying audibly as well, Jada among them. Their failure to save Sunny as she had done for so many of them had rendered them inconsolable. Born, too, felt himself getting choked up with emotion. Sunny and Dorian had raised a generation of hustlers, many of them sleeping on Sunny's couch or in her guest room over the years when they had no place else to go. Knowing that she had died alone and afraid under such preventable circumstances was too much to bear.

Reuben walked to the front of the room and hugged his brother in consolation. He patted Ronnie on the back and then stepped to the mic himself. His voice was wracked with emotion as he spoke.

"The last time I saw my sister," he began. His voice trailed off, and once again the crowd shouted encouragement until he continued. "I was so mad at her for slipping up again. I told her that she was in denial about her problem, that she needed help." He looked out at all of the familiar faces in the crowd. "I told her that if she didn't get the help she needed that I had nothing else to say to her."

Murmurs of pity could be heard throughout the room. Reuben seemed to steel himself before speaking again. "I thought I was giving her tough love. I told myself that she would get her act together so that she wouldn't disappoint me. So that she wouldn't disappoint our whole family. Especially her daughter." Reuben looked at Mercedes then. She stared back at him with rapt attention. "I left that night thinking that I would see her again the next day or the day after that." He shook his head, looking down at his hands. "But I never saw her again until today." He looked out into the crowd. "And now it's too late. I can never tell her the things I had planned to tell her the next time we got together. That I love her more than anybody else in this world. That I'm so proud of the woman she turned out to be, even with all of her struggles. That she was a great mother, who raised a really great kid all by herself. That I'm sorry. Sorry for not noticing that she was in trouble, that she needed help. Sorry for worrying about my own best interests and what I could get out of her lifestyle for my own selfish reasons. Sorry for not protecting her. For not realizing that she really didn't have everything under control like she wanted everybody to believe she did."

Jada wept softly, her head resting on Born's shoulder. Reuben was saying so much of what she, too, was feeling.

Reuben glanced over at his sister's body, and shook his head in disbelief. "Now she's gone. And I will never get to tell her those things." He turned back to the crowd and scanned the room. He saw Olivia, Jada, Born, Lamin, Gillian, his parents, scores of distant relatives, a handful of celebrities, and some unknown individuals he assumed were media affiliated. Finally, he set his sights on Mercedes. He found her eyes, and held her gaze.

"I try to think about the fact that my sister is at peace now. She doesn't have to worry about fighting her addiction anymore. She doesn't have to think about all of the people who she disappointed. No more cameras in her face, no more talk show hosts trying to raise their ratings by bashing her. No more pain. Still, it hurts me to know that she had to leave her beautiful daughter behind."

Mercedes' chin quivered as she fought the urge to break down. She and Sunny had been inseparable for as long as she could remember. She had no idea how she could go on without her.

Reuben's eyes bore into Mercedes. "I know that Sunny wanted to see you grow up. To watch you graduate high school, and go off to college. To see you get married and have a family someday. She wanted nothing but the best for you, and she loved you so much. Now it's our job to pick up where she left off. We can't fix all the things we should have said or done differently. But we can make sure that Mercedes is reminded of her mother's love for her each and every day of her life. That's how we can make it up to Sunny. That's how we can make it right for her, just like she always made things right for all of us."

Reuben stepped away from the podium and returned to his seat amid applause from all of the mourners. Reverend Gibson approached the podium in preparation for the eulogy. But he—and everyone else in the room—paused when Mercedes stood up out of her seat and walked toward her mother's casket. Everyone held their collective breath as she approached Sunny's body, and stared down at her mother silently.

Mercedes gently touched Sunny's face, recoiling a bit at its coldness. Sunny's body felt hard despite the fact that she looked so soft and peaceful laying there. Mercedes hadn't expected that, but was somehow grateful for the reminder that her mother was gone for good. From her seat, Sunny had looked like her usual self. But as she touched the stiff body lying before her, there was no question in Mercedes' mind that this was final. Her heart was racing in her chest. She had to get out of this room. But not before she said what she needed to say.

Mercedes kissed her fingertips and touched them to her mother's beautiful face. She whispered, "I love you, Mommy," and then walked to the podium and stepped up to the microphone. She was aware of the questioning looks from her grandparents and her uncles, so Mercedes avoided looking directly at them. Reverend Gibson stood behind her, praying quietly for her as she gripped the podium for support.

Mercedes looked out at all of the mourners and took a deep breath. She let her gaze rest on her Grandma Gladys as she addressed the crowd.

"Thank you all for coming today," she said softly. "My mother always loved being the center of attention."

Uneasy laughter sprinkled across the room. It was true. Sunny would have loved to see the crowd that had gathered to mourn her. Celebrities and ghetto superstars alike were in attendance.

"Most of you know that my dad was killed before I was born," Mercedes continued. "And my brother DJ was very young when it happened. But he remembers that Daddy was handsome, tall, and strong. He always told me that our father was very respected and very powerful. I never got the chance to know him except for the stories that my mother and my grandmother would tell me." She looked at Born. "His friends loved him and looked up to him. He was a great man, from what I've been told."

She glanced over at her mother's body again. "All my life, it was just me and my Mom." Mercedes looked across the crowd and saw Jenny G, Jada, and Olivia. "We had friends and family, of course. But mostly all we had was each other. I always looked up to her. She was so beautiful, so stylish and bold. She never seemed afraid of anybody. She was always in control. I felt safe as long as she was around. I was never one of those kids who was afraid of the monsters under my bed because I knew that Mommy would kick a monster's ass."

People were laughing through their tears despite the crass language Mercedes was using to get her point across. At fourteen, she was wise beyond her years. And she was speaking the gospel truth about the Sunny they all knew and loved.

"When I was about ten years old, she told me that she used to get high." Mercedes paused. The room fell so silent that only the faint whir of the overhead fans were audible. "She wanted me to know so that I wouldn't have to find out the hard way. She didn't want me to be surprised by some kid in school, or some reporter, or magazine. But she swore that she was done with that life. She said that she cleaned up her act after I was born, and she would never go back to doing that." Tears began to stream slowly down Mercedes' face. She took the tissues that Reverend Gibson handed to her, and thanked him softly. "But, she lied," Mercedes continued. "She lied and now she's dead." Mercedes wiped her eyes and blew her nose gently. "Now both of my parents are gone. I have been trying to find the meaning in this." Mercedes looked at Jenny G, who was crying audibly. "Jenny, you told me that Mommy would want me to grow up and be better and stronger than she was. So I have been thinking a lot about how I can make sure that I don't fall into the same trap she did. And this is what I realized." Mercedes took a deep breath. "My father was a great man, according to everyone who knew him. But he lived a life that was dangerous and deadly. He played with people's emotions and it cost him his life. He was killed before he even got the chance to know me. He never got to see my brother become a superstar." She shook her head, disappointed. "My mother was my hero. I wanted to be just like her. But she was living the same dangerous lifestyle as my father. She got addicted to it. Maybe they both did. And it killed her. So if I want to be better than her, stronger than her, I have to avoid making the same mistakes she did."

Mercedes looked over at her family now. Her gaze rested on her uncle Reuben. "I don't want to be like Mommy when I grow up anymore. I want to be my own person. I want to be the kind of person who doesn't need drugs to have a good time. I want to be like my brother DJ, who works hard to chase his dreams. He's not making easy money in the streets. He's using his talent to become successful." She took a deep breath. "A lot of people in this room let my mother down. They can never take that back."

Reuben stared at his hands, convicted. He thought about his pending legal battles, about the role he played in the crew Dorian had introduced him to. His shame wouldn't allow him to resume eye contact with his niece.

Mercedes noticed and looked away, satisfied that she had gotten her point across. "I love Mommy. I miss her. I feel like I have a hole in my heart where she will always be." She choked back a sob. "But I'm so mad at her. I'm mad because she disappointed me and the people who cared about her the most. I'm pissed off because she was still young, and beautiful, and full of life. And now she's gone. All because of some cocaine." Mercedes' anger rose to the surface and mingled with her grief. The toxic combination caused her to cry uncontrollably, her chest heaving as she fought to control her emotions. She pounded her fists on the podium and cried.

Jada was out of her seat before she knew it. She made a beeline for Sunny's daughter, wanting to shield her from the pain, from the public scrutiny, from all of it. Jada reached Mercedes' side and pulled her into an embrace. As she cried into Jada's chest, Mercedes gripped her tightly and finally allowed all of her anguish to pour forth. Jada stroked her back and kissed her gently on the forehead.

"Okay, baby girl," Jada cooed lovingly. "Come on, let's go outside." Jada led Mercedes out of the room and into the vestibule. They sat together on a cushioned bench and Mercedes buried her head in Jada's chest, crying uncontrollably. Jada comforted Mercedes as she cried for her mother and for the father she had never known. While Jada soothed her, Reverend Gibson continued with the program, giving a rousing eulogy. He reiterated that tomorrow is not promised, and urged everyone present to get right with God before it was too late.

Jada listened, while she waited for Mercedes to calm down a little. Once her sobs subsided, Jada pulled away and held the young lady's face in her hands. Jada smiled weakly at her. "I'm so proud of you," she said. "Sunny would be proud of you."

Mercedes sniffled, wondering if what Jada said was true.

"She raised you to see things clearly, and not to be afraid to speak the truth. And that's what you did," Jada said. "What you said was right. We are all disappointed that Sunny messed up. We all miss her, and all of us are pissed off about it. But I don't want you to be so angry that you lose sight of who your mother truly was. Sunny was an incredible woman." Jada wrestled with her emotions. She wanted to cry, but knew that she had to be strong for Mercedes. "She saved my life," Jada said softly. She thought about the night Sunny put a bullet in Jamari's head in a cold, dark parking lot to protect her friend.

Mercedes looked at Jada, questioningly.

Jada shook her head. "I'll tell you that story when you're older. But what I need you to know right now is that she loved you so much, Mercedes. I know that she never would have gone into that bathroom and did what she did if she thought for one moment that it would cost her a lifetime with you."

Mercedes blinked back her tears. She knew it was true. As mad as she was at her mother, she knew that Sunny hadn't left her behind intentionally. But that did little to soothe her pain.

"I miss her so much," Mercedes whispered.

Jada nodded. "So do I," she said.

"I'm so mad at my family. My grandparents, my uncles. They all let her get caught up in that life because they all benefited from it." Mercedes had learned a lot about the family dynamic over the past week. She didn't like it one bit. "My grandparents practically sold her off."

"That's not true," Jada said gently. "They made mistakes, there's no question. But they loved her, Mercedes. Sometimes parents make mistakes that cost us dearly. But that doesn't mean that they don't love us." Jada thought of her own mother as she said that. She knew that Edna had done the best she could at the time. Forgiveness hadn't come easily, though.

Mercedes nodded. She did believe that Sunny was loved by her parents and siblings. But she didn't want to end up the way that her mother had. Mercedes was determined to go and live with her Grandma Gladys. If only for a little while, she needed to put some distance between herself and the family who had enabled Sunny right up to the grave.

"It's going to be hard to go on without her," Mercedes said softly.

Jada nodded. "But we still have each other." She smiled. "God didn't give me a daughter, and I doubt that I will be having any more children. So now you can consider me your surrogate mom. I will stand in for Sunny and you can call me whenever you need me. Sunny will always be with us, just like Dorian always has been. And I will be there for you the same way that Born has stepped up to be there for DJ. I promise you that, Mercedes. You're not by yourself."

Mercedes couldn't express her gratitude in words. Instead, she threw her arms around Jada's shoulders and hugged her tightly. Jada held her close and together they returned to the service.

The funeral directors were beginning to guide the crowd on one final processional past Sunny's casket. While a soloist sang "Over the Rainbow" in the style of Patti LaBelle, Jada took Mercedes by the hand and led her up to the front of the line. Born remained seated, watching them. Mercedes broke down, her body heaving with the sobs that rose up and overtook her. Jada comforted her as she cried, and then led her past the line of mourners. Born stood and walked over to join them, and together they led Mercedes outside to one of the waiting limousines which would take them to the cemetery.

Olivia stood looking down at Sunny's body, crying not just for the loss of one of her dearest friends, but for the end of what had once upon a time been one big family. None of them would ever be the same again. Sunny was gone for good, and so were the good old days. As Lamin ushered her out to their waiting car, the other mourners filed past until only Sunny's family remained.

Dale helped Marisol to her feet. She looked as if she had aged years in the few days since Sunny had passed away. Sunny's mother looked frail, exhausted, and heartbroken as she was helped to her feet by Dale and Ronnie. Reuben followed them to the coffin. A long, gut-wrenching wail escaped Marisol as she collapsed in front of her daughter's coffin, falling into her husband's arms in hysterics.

"Dios mio!" she wailed. "My God!"

Dale and his sons formed a circle around Marisol, coaxing her to breathe and to calm down. But all of them were overcome by their grief in varying ways. Ronnie stood helplessly with tears streaming down his face. Reuben stroked his mother's back while fighting back tears of his own. Dale, meanwhile, comforted his wife. All the while, he could still hear his granddaughter's words echoing on repeat in his head. *A lot of people in this room let my mother down.* Dale knew that his name was at the top of that list.

By the time they returned home from the repast, Born and Jada were both incredibly drained. Ava and Sheldon were in the living room watching a movie. Jada and Born sat down and gave them the rundown of how the day had gone.

"Sunny looked so peaceful," Born said. "All I kept thinking was that hopefully her and Dorian are together again now."

Jada nodded and they all sat in silence for some time, lost in thought.

Sheldon cleared his throat. "Can I go call Mercedes?" he asked.

Jada nodded, thinking that a call from Sheldon might be exactly what Mercedes needed. She and Born had attended the funeral repast at Gillian's Midtown restaurant *Conga*. As they were leaving, Jada noticed Mercedes sitting in a corner with her friend Adiva. Although the two girls were close, Jada knew that a special bond existed between Sheldon and Mercedes. She was certain that a call from Sheldon would be a welcome distraction for Sunny's daughter.

"Go ahead."

Sheldon got up and went upstairs to his room, where he could talk to Mercedes in private. She was the one person who could get through to him when he was at his lowest, and now he hoped to have the same effect on her.

Born's cell phone vibrated, and he reached into his pocket. He saw Anisa's name flash across the screen, and dismissed the call. This wasn't a good time to talk to her, since Jada was still so upset after burying her best friend. Before he could put the phone back in his pocket, it vibrated again. Anisa had called him right back. He frowned. That wasn't like her. One of Anisa's strongest attributes was her ability to take a hint.

Jada noticed and made eye contact with him. "Maybe it's important," she said, assuming that Anisa was the persistent caller. "You should answer it."

Born felt bad, aware that Anisa was still a point of contention for Jada. Reluctantly, he hit the green button on his phone and was immediately met with the sound of Anisa crying and yelling hysterically.

"Ethan is missing!" she yelled. "Somebody came in here and took him!"

Born shot to his feet. "Calm down! What happened?" His heart was galloping in his chest.

Jada and Ava looked on, confused, as Born was clearly agitated.

Anisa could barely catch her breath. "Oh my God, Born!" Anisa fought to get the words out. "He was downstairs playing his video game. I finished working out, and I went to get in the shower. I was just about to get out of the shower when I heard the doorbell ring. So I shut off the water and wrapped a towel around me. When I got out, I called down to Ethan, but he didn't answer me. I came down here to look for him and the front door is wide open. One of his sneakers is on the front porch, and he's gone! Oh my God!" Anisa was crying uncontrollably. "Somebody has my son!"

Born felt like he was going to have a heart attack. "Anisa, I called you after I left Maury's office yesterday. I told you not to leave Ethan alone—"

"Don't act like this shit is my fault, Born!" Anisa was hysterical. "I just took a fucking shower!" She felt lightheaded. She sat down on the chaise and took a deep breath. "If this shit has anything to do with Jada, I'm going to kill her myself." Anisa's voice was steady. She meant every word.

"Okay, okay." Born took a deep breath, willing himself to calm down. He paced the floor. "Listen," he said. "I'm on my way. Don't call the police."

Anisa unleashed a fury of curse words so powerful that Born held the phone away from his ear.

"If you call the cops, he's gonna hurt him!" The thought of that made Born's hands tremble involuntarily. "Just wait until I get there!"

Jada was on her feet now. Ava was looking like she'd seen a ghost.

"I'm on my way," Born said again. He clicked off the phone and looked at Jada with fear in his eyes. "Somebody took Ethan," he said.

Ava gasped and jumped to her feet. Jada and Born exchanged knowing glances. "You think it's him?" Jada asked, referring to the stranger who had been tormenting them.

Before he could respond, Born's phone vibrated loudly. The caller ID read "private." He answered, and collapsed on the couch at the sound of Ethan's scared voice.

"Dad?" Ethan sounded petrified. "Dad, can you come and get me?"

"Where are you?" Born asked breathlessly.

But he was met by the voice of his son's captor. The same voice of the man he had encountered in the McDonald's bathroom. "I warned you, Born," the man said. "No cops. You didn't keep your end of the bargain."

"What are you talking about? Nobody went to the cops. Bring my son back home." Born couldn't get his words out fast enough.

"I'm smarter than you give me credit for," the man said. "I told you the rules, and you didn't listen."

Born frowned. "You got your information wrong. We were at a funeral all day. We just got back. For the last time, nobody spoke to the cops."

"There are police outside of Jada's house right now," the man said. "Just because they aren't sitting in a squad car doesn't mean that I can't recognize police when I see them. And I specifically said 'no cops'."

Born shot a look at Ava, who was sitting across from him with a strange look on her face. "Cops at Jada's house?" he repeated.

Ava hung her head in her hands.

"Now the game is going to be played differently," the man said. "I do not want to hurt your son. But if I don't have the money you owe me by tomorrow, you will never see this kid again. I promise you that."

"I'll get you your money," Born said anxiously "Just bring my son back safe."

"I will call you back with instructions."

The line went dead. Born roared with frustration. He barreled down on Ava, demanding answers.

"Why is this muthafucka telling me there's cops outside?" he demanded.

Ava was crying. "I thought I was helping," she said. "I just called a friend of mine who's a detective. I thought he could put some undercovers outside to look out for anyone suspicious."

Ava's tears did little to quell Born's fury. He took off his sling and threw it across the room in frustration.

"I was just trying to help," Ava pleaded. "I know that you can't go to the police, but this is crazy. The man detonated a bomb at your house. He attacked Jada at the hospital. He's sending threatening messages, approaching you in the street. I just wanted to do whatever I could to end this."

Born wanted to strangle her. "I *told* you that all of us are being watched. And I specifically said that we can't involve the police. Why the fuck would you go behind my back and call some detective to do some half-assed stakeout?"

Ava shook her head. "I thought that whoever it is would be following you and Jada, instead of watching the house. I thought—"

"Fuck what you thought, Ava!" Born's voice thundered. "Now this man has my son!"

Ava wanted to die. "I'm so sorry, Born. I was just trying to help."

Born blew out a heavy breath and dialed Maury's number, frantically. As soon as he answered, Born dove in, telling him that Ethan had been kidnapped after Ava had been foolish enough to think that she could outsmart the mystery man.

As he spoke with Maury, Jada's phone rang. She picked up the private call and was met by a sinister laugh. "Hello, my darling, Jada." The voice was familiar. For a moment, Jada's heart seized in her chest. She thought it sounded like Jamari back from the dead. She was reminded of the nightmares she'd been having about Jamari taunting her from the grave. But as the caller continued speaking, she realized that it wasn't Jamari at all. Instead, it was another voice from her past.

"Are you ready to give me what you owe me?"

Instantly, she knew who the kidnapper was.

"Elliot!" she said, breathlessly. She looked at Born, everything suddenly making sense.

"Ah, you remember," he said. "It's been a very long time."

Jada clung to the phone, speechless.

"You cost me dearly," Elliot sneered. "You stole my drugs, and then you sent the police after me."

Jada shook her head. "No! No I didn't. That wasn't me who tipped them off."

Elliot wasn't trying to hear her. "They killed my brother and two of my cousins in that raid."

Jada squeezed her eyes shut in despair. This whole thing was a nightmare. Elliot was the Guyanese drug distributor who supplied Jamari and his cohorts with cocaine back in the day. Jada had double-crossed Elliot and Jamari when she stole the drugs that she was supposed to deliver to Jamari, and sold it herself instead. That money had given her the freedom to get away from Jamari once and for all. It was the money that Jamari had come for when he ambushed Jada in a parking lot, resulting in Sunny blowing his brain out in defense of her friend. The newspapers had said that Elliot, too, had been killed in a gun battle with the police all those years ago. As if reading her thoughts, Elliot spoke again.

"The newspapers claimed that I was dead. But it was my younger brother that they turned into Swiss cheese. He looked just like me, and for that he paid with his life. While he was shooting it out with them, I was lucky enough to escape with just a bullet in my back. But then I had to go underground. So far underground, in fact, that I had to leave the U.S. I never even got to bury my brother. Do you know how that feels, Jada? To lose somebody close to you and never get the chance to say good-bye?"

Jada held the phone in silence. She couldn't believe this was happening. Elliot was alive. He knew what she had done. And he had Ethan.

Elliot continued. "Years later, I snuck back into the country, and I went looking for Jamari. I believed that he crossed me. But he was already dead by the time I came back to the U.S." Elliot chuckled at that. He had searched high and low for Jamari, only to find that someone else had beaten him to the punch. "I thought that was the end of it. But then I heard that you are a big-time author now. People told me that you wrote a book about your life as a hustler's wife. Imagine my surprise when I got my hands on your book."

"Elliot, that story isn't true. It's just a book," Jada interrupted.

Elliot laughed. "Your character double-crossed the distributor and sold the drugs to some dealers she knew from way back when. And it just so happened to be the exact same amount of drugs that you stole from me. That's when I realized that Jamari might not have been the guilty one. Did you give my drugs to Born to sell for you?"

"No!" Jada insisted. "I'm telling you that story is not true. Born has nothing to do with this." Jada felt like she was going to self-destruct. It made perfect sense now. Aware that Born used to be a hustler and that Jada loved him, Elliot assumed that he had been in on her scheme all along. It explained why he targeted Born with the bomb at his house, why he approached him at Mc-Donalds and kidnapped his son.

"I thought you were so sweet, Jada," Elliot continued. "You were so young and soft-spoken. I'll admit that I never thought you had it in you. I thought Jamari put you up to it. But the more I dug into your background, the more I learned who you really are. You are a crackhead. And everybody knows a crackhead can't be trusted. You stole my drugs and sold them so that you could get high. And now look at you, Jada." Elliot chuckled sinisterly.

"Jamari is dead, and you got away scot-free. You and your boyfriend are living on top of the world at my expense."

Her hands trembled from the shock of all of this.

"I tried to give you the benefit of the doubt. I thought to myself, *No one is stupid enough to try and cross me.* But you surprised me, Jada. You took my kindness for weakness. So now it's time to pay up. I called you now because I want you to know who you're dealing with. Do not play with me. I want my fucking money. And if I don't get it, I'm going to kill this kid. And then I'm coming for you, bitch."

Elliot hung up. Jada stared at Born in silence, with tears of terror streaming down her face.

"Oh my God," she said. "This is all my fault."

18

RESURRECTION

Born felt powerless. He stood in the living room at Anisa's place, watching her fall apart, and there was nothing he could say or do to make it better. Ethan had been gone for three hours, and with every minute that ticked by Born and Anisa became more anxious. He walked over to where Anisa sat on the sofa and sat down beside her. He pulled her close to him, and held her, comfortingly. Anisa held onto Born for dear life and cried into his chest, her sobs rocking her.

"I'm gonna find him," Born said. "I'm gonna bring him back."

Anisa wanted to trust him. God, she did. But the longer he was gone, the harder it was for her to believe that the outcome would be positive. She pulled away and looked at Born.

"How can you be so calm?" she asked. "That bitch is the reason our son is missing. If anything happens to Ethan, I will kill Jada myself."

Born shook his head. "It's not her fault." Before he could say another word, Anisa lunged at him, scratching, kicking, and punching at him wildly. He held his good arm up to fend off her blows, but it did little to shield him from her vicious attack. Hearing the melee, Miss Ingrid rushed into the room and pulled Anisa off of her son.

"Calm down!" Miss Ingrid demanded. "What the hell are you hitting him for?"

Born stood up and put some distance between him and Anisa. She had hit him hard in the face, busting open his lip. He touched it gingerly, the metallic taste of blood on his tongue.

"It's okay," he said to his mother. "She's upset."

Anisa was far more than upset. She had had enough of Jada. "How fucking *dare* you sit here and defend her after she got our son into this mess? This man is after *her*! He has a problem with Jada, and he's taking it out on your child. And all you can say is this ain't her fault? This *IS* her fault, Born! She owes him money, and she got his brother killed. Why didn't he kidnap her crazy-ass son?"

"Anisa—" Born tried to reason with her.

She wasn't having it. "If anything happens to Ethan, I am going to—"

"*Listen!*" Miss Ingrid interrupted Anisa's tirade. "That's not gonna bring Ethan home. Now just calm down and let's figure out what we can do to get him back."

Anisa sucked her teeth and walked off to sulk in a corner. She was distraught over Ethan's abduction. Hearing that Jada was the reason for all of this, and having Born defend her was just too much for her to accept.

"Anisa," Born said, softly. "I'm not defending anybody. I'm just as pissed off as you are. All I want to do now is make sure that he doesn't hurt Ethan. I just want to get him back home safe and sound. I need your help, though. Please."

Anisa stared out the window.

"Don't go to the police," he pleaded. "Just let me get the money together and I will go and get Ethan back."

Anisa shook her head in dismay. She cried softly. "I keep thinking about how scared he must be," she said. "He's just a kid. He doesn't deserve this."

Born closed his eyes, trying not to imagine that. He hadn't let himself think of what Ethan must be going through. The thought of it was enough to drive him insane.

Anisa turned and glared at Born. "You've put him through so much," she hissed. "Exposing him to that crazy bastard Sheldon."

"Anisa, don't talk about him like that. He's a child," Miss Ingrid said, chastising her.

"Oh, give me a break!" Anisa frowned. "He drowned a damn dog in your bathtub. He took an overdose of prescription pills. The kid is crazy." She turned back to Born. "And his mother is an ex-crackhead with skeletons coming out of her closet left and right. Now Ethan is with some crazy man who has a vendetta against Jada. A man who is threatening to kill him if you don't pay him what *she* owes him plus a shitload of interest. And I'm just supposed to be okay with not involving the police. I'm supposed to trust you. *You?* The same man who lets Jada toy with him like a damn yo-yo, pulling you into her life one minute and pushing you out the next." Anisa shook her head again. "You're pathetic. Any love I still had for you is gone now. And if Ethan gets hurt because of you and your bitch, I will never forgive you."

She stormed out, leaving Born and his mother reeling in her wake.

Jada handed a mug of tea to her sister. Ava hadn't stopped crying since the phone call from Elliot. She felt so bad, knowing that her attempt to help had backfired so terribly. It was late, but none of them could sleep. Sheldon sat on the couch playing Xbox, and Jada didn't even mind since it allowed her to keep an eye on him. Ethan's abduction had put them all on edge.

Jada sat down near her sister and sipped her own tea. "Stop crying," Jada said, sternly. "It's gonna be okay."

Ava sniffed. "How do you know?" Ava was devastated. "If anything happens to that little boy, his blood will be on my hands."

Jada set down her mug. "I know that we're gonna get him back safely. God answers prayers. He won't let anything happen to that innocent little boy. Ethan is going to be fine." Jada was trying hard to convince herself that it was true. She had spent the past few hours pooling all of her financial resources. She certainly didn't have a million dollars. Neither did Born. But they had some savings, a few assets, and a lot of favors that they could call in. Ava had already offered them every penny that she had to her name. DJ, too, had assured Born that he could have anything he needed without question. Jada was certain that they could get the money together in time. The only question was whether or not Elliot intended to keep his word.

"Ma, is Born coming back?" Sheldon asked. He had set the game controller down, and was sitting with his chin resting on the arm of the sofa.

Jada looked at her son. "Yes," she said. She tried not to think about the fact that Born was over at Anisa's house comforting her. Especially since they had only recently been intimate again. To add to the problem, it was Jada's own fault that Elliot was terrorizing them. She reminded herself that she and Born were back on track, and she silently reassured herself that he was not reuniting with Anisa in the midst of their grief.

Sheldon could tell that this situation was serious. He had been instructed not to answer the door or the phone under any circumstances. He was not to go outside or log on to the Internet without an adult present. He had been told that Ethan was missing, but he could tell that this was not the type of random disappearance like he saw on television shows. From the way that Aunt Ava was crying and carrying on, it was clear that this situation had several layers.

Born returned with a downtrodden demeanor. He had left

Anisa locked inside of her home like a fortress. His mother had agreed to stay in Anisa's spare room until Ethan returned. It served a dual purpose, ensuring that no one in their family was left alone for the night. Born reasoned that there was strength in numbers. Even though Anisa hated his guts right now, he wanted to make sure that she was safe. Ethan's return was enough to worry about.

Jada went to him, unsure whether he was in the mood for her presence right now. She knew that somewhere deep down inside, Born blamed her for this. After all, she was the one who had stolen from Elliot. His beef was with her, not with Born or his family. Still, Born pulled Jada into his arms and held her close for several wordless moments. Jada was grateful for his love, even at a time like this.

Sheldon watched them, a dozen unasked questions languishing below the surface. Born noticed him sitting there, and had to fight back his resentment. Sheldon had singlehandedly wreaked havoc on their family, and yet Ethan was the one being traumatized by some disgruntled associate from Jada's past. It was hard not to wish that the kidnapper had chosen a different kid.

Born pushed down those feelings, and greeted Sheldon and Ava. Then he plopped down on the couch and kicked off his sneakers.

Sheldon stared at him for a while before he found the nerve to speak up. "Born, is Ethan gonna be okay?"

Born let out a long sigh. He nodded. "Yeah. I'm gonna make sure he's okay." Born looked at Sheldon and forced a smile. "I'm gonna make sure you're okay, too."

Sheldon was happy to hear that. He was too tough to admit that he was scared. But he was. Ethan's disappearance had unsettled him, and for the first time he was happy that Born was there with them. Having him around, even with his arm in a sling, made him feel more at ease. He picked up the Xbox controller and resumed his game.

Ava glanced sheepishly at Born. "I'm sorry, Born. I know you probably hate me right now—"

"I don't hate you."

"I just wanted to try and help catch this bastard. I never expected anything like this to happen." Ava's eyes misted at the thought of Ethan suffering at the hands of a crazy stranger.

Born shook his head. "I know. It's gonna be okay." He laid back his head against the sofa, a headache creeping up on him.

Jada watched him. "How is Anisa?" As much as she despised Anisa, her heart went out to her. No mother should have to go through what Anisa was dealing with.

Born shook his head. "Not good."

Silence lingered. Ava decided to be the one to cut the tension. "I'm going to bed," she said. "Sheldon, why don't you come upstairs with me? Let's give these two some time to themselves. It's been a long day."

Sheldon didn't argue. He placed the controller on the coffee table and stood up to follow his aunt upstairs. "Good night."

Born and Jada watched them go, and Jada sat beside Born on the couch. She didn't know how to approach him. There was no manual for dealing with things like this. She wasn't sure whether to hug him, or hold his hand, or leave him alone.

Sensing her hesitation, Born looked at her. Despite everything they had been through, he loved Jada so much. "Come here," he said.

Jada scooted closer to him, and laid her head on his shoulder. Born scooped her into the crook of his arm and kissed her forehead.

"It's gonna be alright," he said.

Jada exhaled deeply. "Baby, I'm sorry."

"It's not your fault. Not Ava's fault either. The only person to blame is the muthafucka who did this." Born couldn't bring himself to say Elliot's name. It filled him with an unhealthy rage.

"But this keeps happening. There's always some reminder from my past of who I used to be. It doesn't stop. Charlie, Shante, now Elliot. Plus Sheldon and his nonsense." Jada looked up at Born. "I know you're having second thoughts about being with me."

Born frowned. "Who said that?"

"You don't have to say it. Anyone in your shoes would feel that way."

Born thought about it. "I knew all about your history when I fell in love with you. I might not like it, but I accept it. You made some mistakes, Jada. That don't give nobody the right to do this to you and your family." He looked at her seriously. "I'm gonna kill this dude," he said. "I'm gonna play this little game with him, and I'm gonna get my son back. Then I'm gonna blow his fucking brains out."

Jada watched him closely. She knew that he meant every word.

Born pulled her closer to him and kissed her lips. "I'm gonna handle this. And if somebody else pops up, I'll handle them, too."

Jada felt her heart overflowing. She was a lucky woman. "I love you."

Born looked her in the eyes. "I love you, too, baby. Nothing from your past is gonna change that."

They sat together on the sofa, wrapped in each other's arms, until they both drifted off to sleep.

Elliot watched Ethan closely. The kid was scared, that much was clear. He had cried himself to sleep, and if Elliot wasn't so evil, it might have tugged at his heartstrings. But his rage toward Jada superseded his pity for the kid.

Elliot was furious with Jada. Ever since he'd returned to the U.S. and reconnected with what remained of his old crew, he'd been obsessed with recouping his losses. Truth be told, Jada had made a fool out of him and Elliot had never gotten over it.

Back when he was Jamari's distributor, Elliot had truly liked Jada. She reminded him of his baby sister, a hustler at heart. When Jada had come to him with her plea for five bricks of cocaine, he had allowed himself to be swayed by his sympathy for her. He had always known that Jamari wasn't cut out for the life he was living. Jada seemed like a woman who had gotten caught up with a lame and found herself in an unfortunate predicament. Elliot had given her those five bricks mostly out of compassion. So when he returned to New York and found out that it had been Jada herself who robbed him, he felt particularly naïve. It had been one of the few times he allowed his heart to overrule his mind. He was determined that it would never happen again.

He left the room and went into the kitchen. Retrieving a beer from the fridge, he sat down at the table across from his nephew, Cheo.

Cheo had mixed feelings about his uncle's return. More than ten years had passed since the DEA raid that forced Elliot to go on the run. A lot had changed since then, namely the way they handled things. The eighties and nineties had been a wild time on the streets of NYC. Their crime family had boldly violated anyone who dared to challenge them. They had shot it out in broad daylight with the police and rival crews alike. What Elliot couldn't seem to get through his head was that situations like this were no longer acceptable. The goal was to stay off the police's radar. Kidnapping was not the way to achieve that.

"When are you gonna bring him home?" Cheo asked, gesturing with his chin toward the room where Ethan lay sleeping.

Elliot ignored the question. He didn't like this new version of his nephew. The kid he'd left behind years ago when he'd gone on the run had developed into a young man who didn't seem to respect Elliot's position any longer. Back in the day, Cheo never would have dreamed of questioning Elliot. Clearly, he'd forgotten the established hierarchy.

"I'm thinking about staying in New York after all," Elliot said.

Cheo frowned. That wasn't part of the plan. Elliot's visit was supposed to be just that—a visit. He was supposed to stay for a few weeks at most. Cheo had been counting on the fact that his uncle would be returning to Guyana soon.

"I don't think that's a good idea," Cheo said.

"I didn't ask you what you thought." Elliot guzzled his beer, then tossed the empty can in the trash.

Cheo noted that his uncle didn't use the recyclables trash can, but decided against commenting on it. "I'm just saying that it's not safe for you here, Uncle Elliot. I don't want the cops to find out that you're back. You know they got it in for you."

After Elliot's escape, the heat had been turned up on their crew big-time. Cheo's father had borne a striking resemblance to his brother, Elliot. After the gory bloodbath between the DEA and their crew, the cops had prematurely declared that they had taken down one of NYC's most notorious and ruthless drug czars. By the time lab tests determined that the dead guy was not Elliot after all, the story had been too widely circulated to retract. The police commissioner was worried about being labeled an imbecile. Helped by the fact that the real Elliot had disappeared, the police kept mum about the dead man's real identity and turned their attention to taking down what remained of the crew. It had been years before they were able to operate effectively again. And now, over a decade later, here was Uncle Elliot, back from the dead with a kidnapped minor and an extortion plot, and now it seemed he had plans to stick around.

Elliot let out a loud belch and shrugged. "I'm dead, remember?"

Cheo shook his head. "You know you can only stay underground for so long. These streets talk." Cheo felt like Elliot had forgotten what it was like to run a criminal enterprise on the streets of New York City. Word traveled fast, and it wouldn't be long before Elliot's return was heralded widely. In fact, Cheo felt that his uncle had already overstayed his welcome.

Elliot leaned forward and stared Cheo down. "All these years that I spent back home, I had nothing but time to think. I left a lot of money out here in these streets."

Cheo nodded. "Which is why there's a lot of people who won't be too happy to see that you're back."

Elliot sneered. "Good." He noticed Cheo roll his eyes in frustration. "Listen," Elliot said. "I'm gonna get what's mine. Starting with my little insurance policy in there. Once I get rid of him and Jada and that nigga Born, everyone will know that I'm not the one to fuck with. After that, I'm going to check them all off my list, one by one, until I have everything that's owed to me. I'm taking back my spot at the head of this crew." He smirked at Cheo. "You'd be smart not to get in my way."

Cheo eyed Elliot, but dared not respond. Elliot stood up from the table and pulled his gun from his waistband. "I'm gonna off this kid. Then, when I get the money from Jada tomorrow, I'm gonna put one in her head, too."

Cheo grimaced. He didn't believe that Elliot meant what he said. Not until he watched him march toward the bedroom where the kid was sleeping. Elliot cocked the gun as he walked.

Cheo sprang to his feet. Trotting after his uncle, he followed him into the bedroom. Elliot pointed the nozzle of the gun directly at Ethan's temple, but Cheo slapped his hand away just in the nick of time. A shot went off, the bullet lodging in the wall next to Ethan's head. The round woke him up with a start. Seeing the two men standing over him—one with a gun in his hand—Ethan began to cry instantly. He had never been more afraid in his life. The two men were arguing now. Ethan's body quaked with terror. He shrunk into the corner of the bed, which was pushed up against the wall and cried softly, trembling.

"Yo, Elliot, what the fuck! I respect you as my uncle. But you're bugging right now."

Elliot still had the gun in his hand and he seemed none too pleased that Cheo was challenging him. Cheo perceived the glint in his eyes and changed his tone a bit.

"If you splatter shorty's brains in here, all of that DNA evidence gets spread throughout the whole room." Cheo forced his voice to register lighter. Now more than ever, he could see that his ruthless uncle had gone off the deep end. "Just take him out tomorrow and do what you gotta do in the woods somewhere. Just don't do it in here."

Elliot seemed to consider it for several long, tense moments. Finally, he nodded slowly, grinning. "You're right," he said. "I watch *Forensic Files*, too. That DNA shit never completely disappears. He chuckled a little and, with the gun still in his hand, Elliot patted his nephew affectionately on the head.

Cheo cringed, but kept silent. Ethan continued crying softly in the corner. Elliot winked at Cheo. Finally, he tucked the gun back into his waistband. He looked at Ethan.

"Tomorrow, then."

Elliot left the room.

Cheo watched his uncle leave and knew without question that he intended to kill the little boy. He wondered if Elliot might kill him, too, for good measure. Family or not, he was crazy. Cheo glanced at Ethan and felt sorry for him. Cheo had been around Ethan's age when his own father had died in Elliot's place. He cleared his throat.

"It's alright, Shorty. Ain't nothing gonna happen tonight. Go back to sleep."

Cheo left the room, shutting the door behind him. Ethan stared at the closed door with his heart galloping full speed in his chest. He squeezed his eyes shut tightly and prayed with all of his might.

19

HOMECOMING

Zion stepped off the elevator and walked the long corridor toward his attorney's office. He was relieved to be free. After weeks of hard work, Maury had gotten him another bail hearing. Once the media hype around the mass arrests began to die down in favor of more scandalous headlines, Maury brought Zion back before the judge, and he was granted bail under very strict conditions. The prosecution argued that Zion was a flight risk, so the judge forced him to surrender his passport. The DA was also concerned about Zion continuing to run the crew while out on bail. So the judge ordered that Zion wear an electronic ankle monitor and adhere to a curfew. The judge set bail high at one million dollars, and the DA still wasn't satisfied. He requested a bail-source hearing to ensure that the money used to bail Zion out did not come from illegal means. Gillian and Lamin had stepped up and put up their financial records as proof that the bail money hadn't come from a questionable source. Finally, after all of that, Zion was free to leave the madhouse that was Riker's Island. Maury had sent a car and driver to pick him up from the Queens jail and deliver him to his office in Lower Manhattan.

Zion strolled toward the office, wearing a simple white button-up and a pair of cargo pants from Old Navy—definitely not his usual attire. Maury's secretary had sent the outfit to Riker's so that Zion would have something decent to come home in. His clothes that he'd worn the night of his arrest were covered in blood and dirt as a result of his beating. Those clothes were now evidence in the case Maury was filing against the NYPD.

Zion couldn't wait to go home and take a hot shower—alone. The past few weeks in jail had been hellish. He intended to take full advantage of all of the luxuries he had once taken for granted.

As Zion neared the office, Maury stepped out and smiled warmly at him.

"Welcome back," Maury said. He shook Zion's hand firmly.

"Thanks." Zion's smile was thanks enough.

"Remember, stay home, stay out of trouble, stay out of the spotlight," Maury said.

Zion nodded. "That's exactly what I plan to do."

Maury patted him encouragingly on the arm. "Go on in," he said. "Take all the time you need."

Zion watched Maury walk away. Then he opened the office door, and stepped inside. He smiled at the sight of Gillian and Lamin seated before him. They returned the gesture, and Lamin stood up and greeted his friend with a firm handshake and a hug.

"Welcome home, Zion." Lamin was beaming. He and Zion had been friends since they were teenagers. Although Lamin was aware of what was going on between Olivia and Zion, their friendship remained intact. Relationships had their ups and downs, and Lamin knew better than anybody that Olivia could be a lot to handle. Despite all of that, he was happy to see that Zion was once again a free man.

"Yo," Zion said, shaking his head. "I feel like doing the moon-walk, I'm so happy! Thank you for everything you did to help me get out."

Lamin nodded. "No doubt. But all I did was sign some paperwork and say the right things in a hearing." He aimed his chin at Gillian. "That's who you should be thanking."

Perched regally on her seat, with her legs crossed daintily, Gillian's eyes sparkled like the diamonds on her wrist when she smiled at Zion. He walked over toward her and she stood up to greet him. He hugged her tightly. "Thank you," he said sincerely. "Thank you for everything, Gillian. I mean that."

Gillian pulled back and looked him in the eye. "You okay?" she asked, her voice full of sincere concern.

He nodded. "I'm fine," he said. "But I think we have a problem."

Gillian agreed. "We do. Have a seat." She gestured toward the chair across from her. Zion sat. Gillian and Lamin followed suit.

Lamin spoke first. "Okay, so let me state the obvious. We're meeting here for a few reasons. First, it makes sense that you would go to your lawyer's office straight after your release. They'll be tracking your every move with that ankle monitor. So when this address comes up, it won't raise any red flags."

Zion nodded. "Makes sense."

"Second, any conversation between you and your lawyer is considered privileged and confidential. So you can speak freely here."

"It's probably the only place where we can speak freely at this point," Gillian agreed.

"The final reason," Lamin said. "Is that it's not safe for you two to be seen together. For some reason, nobody has linked Gillian to the crew. The feds know all kinds of other shit about the family. But there's no spotlight on Gillian right now, and it's best to keep it that way."

Zion nodded again. "Yeah, I've been wondering about that," he said.

Gillian frowned slightly. "What?"

Lamin noticed Zion hesitate. Immediately, he understood where Zion was coming from.

Zion cleared his throat. He sat forward in his chair and looked

Gillian in the eye. "I spent a lot of time thinking while I was locked down," he said. "Basically, with the exception of like . . . maybe four or five people, the whole crew got swept up in raids that night. All of us got hit with big charges. Everybody but you, G."

She stared back at him, but didn't respond.

"They got me down on paper as the kingpin of this family. And that's not how it is."

Lamin smirked a little.

Zion continued. "At first I thought they were just trying to shake me up. All of us, really. Trying to see who would get scared and start telling. But then they started telling me what they already know. And they know a lot."

"Like what?" Gillian asked.

Zion was old school. Law office or not, he was being careful. Much of what had gone down was common knowledge within the family. He didn't feel it necessary to get into specifics. He cleared his throat. "Like a lot of old shit. That guy on the jury that time. The situation with Danno. They know about the Russians. And Grant. About your Pops passing over Baron to pick somebody else to take over the crew when he died. I don't know why, but they think he chose me. They know too much for it to just be the result of an investigation. There's a snitch."

Gillian stared back at him. Secretly, her heart was racing. Though composed outwardly, inside she was shaken. She remembered what her father taught her. As a little girl, she watched him closely, awestruck by the way that he made grown men tremble, men twice his size. He was powerful. He commanded respect. She had asked him once how he did it.

Doug Nobles, a strong and handsome man, had looked down at his daughter and smiled: *"Focus. No matter what is going on around you, no matter who's in the room. You have to watch them. You have to learn how to read people, how to sense their intent. You have to listen. And only speak when necessary. Then, when you do speak, everybody listens."*

Gillian stared at Zion. She saw the smirk on Lamin's face, subtle as it was. She tilted her head to the side and frowned a little. "Do you think it's me, Zion? You think I'm the snitch?"

Zion shook his head. "No. I don't believe you're built like that. You're your father's child."

Gillian nodded. So did Lamin.

"You think it's Baron?" she asked.

Zion didn't answer. Lamin stared at the drink in his hand. Silence descended like a plane coming in for a landing. Tension filled the room until finally Lamin cleared his throat and spoke.

"Let's tell the truth," he said. "Baron didn't inherit his father's character, his work ethic, and sense of honor. But you did." He looked Gillian in the eye. "You're the female version of your father."

Gillian took that as the highest compliment.

"Baron is a different story," Zion said.

Lamin sat back in his seat. "Somebody's been talking."

Gillian's mind reeled. "And now all of the major players are locked up. Except me."

"Okay, so let's start there. Why not you?" Lamin asked. "Who would snitch on everyone else but leave you out?"

"Baron," Zion suggested softly.

Lamin winced a little. Although Gillian and Baron weren't close, they were still siblings. Lamin understood family loyalty all too well. In fact, it had been Doug Nobles' downfall. It was common knowledge that Baron was toxic, troublesome.

Gillian didn't even blink at the suggestion. She sat there for a moment, then slowly nodded.

"That's possible," she said honestly. "Only problem is, why wouldn't he throw me to the wolves, too? It's not like I'm his favorite person. He could get rid of me for good if he gave them the information that he has."

Zion nodded. "True."

"How about Olivia?" she countered. Glancing at Lamin, apologetically, she shrugged. "Sorry, Lamin. I know she's your sister and you love her, but she is mean as hell."

Lamin didn't respond, but he knew Gillian was right. Olivia was mean. Still, he didn't suspect her of turning on the family like that.

Gillian continued, addressing Zion. "You said she was nagging you to get out of the game. You've been screwing her so-called friend. Maybe she decided to get payback."

Zion shook his head. "I mean . . . anything is possible. But I just can't see that. Olivia don't hate me. She's just a little mad right now. That's gonna pass."

Lamin nodded. "Sister or not, I would bet my life on Olivia. She's not your snitch."

"Anybody else?" Gillian asked. Ever since the crew had gotten locked up, she had been wracking her brain trying to understand how the hell it happened. If she thought about it enough, there were possible motives everywhere she looked.

Lamin seemed to agree. "I think it could be anybody else, and that's the problem. Is there enough to get everybody out, and see who does what?"

Gillian nodded. "Zion was the only one held without bail. Now that we got that out of the way, I'm ready to get the rest of them out." She looked at Zion. "I wanted to talk to you first. And I couldn't get to you in there."

Zion seemed to grasp the magnitude of what she was saying. But just to make it clear, she said, "I trust you, Zion."

He nodded, gratefully. "It's mutual."

"I feel like my father had a stronger team in the family's heyday. Dorian, Frankie, Born, Grant. And Zion, you were a part of that team, too. I feel like . . . out of everybody who's left in this shit, I trust you the most."

Zion blushed a little. Gillian noticed.

"And it's not a sexual thing, either. 'Cuz you're fine as hell, but Olivia's crazy. I heard about how she did Jada's little sister dirty at the courthouse."

They all shared a little laugh at Ava's expense.

"Anyway, your apartment is probably destroyed. Maury arranged for you to go home and box up what you can. We'll set you up in Fort Greene. Maury owns a brownstone there. Nice neighborhood. Quiet. You gotta keep a low profile."

"No doubt." Zion wanted nothing more than to get out of the public eye and blend in.

"Let's watch and see who does what and who goes where once we let the guys out."

Lamin and Zion both agreed. The next few weeks would be crucial.

Born had risen long before the sun that morning. He was physically exhausted, but he was too wired to rest. Thoughts of his son filled him with worry and robbed him of the sleep that he so desperately needed.

Jada was still asleep on the couch. Born had covered her up with a blanket, and then he spent the rest of the night sitting in his favorite recliner, thinking. He thought about his son, afraid, away from home, in the clutches of a man who had threatened to end his life. Born wrestled with so many different emotions that by the time the sun rose he had laughed at the absurdity of the situation, cried in anguish, and gotten angry enough to hatch a plan.

As the house came alive with the family waking up, Born was in a reflective mood. He didn't have much energy for idle conversation. So after saying good morning to Jada, her sister, and Sheldon, he withdrew to Jada's bedroom for some much-needed time alone.

He sat on the bed, his nerves on edge. It was just after eight a.m. and he was anxious for Elliot to call him with instructions on where to meet him. Born had already secured the money for Ethan's release. He and Jada had pooled their resources, and DJ had contributed a large amount as well. Born had called in every favor he was owed and scraped together every penny of the one million dollar ransom. But he had no intention of giving Elliot anything. The cash was just a guise to get him in the door. Born had every intention of killing him today. Either he would free Ethan and kill his captor, or he would die trying.

Born had spoken to his mother briefly that morning. She told him that Anisa had been up all night, alternating between fits of crying and cursing. Born knew how she felt, and wished that she would talk to him and find solace in their shared anguish. But Miss Ingrid let him know that Anisa had made her refusal to speak to Born very clear.

"Marquis, she's upset right now. This is her son, too. All she can see right now is that he's gone, that it's Jada's fault, and that you don't hold her accountable. Right now, she wants no part of you. You can understand that, right?"

Born did understand. He couldn't even explain it if he tried. His love for Jada overshadowed the fact that this whole situation stemmed from her checkered past. He realized that to Anisa, Jada and her son were nothing but trouble. But Born loved Jada so much that he couldn't blame her for this. Still, he understood how Anisa was feeling.

Jada entered the bedroom, bringing Born a plate of breakfast. Born had no appetite, though. He thanked her, and set the plate down on the bedside table.

Jada sat next to him on the bed. "Have you heard anything yet?"

Born shook his head. "Still waiting."

Jada glanced again at her own cell phone, hoping that it would ring so that they could get this whole thing over with. Elliot was taking his time, and making them suffer with each passing moment. "When are the guys getting here?"

Born stared at her, confused. "What guys?"

Jada frowned. "Well . . . who is going with you?" Jada had assumed that Born would be bringing some of his boys as backup.

Born knew that she wouldn't like what he was about to say. "I'm going by myself."

Jada jumped up, pissed. "No, you're not!"

Born held up his hands defensively. "Calm down," he said.

"Calm down, my ass. You're not walking into a damn ambush by yourself. Why would you even think that was a good idea?"

Born looked exhausted. "Jada, listen. This is my battle."

"No!" She was adamant. "It's *my* battle. It's bad enough that your son is involved. Now you want me to just sit here while you go off *by yourself* to deal with Elliot? You must think I'm crazy."

"I don't think you're crazy," he said, wearily.

"What about Dorian's brothers? Zion? Tremaine? Damnit, even DJ! Why can't any of them go with you?"

Born pulled Jada close and held her tenderly. "Listen," he said calmly. "Those guys have enough problems on their hands with their criminal cases. And how would I look bringing DJ with me to do some shit like this? He's a kid as far as I'm concerned. A kid with a big career and an international spotlight on him." Born kissed Jada softly, which seemed to calm her. "This is something I have to do by myself. Ethan is my son. You're gonna be my wife. It's nobody else's responsibility but mine to protect you guys."

Jada was crying now. "I'm scared, Born. What if he hurts you? Or if he hurts both of you? I couldn't handle that." Jada had never been more afraid of anything in her life.

"Don't think like that." Born knew it was futile to try to convince her not to think of the worst-case scenario, but he said it anyway. Truthfully, he had spent much of the night coming to grips with the fact that he could very well be walking directly into his own demise. But he had no reservations about it. He had to get his son back, and he was determined to make sure that Elliot never terrorized anyone again. He kissed Jada one more time, even more passionately. When he pulled away, he held her face in his hands and looked deep into her pretty brown eyes.

"I need you to know how much I love you, Jada. I don't care what you did years ago. It don't matter to me. I love you. I want to spend the rest of my life making you happy, raising our kids, and making up for every time I hurt you or let you down. I want you to be my wife. There's nobody else I want but you." He thought about Anisa, how she hated him now, and rightfully so. "I played a lot of games, and I shouldn't have. No matter what I did, or who I was with, there was never anybody else in my heart but you." He wiped the tears that fell from her eyes. "After all this is over, I want you to promise me that we'll go and get married. No more games, no more delaying. Just me, you, and our kids. We can move away if you want or we can stay right here. It don't matter. I just want us to have our happily ever after. Promise me that."

Jada nodded. "Yeah," she said, softly. "I promise."

Born drew her close, and she clung to him tightly. This felt too much like good-bye, and she cried out of her deep love for him and out of fear that their happy ending might never be.

Born's phone buzzed, and they both jumped anxiously. He looked at the screen and saw a text from a private number. With his heart racing, he looked at the picture that popped up on the screen. Ethan was tied to a chair in an otherwise empty room. He was bound to the chair with thick rope, his eyes and mouth covered with grey duct tape. The walls around him were gray, and there was no other visible furniture or people. Born and Jada searched the picture for clues, their hearts breaking at the thought of the horror that Ethan must have been enduring at that moment.

While they stared at the picture in silence, Jada's phone rang. With trembling hands and an equally shaky voice, she answered. "Hello?"

"Good morning, dear Jada."

Elliot's tone sent chills up her spine. She activated the speakerphone so that Born could hear what was said.

"I assume that Born is there with you?"

"Yeah," she said tersely. Bile rose in her throat at the sound of his voice.

"Good," he said. "I want both of you to bring the money together. Just the two of you. Nobody else. If you show up with any police or anyone else, I will blow this kid's brains out on sight." Elliot chuckled slightly. "He's a real pussy, you know? He cried all night, and then he wet himself right after I tied him to this chair. Not at all what I would expect from the son of a so-called hustler."

Born squeezed his eyes closed, painfully. He knew that Ethan had to be petrified, but to hear about it in such detail broke his heart into a million pieces.

"Anyway, I trust that you have the money?" Elliot asked.

"We got your money." Born fought to keep his emotions under control. He was afraid that if he berated Elliot the way that he wanted to, Ethan might be hurt. Born willed himself to save all of his rage for when he faced this coward in person.

"Very good. Bring it to West Farms Road and East 174th Street in the Bronx. This is a warehouse that I use from time to time for situations like this." Elliot chuckled again. He was giddy at the thought of all of the money he was about to get. He was also quite eager to exact revenge against Jada at last. "When you get here, park your car behind the silver minivan. Take your keys out of the ignition and leave them on your dashboard. Take only the money with you and nothing else. Then, walk through the alleyway with your hands where I can see them at all times. Walk slowly, and do not make any sudden moves or you will be sorry. Once I have the cash, you will have your son, and we can all get on with our lives. You have until noon. If you are not here by then . . ." The sound of a gunshot pierced the air, echoing in the emptiness of the room Elliot was in. Jada gasped, clasping her hands over her mouth in horror. Born jumped to his feet, panicking.

"Yo, what the fuck!" he roared. "You better not hurt my son!"

Ethan's muffled yet anguished cries could be heard despite the duct tape over his mouth. Born's eyes welled up with tears as Elliot's laughter filled his ears.

"Relax," he said. "The kid is okay. For now. Clock's ticking."

Elliot hung up. Born turned away from Jada and held his head in his hands. His fury was evident so she gave him space. For several minutes, neither of them spoke. Finally, Born turned and looked at her. His tone left no room for debate.

"You're gonna stay here. You, Ava, and Sheldon do not leave this house for any reason. Don't open the door at all. Stay put until I get back."

Born made a move toward the door and Jada grabbed his arm. He turned to her and Jada threw herself into his arms, weeping.

"It's okay," he said, his voice cracking with emotion. He held her tightly and inhaled her scent, aware that it might be for the last time. "I'm coming back to you. Just remember what I said. I love you, Jada."

"I love you, too." She wiped her eyes, determined to be strong for him. "Be careful."

Born nodded. He kissed her on her forehead, then grabbed the duffel bag that sat beside the bedroom door. Without looking back, he headed for the Bronx to bring his son back home.

20

BANG! BANG!

Miss Ingrid hung up the phone and started praying. Anisa stepped into the room and found Born's mother on her knees facing the sofa, praying so hard that beads of sweat formed on her brow. A sense of dread overtook Anisa, and she braced herself against the wall.

"What's wrong?" she asked.

Miss Ingrid looked up at Anisa with eyes full of worry. She had never particularly cared for Anisa. Over the years, Ingrid's allegiance had always belonged to Jada. But in this situation, as a mother whose child's life was in limbo, her heart went out to her.

"Marquis is on his way to meet with the man now. He says he has the money and it should all go smoothly." Ingrid shook her head. "But I know Marquis. He's not gonna pay that man a dime." Ingrid shut her eyes as she thought of all the things that could possibly go wrong. "God, please don't let nothing bad happen."

Anisa stood there for a moment deep in thought. She was furious with Born, but she still loved him. She certainly didn't want to see any harm come to him or to Ethan. Without another moment's hesitation, she dropped to her knees beside Miss Ingrid, each mother praying desperately for the safe return of her son.

———

Born pulled up on West Farms Road and slowly canvassed the block. It was a virtually deserted stretch of industrial real estate, with little thru traffic. Several cars were parked along the street, but there was no one walking about. He saw the silver minivan that Elliot had referred to during the phone call earlier. The vehicle had no license plates, and Born looked around for any clue as to where Elliot might be, or where he was hiding his son. He saw a self-storage facility a couple of doors down from the warehouse, and an auto body shop that appeared to be abandoned on the corner.

Born parked behind the minivan and turned the car off. He took the key out of the ignition and laid it on the dashboard as he had been instructed. He reached over and touched the picture of Ethan that he kept taped to his windshield near his inspection sticker. If he didn't make it out of this alive, he promised himself that he would make sure that Ethan did. He took a deep breath, grabbed the duffel bag sitting on the passenger seat beside him, and climbed out of the car.

Born stood near his car for a few moments before heading toward the alleyway. The walls were all splattered with graffiti, and the warehouse itself looked desolate and abandoned. He walked slowly, with both of his hands visible, struggling with the heavy duffel bag, which was packed with all the cash. As he walked, he kept his eyes and ears open for anything out of the ordinary. With his senses heightened, his heart raced in his chest. He jumped slightly when he saw a man emerge through a gray metal door, which was covered in graffiti. It wasn't the same man he'd met in the McDonald's bathroom. This guy looked a lot younger, somewhere in his twenties—and he stared at Born, icily. With a gun in his hand, the man motioned Born over and held the door open wide enough for Born to peer inside. It looked dark in there, and Born couldn't tell if Ethan was in there or not. But without a word, he walked toward the open door, and made eye contact with the man standing there.

"Where's my son?" Born asked, getting right to the point.

The guy didn't answer him. Instead, he just held the door wider as Born walked past. Born stepped across the threshold and was immediately knocked to the floor from behind. As he tried to get up, he was hit in the back of the head with something heavy and it hurt like hell. He moved to push himself up and was hit again. This time, he lay there on the floor, looking around with his head pounding relentlessly. He recognized Elliot's voice before he saw him.

"You don't ask the fucking questions around here." Elliot kicked him hard in his side. Born groaned in pain. Elliot turned to his nephew and told him to go out to Born's car and bring him the keys from the dashboard. Then he turned back to Born, sneering. "I'm the one that asks the questions. You want to know what my first question is?" He didn't wait for Born to respond. "Where the fuck is Jada?"

Born peered up at Elliot from his awkward vantage point. "She couldn't make it," he said, facetiously. "I'm here. The money's here. Now where the fuck is my son?"

Elliot laughed, looking at Born incredulously. Elliot's amused expression belied his fury. He kicked Born hard in the face, and spat on him as he writhed in pain.

Cheo returned with the car keys and tossed them to Elliot. Born watched them closely, waiting for an opportunity to make a move.

"I specifically told you to bring Jada with you," Elliot said. He picked up the duffel bag that Born had brought in and threw it to his nephew. It landed with a thud right in front of where Cheo stood. "Count every dollar," he ordered. "I don't care how long it takes."

Cheo took the heavy bag to the far corner of the room, and that's when Born saw him. Ethan was strapped to a chair, facing the wall. His back was facing Born, but Ethan knew that his father was there. Ethan's cries were muffled, but he was certain that he was yelling, "Dad!" Born sat up, but stayed on the floor under Elliot's deadly stare.

Cheo cast a sidelong glance at Ethan, as he stood nearby counting the money. His heart went out to the kid. Elliot had slapped him around for kicks while they awaited Born's arrival. Cheo had kept his mouth shut, but he was secretly seething. His uncle was truly a ruthless bastard.

Elliot glared at Born. "I really wanted to see Jada again. I got a good punch in when I found her at the hospital that night. But I had bigger plans for her. I was gonna fuck her while you watched. Then I was gonna put a bullet in her head for that shit she pulled with my cocaine back in the day."

Born stared Elliot down, coaxing himself not to be swayed by his words. Jada was at home, safe. Now all he had to do was get Ethan out of here, and it would all be fine.

"So now, I have to deal with Jada another time." Elliot pulled out a cigarette and lit it, keeping his eyes on Born the whole time. "She will get what's coming to her."

Born frowned. "What happened to keeping your word? You said to bring the money and everything would be done." Born had known all along that Elliot had no intention of going away. It was for that very reason that he had insisted that Jada stay behind. He shook his head at Elliot. "You're taking this shit too far. She owed you money. Okay, fine. You got your money. Now let me take my son home."

Elliot's rage bubbled over then. He pulled out his gun, cocked it, and pointed it in Born's face. Ethan started crying, though his cries were muffled by the duct tape. Elliot's eyes flashed with anger. "Who the fuck do you think you're talking to?" he demanded. Elliot was sick of people acting like they couldn't remember how powerful he was. He put the gun to Born's head, and stared him down. He spoke to him through clenched teeth. "You don't tell me what to do. I'm the one in charge. Not you. I told you to bring Jada *here*!"

Born could see that this man was unstable. The frenzy he had worked himself into was completely unwarranted. His spit landed on Born as he spoke.

"Not only did you not listen to me, but now you want to sit here and tell me what to do?" Elliot shook his head. "Let me tell you what's gonna happen now. We're gonna call Jada and let her listen to you die!"

"All the money is here," Cheo called out. He hadn't really finished counting it so quickly. But it was clear that if he didn't say something when he did that Elliot was going to escalate the situation very quickly.

Born kept staring Elliot down. He was outnumbered, but he couldn't mask his hatred for the man who stood before him.

Elliot held Born's gaze, and waited for him to acquiesce. He took Born's refusal to back down as a sign of immense disrespect. He smirked and shook his head. "What a fool you are. You come in here asking questions, making demands. You don't bring Jada to me like I told you to." He sucked his teeth. "And now you want to stare me down like you got balls of iron. Let me humble you, Mr. Born."

Without taking his eyes off of Born, Elliot walked over to where Ethan sat strapped to the chair. With the gun in Elliot's hand, Born had a clear idea of what was about to happen. He jumped to his feet, and rushed Elliot at full speed. Elliot pointed his gun at Born, with a sinister smile on his face. The sound of the gunshot blast reverberated throughout the warehouse.

Born stopped dead in his tracks. He was certain he had been shot, but couldn't feel any pain. Momentarily dazed and confused, he watched Elliot's face twist in agony. Elliot fell to the floor with a chest wound bleeding heavily beneath him. Behind him, Cheo reached for his gun, but wasn't fast enough. Another shot rang out, the bullet slamming into his shoulder with such intensity that it visibly tore away chunks of flesh as it made contact. Born scrambled to his feet and was shocked to see Jada barreling toward him with a smoking gun in her hand.

Ethan whimpered softly. Unable to see what had transpired, he was certain that his father was dead. Cheo whimpered in pain not far from his uncle lying on the concrete floor

Jada ran toward Elliot, and kicked his gun in Born's direction. Still bewildered, Born scooped up the gun, and trained it on Cheo, as Jada stood over Elliot laying on the ground. He was gurgling on his own blood, and still trying his best to talk shit. Jada stood over him wordlessly and watched him suffer for several moments. Then she shot him through the forehead and watched him die. Urine seeped from his lifeless body as she stepped slowly away.

Cheo writhed in pain on the floor just feet away. "My uncle is crazy," he said, breathlessly. "I did not condone what he did to your son. This shit went too far." The desperation and pain in his voice were evident, but Born and Jada were unmoved.

"You can take your son and lea—"

Born shot a slug through Cheo's throat in midsentence. The young man's eyes flew open in shock, and he clutched his neck futilely before falling in a bloody thud onto the floor.

Born rushed over and untied Ethan, while Jada carefully peeled away the duct tape from his eyes and mouth. Ethan smelled like urine, and he was visibly shaken. But he was alive. Born and Jada's tears of joy mixed with Ethan's as they embraced.

"You're safe now. It's okay." Jada was trembling, even as she spoke the words of reassurance to young Ethan.

Born noticed her shaking. "I told you to stay home," he said, his voice low and steady.

Jada had made up her mind to follow Born the moment he said that he was going to meet Elliot alone. Jada knew that she couldn't let him go alone to clean up her mess. If anything happened to Born or Ethan because of her, she would have died.

"I knew you might need some backup," she said. She forced a smile.

Born shook his head, grateful beyond measure, and upset that she had put herself in danger at the same time. Truthfully, he was shaken, too. But he knew that they had to get out of there in case there was anyone else in that warehouse. He rifled through Elliot's pockets until he found his car keys. Once he had them, Born grabbed the heavy duffel bag, and together the three of them ran for their lives.

Over the next several days, Gillian maneuvered funds through various vendors at *Conga*, calling in debts and favors alike. One by one, she brought the guys home, starting with her brother.

"What did they ask you?" She got straight to the point in the privacy of her all black Range Rover tucked discreetly behind the tinted-out windows of the backseat. Baron sat up front, with Celia driving. The feuding ladies had ridden together in silence to bail out Baron and, courteously, Gillian had climbed into the backseat afterward to allow mother and son to have their reunion.

"Gillian," Celia said, catching her eye in the rearview. "He just got in the car. Give him a minute to breathe. He just got out of jail. Now I appreciate you putting up some of the money. But I'm his mother, and your father did not leave me penniless. So I will give you back your money if you think it entitles you to grill him like a damn interrogator. I don't need your help to look after my son."

Gillian smirked at her. Celia's words were so telling. What Gillian heard was that Celia suspected that her son was guilty, too.

"I was talking to Baron," Gillian said. "Last I checked, he's a grown man." She leaned forward slightly, peering at Baron's handsome profile. "Right?" she asked. "You want to tell me what happened in there, Baron?"

"Not right now," he said. "We'll talk later on."

Gillian sat back in her seat and watched her brother hide behind his mother's skirts. She sat back for the rest of the ride and said nothing. They watched the traffic and the pedestrians through their windows while Celia made idle chat about the weather and whether anyone was hungry. Gillian waited until they arrived at Celia's home, and she moved closer to her brother in the foyer.

"Baron, let's talk."

He looked at her oddly. Gillian couldn't tell what he was thinking. He said nothing, but walked past her and toward the kitchen.

"I'm hungry."

Celia moved after him. "Let me make you a sandwich." She followed him into the kitchen, while Gillian stood pissed in the foyer.

She took a deep breath and followed them. Baron sat at the counter, sulking. Gillian wanted to slap the shit out of him.

"Baron, what's up?"

Celia's eyes flashed as her head snapped in Gillian's direction.

"What don't you understand? He's not going to talk to you about this today, Gillian!"

"With all due respect, Miss Celia, this is none of your business."

"You're in *my* house."

"Baron." Gillian's voice was firm and commanding.

"You never even bothered to ask if he's alright, if he needs anything," Celia continued. All you give a damn about is yourself. Fall back, young lady. Like I said, this is my house. Baron has just gotten home. He's hungry, he's tired, and this is not the time to talk business. Not today. Now, thank you for your help today. Thank you for accompanying us home, even though I offered to drop you off along the way."

Gillian scowled at her. "I wanted to come here and speak to Baron in private." She was trying so hard to remain respectful.

"And that's not gonna happen today." Celia said it matter-of-factly, and smiled victoriously. She turned and walked to the refrigerator to prepare a sandwich for her son.

"Gillian," Baron spoke at last, "I'll call you tomorrow."

She looked at her brother with venom in her gaze. "Don't bother."

She turned on her Brian Atwood heels, and sauntered out of Celia's house for the last time.

Frankie bounced Bria on his lap, trying to get her to stop squirming. She wasn't comfortable with him, and it showed. He was embarrassed by his daughter's unfamiliarity with him. It was no one's fault but his own.

Camille kept her distance, busying herself in the kitchen, watching in silence. Frankie had stopped by soon after his release from jail. She was glad to see him, and happy that someone else—probably Gillian—had stepped up to post his bail. Although she cared for Frankie, she was in love with Eli. She didn't want anything to jeopardize their relationship. Still, part of her was relieved to see that Frankie was okay, and that apparently the letter she had written to him while he was in jail had made him eager to reconnect with their daughter.

Camille's mother, Lily, wasn't as coy. At first she watched while her granddaughter squirmed in Frankie's arms. Then she sucked her teeth and walked into the living room. "Bria, be nice to Daddy," she said softly. "Sit nice."

Bria's lower lip quivered, teetering on the brink of tears, but she stopped squirming.

Frankie looked at his former mother-in-law gratefully. "She listens to you."

"That's because she sees me every day." Lily looked him dead in the eye as she said it. There was no mistake about the meaning behind her words.

Frankie turned his attention back to the baby, ignoring Lily at first. He baby talked and played with Bria, the whole time thinking about what Lily had said.

"You're right," he admitted at last. "I'm ashamed that my own daughter doesn't know me. It's my fault, 'cuz I haven't been around. But I'm gonna change that now."

Lily nodded. "I'm happy to hear that. Bria's getting bigger now. It's important that she knows her father."

Frankie looked around for Camille and, as if on cue, she appeared. She handed Bria a sippy cup full of apple juice, and placed bottled waters on the table for Frankie and Lily.

"Frankie, what happens now with your court case?"

He shook his head. "It's hard to say. I have a hearing on Thursday. I'll have to wait and see what happens."

Lily frowned. "Well, maybe it's time for you to leave those old friends of yours alone," Lily said, speaking in code since five-year-old Shane was within earshot. He sat in the middle of the living room floor, coloring, oblivious to the conversation that the adults were having.

"You have a lot of legitimate businesses, Frankie. It's time to leave the rest of that mess alone."

Frankie nodded, but said nothing. Camille shot her mother an icy look, beseeching her with her gaze to be quiet.

Lily didn't take the hint. "I know it's none of my business," she acknowledged. "You're a grown man, and you can do what you want. But I've known you for so many years. And this family has been through a lot of things with you over the years. So you can take this as some mama wisdom. Motherly advice. If you dodge the bullet this time, you should take it as a sign from The Most High. Get out of any business that you can't run out in the open." Lily shrugged. "That's my advice. You can take it, or leave it." She got up and made her exit, rubbing Shane's head affectionately as she left the room.

Camille watched her go. Bria was wriggling to get free again. Mercifully, Frankie set her down on the floor, then watched as she ran to her mother and raised her arms for Camille to pick her up. Camille gathered her daughter onto her lap, and looked at Frankie. He looked so despondent.

"She'll get used to you, Frankie. The more you come around, the more relaxed she'll feel around you."

He nodded. "I know." He forced a smile. Awkward silence descended upon them. He rubbed his hands together as a way to occupy them. Looking at Camille, Frankie smiled again. "You look good," he said. "I know you're with Mr. NYPD now. But I can still compliment you."

Camille smiled, shyly. "Thanks, Frankie."

He got a kick out of seeing her blush. It was good to see her smile again. "Are you happy?" He didn't know why he asked the question. Camille's happiness hadn't been his concern for quite some time. Still, he wondered if she had found fulfillment since the demise of their relationship.

Camille appeared to be caught off guard by the question. She only gave it a moment's thought before nodding. "I am. Happier than I've been in a long time."

"Good," he said. "Then I'm happy for you." Frankie looked around awkwardly. "Where's Misa?" he asked. The question felt strange to him as he said it. Camille's sister Misa had killed his brother Steven. But facing the truth of his family history had helped him come to terms with what had taken place. While he wasn't yet ready to say that he forgave her, Frankie had somehow managed to forge a relationship of mutual respect with Misa.

"She's at Miss Celia's place visiting Baron," Camille answered.

Frankie looked at her. "He's home?"

Camille frowned. "You didn't know?"

Frankie shook his head.

Camille's frown deepened. She chastised herself silently for spilling the beans about Baron's release. But she hadn't known that it was a secret. "He just came home, too."

"When?" Frankie asked.

Camille stalled. "I'm not sure." She lied, Baron had been home for weeks.

Frankie looked away, seemingly lost in thought. During the two days since Frankie's release, he had been calling Baron repeatedly, calling Celia, too. Neither of them had answered.

For several minutes neither of them spoke again. Frankie watched Bria playing with her mother. He smiled whenever she spoke the few words in her one-year-old vocabulary—"hi," "thank you," and "no." Her voice was so precious that it melted Frankie's heart. He felt like shit for being so detached from her.

"I'm sorry, Camille."

She looked at him.

"Sorry for what?"

"For not being around more. For not being a good father. Or a good husband." He shook his head, his expression full of regret. "I got your letter while I was locked up, and I felt like shit. A real man doesn't need someone to ask him to be a father to his child. I won't sit here and make excuses for what I did and what I didn't do. I'm just sorry for everything I ever did to hurt you. You didn't deserve it. You're a beautiful mother. A beautiful woman, period. Eli's a lucky man. If I was smart, I never would have left my family. It's something I really regret right now."

Camille wanted to cry. Frankie had apologized to her. She hadn't anticipated the emotional impact of his words. Hearing him acknowledge her pain—the pain that he had caused her—made her choke up. "Wow," she managed.

"I'm gonna go." Frankie stood up.

Camille continued to sit. She never expected to be here. The old Camille would have grabbed hungrily at the chance to reunite with Frankie. In that moment, she realized the depth of her love for Eli. Eli loved her deeply, completely, and with no drama. It was the complete opposite of what her life had been like with Frankie. It occurred to Camille that if they were still married, she would have been in the middle of this legal battle right alongside Frankie. It would have been her home that was raided, her assets that were seized. She was grateful that she had gotten out when she did. She surely hadn't known it then, but Frankie had done her a favor by leaving her.

She looked up at him. "What about you, Frankie?" Camille asked. "I mean I know you have a lot going on in your life right now. But, are *you* happy, Frankie? Aside from all the problems?"

Frankie shrugged. "I mean . . ." He sat lost in thought for a long time. So many silent minutes passed that Camille squirmed uncomfortably in her seat. Frankie thought about the state of affairs in his life. His brother was dead. His mother was a recluse, weak and practically dead herself. Gillian had left him, and his marriage to Camille had crashed and burned. He had been dethroned as head of his crew, then arrested and charged with just about every crime he could name. And to top it all off, his own daughter didn't know who he was. "Nah," he said, shaking his head. "Not at all."

He felt himself getting choked up. Then he got angry with himself for getting emotional. Embarrassed, he walked over to where Camille stood. He picked Bria up, ignoring her writhing with discomfort in his arms. He planted a kiss on her chubby cheek, and then handed her back to Camille.

"I'll call you tomorrow," he said over his shoulder as he headed for the door.

Camille watched him go, her heart going out to him. It didn't take a rocket scientist to know that Frankie's life was in complete chaos. Despite the way he had hurt her, Camille did not hate Frankie. She wished him well, and as he shut the door behind him, she said a silent prayer for him.

Born drove home with Ethan in the passenger seat and Sheldon in the back. The three of them hadn't said much since they left the mall. Jada had stayed home to work on the new book she was writing. Halloween was fast approaching, and Born had taken Sheldon shopping for a costume. Ethan wasn't in the mood for trick-or-treating, still traumatized by his kidnapping ordeal.

When Born had returned home with Ethan, he had been terribly shaken. Anisa and Miss Ingrid had rushed over to Jada's house for what turned out to be a very emotional and tearful reunion. Ethan had told them every detail of what he'd endured, including the fact that Elliot had clearly intended to kill him before Jada saved their lives. Anisa's fury toward Jada lessened then. She still harbored resentment toward her. But she had saved her son's life. That softened the blow somewhat.

Sheldon was so impressed by the fact that Ethan had survived an attempt on his life, that he gained a new respect for his nemesis. He thought Ethan might have some grit deep down inside after all. Since Ethan's return, Sheldon had made a conscious attempt to get along with him better than before.

In the weeks since then, Born and Anisa had enlisted the help of a psychologist who Maury recommended. Doctor Reilly specialized in child psychology and post-traumatic stress disorder. Ethan was a bit more withdrawn since his return, but he was coming around slowly but surely. Sheldon even sat in on a few sessions with Ethan, in the hopes that the two boys would bond over what they had been through together, and separately. What made Born especially happy was the fact that Anisa hadn't objected to Ethan and Sheldon bonding, so long as Born was always present with them. She had resigned herself to the fact that Jada was the woman Born wanted in his life. Since Sheldon was her son, she reasoned that it was best for them to try to get along, if that was possible. She was so happy to have her son back safe and sound, that she stopped bitching about Jada and Sheldon. All she cared about was Ethan's safety, happiness, and well-being.

Since their reconciliation, Jada and Born had gotten Sheldon under control. Born left no question about who was the man of the house. So far, Sheldon seemed to be accepting that. He and Ethan were getting along much better. It seemed that things might turn out well for their family after all.

During their search for a costume, Sheldon wanted something gross and ghoulish. Born heard him out, let him describe the blood-and-guts ensemble he had in mind. But when it came time for them to make the final choice, Born had convinced young Sheldon to embrace a different vision for himself. His class was having a costume ball. Sheldon, whose behavior had improved considerably this school year, was being allowed to attend his first school function in quite some time. Instead of showing up as the creepy monster everyone already thought he was, Born outfitted him as a king. Sheldon's costume consisted of a long, plush red velvet cloak, a large golden crown, and a scepter.

"Ghosts, and monsters, and all that are tough. But kings are above other men. They reign over everybody, even the monsters. So when you walk in there with your crown dipped to the side, you gotta own it. You're kings. Both of you. But you gotta act like it. Kings don't raise hell, cuz they don't have to. Kings have armies that do their dirty work. They sit on their throne and they play it cool." Born sold Sheldon on it, and he stood tall in the mirror as he tried on his costume.

Now, as they rode in the car listening to the radio, Born rapped along to a Biggie verse on "One More Chance." Sheldon watched him from the backseat with admiration. Born was cool after all. Sheldon had wanted to hate him. Despising Born had been fun for a while. But now he was enjoying the time they all spent doing guy stuff. Sometimes Ethan came along, and sometimes he didn't. Sheldon didn't really like sharing Born's attention. But he was learning how to keep his impulses under control. When he hung out with his soon-to-be step-Pops alone, it was nice.

"You knew Biggie Smalls?" Sheldon asked.

Born laughed. "Nah, I never met Biggie. But me and your mother used to party with the rich and famous back in the day. We had a lot of fun together. We still do, that's why I love her so much."

Sheldon tried to imagine his mother and Born when they were younger. He had seen pictures of them in their youth. He also heard some of the stories when his mother and his "aunt" Sunny reminisced on the good 'ole days. But now they were moving into a whole new phase. Born had moved into their home, and was now a full-time part of his life. DJ was really famous now. Born had met a lot of stars in his role as his manager. Sheldon hoped that having Born around meant meeting some of his favorite stars, too.

"Are you really gonna get married?" Ethan asked Born. "You and Jada gonna have kids and all that?"

Born smiled. "Well, we're definitely getting married. But I'm not sure about the baby part. We're a lot older than we used to be. And I think we got our hands full with you two."

Sheldon smiled, relieved to hear that.

"Life is fragile," Born said. "I know a lot of people who had plans for their life, but life had other plans for them." Born thought about Dorian. "All you really have is today. So you have to make the most of it. I want you guys to grow up with every opportunity to be great. You guys are kings. Not savages."

Sheldon stared out the window. *Kings.* He liked the sound of that.

21

DAMAGE CONTROL

Baron and Misa lay entangled in the sheets on the king-sized bed. They had woken up early that morning and made love twice. Now it was 11:05 a.m. on a Sunday morning, and the lovebirds were discussing breakfast. Holed up for the past two days at the Hilton in Short Hills, New Jersey, the two of them had big plans.

Things had completely changed between them. Baron was, admittedly, in love with a murderous beauty. He understood Misa, and she him. The two of them were volatile, restless spirits searching for a center, something to ground them. Oddly enough, they had found that in each other. Baron's brush with death, and Misa's troubles with the law had bonded them together. They had come to each other's rescue when it mattered the most.

"So when are we leaving?" Misa asked. I have to go home and pick up Shane, and pack a few things."

"Don't pack nothing," Baron said firmly. "Get Shane, get your passport, your jewelry, and whatever little cash you got, and let's go. I got the rest." He gripped her chin roughly. "Don't say good-bye to nobody. It's not good-bye. We'll come back when things calm down."

Misa nodded as best she could under his firm grip. "I got it."

He kissed her. "Come on, let's order breakfast."

Baron climbed out of bed, perused the hotel menu, and Misa

requested pancakes. She stretched, smiling, and got out of bed. They were going to start a new chapter together. They were going to Miami and meeting up with Baron's friends there. Once everything was set up, they would sail to the Bahamas, and get lost from there.

Baron felt like the family's fall guy. He and others in the crew were being charged with major crimes, while Gillian walked away free. It had taken far too long for anyone to bail him out. It caused Baron to be suspicious of his sister and what her intentions were for him once he got out. Frankie had been calling, but Baron didn't trust him, either. He just wanted to get away. And Misa was coming with him.

"I'm getting in the shower," she said. "Can you ask them to send up some more towels, too? We used a couple last night."

Baron smiled and nodded. The room service operator answered, and he placed their order. He was starving after working up an appetite with Misa all morning. Afterward, he called down and requested that fresh towels be sent up. Baron walked into the living room portion of their suite, and sat down on the sofa. He thought about his mother. She had no idea that he was leaving. She couldn't know. If she did, she would have insisted that he stay and face it all head on. But Baron had made up his mind. It was time for him to go.

A knock on the front door brought him to his feet, and he strolled his sexy limp across the floor. He opened the door, expecting to find someone bearing towels. Instead, when he swung open the door, he came face to face with the barrel of a Taurus 9 millimeter. He glanced at the person holding the gun, and frowned. He opened his mouth to say something, but the words never surfaced. The shot came so quickly, that before he could register a thought, he was thrown back several feet. The shooter walked quickly down the hall before disappearing out of sight. Baron saw the blood seeping from his chest and felt the life slipping slowly out of his body. The room began to look blurry, and then his vision faded to black altogether. Misa came running, naked, to Baron's side, screaming and crying over his bloody body.

"Oh my God, somebody help me!"

Frankie sat transfixed as he sat in the waiting room in Saint Barnabas Hospital watching Gillian wipe her tears. He heard Celia's cries mingled with Misa's muffled sobs. He also noticed the detectives milling indiscreetly nearby. Frankie took it all in.

He wasn't the only one watching everything closely. Camille had come to offer her support to her distraught sister. Misa had been so distressed by Baron's shooting that the doctors feared she might have a nervous breakdown. Seeing so much blood flowing out of his body, and watching him slip in and out of consciousness had taken Misa close to the edge of her sanity. When Camille heard her sister sobbing on the phone, she had dropped everything in order to rush to her side. But the truth, which Camille would never admit to anyone, was that she couldn't have stayed away even if Misa and Baron had not been an item. She couldn't help herself. Part of her was fascinated to watch it all fall down. The Nobles empire was coming apart at the seams.

Camille held Misa as she cried on her shoulder. She watched Frankie sitting on the opposite side of the room, practically drooling as he stared at Gillian. Camille shook her head in disgust. Frankie clearly still had it bad for his former lover. Seeing Gillian cry, Camille did her best to look for signs that she was insincere. She wondered whether Gillian had sanctioned Baron's shooting. Their encounters with one another over the years had never been pleasant ones. Gillian had been a fiery opponent, ruthless when she set her sights on something she wanted. And Gillian had wanted Frankie, and gotten him. She had wanted her father's position, and gotten it. But, Camille wondered, was she capable of killing her own brother?

If she was, she was doing a good job of playing it off. No one had seen Gillian show this much emotion since her father's funeral. To some, it seemed that the siblings had never been particularly close. Baron had been the prodigal son, always having to learn the hard way. Gillian, the doted-upon baby girl, had been the apple of her father's eye. Their sibling rivalry had been understandable. Still, sitting there in the hospital waiting room, Gillian wept bitterly. It was a believable performance to everyone present. Camille couldn't help but feel some empathy for the woman she had once despised.

Celia, too, was so distraught that the doctors had threatened to sedate her. Baron was her only child. As Doug Nobles' first wife, she had experienced the first fruits of his hard work, and Baron was supposed to be the completion of their picture. He was their handsome son, groomed from the womb to be a hustler. But, to Celia, he was just her baby, her only son. The air was thick with heartache as Baron's mother and sister wept for him.

Frankie caught himself staring at Gillian, and forced himself to avert his gaze temporarily. When he realized that he couldn't keep his eyes off of her, he walked over to where she sat crying silently by herself.

She looked up when he stood in front of her, casting a shadow over her seat.

"Frankie," was all that Gillian could manage.

"Are you okay?" Frankie's sincere concern was etched all over her face.

Gillian shook her head. "No." She took a deep breath. "I can't go through this again." Baron had clung to life similarly years earlier. At the same time, their father, Doug Nobles, had also been shot, and later died as a result of his wounds. Ever since his death,

Gillian's relationship with Baron had been strained at best. Knowing that he was fighting for his life again, Gillian felt incredibly helpless and full of regret.

Suddenly, a commotion could be heard as Celia tried to charge Gillian, while Camille and Misa struggled to hold her back. Hospital security had to step in to assist. Celia was irate, and determined to get loose so that she could attack Gillian.

"You privileged, spoiled, little bitch! You think because he's gone now you can get away with it?" Celia's lovely face was twisted into a mask of pure hate.

Frankie's head snapped around, and he hurried over to Baron's mother. The detectives were listening closely. Gillian got up and walked toward the exit.

"Miss Celia, calm down," Frankie urged. Everyone present was riveted as they watched Celia come unglued. Usually so poised and classy, Baron's mother was now hollering at the top of her lungs.

She wailed loudly. "That's my *son* in there, Frankie! That bitch is gonna pay for this!" Celia battled to break free as she watched Gillian walk out the door, with Frankie now hot on her heels.

Zion and Lamin sat together in the kitchen of Lamin's Brooklyn bachelor pad. Despite being lifelong friends, in recent years these types of visits were infrequent. The troubles between Zion and Olivia had put Lamin in an awkward position. Caught between his loyalty to his sister and the brotherly love he felt toward his best friend, Lamin had struggled to stay neutral. But now that Zion and Olivia had officially ended their relationship, Lamin felt free to resume the bond he and Zion had once shared. After Sunny's death, Olivia had found a younger, newer model to be the face of her clothing line, Vintage. These days, she was putting all of her energy into advancing her career. And it was working. Vintage was quickly becoming a fashion staple. She was determined to solidify her position with her upcoming show during New York Fashion Week.

Zion took a swig of his Hennessy, while Lamin refilled his glass. "So how's everything with you and Ava?" Lamin asked.

Zion laughed. "Me and who?"

Lamin looked surprised. "You mean after all of that, it's over already?"

Zion shrugged. During his incarceration, he had come to the conclusion that his relationship with Ava was never going to be more than just a physical one. "I don't think she's cut out for the life I live." He swigged his drink again. "To be honest, at first she was just a distraction for me while Olivia was drifting away. I liked Ava, don't get me wrong. I definitely cared about her a lot." In Ava, Zion had found the complete opposite of Olivia. Where Olivia was fiery and confrontational, Ava was calm and demure. It was refreshing. "But I wasn't in love with her," he continued. "Not yet. I was starting to worry that she was falling hard, though. It seemed like she wanted to get more serious. Then this shit happened." Zion gestured toward his ankle monitor. "I think that was the final nail in the coffin."

"What you mean?" Lamin asked.

"She wrote me a letter while I was locked up. She told me that this was all more than she had bargained for. She didn't want to be in a relationship with somebody who was facing life in prison. She said she wasn't cut out for curfews, or jail visits. Basically, she was like, 'This was fun, but I'm out.'" Zion laughed. "It's all good. I wrote her back, told her no hard feelings."

Lamin shook his head. "Damn," he said. "Any regrets?" Lamin wondered if Zion wished that he hadn't ended his relationship with Olivia now that Ava was history.

Zion shook his head. "Nah, not at all. It was never about me wanting to leave Olivia to be with somebody else. I know she'll probably never believe that, but it's the truth. I was ready to move on. My relationship with your sister was beautiful while it lasted, but I realized that shit was getting so bad that I was falling out of love with her. All those years of arguing and fighting. It's a relief to be free from that." Zion smirked at his friend. "She won't admit it now, but someday she'll tell you how much happier she is now that everything is over between us."

Lamin smiled, too. Olivia did seem much happier these days. It made him wonder if the two of them should have ended things a long time ago.

"I heard Baron ain't doing too good."

Zion shook his head, sadly. "They gave him another blood transfusion yesterday. Gillian said it's not looking good for him to survive this time. Two shootings within the span of a few years? That's a lot for anybody to pull through."

Lamin eyed Zion to gauge his reaction to this next question. "You think Gillian had anything to do with it?"

Zion stopped mid sip and stared at Lamin. Truthfully, Zion did suspect Gillian, but his loyalty to her wouldn't let him admit it out loud. "Hopefully, Baron survives," Zion said. "Then he can tell us himself."

Celia sat at Baron's bedside, feeling a sickening sense of déjà vu. She had held vigil at his bedside the last time he was shot, and had experienced pure elation when he fought his way back to recovery. This time, she wasn't sure that it would happen that way.

Baron was in and out of consciousness, talking gibberish one minute, and then completely out of it the next. He had lost an incredible amount of blood before the paramedics arrived. The doctors were calling it a miracle that he was still fighting for his life. There was no way to know whether he would live, and if he did, what his quality of life would be. It was heartbreaking for Celia to think that she might lose her son for real this time.

Today, Baron was having one of his bad days. He woke now from what seemed like a bad dream, uttering words that made absolutely no sense to Celia. She came closer and pressed her ear to his lips so that she could hear him better. Then, she frowned, certain that she must be hearing wrong.

"Baron . . . what are you saying?"

His eyes looked like they would pop out of his head. He was struggling so hard to get the words out that Celia thought she should probably summon the doctor. But then he said it again. His words stopped her dead in her tracks.

". . . shot me. Tell everybody . . . it was . . ."

Celia clasped her hands over her mouth in shock.

Gillian clung to the phone like it was her lifeline. "Are you absolutely sure about this?"

Maury toyed with the pencil in his hand. "I wish I could say that I wasn't sure. I would love to be wrong about this. But there's no question about it. It's him."

Gillian's hands trembled with a mixture of fury and devastation. "My God!" She had called Maury after Celia had summoned her to the hospital. Gillian had been hesitant to go at first. After all, Celia had all but kicked her ass the last time they'd seen each other. To make it worse, Celia hadn't divulged what the big emergency was. She'd only said that Baron was asking for her and that she needed to get there right away. With her own ears, Gillian had heard her brother tell her who had shot him. Even then, she wanted to believe that it was the medication that was making Baron delirious.

Soon after he told Gillian who his assailant was, Baron had

gone into cardiac arrest. The doctors and nurses had rushed the women out of the room while they did their best to revive Baron. But their efforts were futile. Baron died, and both Gillian and Celia were inconsolable.

Gillian had called Maury with tears cascading down her face. She had given him the name that Baron had uttered in his final moments, and sent Maury on a wild-goose chase to see if he could garner some information on whether Baron had been right about who the snitch was.

"Now," Maury continued. "The good news is that none of this appears to be a problem for you personally."

Gillian frowned. "What do you mean?"

"I mean, your name isn't mentioned anywhere in any of the recordings, or in any of the statements. For whatever reason, you've been left out of this. There's no indication that you have anything to worry about."

Gillian scoffed at that. She had plenty to worry about. "Everything my father spent his whole life building . . ." She felt a tear fall from her eye. "My brother. He's dead, Maury. I think I have plenty to worry about."

"I know, Gillian. I'm not trying to minimize any of that. But let's look at the bigger picture. You could be facing a lifetime in prison. You could be facing an astronomical amount of legal bills, asset seizures. The silver lining, if there is one, is the fact that your name appears nowhere in any of the evidence that exists. The same can't be said for many of your friends."

Gillian closed her eyes, her head suddenly pounding. Her worst fears had been confirmed. There was a snitch in the family, and it was someone with extensive knowledge about the operation. The whole crew was fucked, and Gillian didn't care how Maury tried to reassure her. She knew that life—her life—would never be the same.

"Thank you," she said softly. "Thanks for letting me know, Maury." She hung up the phone and cried.

Gillian watched from across the room as Frankie stepped into *Conga*. He walked at a leisurely pace, greeting the maître d' along the way before continuing on in Gillian's direction. She had always loved Frankie's walk. He had the ability to make her weak just by strolling across a room.

He drew near and she watched as a slow smile crept across his handsome face. She smiled back, and greeted him with a hug.

"Happy Thanksgiving," she said.

Frankie kissed her on her cheek. "Happy Thanksgiving, Gigi." He was so happy to be in her presence. Things had been tense between them ever since their split. The criminal case against the crew had only increased the distance between them, since Gillian was doing her best to keep a low profile. The last thing she wanted was to be on the feds' radar. Frankie understood her dilemma, and had kept his distance. But he had missed her, and was glad to be with her now.

Gillian led Frankie to a corner table. He pulled out her chair and she sat down. Frankie sat across from her, and glanced around at the handful of patrons dining out for the holiday. Only a skeleton staff worked the room, and the atmosphere was cozy and warm. A waiter came over and greeted both of them by name, before pouring their glasses full of Perrier. Once he was gone, Frankie stared across the table at Gillian.

"I was surprised to hear from you today," he admitted, then sipped his water.

Frankie had spent most of the day at Camille's mother's house, playing with baby Bria. It had been awkward for him at first, seeing Camille with the next man; spending the holiday with Misa, the woman who had killed his brother. Eli had been polite, and Camille had done her best to make Frankie feel at home. Still, you could cut the tension with a knife. Misa was mourning the loss of Baron, too, and in her misery, she had secluded herself in her bedroom for the majority of the day. The mood in Miss Lily's home had been solemn at first. Frankie had left a similarly somber scene at his mother's house earlier in the day. Without Steven, Frankie was all that his mother Mary had left, and the few hours he'd spent with her had taken a toll on him.

By the time he arrived at his former mother-in-law's house and sensed a similar sadness in the air, Frankie had made up his mind that he wouldn't stay long. But the moment Bria saw her father walk in the door, she got excited. It seemed that his consistent visits over the past few weeks had paid off. Bria had insisted that he sit at her little table with her and eat dinner. It was the first time that she was happy to see him, and it made Frankie smile so hard that his cheeks hurt. Camille and Eli encouraged him to stay and indulge her, and Frankie had relented and enjoyed the best Thanksgiving dinner he'd had in years, as well as the company of his baby girl. It was strangely like old times spending the holiday with Camille and her family—although watching Eli steal kisses from Camille when he thought no one was looking was somehow unsettling for Frankie. He still thought of Camille as his own, though he knew that he'd forfeited those privileges long ago.

He had been surprised when he got the call from Gillian after dessert. She called from an unfamiliar number, taking no chances in the wake of the crew's legal troubles. She asked him to meet her at *Conga* in Midtown Manhattan, and he had happily come to meet her there. Gillian was in a tough position, and they had to be careful not to be seen together with all of the police surveillance lately. They were taking advantage of the holiday, the late hour, and the familiar location to finally have a chance to talk now that all of the smoke was beginning to clear.

"I thought you might be lonely," she said. She looked him in the eye. "The holidays are a tough time for both of us. Me, without my father and Baron; you without your brother. I figured we could find some comfort in one another considering that we've both lost so much."

Gillian's eyes were downcast, her voice soft and sad. "I can't believe Baron is gone," she said. "I think about the holidays . . . what it used to be like." She shook her head.

Frankie understood completely. Everything had fallen apart. He nodded. It was true that the two of them were existing in fractured families. He smiled, hoping to lighten the mood. "I spent time with Bria today. For once, she was happy to have me around." He looked at Gillian seriously. "That wasn't always the case. I was a stranger to her, really. But since the raids, I guess . . . I put some things in perspective. Started spending more time with my daughter, and now we're finally building the relationship we should have had all along."

"That's great, Frankie," Gillian said. "It's never too late for a new beginning."

Frankie's smile faded a little. "Is that true for us, too?"

Gillian sipped her water rather than respond right away. She was grateful when her mother approached the table, at that moment.

"Frankie!" Mayra's smile outshined the candle flickering in the center of their table.

Frankie rose to greet her, wrapping Mrs. Nobles in a warm hug.

"How are you, Mayra?" he asked, smiling down at her.

"I'm good. I'm praying that everything works out for you, too." Mayra was no stranger to the turmoil going on within the family. "I'm glad you stopped by today. Gigi and I had an early meal together this afternoon, and then we came in here and got to work." She touched him gingerly on the arm. "I'm glad you're here, Frankie." She smiled at her daughter. "So now, Gigi can have some time to relax."

Gillian smiled back at her. She was happy that the two of them had worked through their differences. It was nice having her mother back in her life again.

Mayra gestured toward Frankie's seat. "Sit down. I'm going to send Javier over with a bottle of wine."

Frankie thanked her, and sat back down as she hurried off. Gillian smiled after her mother.

"You're not the only one whose parental relationship is improving," she said. "Me and ole girl are closer than ever these days."

Frankie laughed. "If she heard you call her 'ole girl,' she'd be pissed."

"I know!" Gillian laughed in agreement.

"That's good, though," Frankie said, nodding. "It's long overdue. Your father would want it that way."

Gillian's smile faded, hearing Frankie mention her father. Javier arrived then with a bottle of 2008 Emilio Moro red wine. Ceremoniously, he uncorked the bottle and poured the wine in both of their glasses. He set the bottle down on the table and hurried off, leaving them shrouded in silence and candlelight.

Frankie took a sip of his wine and sat back in his seat. "He'd be so proud of you. You realize that, don't you?"

She nodded. "He always was. No matter what."

Frankie agreed. "Doug Nobles was a great man. He raised a great daughter." Frankie held up his glass as if to toast. Gillian slowly raised hers and they clinked their glasses together.

Gillian's eyes bore into his over the rim of her glass as she took a sip. Setting her glass down, she licked her lips, frowning slightly. "My father loved you, Frankie."

He nodded. "I know he did. I loved him, too. The man practically raised me." Frankie had nothing but the utmost respect for Doug Nobles.

"He told me once that he had failed with Baron," he continued. "His only son, and he was nothing like him. Doug was strong and in control. He was honorable. He commanded respect without being resented for it. Baron was nothing like that. Baron was weak. He thought he should be respected just because he was Doug's son. That was never enough. With you, Doug felt like he got it right."

Gillian didn't respond.

Frankie silently chastised himself for speaking so negatively about her brother, who was so newly deceased. He stared at her for several long moments. "I still love you, you know?"

Gillian met his gaze. She nodded. "I know."

Frankie waited, hopeful that she would return the sentiment. When she sat silently, he sighed. "We had a good thing, Gigi. Don't act like we didn't."

"It was good while it lasted," she deadpanned.

Frankie didn't respond, but his expression was grim.

"Things got twisted. We lost focus, and let our hormones take over. A lot of people got hurt. We never should have crossed that line."

Frankie disagreed. "Everything was fine until Camille got pregnant. Once Bria was born, you . . ." He paused and looked at Gillian. He didn't want to rehash the past. "We were good before that."

She stared back at him, searching his demeanor for answers to questions she hadn't asked yet. "Is that what you think?"

He nodded. "It's what I know."

"Is that why you took it out on them? On Camille and Bria? Because you think they're the reason why we didn't work?"

Frankie shook his head, but then stopped and thought about

it for a moment. "Maybe . . . at first. Maybe that's why I wasn't there in the beginning." He shrugged. "But really I think it had more to do with me not having a good example with my own father. But I'm changing that."

"Everything is different now, Gigi." Frankie leaned in closer. Although the restaurant was nearly empty, he still kept his voice low so that only she could hear him. "I'm about to disappear."

Gillian's brow furrowed. "What are you talking about? You can't go anywhere. You're out on bail."

Frankie shook his head. "I know it sounds crazy, but I have a plan. I'm not waiting around for them to lock me up. I'm getting out of here."

Gillian stared at him, speechless. After a few moments of silence she sighed and stared at her hands, which were wrapped around the stem of her glass.

Frankie watched her. "Do you still love me, Gigi?"

She looked away. The years had taken their toll on her relationship with Frankie. Once inseparable best friends, she had begun to lose respect for Frankie. His handling of his marriage's demise and Camille's pregnancy, Misa's trial . . . it had clouded the lens through which she viewed him. Still, she couldn't deny that she still had some strong feelings for him.

She sighed. "You'll always be special to me," she said. "But I know that we could never go back to the way it was."

"Why not? Everything is all fucked up now, so what have we got to lose?"

Frankie reached across the table and took her hand in his. She didn't pull away.

"Come with me," Frankie whispered, anxiously.

Gillian shook her head, frowning. "Frankie, I can't just pick up and leave town for good. Neither can you."

He nodded, and his eyes widened as if their intensity might

convince her otherwise. "We can! What if we just pack a bag and leave tonight? We don't have shit to lose."

Gillian shook her head again. "What about your daughter, Frankie? You just finished telling me how you're finally bonding with her. Now you want to just up and leave her behind?"

Frankie let out a long breath and sat back in his seat, seemingly defeated. "I can come back and visit her. Or I can send for her to come to us." He shrugged. "I don't know how, but I'll see her." Frankie watched Gillian's facial expression and sensed that she was apprehensive. "Listen, I have to get out of here, Gigi. Come with me."

Gillian shook her head. "Frankie, have you lost your mind?" A look of genuine concern was etched on her face.

"Listen—"

"No, *you* listen!" Gillian spoke in a hard whisper, and Frankie could tell she meant business. "Nobody's going anywhere. Shit is bad right now. I'll give you that. But running would only make it worse." She sighed, frustrated. She took his hand in hers across the table. "I care about you, Frankie. I don't know what the future holds for us. But I can't stand by and watch you run away."

Frankie looked like he was on the verge of tears. Gillian studied his face, aware that he was struggling to keep his composure.

"Frankie, what's wrong? What aren't you telling me?"

He shook his head and avoided her gaze. He watched a couple chatting with Mayra as they made their exit. As he watched the couple, Gillian watched him.

"Let's go downstairs where we can have some privacy," she suggested softly.

Frankie looked at her, his eyes searching hers. For the first time in months, he felt a glimmer of hope that Gillian might be willing to be more than business associates. The thought of being alone with her made his heart leap in his chest. He nodded.

Gillian waved Javier over. "I'm stepping away for a little while," she said to him. "Let my mother know that I'll be back in a few."

Javier nodded, and collected the wine bottle and their glasses. Gillian led the way to the back of the restaurant and down three flights of stairs heading to the quiet and seclusion of the wine cellar. As they reached the landing, Frankie grabbed her from behind and spun her around to face him. Caught off guard, Gillian gasped.

Frankie covered her mouth with his own. Gillian didn't protest. Their tongues intertwined as they kissed each other passionately. Frankie's jeans could barely contain his erection as he grabbed a fistful of her hair, and tilted her head back. A soft moan escaped her as he licked and sucked her neck. Frankie's touch, his scent, his lips were all so blissfully familiar to Gillian. Reluctantly, she pulled away, took his hand in hers and led him down the long, dark hallway to the wine cellar.

Frankie was familiar with this room. The ultra-exclusive space had been the venue for many of the crew's big meetings over the years. The large room was insulated to protect the many expensive bottles of wine lining the walls and shelves.

Gillian led the way to the back where a sturdy, round oak wood table stood near one corner. He scooped her up into his strong arms easily, and sat her on top of the table. Gillian spread her legs apart and Frankie positioned himself between them. His lips found hers again, and his erection grew stronger as she tore at his clothes, peeling him out of his blazer and frantically tearing at the buttons on his shirt. She ran her fingers across his chest and gripped his back. Eagerly, she unbuckled his belt while his hands slid beneath the turtleneck she wore. She unfastened his jeans and pulled them down, then his boxers. Boldly, she took his hard dick in her hands and felt it grow even harder, until it felt like steel in her hands. Frankie closed his eyes and let out a sigh of pure ecstasy. Gillian's touch still had the power to make him weak.

Suddenly, she stopped and pushed him backward so hard that he practically fell, tripping on his pants around his ankles. Frankie's eyes flew open in shock, and he stood speechless, staring at the silencer on the end of the Taurus 9 millimeter in his face; confused until he saw Biggs holding the gun, and it finally occurred to him that he had been set up.

Gillian stood up from the table and wiped her mouth, her expression one of pure disgust as if she had just been kissing a monster. Frankie's mind moved in slow motion. Aware that his erection was gone and that his limp penis hung sadly between his legs, he reached down to pull up his pants.

"Don't move," Biggs warned.

Frankie froze.

"Step out of your clothes, your shoes, everything," Gillian ordered him, calmly. Gillian's voice had the cold ease and nonchalance of a doctor instructing her patient to disrobe. Frankie stood speechless, his gaze alternating between Biggs and Gillian. Slowly, he did as he was told, aware that his only chance at getting out of this was to talk his way out.

"Gigi, what's going on?" he asked, although he already knew. His heart galloped in his chest, and sweat pooled all over his body, despite the cool temperature of the wine cellar.

Gillian calmly pulled up one of the leather chairs surrounding the table she had just been spread eagle on. She placed it in front of Frankie. "Sit," she ordered.

Nervously, Frankie sat down while Biggs kept the gun trained directly on him. Frankie looked up at him. "Biggs, you know me—"

"Don't talk," Gillian sternly. "None of us knows you. Not really. Do we, Frankie?"

Frankie watched as Gillian searched his clothes. She went

through his pockets, tore the lining out of his blazer. She took apart his cell phone, removing the battery, the SIM card, the memory card. Satisfied that there was no wire, Gillian threw everything in a corner, and stood facing Frankie with her arms folded across her chest.

"So, you want to leave town, huh?" Gillian smirked. "How convenient." She shook her head. "You know, when everybody got arrested except me, I didn't know what to make of it at first. After all, everybody knows that I'm running everything. So, why would the feds sweep everybody but me? I couldn't figure it out." She paced the floor a little. "From the start, Maury warned me that we were probably dealing with a snitch. I even mentioned that to you, when you came home on bail. You tried to convince me that it was Zion. Or maybe one of the Douglas brothers. But honestly, I thought all along that it was Baron."

Frankie was nervous, and hearing Gillian mention her brother's name only made it worse.

She chuckled a little, though her countenance was sinister. "My big brother. He was a trip, but he was my blood. I hated to think that he might flip and start snitching on the very people we called family. But you were right about what you said upstairs. Baron was never like our father. He was weak, and he was unpredictable. Plus he was avoiding me, and that made me suspicious of him. Then somebody shot him point-blank, and that changed everything. Who would have the motive to do a thing like that? Who but me?"

Gillian stopped pacing and glared at Frankie. "The only problem was, it wasn't me. So then . . . who?"

Frankie stared at the floor, convicted.

"You killed my brother, didn't you, Frankie?"

Frankie sat silently, and bit his lip to keep it from quivering.

"Answer me," she said through clenched teeth.

Frankie looked sheepishly at her, and slowly nodded. "I was

in a fucked-up spot, Gillian. They had me, and they were gonna move in on everybody with or without me. I did what I had to do to make sure that you could walk away. You have to understand that I was trying to protect *you*, Gigi. I swear it was always about protecting you."

Gillian nodded. She leaned against the table and shook her head sadly. She looked at Biggs. "Do you get it now?" she asked him. "Do you understand what happened?"

Biggs shook his head, his eyes still trained on Frankie. "Nah," he answered honestly. "All I know is you told me Frankie here is a snitch. That's all I needed to hear." Biggs looked disgusted and disappointed at the same time as he looked at Frankie. Biggs had been with the family for so long, and had been the muscle in the operation for a very long time. He was only called when the time had come for slow singing and flower bringing. He hated that it had to be his man Frankie. But snitches were a thing that could never be tolerated.

"Let me fill you in," Gillian said. She glanced over at Frankie. "Stop me when I get it wrong, okay?"

Frankie didn't respond.

"A while back, Grant Keys let us know that Angelle and the doctors she works with couldn't be trusted. They were under investigation for pushing illegal prescription drugs. Zion and I discussed it, and decided to cut ties with them. Wasn't worth the risk. We told good 'ole Frankie here that the fam was no longer doing business with Angelle. Frankie didn't listen, and he kept moving pills with Angelle and her doctors, never knowing that they were not just under investigation; the feds already had enough evidence to put them all away for a long time. So they struck a deal and agreed to set us up as the distributors who were moving those pills on a very large scale."

Biggs shook his head, as the picture started coming into focus.

"So my dear Frankie walked right into a trap. Every conversation he had with Angelle from then on was recorded, and Frankie was arrested. According to Maury, they offered him a deal, too. All he had to do was point the finger at the people who were at the top. Help them bring down the kingpins."

She turned and narrowed her eyes at Frankie. "They knew you weren't the top guy because you kept saying *they* on tape. *They don't want to take the risk. They act like they're scared. They don't have to know.* So they wanted to know who *they* were. And you folded." She shook her head in dismay.

Frankie cleared his throat. He spoke softly, aware that Biggs was barely blinking as he kept the gun aimed right at him. "I didn't tell them anything about you . . . about neither one of you."

"You told on Zion. On Grant. Tremaine, Baron, the Douglas brothers, Reuben Cruz. You wore a wire. You killed my brother."

"Only to protect you," Frankie insisted. "Baron wasn't gonna keep quiet. You *know* he would have told on you. It was just a matter of time. The kind of time the feds were talking . . . if Baron was under that kind of pressure much longer, he was gonna tell them that you—"

"So you took it upon yourself to kill my brother to protect me from going to jail." Gillian hoped that hearing it said aloud would help Frankie realize how crazy it was.

He nodded. "Yes," he admitted again. "I did it to protect you, Gigi."

She scoffed at that. "You did it to protect yourself."

Frankie gripped his hands together, pleadingly. "Okay," he said. "I was trying to protect *both* of us, G. We could walk away from this. We can get out of here, and never look back."

Gillian's eyes narrowed as she looked at him. "You're crazy."

"Crazy about you," he said. "I swear, G . . . all I wanted to do was protect you so that me and you . . . we can go back to being like we were before. Bonnie and Clyde, you know? I love you, Gillian."

Gillian laughed. "I loved you, too, once," she admitted. "But I wasn't looking at the whole picture back then. Camille is softer than I am, and I used to think that made me better than her. The way she'd cry all the time, letting you know how powerless she was, begging you to give her one more try."

"Camille's with somebody else now." Frankie's eyes pleaded with hers. "I'm talking about me and you."

Gillian smirked, proud of Camille for finding the guts to let Frankie go for good. She was better off without him. "I expected her to take you back after we broke up," she said. "But she surprised me." Gillian moved closer. "You surprised me, too."

She walked over and took the gun out of Biggs' hand. Biggs looked at her, surprised, but didn't protest. Instead he took a step back, and let her do her thing. She gripped the gun tightly in her manicured hands and took one step closer to Frankie.

"My father knew you as a man of strength, integrity, and substance. He told me once that you were the son he should have had."

Frankie's heart raced. He stared back at her. "Gigi, please . . ." His voice wavered. "Please, don't do this."

Gillian's rage bubbled over. "So I'm supposed to just ride off into the sunset with you after you snitched on everybody in our family? After you killed my brother, you *bitch*?"

Gillian hocked back and spat in Frankie's face. When he lifted his hand to wipe it, she shot him point-blank, just as he had done to Baron. The muffled sound of the gunshot echoed in the cellar. To Gillian, it sounded like a gavel in a courtroom, signaling Frankie's final exit from her life.

Biggs walked slowly over to her, and took the gun out of her hands. Frankie's face was wide open, his blood and brains oozing out of him. Gillian didn't look away. Instead, she stared at the mess of what had once been the man she loved.

Biggs wiped down the gun. He placed it in a duffel bag along with Frankie's clothes. He placed his hand gently on Gillian's shoulder. "Let's get you out of here," he said. "I'm gonna take care of this."

Gillian looked at him, and nodded calmly. Slowly, she began to walk toward the exit. Biggs stopped her.

"Your father was a great man. He would be real proud of you, Gillian. You did what you had to do."

She didn't answer for several moments. Her expression was blank when she finally did. "My father didn't raise me to be a killer," she said softly. "He didn't want this life for me, but I chose it for myself. This was for my brother. For the work my father put in that this nigga just flushed right down the toilet." She reached up and touched Biggs' cheek, smiling weakly at him. "Make sure his body disappears completely. Not a trace. Then take the money my mother has for you and get the fuck out of the country. Go somewhere and start over. Keep your hands clean, and live a good life. You deserve that. We all do."

She kissed Biggs on the cheek, and thanked him. Biggs had been loyal to her and to her father for many years. She had rewarded him with a very large payoff for this final act of loyalty. As he watched her walk out, Biggs knew that this was the end of the family for good. Gillian had settled the score, and now there was no turning back.

22

EVER AFTER

Night had fallen and so had the temperature by the time the dinner dishes were washed and Jada's house was quiet. It was late, and she was emotionally and physically drained. Everything was peaceful for once. Sheldon and Ethan were asleep, and Born lay awake in bed, watching a late night airing of *It's a Wonderful Life*. Jada stood in the doorway of their bedroom and looked at Born in the glow of the light from the TV.

Jada smiled and crawled into bed beside him. Even with no makeup on and an old T-shirt, he thought she looked beautiful.

"Hey, baby." He smiled at her.

"Hey." Jada kissed him, clutching his face between her hands, longing to devour him. She pulled him toward her. She had been waiting for this all day long.

Born kissed her deeply, and gripped her body so firmly that a moan escaped her lips. He scooped her up easily, pulling her on top of him, palming her ass. Jada wrapped her legs around his waist.

"I'm a lucky man," he said.

Jada smiled back. "I think I'm the lucky one."

Born looked in her eyes, his expression serious.

"Everything is different now," Born said. "I think it just hit me today. I looked around at the kids, Ava, my mother. Even with all of them here with us, there were still a bunch of people missing. I thought about the way things were, and how they are now. Dorian, Sunny, Doug Nobles, Baron, they're all dead. Sunny's brother, Reuben, Dorian's brothers, Zion, Frankie, and damn near everybody else is facing jail time. All of our kids are growing up." He shook his head. "Everything is different. The only thing that hasn't changed is the way I love you."

Jada kissed him. "I love you, too."

Born pulled her even closer. "You promised me something a few months ago. I want to marry you. And I don't want to wait. Let's do it now."

Jada frowned a little. The last time they discussed marriage, they agreed that they would wait until things settled down, and they knew what the future held for everyone around them. "What about—"

"Forget everything, and everybody else. Just me and you. Let's just do it." Born had a mischievous grin on his face. "I was thinking about us the day we first met each other. I saw you walking down the block, sexy as hell. You tried to play hard to get."

Jada laughed. "You thought you were all of that, driving around in your fancy car, calling out to me like I was supposed to drop everything and come running. I was like, *Who does he think he is?* You were so cocky!"

Born shook his head. "Confident, not cocky."

"No," Jada insisted. "You were *cocky*." She laughed at the memory. "But I grew to love it."

"We came a long way since then." Born grew more serious. "We've hurt each other, over and over again."

Jada tried not to dwell on Born's recent indiscretions with Anisa. She took responsibility for her role in isolating him, and she had forgiven him for it. But the thought of him in Anisa's arms still stung Jada greatly. She shook the thought away, and nestled deeper into Born's embrace. "That's all behind us now," she said. "New start."

"So come on! This week. Let's just go get married, Jada. We don't have to make it a big show. For what? All we need is me, you, the kids, and God." He was so excited by the idea that his voice had risen without him realizing it. He searched her eyes, anxiously. "You with me?"

Jada smiled. She loved Born so much that she would do anything to guarantee that he would be in her life forever. "Yeah," she said, nodding. "Let's do it."

Born's kiss left no doubt that she had just made him the happiest man alive. They made love all night, anticipating the bliss of knowing their story might have a happier ending than they had allowed themselves to dream possible.

Born stood watching as Jada slowly made her way down the aisle of the church. Mary J Blige's "Share My World" played from the speakers that were hooked up to the Bose system in the pastor's office. Jada looked so beautiful that it took Born's breath away. She wore a gold-beaded, floor-sweeping Jenny Packham gown that hugged her curves perfectly. Jada carried a simple bouquet of purple wine Calla lilies. Her hairstylist, Ramiek, had styled her long hair into a sophisticated updo, and her makeup was minimal. To Born, she looked like an angel.

While the chords of the instrumental played at the beginning of the song, Jada stood in the doorway of the church and stared, smiling at the man who would be her husband. Born was a good man. And he looked *good* on this day.

Born wore a black Tom Ford suit, and sharp Prada shoes. Jada knew that her man didn't enjoy getting dressed up. He had even suggested that he might wear jeans to the ceremony. But he had set his comfort aside for the woman he loved. Jada adored him.

Promise I'll be here.
Whenever you need me near.

Jada had requested the song and was so glad that she did. Mary was singing her heart out, and Jada felt as if she was singing it just for them. She arrived at the altar and faced Born. She clutched her bouquet tightly, her hands shaking from the nervousness every bride feels on their special day. But despite her trembling hands, Jada was bubbling over with pure joy. It took all of her willpower not to kiss him before it was time.

Ava stepped forward and held Jada's bouquet for her. Born took Jada's hands in his own. As the song continued to play, the couple sang along and two-stepped a little. It was as if they were alone together, as the two of them rocked together and vibed with Mary. There was barely a dry eye in the house, since everyone present knew the long road this couple had traveled together.

Ava, Sheldon, Ethan, Miss Ingrid, Sunny's mother Marisol, Mercedes, and DJ were the only guests present at the simple, quiet ceremony in the otherwise empty church. It was Friday, December 3, a week after Thanksgiving. And this year, the couple had so much to be thankful for. After all of the ups and downs, they were finally getting their chance at happily ever after.

Even Reverend Gibson was emotional. He cleared his throat as he began.

"You're gorgeous," Born whispered.

Jada blushed, and smiled at the fact that he still had that effect on her after all of these years. Together they faced the minister.

"Dearly beloved . . ."

Her mind wandered down the road that she and Born had traveled together in the years since they first met.

"We're gathered here today to join Jada Noelle Ford and Marquis Lamont Graham in holy matrimony."

She smiled as she thought of the day in 1995 that Born pulled up alongside her in his black convertible E320 Benz, cocky and brazen as he spoke to her. She thought back to their first date and how she had balked at the way that he talked with his mouth full. She recalled the first time they made love, the first time he professed his love for her, the first time they'd seen each other again after cocaine tore them apart.

"If anyone believes that this couple should not be united in holy matrimony, speak now or forever hold your peace."

Born, too, was reflecting on their history together. As the preacher instructed them to bow their heads in prayer, Born peeked and looked at Jada and thought back over all of their years—for better or for worse.

He reminisced on the early days—before they hooked up with Dorian and Sunny, before Born's rise in the drug game. He remembered the way that his love for Jada had crept up on him, taking him hostage against his will. Eventually, though, he had surrendered to it, and the days he spent in her arms had been pure bliss in comparison to the ones he'd lived without her. He looked at her now, standing beside him looking lovelier than ever. Born felt like the happiest man alive.

The minister finished his prayer, told Born to repeat after him, and began to recite the usual vows common in most Christian ceremonies. Born cleared his throat. "Excuse me," he interrupted. Seeing the confused look on both Jada's and the reverend's faces, he explained. "I want to say my own thing. My own . . . vows . . . is that all right?"

Jada's eyes widened. "I . . . I didn't write anything . . ." she stammered.

Born smiled at her. "Neither did I. I just want to say what's on my mind." He looked at the reverend. "Can I do that?"

The reverend nodded, smiling. "Yes, yes," he said. His smile broadened. "Go ahead."

Born cleared his throat again. He looked at Jada, beaming. "I know we didn't plan on saying our own thing. But nothing about us is ordinary. So I don't think we should just say ordinary things. I want to speak from my heart." Born looked at the handful of guests assembled in the two front pews of the church and smiled. Every one of them was aware of the journey he and Jada had taken together. They knew how special this occasion was, how long they'd fought for it. His gaze settled on Sheldon and Ethan, both of whom personified the rough road the couple had traveled to get here. Looking again at his beautiful bride, Born took a deep breath. He searched his mind for the right words to express what was in his heart, and then began his vows.

"We've been through it all, Jada. We had some good times and some bad. We wasted a lot of time that we can never get back again. Now that I have you back, I'm never letting you go again. I'm never gonna take what we have for granted." His gaze was direct and so was his delivery. "I promise to love you, and protect you, and respect you until the day I die. I'll take care of you and the kids until we get so old that the kids have to take care of both of us."

Jada laughed through the joyful tears that puddled in her eyes. "I'll do my best to remember to put the toilet seat down after I'm done."

The reverend and all of the guests were smiling and chuckling as they listened to Born's impromptu vows. It was spontaneous, romantic, and the sweetest thing any of them had ever witnessed.

"I'll buy you flowers just because you deserve it. I'll never keep any secrets from you. Unless it's to surprise you, 'cause I know how much you love surprises." He squeezed her hands tightly.

"I'll never cheat on you." Born's expression was serious as he said it. He knew that his recent dalliance with Anisa had hurt Jada terribly. "I'll never cause you pain again. And I'll never leave you. I'll be the husband you deserve—the husband you always deserved." He started to get emotional, but manned up quickly. "I'll take care of you. I'll take care of our kids. We're a family, and I promise to always put my family first—before anything or anybody else. I swear I'll make you happy. Always. So help me God." Born brought Jada's hands to his lips and kissed each one. The pastor handed him Jada's platinum-and-diamond wedding band, and Born placed it on her finger.

Ava, Miss Ingrid, and Marisol dabbed at the tears in their eyes, but Jada didn't bother to control hers. Joyful tears spilled forth, until Born reached forward and gently wiped them away with his handkerchief. Jada's heart nearly burst with all of the love she had inside.

The reverend turned to her. "Would you like to say your own vows, too?" he asked.

Jada nodded. "I don't think I can talk without crying, but I'll try." She looked at Born, and her smile widened. "I love you," she said. "God blessed me when he sent you into my life . . . into me and Sheldon's life." She took a deep breath. "You've been so patient with me. From the very beginning, you've been my best friend. You treat me better than I treat myself at times." Her gaze lowered, Jada choked back a sob. "I don't know *why* you love me, but I'm so glad that you do. You know everything there is to know about me, and still . . ." She looked at him again. "You love me." She shook her head at the magnitude of that. "And, my God, Born, I love you, too. I love you so much."

She took another deep breath. "I promise to keep you happy *forever*. I will respect you, honor you, and take care of you all the days of my life. I'll never hurt you again. When things get hard, I won't run. I swear." She smiled at him. "I won't complain when you spend Sundays watching football all day."

"Yeah, right," Sheldon said, louder than he meant to. Still, everybody laughed.

Jada's smile was wide as she continued. "I won't complain when you talk with your mouth full. I love you for who you are, for who you've helped me become. And I will never let anyone or anything ever come between us again. I love you." She took Born's matching wedding band and placed it on his finger.

The minister spoke again, blessing their union. He pronounced them man and wife at last, and Jada rushed into Born's open arms. They kissed and held each other close. Born forgot about everyone else present as he looked into Jada's eyes and kissed her over and over. Jada was weak with joy.

They turned and faced their loved ones at last, and were surrounded by hugs and kisses all around. In that moment, though neither of them knew it at the time, they were both having similar thoughts. It was as if Sunny and Dorian were there in spirit, surrounding them with love, and blessing their friends as they began their lives together as husband and wife.

EPILOGUE

Gillian sat in the small office with her mother and her attorney—an associate of Maury's—as the agents grilled her relentlessly.

"I'm telling you what I know," Gillian said, sincerely. "Frankie came by the restaurant on Thanksgiving. I was surprised to see him, since we hadn't spoken to each other in months. He was upset."

"Very upset," Mayra interjected. "He insisted that he needed to speak with Gillian right away. So she sat with him at one of the tables in the corner."

Agent Payne watched the women closely, glancing at his notes periodically to see if they would switch up any of the details of the last sighting of his star witness.

"You said that he asked you to leave town with him. Did he say where he was going?" Payne asked.

Gillian shook her head. "No. Honestly, it didn't seem like he really knew where he was going. He just kept saying that we could disappear; that the case against him was serious and he couldn't stay here and stand trial. I reminded him that his daughter is here, and she needs him. He just said that he would find a way to see her, but he had to get away. I told him that I couldn't just up and leave. I've got the restaurant, my home, my family here. I told him that he was crazy. So he left. And I haven't heard from him since."

Gillian dabbed at the corner of her eye with a tissue. "My God, I hope he's okay. I didn't really think he would just up and leave like that."

Mayra stroked her back, comfortingly.

"My daughter is very upset. She loved Frankie very much. They broke up years ago because he wouldn't get out of that life. She warned him that things would get out of hand if he kept living like that, but he didn't listen. And now look!"

"Mama, don't," Gillian protested.

"No, Gigi; there's no point in pretending anymore. He's a fugitive."

"We're still trying to determine if that's the case," Agent Payne insisted. "Right now we're piecing together his movements on the last day anyone saw him. His ex-wife tells us that he spent the day with their family, and then left after dessert. We know that he came to see you after that."

"You only know that because my client told your investigators that. She's been very forthcoming and candid. But this has been a very long day, and she is clearly overwhelmed. She's told you everything she knows. Can we wrap this up?" Robert Nestlebaum was no Maury, but he came damn close.

Agent Payne didn't look too pleased, but he threw up his hands in surrender. "Sure. Listen . . . it's just that Frankie hasn't been home, hasn't checked in anywhere in the past four days. No trace of his car or his cell phone. His mother hasn't heard from him. We're concerned that he may have met with some type of foul play."

Gillian frowned. "Why would anybody want to hurt Frankie?" she asked.

Agent Payne looked over at his colleagues. They knew that

Frankie was a government informant, but that fact hadn't been made public.

"That's what we're trying to figure out Ms. Nobles." Payne stood, signaling the end of their questioning. Gillian, her mother, and her attorney stood as well. "If we have any more questions, we'll give you a call."

Gillian nodded. "Please let me know as soon as you know something. I'll be worried sick about him until I know where he is."

Agent Payne agreed. "Will do, ma'am. Thank you for your time."

He watched the three of them as they left, something in his gut telling him that Frankie hadn't made it out of town. He believed that Frankie was dead.

"Back to fucking square one." He slammed his fist on the table and sat back in his chair, frustrated.

Meanwhile, as Gillian exited the building with her mother and her attorney, she continued to play the part of the concerned friend. On her face was an expression of worry and concern. But in her mind, she was thankful to Biggs for a job well-fucking done.

Once in the car, Nestlebaum filled them in on what they could expect next. "Without him, they don't have much of a case. As long as he doesn't show up anytime soon, it's safe to say that their case is significantly weaker against everybody."

Gillian smiled for the first time all day. "Now, that's good news."

In the months that followed, the majority of the charges against Grant, the Douglas brothers, Tremaine, and Reuben were dropped. With no informant to implicate them, the feds' case was all but done. A few of the charges stuck, particularly those for weapons and drug possession. When the dust settled, Grant's case was dismissed for lack of evidence, but he was still released from his job in the D.A.'s office on the grounds of illegal drug possession for the pills they'd found in his home. He went into a court-mandated rehab facility and emerged thirty days later a free man. Sunny's brother Reuben, and Dorian's brothers Patrick and Christian were each sentenced to two years in prison for the drugs and guns found in their homes at the time of their arrests.

Zion was hit the hardest. The pills and gun found during the search of his home didn't bode well with the judge. He was sentenced to eight to ten years in prison. Olivia kept a stiff upper lip as she continued to take her clothing line to the top of the industry. But inside, she was crushed. She would always love Zion, and without him she felt a void that no other man could fill. She focused on taking her fashion career to the next level, determined to give Adiva a positive role model to emulate as she grew older.

Frankie's body was never recovered, and rumors abounded about what had become of him. Some imagined that he had fled to avoid prosecution. Others wondered if Frankie had met with a more unfortunate fate. Camille, for one, was convinced that Frankie was dead. Nothing else could explain his sudden disappearance from Bria's life. It was tough on Bria. It took months before she stopped asking for him. Camille and Eli did their best to compensate for Frankie's absence. And as the weeks turned into months and the reality set in that Frankie was never coming back, Eli proposed to Camille.

"Let me be the man in your life, and the father figure in Bria's," he asked. "Marry me."

With tears streaming down her face, Camille said yes. She had never expected to marry again after having such a tumultuous union with Frankie. But when she said "I do" to Eli on August 4, she entered into a marriage unlike the one she'd endured previously. Eli was patient, kind, gentle, and attentive to both Camille and Bria. Their love provided the perfect atmosphere for her to grow up a happy and healthy young girl in the absence of her father.

Born, Jada, and their sons were officially a family now. Although Ethan was still a bit leery of Sheldon, they had managed to squeeze some normalcy out of what had once been an insane existence.

Anisa was none too thrilled with Born and Jada's marriage. Out of spite, she had threatened to move to California with Ethan. Anisa's parents had purchased a home in Anaheim, and she determined that since Born no longer wanted to be in her life, she may as well move to the west coast and start over. She was angry that Born had married Jada without warning. By the time Anisa found out about it, there was nothing she could do to stop it. Angry and jilted, she began to pack hers and Ethan's bags for the trip to Cali. But Born's mother, Miss Ingrid, had gone to talk with Anisa. Always one to keep it real, Miss Ingrid had pulled no punches.

"Do you know how many kids out there would love to have a father in their life? Whether he's with you or not, nobody can argue that Born is an excellent father. He takes care of you and Ethan financially, and he spends more time with him than most fathers I know. Don't let your pride cause you do something you'll regret. If you move Ethan all the way to the other side of the country, who do you think it's really gonna hurt? Huh? Born has already moved on. He's happy with Jada, so you might as well get over that. The only person who'll be hurt by that is my grandson. And I would really hate to see that happen."

Anisa had stared at the floor, convicted. Two days later, she had called off the move to California. But she did pack up and move back to Queens, where she had grown up. She no longer wanted to live in the house Born owned, which now felt like an ungratifying second prize in a contest she had once been so desperate to win.

Born and Jada were glad to see her go. Jada needed no reminders of Born's trysts, and Born was happy to have a reason to sell the house on Bement Avenue. Ethan came to stay with them every other weekend, and as often in between as Born could manage. They split holidays 50/50, and the absence of Anisa gave them the chance to enjoy their relationship with no outside interference. They were finally beginning to settle into a peaceful family existence for the first time ever. They were ecstatic as they enjoyed their renewed romance, and it showed. They had come through all of the twists and turns of their lives—not unscathed, but certainly not destroyed.

Gillian's life as the head of a crime family had come to an end. Baron's death, the case against the crew, Frankie's betrayal, and her progression from queenpin to cold-blooded killer had forced her to accept one crucial truth. The drug game would never be the same again. There was no honor among thieves, no integrity to be found in a life that had once been the source of her family's wealth, power, and prestige. In Gillian's mind, when her father died, he took with him the last bit of glory that would ever accompany a life of crime. Baron and Frankie were dead. Zion was in jail. Born had settled into a life of domesticity, and Biggs had taken the ticket to freedom she had offered him and never looked back. Gillian found herself feeling lonely and unimportant for the first time ever. And it was ironic that the person she found herself clinging to was her mother, whom she had once reviled.

Mayra had helped Gillian cover her tracks in the weeks following Frankie's disappearance. She had been eager to forge a stronger bond with Gillian, and the crew's troubles had given her the perfect opportunity. Mayra spent less time with Guy London, the man she had been involved with for years. Instead, she and her daughter spent their days shopping, having lunch or dinner dates, getting their nails done, and making up for lost time. Mayra sold *Conga*, which was the source of understandable angst for her daughter. And now she had opened a new upscale eatery called *Monte Cristo*, named after a popular cigar from Mayra's native Cuba. Since Gillian had earned a college degree during the years before her ascension to the Nobles throne, Mayra brought her in as co-owner, and together they took the restaurant to the top. *Monte Cristo* became so popular among the who's who of New York City that it garnered rave reviews and became the toast of the town.

Still, Gillian wondered if her life would ever consist of the astronomical highs that she had enjoyed as a member of the Nobles crime family. Wondered, too, if she would ever find love again. She had no regrets about the blood she had shed to protect those she loved. But, every now and then, she found herself daydreaming about her life in the fast lane, and secretly she wondered if she would ever find fulfillment in the ordinary existence she enjoyed now. While she was grateful to have landed on her feet, free and clear, there still remained a yearning in her heart for the power and the danger that life on the edge had given her. In her heart, she knew it wouldn't be long before she found some new way to quench her insatiable thirst for what had been taken from her far too soon.

In the meantime, she made do with what she had, and quietly plotted and planned for the day when she would once again take over the world.